3/21

CAN'T TAKE THAT AWAY

STEVEN SALVATORE

BLOOMSBURY

NEW YORK   LONDON   OXFORD   NEW DELHI   SYDNEY

BLOOMSBURY YA
Bloomsbury Publishing Inc., part of Bloomsbury Publishing Plc
1385 Broadway, New York, NY 10018

BLOOMSBURY and the Diana logo are trademarks of Bloomsbury Publishing Plc

First published in the United States of America in March 2021 by Bloomsbury YA

Text copyright © 2021 by Steven Salvatore

Bloomsbury books may be purchased for business or promotional use.
For information on bulk purchases please contact Macmillan Corporate
and Premium Sales Department at specialmarkets@macmillan.com

Library of Congress Cataloging-in-Publication Data
Names: Salvatore, Steven, author.
Title: Can't take that away / by Steven Salvatore.
Other titles: Cannot take that away
Description: New York: Bloomsbury, 2021.
Summary: When Carey Parker, a genderqueer teen who dreams of being a diva like their hero
Mariah Carey, is cast as the female lead in the school musical, they must fight against
discrimination and injustice from their closed-minded school administration.
Identifiers: LCCN 2020034735 (print) | LCCN 2020034736 (e-book)
ISBN 978-1-5476-0530-9 (hardcover) • ISBN 978-1-5476-0531-6 (e-book)
Subjects: CYAC: Gender identity—Fiction. | Identity—Fiction. | Prejudices—Fiction. |
Social action—Fiction. | High schools—Fiction. | Schools—Fiction.
Classification: LCC PZ7.1.S2543 Can 2021 (print) | LCC PZ7.1.S2543 (e-book) |
DDC [Fic]—dc23
LC record available at https://lccn.loc.gov/2020034735

Book design by Jeanette Levy
Typeset by Westchester Publishing Services
Printed and bound in the U.S.A. by Berryville Graphics Inc., Berryville, Virginia
2 4 6 8 10 9 7 5 3 1

To find out more about our authors and books visit
www.bloomsbury.com and sign up for our newsletters.

For every Carey Parker:
You are loved, worthy, *enough*

I'M READY

CAREY PARKER, lyrics and vocals

CRIS KOSTAS, guitar

Spotlight on, am I ready?
The world a stage, waiting for me
But the darkness creeps in, slowly
Devouring the light until I
Stay inside the lines
And play the role assigned

I've been too
Scared to live
Scared to die
To forgive myself
I have to try
One day I'll be stronger
Maybe I already am

I wonder if I'll ever fly
The open air calls out to me
But I get tangled in branches
Too afraid to spread my wings and
Take that first leap
What if I fall?

No longer
Scared to live
I want to try to
Be true to me
It's time to fly
One day I'll soar higher
Maybe it's time

You want me to believe
I'm not good enough
But you won't
Ever get the best of me
Because my voice is
the one thing
You can never take from me

One day I'll be louder
Maybe I'm ready

I'm ready

I'll scream out loud
I'm done apologizing
For wanting to shine
For wanting to fly
For being myself
No day like today
I'm ready

TRACK 1
THEY/THEM/THEIR

I should probably pay attention to Mr. Kelly's lecture right now, but I'm struggling to focus; I stare out over mountains blanketed in dead trees, his voice nothing but static as I follow a lone bird soaring above the Hudson River. I'm too far away to hear its melody, but I'm sure this bird has a song; every bird does. I take a deep breath, close my eyes, and attempt to remember a time I felt that free. No matter how hard I try, I come up short. I've always felt trapped in a cage, with clipped wings.

"Carey?" Mr. Kelly is standing in front of the whiteboard, arms folded, lips pursed.

I blink. "What?" A few assholes snicker, as if they've never daydreamed in class. It's nothing against Mr. Kelly—he's pretty cool, for a teacher—but why do I need to know what a symbol or a motif is?

Mr. Kelly clears his throat and my face heats. "We were discussing the significance of Holden Caulfield's red hunting hat, and Phoebe said that she thinks Holden uses it as a crutch to hide from the world." Phoebe Wright's tight curls bounce as she turns to look at me. "Do you agree?"

I first read *The Catcher in the Rye* last year on Mr. Kelly's recommendation. He said it helped him when he was in high school and thought it might do the same for me. The thing is, Holden Caulfield whined so much and overthought everything. I ended up skimming the novel because I couldn't stand his character. I never had the heart to tell Mr. Kelly. He lets me eat lunch in his classroom because my only two friends in the world, Monroe and Joey, are scheduled in different lunch periods, and he stays after school with me if I have a panic attack, talking to me while I wait for Mom to pick me up. I can't tell him I hate his favorite book.

"I don't know," I start. "I don't see why everyone makes such a big deal about his hunting hat. I get why people call it a security blanket or whatever, but it's not like Holden isn't out there, living, trying to figure out what the hell the world is all about. Pretty much everyone besides his sister is faker than a Kardashian. He knows that. He's very aware. He just wants to feel safe, I think." My mind drifts to the lone bird. Is it lonely, the other birds having migrated south for the winter? Is it vulnerable, by itself, looking for a safe place to land? "There's nothing wrong with trying to protect yourself."

"I can see that," Phoebe concedes, a bit too quickly for my liking. "And that would be true if Holden actually, like, dealt with his problems. But he doesn't. He hides."

"Why shouldn't he?" I say. "The world is harsh and cold, and the colder it gets, the less he can protect himself. Basically, the world sucks." Most of the class laughs. Even Mr. Kelly cracks a smile.

"That's for sure," Phoebe says.

There's an under-the-breath comment from behind me, loud enough to get Mr. Kelly's attention. Max McKagan's greasy fingers grab my earlobes and tug on my black diamond earrings. "Maybe it wouldn't suck so much if you weren't so . . . *defective*." He beeps like a malfunctioning robot, and the stench of Cool Ranch Doritos on his breath lingers as he follows it up with a repulsive term I won't repeat. I curl back into myself, shutting out the rest of the class.

But Mr. Kelly *has* to go and address it. "Do you have something you want to share with the class, Max?" I hate when teachers do this. Bringing everyone's attention to a problem always makes the situation worse. This isn't a wholesome family sitcom. We're not all going to learn a valuable lesson about tolerance in fewer than twenty-five minutes. This is eighth-period English, and Mr. Kelly is lucky most of us stay awake.

Max, of course, doesn't say anything.

My hands start to tremble. I shove them under the desk. "He called me a word I won't repeat in an attempt to make me feel . . ." *Broken.* My breath catches in the back of my throat, which prevents me from launching into Max's frequent and sustained microaggressions. I feel his stare on the back of my neck, but I don't turn. "Give it up, Max."

His desk skids forward, screeching against the floor, making Mr. Kelly jump. "At least I'm not *you*."

I laugh, because it's easier than crying in front of everyone.

"At least I'll get out of this town one day, unlike you, who'll live in your mom's basement until you Norman Bates her."

A few students gasp; a few make "*Ooo*" sounds like guests on a gossipy talk show. Phoebe's eyes widen as she covers her mouth to trap her laughter. The girl next to her, Blanca Rodriguez, elbows her in the ribs and they whisper to each other.

"Shove it, Mariah *Carey*," Max hisses.

"Good one," I say. "Very original." It's no secret that I love Mariah, and I'm no stranger to being called by the queen's name. Mom set me up for that with a first name like Carey. I *was* sort of named after her. Mom was obsessed with her music in the nineties, and she indoctrinated me into her fandom before I sashayed out of the womb. Sometimes she claims I was named after an old Hollywood star named Cary Grant, but the spelling tells a different story. Besides, newsflash! It's a total honor, Max!

"Mr. Kelly," I say, "Holden Caulfield thinks the world is full of fake people, so it's not a place he feels he belongs, right? What if *he*'s the fake one? Maybe it's the plight of the straight cisgender *bro* that, instead of trying to make room for anyone who's different, he's going to claim everyone else is fake. Like Holden, Max is telling on himself, letting the world see exactly who he is. I don't think this conversation will change his mind."

"You don't know shit. Are you gonna let he/she/*it* talk to me like that, Mr. Kelly?" Max is standing up now, hovering uncomfortably close.

Sweat trickles down my neck.

I try to breathe.

Steady myself.

4

I resist the urge to turn around and face him. I haven't looked directly at Max since . . . well, for a long time.

"Max, Principal McCauley's office, now!"

"Are you kidding me?" Anger tugs at the corners of Max's mouth. "This is ridiculous!" Max goes out of his way to shove the back of my chair as he walks out. He hovers in the doorway, looks at me, and making a camera-clicking motion with his fingers, mouths, *Click-click*.

Max has no power over me.

The whispers from everyone around me grow as Max slams the door behind him.

Mr. Kelly walks over to me and places a hand on my shoulder.

I flinch. I don't want any more attention.

Click-click.

"Carey, hang back after class," Mr. Kelly says before walking back to the whiteboard and writing out the homework for tomorrow.

Click-click.

I can't breathe.

Max does *have power over me.*

There are two coping tricks Dr. Potter taught me when my body shuts down from a panic attack: 1) Loudly say random Mariah Carey facts until the world stops buzzing, or 2) Sing a song in my head from start to finish. I can't exactly spout that when Mariah was married to her emotionally abusive record executive husband in the nineties, she called their New York mansion "Sing Sing" because it felt like a prison where she was forced to sing. Instead, my mind presses play on Mariah's "Close

My Eyes," the lullaby-like melody unable to drown out the sound of Max's voice calling me "defective," until the bell rings.

Mr. Kelly is still talking as the class funnels out the door. I close my notebook, which is covered in scribbles of music notes, song lyrics, and half-assed doodles of stick figure me in ball gowns. Phoebe waits by Mr. Kelly's desk until we're the only two people left. "How can I help you, Ms. Wright?" he asks, looking at me, not her, to make sure I know not to leave.

"Did you get the fliers printed yet? I wanna post them so we get a good turnout." She bounces on her toes and adjusts her backpack.

Mr. Kelly hands her a thick stack. "Hot off the presses."

"They're perfect!" Her eyes widen. "I *really* appreciate you volunteering to direct the musical. When Mrs. Piper dropped out—"

"Had a heart attack?" Mr. Kelly interjects.

"Right," she says. "I thought the spring musical would be cancelled."

"Well, I've never directed a musical, but I'm bringing someone in to help out. Together, we'll make sure it's a great show." He offers a tight-lipped smile, and his leg shakes restlessly.

Phoebe demonstrates a scale. Her voice is incredibly rich and powerful. "It will be." She hugs the fliers to her chest. "See you tomorrow, Mr. K! Bye, Carey!" She smiles and waves to me as she bounds toward the door, which is totally weird because I've never actually spoken to her outside class.

Mr. Kelly leans back and rocks in his chair before taking a deep breath and turning to me. "How are you, Carey?"

What a stupid question. "Fabulous," I deadpan.

"Mind if I shut the door?" Mr. Kelly asks, and I shake my head. As the door whooshes toward the jamb, his face drops all pretenses and I sigh, tears running down my hot cheeks. He leans against his desk at the front of the room. "People are afraid of what they don't understand. It's not an excuse, it's a sad truth. I'll have a talk with Principal McCauley about what happened."

I quickly wipe the wetness off my face with the back of my hand. I don't need people like Max to understand me. I want them to leave me alone.

"I got you something." Mr. Kelly pulls out his desk drawer. "My husband and I were in the West Village last weekend and came across these." He walks over and places a rainbow velvet pouch on my desk. "The shop owner is genderqueer too, and they explained how they made these for other genderqueer people to express their gender identity on any given day."

I open the pouch and tap the contents onto the desk. There are four macramé bracelets, each one woven in a different pattern. The first is a zigzag of different blues, from baby blue to sapphire, like the ocean.

"On a day when you feel more male energy and want to be identified by he/him pronouns, you would wear the blue bracelet," Mr. Kelly explains. I pick up the pink one, which is a Barbie DreamHouse of pastels. "The pink, is, well, you get the gist."

I resist the urge to comment how binary the pink and blue bracelets are, and while I realize that colors aren't gendered, most people associate the two with gender traits, and the whole point is to signal my pronouns without having to state them. So, it works.

Mr. Kelly continues. "And the green, white, and purple one is—"

"The genderqueer flag." My eyes open a little wider, and I sit up a little straighter in my chair. "So, when I want everyone to use they/them pronouns, like most days . . ." I slip that one around my wrist. Immediately my body relaxes.

"The rainbow bracelet is just fun." Mr. Kelly flashes his wrist to show a matching bracelet. "I had to get one. My husband did too." His face softens into a smile. "I hope this is okay and I'm not overstepping. You shouldn't have to explain yourself every day."

My thumb strokes the bracelet on my wrist. Something inside me is suddenly visible on the outside. It's a strange and beautiful feeling, though a bit uncomfortable. Like how I imagine the glass slipper felt on Cinderella's foot—it *was* glass, after all. My lips tremble. "Every day is like coming out again. Having to tell my friends which pronouns to use, wanting to correct the teachers who call me 'he' when I'm 'they,' but being too afraid to do it in the middle of class, and feeling like it doesn't matter once the bell rings. But it does matter." Tears bubble up as I talk. "I want to feel like I matter. People pretend to see me, but nobody *knows* me." I look up and Mr. Kelly's eyes are wet. "I guess I'm trying to say thanks."

He clears his throat. "You don't have to thank me. Just promise me you won't let"—he hesitates, then lowers his voice, as if someone is listening—"the *bastards* get you down. You're going to take the world by storm, Carey Parker. Once you believe in yourself." He hands back a poem I wrote for an extra-credit assignment.

It's littered with little red marks correcting my punctuation and grammar, but my eyes are drawn to the bright red A- circled at the top. I read his comments:

Carey, your poem is exquisite. There's a musicality here when I read this out loud. Except it seems as if you're holding back. There's a feeling of being trapped between the lines, as if you brought yourself to a certain point in the subject matter, then shied away. Continue to push this further. So much potential. Great job! ☺

"You really think it's good?"

"It needs a bit of work, but yes." Mr. Kelly points to the last stanza:

> *I've been too*
> *Scared to die,*
> *But afraid to live.*
> *I have to try,*
> *to forgive myself.*

"Are you doing okay?"

"I'm *fine.*" I smile as big as I can without being too extra.

There's still tension in Mr. Kelly's upper body. "Do you write poetry a lot?"

"No. Yes. I don't know. They're not so much poems as song lyrics."

"I didn't know you write music. What instrument do you play?"

"Uh, I don't. But when I write, I hear music. Big ballads. You know, like Mariah, Lady Gaga, Sam Smith."

"Is that where you go in class when you look like you're somewhere else?"

I nod. "That was my dream. To be a diva. Sing. Write my own songs. But everyone sees a boy, and what *they* see holds *me* back." I've never said that out loud to anyone but Monroe, but I can be honest with Mr. Kelly. "My old vocal coach used to tell me I had a gift." It feels awkward praising myself, almost like telling a lie.

"Used to?" he asks. "Forgive the English teacher in me, but there was a lot of past tense in what you just said."

"I, um, had to stop going." I try to think of a way to get off this topic because I really don't want to go there. Not now. But he asks why. "My, uh, mom couldn't afford it anymore." Which isn't a *total* lie, because it *was* expensive, and Mom already worked too much to support our family. It just isn't the whole truth.

He hums. "I'd love to hear you sing. You should try out for the musical."

"I love *going* to musicals, but . . . put myself out there like that? No."

"Why not?"

Shit. Now he's prodding, like Dr. Potter.

"They're not diva enough for me." I laugh it off instead of explaining that though music is everything to me, lately I only sing when I'm alone; I'm too scared to sing in front of anyone else.

"Let's reframe: Musicals are filled with divas; big, bold personalities, tours de force, with booming voices and songs in their souls. Like Mariah, they're unapologetic and fierce and—"

There's a knock on the classroom door.

Monroe Cooper is standing on her tippy toes, peering through the glass window, black liner highlighting her cat eyes. Mr. Kelly motions for her to come in, and Monroe pushes open the door. Her bubblegum-pink hair, choppy and layered, swishes against the collar of her cropped leather jacket, and her red, gator-skin heels clack against the tiles as she walks. She tugs on the bottom of her ripped The Clash crop top so it covers her stomach. The only reason she can wear a crop top to school is because last year, she single-handedly organized a student walkout to protest the sexist-as-fuck dress code for unfairly targeting girls because apparently boys "can't concentrate" when girls show skin.

Everyone needs a best friend like Monroe.

"Ms. Cooper," he says. "Sorry for keeping your friend after class."

She plays with the hoop dangling from her nostril. "No worries, Mr. K. I heard about what happened in your class, and when Carey didn't meet me in the parking lot, I figured I needed to come in." Monroe doesn't give him a chance to respond because she pivots to how she wishes she had him for English this year. Mr. Kelly struggles to keep up with her rapid-fire sentences when she says, "At least I don't have Mr. Jackson."

I shudder when she utters *that* name.

"I probably shouldn't be listening to this," Mr. Kelly says politely.

"Come on, he's the worst." Monroe turns to me, and I nod in confirmation. "Carey, we should go. I'm illegally parked out front." She offers Mr. Kelly a polite wave and doesn't wait for me to gather my things before she's out the door.

Mr. Kelly looks exhausted from their exchange, and I stifle a laugh as I hoist my backpack over my shoulder to follow her.

"Carey."

I turn. "Thanks for the bracelets, Mr. K."

"Anytime. But one more thing. If you have to sing, sing. Don't let anyone take that from you. Be the diva you wish to see in the world."

TRACK 2
THEY/THEM/THEIR

Monroe's rusty, dented Oldsmobile is double-parked in front of Sunnyside High's main entrance. Monroe whips around the car and yanks at the driver's side handle until her door pops open, nearly sending her flying on her ass. She crawls in on all fours and tosses a stack of colorful papers on the backseat with her backpack. The inside of her car is filled with empty Yoo-hoo bottles and half-eaten bags of zesty vegetable chips. Notebooks are scattered atop bolts of fabric on the backseat. I slide into the passenger side before the door can fling shut. Like everything else about this car, the suspension in the hinge is shot.

"Can we stop at Exile and get some tea before you drop me off?" I ask.

"That's perfect because I needed to go there anyway. My fucking boss is withholding my paycheck because I said I couldn't work this week with second-quarter exams and college applications due. He's such an ass and . . ." Her words gush out so fast that the untrained ear would have trouble understanding her, but Monroe has been my best friend since we were zygotes. Our moms are best friends, and we were raised basically as siblings. I'm used to Monroe always talking like she's in a panic.

"Where's Joey?" I ask once she's finished ranting.

"Ugh. Basketball practice. Then football."

"Football? It's December." Monroe's twin sister, Joey, is the school's all-star athlete and has played every sport imaginable. They have cheerleader parents who build them up, make them think they can do absolutely everything, like sewing Met Gala–style gowns or joining an all-boys football team. When Joey petitioned the school to try out, she made the roster over some of our biggest jocks. She's a natural athlete. For her, football is fun, a break between cross-country and her meal ticket, basketball.

"Some end-of-season dinner or something. I wasn't listening." She slams on the gas and the car jerks forward like an old amusement park ride. She banks a hard right out of the school parking lot and races at the speed of fucking light down High School Hill toward Main Street. She brakes hard at the bottom. "What's that?" she asks, glancing at my new bracelet.

"Mr. Kelly gave it to me." At the stoplight, I pull out the velvet bag and explain. Monroe is the only person besides Mom who asks which pronouns she should use each day. Monroe has been incredible since I came out last year, which isn't all that surprising because when we were kids, I sneaked a pair of red, glittery slippers she had in her closet, and when she caught me modeling them in her bathroom, she made me do a runway walk. She knew more about me than I was ready or willing to confront. Joey, on the other hand, was blindsided and has avoided me at all costs since prom; tension pulls at my jaw as I think about it. I want to ask Monroe what happened between Joey and me, but I'm afraid. Joey is her sister. Monroe may call me her "sibling," but we're not actually related. If it came to picking sides, I know whose she'd choose—and it wouldn't be mine.

Monroe pulls into the no-parking zone in front of Exile Records, the record shop–café where she works.

Exile is pretty much the coolest place in town. There's nothing better than a good vinyl record; the earnest crackle, the rawness of the instrumentation. The vocals are more real, like whoever is singing is right in front of you. There's nowhere to hide on a vinyl, not like so many of the muddled, robotic autotuned Top 40 songs that hide any hints of artistry or a lack thereof.

A lot of people come here after school to hang out and do homework in the café. Monroe, Joey, and I have spent the better part of our childhood perusing their racks of records and shelves of toys—vintage *Star Wars*, Marvel, and DC superhero figurines; Funko Pops—before purchasing overpriced artisanal coffees from the café like we were actual adults. Monroe always gets a triple shot of espresso and mixes it with brown cane sugar. Joey's drink of choice is an iced latte with two shots of vanilla syrup and so much half-and-half it's basically a cup of vanilla cream. I read a rumor once that Mariah Carey has an assistant whose job it is to prepare tea at the perfect temperature with a squeeze of honey and lemon before all her shows to soothe and preserve her voice, so that cemented it as my forever drink.

I pull on the tarnished brass handle, and we enter the busy shop. Golden rays stream through large picture windows at the front.

"So, what's your plan?" I ask her.

"I'm not leaving without my paycheck. Or I'll quit. And good luck finding someone as good as me. Whatever. Next year I'll be at the Fashion Institute of Technology, *not* working here for the rest of my life," she says without so much as a breath. "I don't see him. He's probably in the office. I'll be back."

While I wait for her, I browse the familiar stacks, not looking for anything in particular. I want everything and nothing. I run my fingertips across the records, some shrink-wrapped, some in hard plastic, some exposed to the elements. Small, hand-written cards let me know which artist or band I'm currently touching. Half the fun of being in a record store is finding an obscure artist or buying an album for its killer, quirky artwork. I have vinyls from every major diva from Freddie Mercury to Lady Gaga. I come across Sam Smith's *The Thrill of It All*. I bought this record after they came out as genderqueer and wore it out. When I realized I could no longer hide anymore, I sat in Dr. Potter's office with Mom and asked her to listen to the album's coming out anthem "HIM," because music has a way of saying what I can't. By the end of the song, Mom had tears in her eyes and asked me if I was gay. It was a complicated question. At least, I thought it was, because it took me so long to put words to my identity. I told her I was genderqueer and androsexual.

"What does that mean?" Mom leaned in closer.

I looked to Dr. Potter, who nodded in support.

"Sometimes I feel very male, and sometimes more female, but most of the time I'm somewhere on a spectrum I can't quite pinpoint or define."

"I don't understand." Her voice, though shaky, was soft, curious, unafraid.

I sucked in a breath, bracing myself, nails digging into the leather, sweating. When I was ready, I exhaled. "I feel like, sometimes, my skin doesn't always fit how I feel." I tried to explain how growing facial hair made me feel icky and fraudulent, and how, though I didn't believe in God, I would pray to Her, hoping I'd wake up with a smooth, hair-free face, or how my stomach would cave in on itself whenever someone would refer to me as a "man," as if that were my defining characteristic. "I don't feel like I'm part of the binary, *just* male *or* female. It's hard to describe, but there are days when I wake up and my energy is female, but I have to dress like a boy and can't express how I feel inside, so every step I take feels wrong, like I want to crawl out of my own skin. But it's not about my body or even superficial stuff, like clothes." Dr. Potter helped me practice saying this a million times. Still, I was breathless saying it out loud, and I braced for impact. "It's like the entire world has had its collective hand over my mouth and I've been gasping for air."

She grabbed my hand and squeezed. "And androsexual?"

"I'm attracted to masculinity."

"So, you're gay?" I could practically see her mind spinning, like the pinwheel on my laptop when it's trying to process information.

"I guess. It's not wrong, but it's not the complete picture."

"You're not a boy, not a girl," Mom whispered.

"I just *am*."

Mom stared at me, as if she was finally seeing the real me. "I love you, my beautiful child." That was all I needed.

I file the Sam Smith record, and I feel someone standing behind me.

"Sam Smith. Killer voice. But they've got nothing on you."

I turn. Cris freaking Kostas is smiling at me. My mouth goes dry. He's shorter than me by a good six or seven inches and breathtaking. His face pulls me in like dark magic—the honey brown of his irises gleaming behind black-rimmed glasses. He runs his fingers through his mop of messy dark brown hair, and the wrinkled, tight white V-neck undershirt he's wearing rises, exposing the light brown skin of his stomach.

"Favorite Sam song. Go!"

"What?" Something catches at the back of my throat. "Um, hey . . ." I *know* his name, but my mind is a baked potato because he's too damn beautiful. It's not like we go to a big school or anything, but we don't have any classes together, and I don't make a habit of lingering in the hallways at school. I keep my head down and zip to class as quickly as possible. But we *are* in the same grade and used to go to the same vocal coach, so I have no excuse except that he caught me off guard. But I can't tell him that.

"Cris." His head dips, like he's disappointed I didn't remember his name. My mind reels in embarrassment, and I have a total out-of-body experience where I'm floating above us, binge-watching my awkwardness like a Netflix show. I want to start again, but, you know, you can't rewind life.

"Yes. Right. Cris. Sorry. I have social amnesia."

He laughs, but I can tell it's a product of nerves, like he's not quite sure what to say next but wants to keep talking. So, he fills the space. "No worries. Haven't seen you around much. Not since summer. At the studio, I think."

I know the exact day he's referring to: when I told our vocal coach, Will Trevisani, I couldn't attend lessons anymore. It was right after junior prom. Coach told me he was planning a winter showcase for his students. At Carnegie fucking Hall. He wanted to feature *me* as one of the last singers, to spotlight *me* for an audience of industry professionals and recruiters at prestigious schools like Juilliard. As he told me this, sweat trickled down my face, and I couldn't tell if it was the heatwave or my nerves. Then the sweat became tears. The thought of putting my whole genderqueer-self, uncensored, onstage to be judged by what felt like the whole world paralyzed me. I told him I couldn't participate and ran out of the room. Cris was waiting on the couch for his session. He stood as if he wanted to ask what was wrong, but I had to get out of there. I bolted.

"You looked so sad that day," he says, his voice full of concern.

The thing about insanely cute people like Cris Kostas is that I never in a million years thought *they*'d ever notice *me*. Cris is the kind of guy who makes jokes at his own expense to make people laugh. He brings his guitar to school to play during lunch and runs from Mr. Jackson before it gets confiscated. Cris moves between friend groups, blending in with ease. I eat lunch with my English teacher. We couldn't be more different.

"You remember?" I ask.

"Some things you don't forget." He notices my bracelet. "Can I?" I hold out my wrist. The calloused tips of his fingers lightly graze my bracelet. "I like that."

I don't realize I've stopped breathing until he retracts his hand and I exhale.

"I heard what happened in Kelly's class today. Max is space junk."

The world goes dark again; I hate the idea of Cris knowing even a fraction of the awful shit Max says about me. "Word travels fast."

"You can count on Sunnyside for two things: gossip and how fast that shit travels," he says, the way only a victim of the Sunnyside chatter can. "I love what you're wearing, by the way." He studies my short-sleeve white button-down with geometric-print skinny black overalls and pink floral-print jacket. This is the first time anyone from school has ever said anything nice about my clothes.

"A Monroe Cooper original. Couture."

"Fierce, Carey." He leans in and his voice gets lower, huskier. I can feel sweat beading at the back of my neck. "*Seriously.*" I try not to stare at his lips, so my gaze wanders to the chest hair poking out of his V-neck. "Stay for my set."

"Your what?"

"I'm performing in the café in a few minutes. You should stay. It's my first time playing here. I could use a friendly face in the crowd. Who's your favorite artist? If I know something, maybe I'll play it."

What the hell is happening right now? This must be a daydream. I reach into the pocket of my overalls and pinch my leg. *Fuck, that hurt.* I guess this *is* real. I debate whether I should divulge my love of Mariah, since most people use her as a punching bag instead of treating her like the timeless legend she is. But Cris doesn't seem the type to dunk on her.

"Mariah Carey."

A smile spreads across his lips. "Interesting choice."

"A legendary choice," I correct.

"I like *all* music. Legends included." There it is again. That smile. Fuck. "I don't know much by her, but her *Caution* album is fire."

"Agreed." I check the time on my phone. "I can stay for a bit, but I have a . . . doctor's appointment."

"Oh." He looks disappointed but shakes it off. "I'll play you something at the beginning of my set, then. Hey, wanna hang tomorrow after school?"

I say yes, perhaps a bit too quickly, and he adds, "Meet me here," before turning toward the café.

"'How Do You Sleep?'" I shout breathlessly, answering his earlier question about my favorite Sam Smith song. I hate myself for the randomness of it all.

He turns and laughs. "That's a good one."

A good one!

Then the realization that Cris just asked me out slaps me across the face.

He *did* ask me out, right?

I look around for Monroe to see if maybe she caught any of that, but there's no sign of her anywhere, so I make my way toward the café. Cris tunes his guitar and fiddles with the microphone stand as people sit with their coffees, waiting for chords to carry them somewhere, anywhere.

As Cris strums, I close my eyes, steadying myself against the wall. I know my feet are on the ground, but suddenly I'm flying on the backs of his melodies. The sweet smell of cinnamon makes me forget about everything else. His voice, like melting butter on fresh-baked banana bread, fills the space, and my entire body breaks out in goose bumps. I don't know the song (it sounds like an original, his voice somewhere between Darren Criss and Harry Styles), but I want to sing alongside him, to harmonize and riff off his notes. I want to freeze time and stay in this moment for as long as I can.

Then a hand grabs my arm and yanks me back to reality. "Can we leave? I'm done with this place," Monroe whispers.

"What happened?" I ask quietly, my body following her to the front of the store, though my soul is still watching Cris.

"They don't appreciate me. I'm done." Monroe slides behind the counter and grabs a piece of blank computer paper and a red pen. HELP WANTED! She sticks some double-sided tape to the front and slams it to the window by the door. "I quit."

"Roe, you sure about this?"

"They'll come to their senses. I can't stand to be here anymore." Her shaky voice betrays her.

Cris's voice booms through the speakers. "This one is for Carey."

Monroe shoots me a confused look as Cris plucks his guitar strings, and I immediately recognize the song. Troye Sivan's "FOOLS." The lyrics are about a crumbling relationship, how he saw a future with this person, calling himself a fool for both falling in love and for messing it up. Then, midway through, the chords change to a lesser-known Mariah song, "Caution," about a love interest needing to proceed carefully because they've been hurt before. My breath catches.

I grab onto Monroe to steady myself.

"We have to go, Carey. You have therapy." She shoves her

phone in front of my face so I can see the time. "And we're gonna talk about this the whole way there."

"Wait," I say, hoping Cris glances my way.

Monroe hooks her arm into mine, and though I know she's impatient to leave, she stays with me until Cris's song ends, and his eyes meet mine. I offer a small wave, and he smiles; my chest flutters.

His brilliant mash-up echoes in the back of my mind for the rest of the night.

TRACK 3
THEY/THEM/THEIR

"I met someone today."

Dr. Potter lets a smile slip.

"He's cute and perfect and I have zero chance with him. I heard he has a girlfriend. Or maybe a boyfriend? Or isn't into nonbinary people? No way I'm good enough for him."

She leans forward. "What makes you go to that place first, where you're not good enough? You're making up scenarios and trying to label him to build walls around yourself while beating yourself up. Remember what we said, Carey. Put away your stick."

The stick. Apparently, I beat myself with an invisible stick. Dr. Potter instructs me to leave it in her office so I'm not tempted to tear myself down when I'm out in the world. But logically, when I'm in her office, shouldn't I be allowed to pick it up?

I examine the fancy lettering on her diplomas on the wall behind her. An undergraduate degree from Hunter College. A masters from Baruch College. A PhD from NYU. When I've successfully memorized them, I move on to the picture of her and her wife in Barcelona, Spain.

"Do you think you're not good enough?"

"Yes." My voice is so small it lingers in the empty space between us like an echo.

She scrunches her freckled face. "How does that make you feel?"

I hate that question.

I stare at her messenger bag with the I'm Still with Her and #MeToo buttons pinned on either side of the zippered pouch.

"Did I lose you?" she asks, running her hand through her fiery orange hair, her big, controlled ringlets bouncing as she repositions her body.

I mimic her movements, twirling my own rusty hair. I like that she has red hair, like me, except mine is super short on the sides and long and wavy on top. When I can't avoid her anymore, I whisper, "I hate that I think I'm not good enough."

"What *or who* aren't you good enough for?" she prods.

"I don't know."

"Are you afraid to say it out loud?"

Yes. I will myself not to think about all the reasons I believe I'm not good enough. I delete thoughts like files on a laptop.

"Do you think you're not smart enough?"

"I'm pretty smart. I practically get all As and Bs. One C. That's pretty good."

"That's pretty *great*," she corrects. "So, if school isn't the issue, who aren't you good enough for?"

"I don't know." I pause. "Maybe the people in school. They don't get me. They see the outward stuff: the nail polish, the pierced ears, the occasional makeup, what they consider 'girl' clothes." I roll my eyes. "They don't get that I have mild gender dysphoria. How can they? They'll probably never experience that. So, they judge me by what they see. And if what they see doesn't match whatever ideas they have about me, I'm somehow *defective*." I wince, but it quickly turns to anger. "As it is, on days I feel more masculine energy, I think I'm not *boy* enough, and on days I feel more feminine energy, I think I'm not *girl* enough. *Every day*, I worry I'm not genderqueer enough."

"So, it *is* a matter of *who* you think you're not good enough for, then?" she asks. I nod, hoping she'll give me the answer to that. "Stand up," she instructs, and I do. She motions me to step forward. "Stop. Turn to the right. What do you see?"

I am face-to-face with a mirror. Fuck. She caught me.

She repeats, "Take a deep breath. What do you see?"

"I see me."

"Do you like what you see?"

That's a loaded question. "Today, yes." My own answer catches me off guard.

"Okay, sit back down. I want you to think about what you just said, and how far you've come. A little more than a year ago, you told me you couldn't look in the mirror because you hated what you saw. Now I want you to close your eyes and think about everything you want for yourself."

I hear Pray Tell, the ballroom announcer from *Pose*, my favorite TV show, telling me that if the world refuses to see me, I better make them unable to deny my power. I imagine myself strutting across a stage about to open my first concert at Madison Square Garden, where I'll sing a duet with special guest Mariah Carey.

"What do you see?" she asks me.

"I'm under a spotlight, in a black sequin tuxedo gown."

Her voice is warm. "I love that confidence." Though my eyes are still closed, I bet she's smiling because *I'm* smiling. "Performing? Singing?"

I nod.

"Go ahead, sing," she encourages.

I see what she's doing. I wish it were that simple. I open my eyes. "That's the whole problem . . . *that* confidence exists only in my head. I'm a hot fucking mess." I look out the window. I'm a bird trapped in a cage of my own mind.

"How do you live that confidence *out loud*? I ask you every session if you've thought about resuming your private vocal lessons. Didn't your mother say she would send you back whenever you were ready? Where are you on that?"

I don't know what to say.

"Are you still avoiding it?"

I nod.

"Why do you think that is?"

I run through a list of excuses, like Mom not being able to afford it, but Dr. Potter knows it's not the truth. "I'm afraid."

"Of what?" she pushes.

"Everything." I barely hear myself, but Dr. Potter hears. She sits back and cocks her head, and though she's not supposed to show emotion, her eyes betray her. "I've lost so much since I came out," I whisper.

Joey doesn't pop to mind because she's always there, hovering like a ghost who just won't leave. And I don't want her to leave. I'd just rather not be haunted by her anymore.

I'm waiting for Dr. Potter to launch into a "look how much you've gained" speech, but she asks, "Like what?"

"Joey."

She nods like she's been waiting for me to bring up Joey. "You've avoided talking about Joey for months."

"What do you want me to say? She was my best friend and now we barely talk. She doesn't look at me. She avoids me. It's like she's . . . disgusted by me." My fist clenches and I mash it onto the leather arm of the chair.

"You know that because she's said so, I presume," Dr. Potter says gently.

"Well, no. But what else could it be? We were so close until I came out. It was always different with Joey than Monroe. Something between us I could never quite define, but more than a sister. She was a soul mate."

She twists her body and tosses her pad on her desk. "Walk me through what happened the last time you hung out and everything felt 'normal.'"

I do quick math in my head. "Like, seven months ago, the night of junior prom. We were going together—me and Joey. Everyone said how cute we looked, and all I kept thinking was that I hated those damn boy clothes, the monkey suit, you know? Joey looked incredible, though. She wore this emerald green form-fitting dress. She owned the whole damn night. And then—" My mind switches lanes. "Well, you know what happened. I don't want to get into Max again." I wince at his name. "I came out to Monroe that night. She was so supportive, and when I told her about my dreams of being a diva, she said she would make all my outfits. She's my personal fashion designer-slash-stylist-slash-everything. I tell her what I like or want, she designs it. *Couture!*" I stand to flaunt the androgynous realness for Dr. Potter.

"There's that confidence—it's nice to hear you compliment yourself! But what happened with Joey?" She glances at the digital clock behind me. "We're out of time." She stands and offers me a warm smile. "Your homework is to talk to Joey. Maybe getting back on track with her, or getting closure and moving on from the friendship, will remove the mental block that prevents you from singing. Plus, you're ignoring one vital part of this situation with Joey: she's still around you all the time, she hasn't completely cut you off. And in all of this, you haven't asked Joey about *her* side of the story."

"Do I have to?" I grind my teeth and it sounds like shoes skidding across a gym floor.

"You already know the answer to that."

Well, that's unhelpful.

Monroe's car is waiting in the parking lot after my session. Joey's in the front seat, flashing me a smile, the skin around her mouth pulled too tight to sell it.

Joey looks nothing like Monroe. She's about a foot taller, with long, curly blond hair, and she almost always wears jeans and a shapeless T-shirt with a sports team logo. Borderline hopeless, bless her soul. Monroe has tried to make her over, but part of what makes Joey so incredible is that she doesn't care what anybody thinks of her. She's the most confident person I've ever met, and I admire that.

"Hey, friends," I say as I climb into the back seat, weaseling my body uncomfortably between mounds of crap.

"Carey will appreciate this," Monroe says.

"You're gonna love this." Joey doesn't bother to look back at me.

What the hell did I just walk into?

"Can *I* tell *my* story?" Monroe hisses. "So, Car, I didn't tell you or Jo because, whatever, I have a billion things going on. So, don't get mad. But a few weeks ago, Phoebe—"

"Phoebe?" I cut her off. "As in—"

"Wright," Joey finishes.

"Yes, Phoebe Wright. *We all know her name, can I finish?*" Monroe yells before taking a deep breath. "She asked me to be the costume designer for the spring musical."

Joey tosses a stack of fliers onto my lap. "She has to post these around town."

"That's awesome!" Since the sun is already down, I take out my phone and tap the flashlight button. "*Wicked* is the musical this year? That's a pretty big deal." I remember Mom took Grams and me to see it on Broadway when I was in middle school, and I cried through the entire show. I *was* Elphaba, and it was the first musical I saw that sounded like pop music. Elphaba was the ultimate diva. I used to spend hours pretending to be onstage belting "The Wizard and I" for Grams, who watched wide-eyed with unwavering awe. That was a long time ago.

"It was announced last quarter in the *Sunnyside Up! Report*," Monroe says.

"Who reads that?" The school's digital newspaper sends

blasts every Tuesday, which I immediately delete. "I hate reading the news. It's depressing, and I already have enough triggers."

"That's no reason not to be informed," Monroe states.

Then it hits me. "I can't believe you didn't tell me. You *hate* musicals. Like, with a passion. Remember when our parents took us to see *Hamilton* on Broadway, and you fell asleep! During *Hamilton*! Who does that?" Monroe and Joey's parents always get free tickets to concerts and shows through work, and they're always inviting Mom and me.

"I hate sung plots," Monroe says. "But the costumes!"

Okay, that's fair. "And Phoebe?" Monroe and Phoebe couldn't be more different if they tried. Monroe is rough around the edges, where Phoebe is poised and polished. Monroe never studies and could be valedictorian if she spent less time in the art room sewing, while I've seen Phoebe pore over textbooks in the library and she is the kind of student who always raises her hand first, asks twenty questions, then requests *extra* assignments. When Phoebe ran for student body president, her slogans were, "Vote Phoebe, Vote (W)right!" and "Phoebe Is Always (W)right." I mean, I totally voted for her because I love a good pun, but Monroe and I made fun of her for ages. Life generally seems so easy for Phoebe, who is super popular and has an actual social life, unlike us, who only spend time with each other.

It feels like a mini-betrayal that Monroe didn't tell me she was hanging out with Phoebe. Or that she joined the musical.

"She's weird like me. You'd like her, I think. She saw my portfolio in art class and was dying over my sketches—especially the ones I've been doing for you. She asked me to do the costumes for the show, and I figured my FIT application would benefit from an extracurricular boost, so why the hell not?" Monroe banks a hard right, and my body slams against the car door.

"Oh, relax, you're gonna get in. How could you not?" Joey adds.

"Says the person scouted by colleges *last year* for basketball," Monroe says. "Not all of us are so lucky, Jo."

"It *is* nice having zero applications to turn in." Joey puts her hands behind her head and kicks her feet up on the dashboard.

"I bet Phoebe has all *her* apps in." I'm so Queen of All Things Petty right now, but it hurts to feel left out. Nobody knows the Cooper twins better than I do. From the way they eat cookies (submerging the entire thing until it's soaked with milk, then shoving it in their mouths before it falls apart) to their career goals—Joey playing for the WNBA and Monroe wanting to be a platypus (like, the animal, which nobody told her was impossible until she was eight) before discovering fashion. But at some point, we all started to keep secrets from each other. I guess I've been doing the same thing by not talking to Joey. Is it possible for best friends to tell each other everything, and if not, is that bad? Soon we'll be going our separate ways. Maybe we won't be the ones who know each other best.

Maybe we already don't.

Maybe the reason I'm afraid to sing is right in front of my face, or rather, *she*'s in the seat in front of me. How can I put myself out there, under a spotlight, in front of an audience, if my own best friend isn't ready to see the real me? The way things are now, Joey and I coexist. It's not perfect—it's actually pretty unbearable, but at least she's still within arm's reach. If I confront her and our entire seventeen-year friendship dissolves, I don't know if I can recover from that. The thought of losing her for good makes me feel like a balloon inflated within breaths of its elastic limits.

The car goes quiet.

As we roll to a stop at a red light, Monroe breaks the silence. "We need a pick-me-up." The light from her phone beams through the darkness, and I know exactly what she's going to play. "A little blast from our childhood!"

Lady Gaga's monstrous voice booms through the speakers, and the three of us start singing the opening *Oh*s and roars of "Bad Romance." For exactly four minutes and fifty seven seconds, we're kids again, jumping on our beds and scream-singing the words: Joey leading the pack with the first verse, Monroe croaking the eerie Hitchcockian lyrics of the second verse, and me talk-singing the fashion show–inspired bridge, all of us coming together for the chorus.

Though I'm not really trying, I *am* singing out loud for the first time in forever, and it feels right. While this one song doesn't mean that everything between Joey and me is good, it gives me hope that it can be, that despite all the tension and hurt between us, our friendship is still tethering us together.

Maybe that's enough for now.

TRACK 4
THEY/THEM/THEIR

I walk up the narrow staircase to our apartment. We live on the second floor of a carriage house from the 1800s. It used to be a servant dwelling for the small castle-turned-museum a mile down the road and has some historical remnants, like a random set of stone steps where men would mount horses and an old post for tying them up. The stairs creak and the carpet smells like mothballs, but our space is pretty big. Well, for what Mom can afford, anyway.

The apartment is dark when I unlock the door, save for the blue light emanating from the TV in the living room. Mom isn't home yet, probably working overtime. I make myself a large bowl of Fruity Pebbles and take it to the living room to sit with Grams and relieve the home health-care aide.

"Hi, Grams!" I bend down and kiss her forehead. "How was she today?" I ask the aide, placing my bowl on the coffee table. Grams looks so much older than she did a year ago, and smaller, like her body gave up on her. A few years ago, Grandma Rosemary was vibrant, two-stepping into bingo night at the local church, where she took up an entire folding table with her cards, blotters, and colorful Treasure Trolls for good luck, and strutting around the mall in oversize tortoise sunnies. She'd spend hours primping her once jet-black hair and applying makeup, pursing her lips like an old Hollywood starlet in the mirror. Rosemary was everything. This feeble version with brittle bones, sunken skin, and straw-like white hair that barely covers the bald spots? This is not *my* grams.

"She had a few accidents, didn't you Miss Rosemary?" The nurse brushes the hair from Grams's forehead. "She's still having trouble eating. I told your mother. She barely swallowed her food. Choked a bit, too. But she's all right, aren't you, Miss Rosemary?" The aide gathers her bag and coat. She doesn't bother to ask if I'll be okay when she goes. She knows I'm expected to take care of Grams until Mom gets home.

I sit next to Grams. She's slumped a little, so I hoist her up. She gently grabs my arm and pulls me down to her with surprising strength. She puckers her lips, so I lean my cheek against them for the most delicate of kisses. I pull away, and she smiles weakly before opening her mouth. Her lips move, trying to find words, but words are lost to her; now, she's a human parrot, only able to repeat a few phrases she hears spoken directly to her. The skin around her eyes crinkles, a sign that she's trying to talk. It's up to me to figure out what she's saying. Her fingernails dig into my skin.

"What's going on in there, Grams? What do you need?"

"Wha-wha-wha you need?" she croaks.

"Are you hungry? You need to eat."

"Ar-ar-are you hungry?" she says, and then, like she

understands, her eyes widen and she nods, maybe even smiles. It's hard to tell anymore.

"Would you like some oatmeal?" She digs her nails deeper into my skin. "Stay there," I command, but it's not like she can go anywhere. I go into the kitchen and make a bowl of instant oatmeal that's ultramilky, the right consistency for her to swallow. Before I start to spoon-feed her, I say, "I love you, you know that?"

"I—I love—love y-you kn-know at-at?" The syllables jumble together at the end.

"I do." Sometimes I tell Grams "I love you" just to hear her say it back. I pretend she's saying it because she knows I need to hear it. Before the Alzheimer's, she said it all the time, so I don't feel guilty. It's nice hearing those words.

When Mom gets home, I help bring Grams to the bathroom so Mom can wash her, change her diaper, and dress her in a velvet nightgown for bed. Once Grams is secure in her hospital cot at the far corner of the living room, Mom collapses on the couch.

"How's my baby?" She stretches her legs before curling them underneath her body. She motions for me to sit with her.

"It's been a day. You?" I could tell her about Joey or Max or Cris, but I can't talk about any of it right now. "Look what Mr. Kelly gave me." I flash her my wrist.

"I love them! Where can I get some?" That's what I love about Mom. She's pretty much the best ally in the world. "I get asked about my Ask My Pronoun button all the time, and it gives me another excuse to brag about my baby." She plants a wet kiss on my cheek, which I promptly wipe away, even though I secretly love it. She clears her throat, Mom Code for *I'm about to bring up something you won't like.* "How're your college applications coming? I know we agreed I wouldn't pester you, but I'm your mother and I get to bring up what I want to bring up."

Here's the thing: Mom is Wonder Woman. Ever since deadbeat BioDad left when I was five, she's had to work at least two jobs at a time to keep us afloat. She was able to squirrel away small chunks of her paychecks for state or city school tuition, and since I'd be the first in our family to go to college, I crushed her dreams when I told her I wasn't sure college was right for me. I wanted to make it as a singer. But then prom happened, and I dropped out of voice lessons with Coach Trevisani, so we came to a compromise: I would apply to a few colleges and attend the most sensible choice while I worked through my performance anxieties, among everything else, with Dr. Potter.

"Finished last week," I say earnestly, with an exhausted groan. "Didn't wanna worry about them over Christmas break."

She grins proudly. "How was therapy?" The skin around her eyes is dark.

"Fine." I sigh. It's exhausting to talk about how I bared my soul after baring my soul.

She gives me The Look and ignores my terse one-word answer. "Have you talked about Grams?" I shake my head. "Carey . . ." her voice does this thing where it gets super serious super quickly, and it's pretty much the scariest thing in the world. "You heard what the doctor said last week. Grams might not make it to her next birthday. She's not really eating anymore, she's basically skin and bones." Mom's whispering now because she's concerned that Grams, on some level, can understand everything we say. "You need to be prepared."

"I don't want to talk about this." I move off the couch and start toward my room, but she grabs my arm.

For a few seconds, she doesn't say anything. "This apartment used to be filled with music." Sorrow drowns her voice. Before Grams lost the ability to have a conversation, all she did was sing. Every morning, we awoke to the sounds of Nat King Cole or Dean Martin playing in the kitchen as Grams made her special savory French toast with fresh mint and sang along to every song. I joined in, harmonized with her. After every voice lesson, I came home and practiced my scales, and Grams would listen and clap for me before joining in. Then Grams got sick. And my world got smaller, the spotlight brighter, and I denied the only thing that made me happy to protect myself.

The air in the apartment is thick. I kiss Mom and Grams and head to my room, where I can at least pretend everything is normal.

I dream about Cris. He's singing at Exile, his voice blending with Grams's, begging me to sing too.

I reach for the microphone, and as I grab it, Cris and Grams disappear. I turn to see Max's face in the crowd. He's sitting behind Joey and pulls her toward him. I look at the crowd, who aren't people at all, but dark, shadowy demons with red eyes. And the more Max pulls on Joey, the more darkness devours her until she's another red-eyed shadow demon. I try to open my mouth to sing or scream, but all the oxygen is sucked out of my lungs like a vacuum. Like Ursula stealing Ariel's voice.

I try to open my eyes, but I can't. The dream won't let me.

Then I hear Grams. I can't make out what she's saying. The shadow demons fade until all that's left is the sound of her voice; it's far away, like a breeze through rustling leaves, but it's there.

I wake up in a cold sweat to the familiar creaking of a thin mattress against a hospital cot. Grams must be restless. I make my way to the living room, and like a baby attempting to get out of its crib, Grams is trying to escape her hospital bed. Except she has no upper body strength, so it's not like she can get far.

"Grams." I pull up next to her. "Shh, it's okay."

She doesn't stop. Her eyes are wide, her face panic-stricken. Her thin fingers shake the rails. I should wake up Mom, but Mom works so much. She deserves sleep.

I start to hum "My All" by Mariah Carey. This was one of Grams's favorites. She always said it was full of raw emotion and pain because, "she really loved that Derek Jeter," whom the song is about. She recognizes the haunting melody and starts to hum along. It's froggy but right on pitch.

Grams's eyes soften. I can't stop now.

The words of the verses build. Slowly, at first. When I reach the thunderous final chorus, I don't hold back, because Mariah wouldn't. That's the one thing nobody could ever take from her: her voice.

She would belt out the words, even if they hurt her. Even if she couldn't have the person she needed so desperately.

I have no choice either.

There in the dark, with an audience of one, I give in to the music.

TRACK 5
HE/HIM/HIS

I wait for Cris in the stacks of Exile Records, tugging at my blue bracelet. It's rather empty in here. The café, usually swarming with Sunnysiders, is slow. In the corner of the store, an automated record player is hooked up to headphones where anyone can try out the used records. I want to listen to something that will calm my nerves. I pick up a Queen record, *The Works*. Freddie Mercury. The OG male diva.

The crackle of the needle against the vinyl makes my eardrums buzz.

Queen, like Mariah, is transcendent. Their songs resonate long after the final note or fade-out; they often crescendo and, just when you think they're about to end, take a turn to someplace magical. When their songs are over, I either feel whole, like with "Don't Stop Me Now" or "Killer Queen," or a sense of loss, like with "Who Wants to Live Forever."

The record spins through "Radio Ga Ga," but I need something more urgent. I set the needle down again. It hisses and sputters the first note of "I Want to Break Free." The aggression of the drumbeat and the guitar plunk before Freddie Mercury growls the first verse. The beat pulses through my veins, pumping notes like blood from my feet to my head to my heart. I look around and don't see a soul, so I start to mumble the lyrics until all the tension in my body melts away. I think about Grams last night trapped in bed, unable to talk, let alone sing.

She can't sing. But I *can*.

I belt out the words and feel like the sun emerging from behind clouds on a cold day. My body feels warm again.

I use a stack of old records as a drum and tap my hands, then switch to air guitar, strumming like I'm onstage, but I'm no drummer or guitarist or background bitch. I'm a fucking diva. I'm Freddie Mercury, and every spotlight is on me in a black, diamond-studded one-piece suit and a tall, black crown, holding the microphone stand, serving up sex and glam and everything.

The track fades. I'm panting, my lungs expanding and contracting.

All the workers, wide-eyed and breathless, break into slow applause that quickly turns thunderous. It seeps into my soul, and I pretend that the few onlookers are a few thousand inside a stadium.

"Damn. Your voice is better than I remember," Cris says from behind, and I whirl around to face him, my cheeks flush and hot, my entire body tense.

Cris motions for me to bow, but I'm suddenly too embarrassed, so I dip my head.

"How much of that did you hear?"

"Enough." He smirks and bites his lip. "Next time, don't hold back."

I swallow hard. "Hold back?"

"You sounded a bit sad. Hesitant." He runs his fingers through his hair. "Not to sound creepy, but when I used to wait for my lessons, I could hear you sing like you were Lady Gaga at the Oscars. Your big-ass voice exploded!"

Holy shit. He's right. It's like he sees parts of me that I'm not even aware of. I wonder what else Cris observed about me when I wasn't paying attention. I fight the urge to run.

My hands and voice tremble. "Did you know Mariah Carey didn't tour until her third album *Music Box*, and then she only did six shows? There are rumors she was afraid to sing in front of that many people."

He chuckles. "You're fucking weird." He stares at me, and I'm pretty sure he's hypnotizing me with his eyes like Kaa, the giant snake from *The Jungle Book*. "I appreciate the random Mariah factoid."

"Plenty more where that came from." I exhale. "So, you were saying I sounded sad."

He winces. "That came out wrong."

"Can't sadness be good? Like, think about Mariah. She has a song called 'Outside' about how she never fit in, always feeling between identities." Cris scrunches his face, seemingly unfamiliar with the song, which is not all that surprising since it was an obscure track off *Butterfly*, an album that came out long before we were born.

I take his hand. "Come on, I'll show you." He trails behind me as I head toward the *C* stack and flip through until I find *Butterfly*. We head to the record player at the front. I place the vinyl on the turntable and gently place the headphones over his ears. "Listen to the words. And how her vocals tell the story," I instruct. As he listens, he keeps looking at me, and every so often, his face twitches in sadness.

When he's done, he grabs my hand. "That was beautiful. Hauntingly sad."

"It's the closest I've ever come to having how I feel inside expressed in a song."

"I could hear the pain, mostly when she launched into that final verse. It's like she was screaming for someone to see her," Cris says. "And the way she ends, so small, almost meek in comparison to where the song peaked? I got chills."

I smile. It's not every day I can talk music, especially Mariah's, with someone who gets it. "So, can't sadness be good?"

"What would Coach Trevisani say?" Cris asks.

I sigh. "A diva of her artistry knows how to utilize sadness when it's appropriate," I say, mimicking his deep voice. "Maybe that's the difference."

He leans against the table next to the record player. "Exactly. 'I Want to Break Free' is a song about shattering constraints and moving forward. Freddie's a caged animal who has *already* broken free. His vocals are controlled, focused, but wildly powerful. 'Outside' is a song where the animal knows it's in a cage but is almost . . . resigned to that. Her voice is soft and pained until it becomes loud and pained. In each song, the emotion comes through differently, you know? I've heard you let loose before. This wasn't it. It was like the words were being pried from your body." He shoves his hands in the pockets of his skinny jeans and looks around the room awkwardly as he shuffles his weight from foot to foot. "I'm fucking this up, aren't I?"

I shake my head. "I haven't sung in a while."

"Maybe we can change that." He nods toward the exit. "Wanna go for a walk?"

He stops by the exit and points to a poster for Mariah Carey's latest concert tour.

I will my body to move forward, even though I want to stop and stare in lust, and sigh.

"Was that . . . a . . . snub to your queen?" he asks.

I turn on my heels. "Never. I just hate seeing that poster because—" I debate how much information to give him about Mom and Grams and our financial situation and settle on, "I can't afford it. Tickets are ridiculous. I would give my right hand to see her."

"Why the right?" he asks.

"It's not my Mariah hand. It's dead weight."

"Mariah hand?"

"You know, the hand jiggle Mariah does when she sings. I use my left hand for that. The right is basically useless."

"Noted." He knocks his shoulder into mine. "Legends only."

"It's nice to find someone else who likes the Legend."

He crinkles his nose. "I wouldn't say I like her. I mean, I appreciate the greatness, no doubt. But I'm more into moody pop." He must see the confusion on my face. "Years & Years. Troye Sivan. Or atmospheric R & B, like Frank Ocean and dvsn. And I looooove when the two styles blend." He makes a chef's kiss motion with his hands. "Like Labrinth. Or Mariah's *Caution* album. I like songs that speak human."

"Huh?"

He laughs as he pushes the handle on the door. A rush of cold air envelops us. "Sometimes it's easier for me to communicate through songs than anything else. Talking about music, saying what I need to say through lyrics. Sounds weird, I know."

You get it, too, I think. "Not at all."

We walk across the train tracks to the park, a stretch of grassy land along the Hudson River. During the summer, it brims with older couples walking arm in arm, parents in flip-flops with their leashed kids and unleashed dogs, and city commuters in three-piece suits. Bright yellow, pink, and purple flowers bloom in carefully planted designs around memorial trees. The park is quieter in the winter. Everyone is bundled up, with scarves and gloves to protect from the wind's frosty lashes. Beyond brown grass, in the river, chunks of ice float downstream. The sun is already setting behind dull clouds, which glow orange and pink.

"I hope you don't think I'm a weirdo," he says as his shoulder bumps into my upper arm again.

"Aren't you?" I want to add, *"You're with me,"* but I don't. "Why a weirdo?"

He sucks cold air in and lets out a long, steady breath that swirls into the air above us. "I'd been in this relationship that was . . . whatever. I was having a shitty day yesterday, and then I saw you in Exile. I don't normally ask out someone so quickly, but I couldn't help myself."

His admission stops me in my tracks. "So . . . this is a date?"

His gaze holds mine, and I realize now if I'm not careful, I could lose myself in his eyes. "If you want it to be."

"D-do you?"

He shrugs and follows it up with a devilish smirk and a nod.

"I've never been asked out before." I cringe at my overshare.

"I like your honesty." He clears his throat. "Carey Parker, would you do me the honor of going out on a date with me?"

My cheeks heat. "When?"

"Right now."

"Hmm . . . I'm sorta busy." I grin.

"Fair. All right, see ya later." He waves and backs away slowly.

I let him get far enough that his face scrunches in worry. He turns his back to me and when his shoulders slump, the bottom falls right out of my stomach because I don't want to mess this up. Or get left behind again.

"Wait!" I yell, perhaps a little too desperately, and trap whatever air I have left inside my lungs.

He turns slowly like one of those animatronic dolls on a Disney World ride to reveal a cheesy grin. "I knew you couldn't resist my charm."

I exhale. "Let's not get ahead of ourselves."

He skips back to me. "My turn to be honest. You make me nervous."

"Why?" My chest starts to flutter, but not with clichéd butterflies. It's the inescapable thought that my identity scares him. I brace myself for the hit.

"I've been crushing on you for a long time, but we've never really talked until yesterday." He awkwardly shifts closer, but not too close. He's not sure what to do with his hands, so they fumble trying to grab mine.

My mouth is dry. "Forward."

He laughs. "I hate playing games." His eyes avoid mine, staring down at the dirt. His hands quiver. "I've learned to say what I mean."

I can't help but wonder what he's been through. "What *do* you mean?"

"You're cute. I've *always* had trouble getting you out of my head."

"What else?"

"You want more?" His eyebrows arch. "That's all I got. For now. TBD."

If this were a rom-com, he'd lean in, and I'd lean in, and our lips would touch and fireworks would go off in the background. It's heady to imagine what that might feel like.

Too much time passes though, because he says, "Say something."

I resist the urge to question his choice in dates because Dr. Potter's voice pops into my head: *Listen to what the boy is saying!*

"You're the first person in a long time who sees me as someone *worth* seeing," I say.

"Fuck, that was deep." He takes off his glasses, blows on the lenses, and wipes them with the sleeve of his jacket. Placing them back on the bridge of his nose, he says, "Yep, you're definitely worth seeing."

Cue the clichéd butterflies. "I want to know you, too," I say softly.

He puts his hands in his pockets and rocks back and forth, deep in thought. After a moment, he says, "See that willow over there?" He points to a large weeping willow at the far end of the park, near the water. "I spent all my time there when my mom passed away. I'd go to disappear from the rest of the world. She loved that spot, so it felt like she was there with me. I know that sounds weird."

"Not at all." I think about Grams. Sometimes I feel her old spirit in the apartment with us, like her physical body has been possessed by someone else, and Grams's true spirit is trapped on the outside, begging to be let back in. It's not the same as what Cris went through, but I get it on some level.

"Show me." I hold out my hand and he takes it. Our fingers intertwine. It's so intimate, more than any kiss.

Cris holds open the branches, sheathed with ice, for me to slip inside. The ice is so thick and crystallized white that even without its leaves, the tree shields us from the outside. A cold breeze rushes in and fallen leaves dance on the ground like a scene from a fairy tale. But this is real-world magic.

"Nobody could find me in here," Cris says.

I follow him to the base of the tree and sit beside him. I remember hearing about Cris's mom passing away from cancer. It was the first time anyone I knew of, even peripherally at school, had lost a family member. My grandfather died before I was born, and my dad and his parents are alive somewhere, but I don't have a relationship with them. I never spoke a word to Cris, besides the occasional "hi" after voice lessons, before his mom passed, so I didn't know what to say to him when she died. I remember crying myself to sleep because I thought about losing my own mom, and it felt like a black hole of anguish.

I couldn't imagine what he felt and my "sorry" wouldn't have brought her back to him.

"It's fine." He sighs. Hard. Like it's painful for his lungs and his chest. "No, fuck that. It really fucking sucks." I put a hand on his knee, and he screams, long and guttural. I don't flinch, because instinct tells me he needs my steadiness. After a few seconds, he says, "That felt good."

"Preach." I shift to recirculate the blood to my butt, which is frozen from the cold ground.

"Your turn."

"Seriously?"

He stares at me until I concede. My yell starts as a timid, pitchy howl, but his hand coaxes more out of me like a conductor's, and I let out a twisted melody that's been inside me for a long time. My throat is hoarse when I'm done, but I needed that.

"I try not to think about my mom too much," he confesses. "I have my dad. He's pretty chill. Lets me do what I want, doesn't ask questions. But he isn't around that much, either. I'd give anything to see her again."

Another breeze from the river gusts around us, and the tree sways, icicles clanging like chimes. Shards from branches tinkle to the ground.

"I don't know what I would do if I lost my mom." I wince, wanting to take it back, but words are tricky like that.

"You close to your mom?" he asks.

"She's everything. Mom, dad, aunt, uncle, brother, sister, best friend, giver of piggyback rides. When I was younger," I add. "Not now, obviously. That'd be creepy."

"Nice. I love piggyback rides. What about your dad?"

"BioDad exists. Somewhere. He left when I was five. Sends birthday cards every year with a hundred bucks in them and a 'Love, Dad.'" I roll my eyes, thinking of his fake valedictions. "The fucked-up thing is that he lives an hour away and never tries to see me."

"He doesn't know what he's missing," Cris says.

I grind my teeth. "The only thing I remember about him is that he had red hair, like me, and he used to sing 'Winnie the Pooh' with me on Sunday mornings. The rest I know only from pictures and fragmented stories. I used to dream of meeting him again. We'd, like, bond over something ridiculous, like a mutual love for *Stranger Things*." Cris laughs. "He'd tell me he left us because he was fighting in a war, or discovering an alternative for fossil fuel, or went deep undercover as a spy." I take in a deep breath and hold it steady. "But he's not a scientist, or a secret spy, no more than he is a father." I lick my dry lips. "Is it sad I feel nothing for him?"

He doesn't say anything. I don't expect him to, not after telling me about his mom. Is it selfish not to want anything to do with BioDad when someone like Cris would give up everything to have his mom back?

"I think what's sad is that he'll never know you." Our stories are very different, but being here with Cris makes me feel less alone. "After my mom died, I was scared I would forget her, but every day, I remember something new about her. Like the way she taught me how to play piano but wasn't sad when I switched to guitar. The way she'd move her hands like she was conducting an invisible orchestra when she listened to me play guitar, or how she'd crinkle her nose when cooking. It used to make me really sad, but the memories are a gift."

"They're her legacy," I say.

"Exactly. She was an immigration lawyer. She was doing good, you know? Which just made it more unfair that someone so good . . ." He doesn't finish. He doesn't have to. "Makes you think about the kind of person you want to be."

"Who do *you* want to be?" I ask.

He pauses. "Someone she'd be proud of." He wipes his eyes with the sleeve of his jacket. "What about you?"

I lift my face toward the willow's canopy and close my eyes. In the darkness, I envision myself onstage. When I open my eyes, the afterimage remains, like a ghost.

"I want to feel seen."

"What do you mean?"

I contemplate telling him what I went through last year, but I'm not ready to share yet. Instead, I hold out my wrist and play with the blue bracelet. "This is what people see every day. If I'm not wearing makeup or something androgynous, they see me as a boy. If I do dress more feminine or androgynous, they still see a boy, but a boy wearing eyeshadow or nail polish. It's easier for people to see what's on the outside than what's on the inside." I try to explain the layers of my identity. I lay my head against the tree trunk. "You know how most people hear a song and only remember the thumping piano melody? I'm more than just that one instrument or one key. I exist in between notes, with backing vocals and lush harmonies."

"You *are* music." He squeezes my hand. He understands. "What do you want most in the world, Carey Parker?" he asks.

Dr. Potter's voice rings in my head, telling me that giving voice to my dreams won't make them come true, but it will make them real.

"I want to be Mariah." He looks at me cross-eyed, so I clarify. "I want to be a legendary diva. A singer."

He smiles. "Do it!"

"Oh, okay. Easy." I snap my fingers, stand, and twirl in front of him like Cinderella under her fairy godmother's spell. When I stop, though, I'm still Carey Parker. No sequined ballgown. No pumpkin-drawn carriage to take me to Madison Square Garden. No rhinestone microphone or mice-turned-background singers. I purse my lips and cock my head. "Didn't work."

"I dunno. That was *very* diva-like." He hops to his feet, bows gracefully, and holds out his palm, Prince Charming–style. When I don't reach for his hand, he clears his throat rather loudly until I take the hint. Then asks me to close my eyes. When I do, he folds his free hand around mine, molding it into a fist and positioning it inches from my lips. "You've got the mic and the voice," he says, and my palms get sweaty. "The spotlight is yours. Demand the stage. The best way to show people who you are is to sing."

I let that sit for a moment before opening my eyes. Is it that simple?

"Oh!" he exclaims, like an invisible light bulb has gone on over his head. He digs into his pocket and pulls out a flier for the musical. "You should try out."

"Why does everyone have that flier? What kind of conspiracy is this?"

"*Wicked* is wicked."

"Nice dad joke," I say, and he smiles. "Why don't *you* audition?"

"I am. What other excuse you got?" He sticks out his tongue. Fuck, he's cute. "I'd only do it if I can play Elphaba. But that'll never happen."

"You'll never know if you don't try. Auditions are next Tuesday. Let them see you the way I see you." He pulls me closer until we're practically hugging. It's awkward because I want him closer, and maybe he wants that too, but our bodies hesitate.

When he pulls away, I squint at the *Wicked* flier, but the sun is disappearing fast, so it's hard to see much. I fold it and shove it into my pocket. "I don't know if I can."

He pulls back the curtain of icy branches and we walk along the edge of the park.

"After Mom died, I started asking myself, Will I regret *not* doing something?" When I don't respond, he says, "Yes, I just pulled the dead mom card. No, I'm not sorry about it."

I crack a smile. "No fair." But he has a point. Will I regret not trying out? "My grams is a singer. *Was.* She had the most incredible voice." I take out my phone and scroll to the pictures-of-old-pictures I have of Grams in tight black dresses that bared her shoulders and a short black bob and whimsical bangs. "She used to tell me stories of how she'd sneak out of her house at night to sing at smoky clubs. She said people would line up around the block to hear her sing. She was . . . never afraid of the spotlight." My hand falls and Cris reaches for it, but not to hold it, to get a better look at the pictures.

"She looks fierce as fuck," Cris says. "And if her voice is anything like yours . . ."

"*Was*," I correct. "It was better. She was better. Unafraid. If you told her she couldn't be onstage, she found a way to elbow herself in."

"What happened to her?"

"One night, after a sold-out set, a tall man in the finest suit she'd ever seen came up to her after her performance and offered to sign her to his record company." Grams told me this story so many times, I know it by heart.

"A modern fairy tale," Cris says.

I sigh. "If only. They had a meeting all set up. But he never showed. He was in a car wreck *that* day. Didn't make it."

"Brutal." He motions to a nearby bench, and we settle in.

"She never got to make a record. She took it as a sign. She gave up on her dream of making it. She sang at home, and to anyone who would listen, but never professionally. When I started to sing, she was my audience, watching intently as I performed for her in my living room, singing songs from Disney movies, draped in a bedsheet I would pretend was a gown. Sometimes she would sing with me or scat over my words." A tear spills down my cheek. "You know, one day, she sat me down and said, 'Don't ever give up on yourself.'"

All Cris says is, "*Hmph*." He sidles up beside me so close that when he stretches out his arm to wrap around my shoulder, he fumbles awkwardly, and his elbow bashes into the metal bench. I pivot so he can maneuver his arm properly, and when we settle back into each other and he pulls me closer so that I'm resting in the crook of his armpit, he doesn't feel close enough. I need to be closer, and I don't know how that's even possible, but there's a pounding in my chest that drowns out everything but his breathing. I want to slip my hand behind his back and hold on to him so tight and never let go. This feeling of needing him this much, this soon, both scares and excites me.

"So, are you?" he asks.

"Am I what?"

"Gonna give up on yourself? Or will you audition?"

"I see what you did there." I look up and see he's staring down at me, waiting for my response. "I'll think about it."

———————

At home, as I sit with Grams, my phone buzzes.

CRIS: thought you'd like this

CRIS: (YouTube link to Troye Sivan's "What a Heavenly Way to Die")

CRIS: reminds me of you

ME: Thanks. Can't wait to listen!

CRIS: what's your fav mariah song besides "outside"?

ME: OMG too many to name . . . I think you'll love this one, very much a #mood:

ME: (YouTube link to Mariah Carey's "The Roof")

ME: But this one was written FOR me:

ME: (YouTube link to Mariah Carey's "Close My Eyes")

I play each song as I wait for him to text back; it's like we're listening together.

CRIS: wow. those lyrics 😭 make me like you even more

CRIS: tho I wouldn't sing that at the audition 😳

ME: 🎧

My heart races and I wish I could ask Grams her advice about auditioning as she stares straight ahead, her face blank. I wonder if, in the far reaches of her mind, she's singing onstage at Madison Square Garden, holding tight to the mic stand.

Give me a sign, Grams.

I start humming a song she wrote for Grandpa when he went to war in Vietnam.

She turns her head and opens her mouth to sing along with me. The words are jagged, the lyrics incomplete, but she's *singing.* And keeping pitch! She reaches the climax like an old Broadway star.

A tear falls down her cheek. I'm an absolute hot mess because I haven't heard her speak a full sentence for the better part of a year, so I bury my head in her lap and she methodically rubs my head, soothing me with a quiet, "Shhhh."

"Grams?" I pick up my head.

She looks at me, registering my face, and brushes her thumb against my cheek. She makes a hard *C* sound.

"*Carey,*" I help.

"C-C-Carey. I love you."

Hot. Mess. Tears.

The doctors told us this could happen, that Grams might experience fleeting moments of lucidity. At first, her forgetfulness was small. She'd get into her car and drive around town for hours, uncertain of where she was headed. Then she started staying in bed all day, head plastered to the pillow like she'd become a part of it. She spent less time primping in front of the mirror and more time wandering around her bedroom, unsure of what to do. But she always knew us. Until one day, she didn't. I'm convinced she knows us by feeling, if not by name. Mom and I tell ourselves that she can feel our love, and even if she might not know us by name, she still knows us on some level. And that has had to be enough.

But now she's singing again. I don't know how long it'll last, but I want to soak up every single minute of it.

I launch into Lady Gaga's "Always Remember Us This Way," a favorite song of hers from *A Star Is Born*. Grams used to watch that movie on an endless loop and she always paused at this song so we could harmonize and duet together. When the movie ended, she would say that she could hear me singing Gaga's finale, "I'll Never Love Again," on a stage someday.

She mumbles, "Louder," before harmonizing with me.

When the song's over, I don't waste any more of this precious, unpredictable time.

"What should I do?" I ask, softly, afraid she'll drift back into her fog, but she acknowledges me again, so I quickly tell her about Cris and the musical.

She goes quiet for a while.

My heart sinks.

I've lost her again.

Except then her lips move.

All she says is, "Sing."

It's not a request but an answer.

TRACK 6
THEY/THEM/THEIR

I always make sure I'm first in the cafeteria. Get in, get whatever horrible food facsimile they're serving, and get to Mr. Kelly's room before Max or some other ogre sees me.

I'm almost out the door when someone calls my name and every muscle in my body tightens. I'm preparing to run when I hear Cris's voice more clearly.

"Carey? I didn't know you had lunch this period." He runs up beside me, and the tension in my body melts. "Wanna come out to the quad with me? It's warm as fuck outside." He smells like ivory soap and coconuts, and honestly, I'd go anywhere with him if he asked.

"Fresh air sounds epic right now." *"Fresh air sounds epic?" Did I really just say that?*

There are loads of students on the lawn, sitting in small circles on the dead grass, taking up space on weatherworn picnic tables. We find an empty one and he pulls a brown paper bag out of his backpack. Peanut butter and jelly sandwich. Somehow, his classic lunch choice makes him exponentially cuter.

"Why don't I ever see you in the cafeteria?" he asks.

"I usually eat in Mr. Kelly's classroom."

He crinkles the bag but doesn't say anything for the longest time. It feels like I actually might die when he finally says, "You have a thing for Mr. Kelly? I just wanna know my competition." He takes a bite of his sandwich.

"Not. At. All," I say. "The universe finds it hilarious to separate me from Monroe and Joey by giving us different lunch periods every single year."

His mouth is full of sticky peanut butter, but he gets out, "You have me now." He takes a drink of water. "I had fun yesterday."

I feel an overwhelming urge to smile. "Me too."

He leans in so only I can hear. "I wish I could've kissed you. Did I just say that out loud?"

"Can't take it back."

"Fuck." He laughs. "Well, might as well."

"Might as well what?" My breath is ragged. Is he really going to kiss me? Right here? Now? My leg shakes restlessly. It makes my whole body vibrate.

He puts a hand on my knee, and it stops. He leans in, super close—then grabs one of my French fries. He shoves it into his mouth. "Thanks."

This must be what it feels like to have a stroke. "Not funny."

"What?" Cris says. "You think I'd be that tacky? We're not Lauren and Steve." He points to the couple across the quad, mauling each other's faces.

"Gross."

"Ahem." A rough cough interrupts us, and I recoil when I see the source.

"Afternoon, Mr. Jackson," Cris says.

Mr. Jackson is a burly man with a long gray beard and a penchant for flannel. But not the cute flannel that emo guys in bands wear, the kind you would see on a far-right conservative holding a sign that says, God Hates Fags on the side of the road during Pride month. He has probably been watching us, waiting for the perfect moment to ruin absolutely everything.

I slide away from Cris.

"You *boys* enjoying your lunch?" His voice drips disdain.

"Yes, sir," Cris says. "We *humans* are enjoying our lunch. Want a fry?" He pushes my basket toward Mr. Jackson, and I look at Cris like he just betrayed my entire family.

Mr. Jackson ignores the fries. "The school has a no-tolerance policy for PDA."

"Great, can you tell that to Lauren and Steve?" Cris points across the way. Everyone in this school runs into Lauren and Steve making out at least once a day. Mr. Jackson doesn't bother turning his head though, because this isn't about Lauren and Steve; this is about me and Cris. "Seriously, Steve is dry-humping her, and you're not even gonna turn around?"

Mr. Jackson frowns. "Keep it school-appropriate." Then he walks away in the opposite direction.

"What the hell is his problem?" Cris clenches his fist.

"Jackson is a homophobe," I say.

"I know, but . . . he's starting to be more obvious about it." He steals another fry. "At least have the decency to fly under the radar."

I tell Cris about how, in tenth grade, I wrote a short story for Mr. Jackson's class about a boy who wore dresses and had a lucky pair of sparkly heels that made him feel invincible. When I got my assignment back, it had a big red *F* on it. I waited after school to see Mr. Jackson in his office so that I could ask him how I could improve my writing, because I'd never written a short story before and wanted to learn. I thought I'd done something wrong, like maybe the structure was off.

He asked me, "Why did you write this?"

I said, "Because it's a story I've had in my head that I wish existed so I could read it."

He raised his hand to silence me. "I'm going to stop you right there. Too many people think they have what it takes to write." His glasses fell to the tip of his nose. He stared at me over the frames. "Not everyone does. Talent can't be taught. Frankly, *this* story . . ." He paused before continuing, "I don't see the merit in exploring this subject."

It felt like I got slapped in the face. "Maybe if you gave me pointers, I could improve."

"Too many mechanical errors. Unacceptable. *Inappropriate subject matter.*" He blinked until his point was made. "If you'll excuse me, I have papers to grade." Mr. Jackson didn't even bother to look up at me. I stood still in his thick, uncomfortable silence as he waited for me to find the courage to walk away.

Anger pools in my stomach and my fists clench. "Mr. Kelly is the only one who has seen my creative writing since. And that's only lyrics. Poems, I guess. I've never written another story."

Cris shakes his head. "I *hate* that guy."

We spend the rest of lunch a full foot apart, wishing we were together, anywhere but here.

––––––––––

Mr. Kelly is *still* lecturing about Holden Caulfield's red hunting hat in English. Like, seriously? Is it possible to spend an entire week's worth of class talking about a hat? I wonder if J. D. Salinger put this much thought into it when he was writing *Catcher in the Rye*. Did he imagine that generations of students would be studying one article of clothing in this much depth? Doubtful. Then again, I live and die by the (admittedly, fabulous Monroe Cooper original) clothes on my freckled back, and I exhaust everyone with my Mariah Carey facts, so I can appreciate his Holden Caulfield obsession.

"Mr. Kelly, haven't we exhausted Holden's hat?" Phoebe asks, looking bored and borderline pissed, like he's wasting her time. "When will we need any of this?"

Mr. Kelly chuckles the way teachers do right before a pop quiz. "How about right now?" He smirks and grabs a stack of handouts on his desk. "Here's your next project. It's not a traditional essay. I want you to have fun with this. Holden Caulfield's red hunting cap was his security blanket. I want to know your security blankets. Develop a thesis statement that both introduces your security blanket and describes its function. It could be a literal blanket or a more abstract coping mechanism. Explore your psyche the way we've been exploring Holden's. Learn why you resort to these measures of self-soothing and how they function in your day-to-day life." He paces the classroom as we collectively panic. "You can hand in an actual essay, a series of poems, a short story, a video project, or do a performance in class."

"I see what you did there," Phoebe says. "I'm here for this." This elicits groans from every corner of the room.

"When is this due?" I ask.

"The week after we return from winter break, which should give you more than enough time to wow me. Everyone will present. If you have questions, see me after school."

The bell rings. Everyone gets up and walks out like a herd of zombies, but not the fresh ones, the ones that've been roaming since the beginning of the apocalypse. I walk up to Mr. Kelly's desk as he shuffles stacks of papers.

He looks up. "Missed you at lunch today."

I laugh nervously. "I sort of . . . met a boy?"

His eyebrows arc. "Congrats."

"I have two questions. Well, one is more of a statement, I guess." He motions for me to sit down, so I plop on the nearest desk. "First, I have no idea what to do for this project, and I'm kinda freaking out. So, help?"

He chuckles. "I don't expect everyone to have an idea right away. What in your life has provided you security or reflects your identity? You don't have to answer me now, just think about yourself a bit. Next question? Or statement?"

I look at the floor. "I think I'm going to audition. Is that okay?" I don't wait for him to respond. "But . . . I don't want to sign up. I don't want anyone to know I'm auditioning." I take a deep breath before the final plunge. "*For Elphaba.*"

When I look up, he's smiling from ear to ear. "Fantastic!"

Before I leave, he says, "I'm proud of you for putting yourself out there."

His words of pride fill my head as I amble absentmindedly to meet Monroe at her car, my chest puffed and ready to take on the world.

Until I bump into Joey.

"Oh, hey." I almost rebound off the imaginary, impenetrable force field she's created around herself. I deflate.

"Roe had to run to Exile. Her boss groveled, apparently." Her voice is matter-of-fact. Not exactly cold, just distant. "I have Roe's car. I'll drive you home before basketball practice." She pauses. "If you want."

This'll be fun and *totally* not awkward at all since Joey and I haven't spent time alone since junior prom. But. Maybe it's a chance for us.

"She called it," I say. "I think she has a thing for her boss."

She raises her eyebrows. I hear Dr. Potter telling me if I act like everything is fine, everything *will* be fine.

"Tell me I'm not the only one who's noticed that," I add. "She's constantly babbling a million miles an hour about *Thom this*, *Thom that*, how much she hates *Thom*, but then—"

"She totally lights up," Joey says, finishing my thought. It's working. She's dropping her force field.

"Exactly."

"We both know better. Oh! And he picked her up from school. That's why I have her car." Joey holds up Roe's car keys and jingles them. "She'll kill us if we bring him up. You know how private she is with stuff like this. Remember when she first told us about him, and you freaked out because you thought he was a creepy old dude?"

"How was I supposed to know he's barely two years older than us?"

She laughs, though it's timid. "We got a two-hour lecture about how even if there was something going on, the age of consent in New York is seventeen and blah blah blah. She was adamant there was nothing going on."

"Still is," I add, hiking up my backpack so it sits more comfortably on my back. "She can't hide anything from us. Who does she think she is?"

Joey starts humming Lizzo's "Truth Hurts," our freshman-year anthem, off-key. I playfully knock my shoulders into hers as I launch into the first verse. Singing with Joey is easy, comfortable. We riff together, trading verses, and it quickly turns into a hallway dance party. I drum on the lockers. Joey hops along in step, doing the shopping cart, her hands taking turns grabbing at the air, her signature white-girl dance move. Then, the running man. Joey and I are choking on laughter, the way we used to. The lines around her eyes are so beautiful and innocent. The redness in her cheeks reminds me of the fun we used to have. Little by little, brick by brick, the walls we'd built are crumbling.

"I've missed you," I say.

Her laughter ebbs, and she sighs. "I've been right here, Carey." And just like that, I'm shut out again.

This is going to be harder than I thought.

TRACK 7

SHE/HER/HERS

I'm freaking out.

Full-on National State of Emergency–level panic attack.

Wicked auditions are three days away.

I have nothing to wear.

I've ripped apart my entire bedroom, Mom's room, Grams's huge oak wardrobe, and found nothing. I had a fleeting thought that Grams's plush black mink coat would be good, but not for Elphaba. Mink for a witch? Maybe a Betty White biopic.

"What the hell are you doing?" Mom looks horrified by the tornado-level destruction I've waged through the apartment. "If Grams knew you were rummaging through her stuff . . ."

"Good thing she'll never know." I immediately regret what I said. "Sorry."

"It's fine, baby. What *are* you doing though?" She pulls one of Grams's old trench coats to her face and breathes in. "It still smells like her old perfume. When I was your age and would sneak into the house in the middle of the night after partying and smell that lilac perfume, I knew she was still awake. Sure enough, she'd be at the kitchen table in her housecoat, tapping her foot." She laughs, lost in memory.

"I'm an angel compared to you."

She grabs my whole head and kisses my forehead. "I lucked out."

"Lottery-style," I say. "I'm looking for an outfit to wear. Help?"

"In Grams's closet? For what, a *Golden Girls* revival?" She smiles, pleased with her expert-level shade.

"Ha-ha. Very funny. No. Although, I did have the same thought."

"Twinning." Mom offers a fist bump. "What do you need this outfit for?"

I haven't told Mom about *Wicked* yet. Part of me wants to audition and wait for the casting notice before telling her. In case I don't get the role. But that seems stupid. Mom would be supportive no matter what. "I'm auditioning for the spring musical."

Mom's entire face lights up. "Really? Oh my God. I had no idea. You're definitely going to get cast." She's being extra dramatic. Wait. She already knew about my audition.

"You're a horrible liar. How did you know?"

"I had coffee at the Coopers' and heard Roe was doing the costumes, and that you're auditioning. I figured you'd tell me when you were ready. What part are you going for?"

"Elphaba."

She takes a few seconds to process what I've said. I can practically hear her inner conversation:

Mom, pre–me coming out: But that's a "girl" part.
Mom, post-out ally: Carey doesn't identify strictly as male.
Their gender identity is fluid. Look at the bracelet on
Carey's arm. Today it's pink, which means she uses she/her
pronouns.
Mom, pre–me coming out: I don't get it.
Mom, post-out ally: But I want to.

She nods methodically. "I'm excited for you. But why are you rifling through these old clothes when you have your own designer?"

Total cliché light bulb moment: Monroe! "Can I borrow your car?"

––––––––––––

"Roe, I need an outfit!" I shout, rushing into the Coopers' house without knocking. The back door is always unlocked. Monroe is lounging on the couch in the living room, watching old episodes of *Project Runway* in a pair of fuzzy pink flannel pajamas. Today, her hair is a vibrant aqua, wavy curls spiraling off her head. "Oh my God, I love that color!"

"I did it last night. I needed a change. My mom thinks my hair is gonna fall out from how much I bleach and dye it." Her fingers comb through her hair. "Wait, what do you mean, you need an outfit? I'm one hundred percent on a staycation for the rest of the year."

"*Please.* I need to embody Elphaba for my audition. I need to feel like a diva when I walk on that stage, and I thought I could pull something together from my closet full of Monroe originals, but nothing feels right."

She scrambles to her feet. "That's because nothing I've made you is right for *that*." She flips through a lookbook in her mind and races to the stairs. "Follow me. Obviously, you want Misunderstood Activist Witch Realness, but you want to slay Mr. Kelly and the Broadway chick he's bringing in to help him direct by putting your own spin on the character."

"The who now? What Broadway person?"

"Mr. Kelly is, like, best friends with this woman who stage-manages actual Broadway shows. She just finished a run on *Straight Up! The Paula Abdul Musical.* I met her last week when Mr. Kelly assembled the stage crew."

"Great. So, I need to impress, like, everyone."

"That's the actual point of an audition." When we reach her room, she holds up a finger and directs me toward her bed. "Sit."

Her bedroom is a disaster, like a department store floor on Black Friday. I hop over pincushions and dress patterns and creepy mannequins half dressed with patchwork garments to get to her bed.

"I worked on this piece for my FIT application. Good thing you're my muse, bitch, because you can wear anything I make." She mumbles incoherently. "This is one of my absolute favorites. It'll be perfect for your audition. Close your eyes."

"Seriously?"

"Carey Parker, if you want my help, do as I say or I'll hurt you." Garment bags rustle, and hangers click against metal rods.

She guides me to my feet, spins me around, and threads my arms into something tight. "Open," she commands.

I'm wearing the most incredible black jacket straight out of the Haus of Gaga. It's super rigid and angular, with a high neck jutting upward like a crown, and I look like a deconstructed avant-garde witch on a Paris runway. The bottom is encrusted with tiny black crystals that almost make the piece look frozen midspell.

"This is perfect." With a little emerald-green eye shadow and dark black liner around my eyes, I'd be the Supreme. "Black leggings would be perfect. Fuck, what shoes?"

Monroe doesn't miss a beat, diving back into her closet like a raccoon into a dumpster. She emerges with two boxes, one regular-size and one haphazardly wrapped with pink glittery paper. She hands me the wrapped one first.

"When you came out and told me your dreams, I remembered all the times you used to perform for me and Joey when we were little—and how happy you were. When you said you were auditioning for Elphaba, I couldn't resist."

I rip through the paper to find a generic cardboard box. Inside are the kid-sized sparkly red heels I used to steal from her. I tear up. "Where did you . . ."

"I found them cleaning out my closet over the summer and was waiting for the right time to give them to you." She continues. "I know it's been hard with . . . everything and stuff, but your wings are sprouting, Carey Parker, and I'm so glad you found the confidence to try out for the musical. I hope these remind you that you're perfect the way you are."

I squeeze my eyelids shut to stop tears from leaking and choke out a thank-you. She hugs me, but only for a moment.

"Enough of that. These," she says, handing me the other box, "are what you're wearing on Tuesday." Inside is the most fabulous pair of glittery, adult-sized red heels. "They're flexible, and luckily you have Cinderella feet. They may be a little tight, but you'll survive the pain. These are the prototypes for the Nessarose character, you know, when Elphaba puts a spell on the shoes so she can walk. I legit *just* finished making them. I used my foot as a model, and we're basically the same size, so . . ."

I carefully slip into the shoes and look in the mirror. I spin in circles and hold my breath, ignoring the voices in the back of my head, whispering that I'm not talented enough or worthy of the role.

"What do you think?" I ask her.

"You're so fucking ready."

TRACK 8

SHE/HER/HERS

Dr. Potter leans forward in her chair. "Did you do your Joey homework?"

I chew on my tongue. *How can I get out of answering? Pivot.* "I definitely went out of my comfort zone. I went on a date with that boy, Cris. I really like him, but I'm so awkward. He's so brave. You know, the cool, calm, collected type. Pretty much nothing like me."

She clears her throat to stop me. "Put down the stick, Carey."

"Right." I sigh. "We had a run-in with the homophobic jerk-bag Mr. Jackson during lunch last week, so that was fun."

"You're not spending lunches in Mr. Kelly's room anymore?" she asks, leaning back in her chair. "*That's* something." She does this thing where she'll respond neutrally to something good that's happening in my life so that I reinforce out loud why it's so good.

"Not since I met Cris. We've eaten lunch together every day since our date. Now I can't wait for lunch."

She smiles. "I'm proud of you. Though, Mr. Jackson? Isn't

he the teacher who—" She knows how he crushed my writing dreams, and I tell her what happened at lunch. "Did you report him?"

"What good would that do? I tried last time, remember?" Or, rather, Mom tried. She marched right into the principal's office and demanded he be fired. She even wrote a letter to the superintendent. Hell hath no fury like Mom when her baby's been scorned. "He has tenure. He can't be fired, which is kinda fucked up."

"Why don't you think speaking up would do any good? It may be true that tenured teachers aren't often fired for these . . ." She chooses her words carefully: "*situations.*"

"Bigots like Mr. Jackson are never going to change, so why should I stick my neck out there? Put a larger target on my back?"

"Haven't you told me that Joey petitioned the school to get onto the football team? And Monroe protested against the girls' dress code? Those rules changed, did they not?"

She's backed me into a corner again with her logic. "Yes, but . . ."

"But what?"

I take a deep breath. "Why is it on *me* to get other people to change? It shouldn't be on me or any queer person to make people treat us like . . . people."

A breath escapes her lips. "I'm going to step out of my therapist role for a second and say I know how you feel. As LGBTQ people, our lives are a constant frontline protest. Being out and living our lives is a political statement. It shouldn't be. And for people who don't exist within the binary"—she nods toward me—"even in spaces that are quote-unquote tolerant, there can be a barrage of microaggressions. It's hard to expect anything to get better if we don't speak up against injustices—especially from the very people who *should* know better." She adjusts her glasses. "You shouldn't be targeted at school by your teachers. School is supposed to be a safe space for *all* students."

I laugh. "Microaggressions are, like, the best we can hope for sometimes. What most people don't get is that I don't feel safe in most spaces. Even Mom and Monroe, as amazing as they are, can't know how paralyzing that lack of safety feels. How could they, unless they know what it's like to be gay and gender-queer? And that sucks. Especially because so many perceive me as male, and I *know* I get to benefit from white male privilege in order to feel physically safe, but . . ." I bury my head in my hands and massage my temples as my heart starts to race. My skin prickles with heat. Describing myself as male doesn't align with my gender identity today, so it's like I'm driving and the gears shift without warning and I have to figure out how not to crash. It's exhausting.

"What's wrong, Carey?"

I shake my head, not wanting to speak.

"Feel your feet on the ground beneath you." Her voice is a steady, calming hum. "Take a deep breath and listen to my words: *You are valid.*"

After a few breaths, the light-headedness subsides. "I want to try out for the musical, but I'm worried about being mis-gendered and having my identity used against me."

"Tell me about that."

I tell her about the nudges from Mr. Kelly, Cris, and even Grams. "I don't want to give up on myself and live with regret my whole life. And it's pretty clear the universe is pointing me toward Elphaba."

"Could it be easier to sing as a character, rather than as Carey Parker?" she asks.

"Wouldn't be much different than what I've been doing every day of my life." I chew on the inside of my cheek. "What if I get up on stage and choke? What if everyone laughs at me? What if people heckle me? What if I don't get the part? What if I *do* get the part?" I think about Max and Mr. Jackson and how I could be opening myself up to a lot of scrutiny. My palms are sweaty.

"You know what I think?"

My slick grip tightens on the arm of the leather chair. "I've been dying to know!"

"You've come a long way since we first started our sessions. Maybe you don't see that now, but the character you've been playing every day is tired. It's time to leave that part behind. You avoid the potential for rejection by not singing in public or confronting what haunts you head-on." She waits for me to say something, but all I can do is hum low because, duh. "But rejection is not avoidable. So, let's tackle that. What's the worst that can happen if you get rejected?"

Suddenly it feels like we're not *just* talking about the musical or Mr. Jackson or Max; visions of Joey and I doing the shopping cart in the hallway dance in my head. I pick at my cuticles. "I'll literally die."

"You *won't*. You have the tools you need. You have command over your voice, right?"

I nod.

"And your voice is a gift that shouldn't be wasted, right?"

I nod again.

"Repeat after me: I already have everything I need."

"I already have everything I need."

"When you feel overwhelmed or nervous, I want you to say, *I already have everything I need*. Because, Carey, *you already have everything you need*." Her words warm my body like hot chocolate.

I close my eyes and repeat the phrase silently to myself, adding in what I've been afraid to claim:

I am fabulous.

I am Freddie Mercury, a trailblazing icon who comes alive onstage.

I am Sam Smith, unafraid to unlock and discover new aspects of my identity.

I am Mariah, effortlessly commandeering the spotlight, with no apologies.

The diva has been waiting to burst out of me.

Now, I just have to believe that.

———

The next day, Cris has the idea to skip lunch *and* gym and head into town. I've never skipped class before, but who am I to object to a handsome guy with a car? I assume we're going to the pizza place on Main Street because that's where most Sunnysiders go, but he takes a detour across the train tracks and parks in a largely empty lot.

I look around. "What're we doing?"

"Ever been to Arcadia?"

"That's still around?" Arcadia is a vintage arcade wedged between two industrial work complexes near the river. Mom used to bring me, Monroe, and Joey here when we were younger. "I thought it got shut down."

"Crowdfunding saved it. It's an institution," Cris says. "I come here all the time to clear my head. It doesn't get much action during the week, and it's mostly older townies, but they have the best French fries. And the raddest games."

I look down at the pink bracelet on my wrist, my skinny jeans, flowy black shirt, and suddenly I'm very aware of the thin layer of makeup I applied this morning. I can't move as I stare at the neon entrance to Arcadia. I hide my polished nails, curling my fingertips into my palms. I try to remember what Dr. Potter told me last night and shift my weight to feel the car beneath my feet.

"What's wrong?" he asks.

My voice is so low that I'm not sure he can hear me. "What if something happens in there?" I'm almost afraid to make eye contact with him. He can't possibly understand, and I can't bear the thought of explaining it to him.

He scrunches his eyebrows, then takes my hand and squeezes it. "They're cool. Trust me. I wouldn't go to a shitty place. And if it becomes shitty, which it won't, I'll protect you."

I roll my eyes. "Sure."

His brows furrow. "You don't believe me?"

"No, it's not that. I just learned a long time ago that I need to protect myself."

He leans forward and pulls my hand to his chest, right above his heart, which is racing. I don't know what he's doing, but if he's trying to make me less nervous, this isn't the way to do it. "I used to be in a band, the Douche Nozzles, with a bunch of guys who go to Wicker High and were my friends since I was a fetus. Like, two years ago, I told my *best* friend that I was bisexual. He totally freaked out and told everyone in the band that I hit on him. They kicked me out. I wandered around town and ended up here. Played games all night to escape and ended up spilling my guts to a bunch of strangers who didn't give a shit if I were bi—they even do a whole thing for Pride month now!" He goes quiet. "Isn't that fucked up, that strangers at an arcade would be cool about my sexuality, but not my so-called lifelong friends?"

That must be why he drifts between friend groups at school, never sticking with one for too long—out of fear that they might reject him.

"It's hard for me to trust people." He squeezes my hand tight. "But you're . . . different."

I move closer to him, as close as I can get with an armrest between us. "I would never reject you," I say, and his heartbeat slows.

He blushes, then clears his throat. "Shall we?"

Arcadia is dingy and dark but bigger than I remember it. It's industrial-chic-without-trying, with exposed brick and rusted pipes on the ceiling that snake around each other. Bright neon signs on the walls illuminate old arcade games from the eighties and nineties. Past *Space Invaders*, *Donkey Kong*, and *X-Men*, I spot a *Ms. Pac-Man*, and I race to the well-worn red joystick. Cris disappears and reappears with a bucket of quarters, popping a few into the slots. He watches as I wind through the 8-bit digital maze, dodging colorful ghosts until I eat the big dots, and then chase them down. Cris leans against the side of the machine, draping his arm over the top, impressed with my skills. Or so he says. I let him compliment me.

He insists we battle each other in *Mario Kart*, where he proceeds to kick my ass.

"It's because you got Princess Peach before me," I say.

"I'm always Peach," he says over the swell of plinking music and grunting sound bites from nearby games.

"Is this how you impress all your dates?"

"Next time, you're Peach."

After a round of Skee-Ball, we sit at a high-top table on swiveling, sparkly red stools with a large basket of French fries.

"You ready for the audition?" he asks.

"I didn't sleep at all last night, thanks to you." I lay in bed, texting Cris different songs I thought he'd like, which distracted me from running through my audition song, until Cris went to bed and I had a panic attack. When deep breathing didn't calm my nerves, I looked around at my posters of Mariah Carey and thought about how by 1992, she had already amassed five number ones on the Billboard Hot 100, had two massive albums, but had zero concert performances, so there were rumors that she was a studio creation and couldn't sing live. Totally ridiculous, I know. So, she did *MTV Unplugged*—flawlessly, might I add— and her cover of the Jackson 5's "I'll Be There" became her sixth Billboard Hot 100 number one. I popped in my DVD of the show and kept thinking about how nervous she must have been, given what was at stake, but you'd never know from her delivery. Basically, I just have to think, *WWMCD* at my audition today. But I don't tell him this.

Cris is staring at me. A French fry dangles from his lips, and he's got this goofy look on his super-cute face, his pupils dilated.

"I couldn't sleep either. I kept thinking about you."

"What about me?" I grab the fry from his lips and eat it.

"Not telling." He shoves two more fries under his lips like walrus tusks and shakes his head. I don't know why, but this makes me want to kiss him. But we haven't done that yet. I playfully bat at the fries. "She's feisty today. Now I'm definitely not telling."

I look around Arcadia. There are a few older guys at some of the older machines and a punk rocker girl behind the counter on her phone. Nobody is staring at us, so I grab his hand. It's a simple move but a bold one for me.

He looks down, and surprise fills his face like a kid on Christmas morning. "You wore me down. You make me feel things I've never felt before. Like I'm more alive, more aware, or something. I want to know everything about you."

I lose my breath. "Creeper," I say with a punch of sass, and move in closer, so close that I'm inches from his lips. Our noses graze. I've only kissed one other person, and that was a disaster, so I have no idea if I *can* kiss.

Cris is so damn beautiful, and he's into me, but oh my God, what if I taste like ketchup? What if, midkiss, he realizes he doesn't like me at all and that I'm too hideous to be in the same zip code as him? And then my head is screaming, OH MY GOD, PLEASE STOP THIS BEFORE IT HAPPENS BECAUSE HE'S TOTALLY ENRAPTURED BY YOU AND IF HE KISSES YOU IT COULD ALL GO AWAY.

When he puts his palm against my cheek, my brain goes quiet for a moment.

I ask him to take off his glasses, because maybe if he can't see me, I'll be less nervous.

"I want to see you." His salty lips lightly graze mine as I stare at his perfect, angular face.

Should I close my eyes? Isn't that what you're supposed to do? So I do, and my body relaxes enough that I grab his face and kiss him back.

He gently nibbles my lower lip and finishes with two soft pecks before letting me go. He goes right back to his French fries, but I'm paralyzed, my body a puddle of goo. He grabs my hand and intertwines his fingers with mine.

Best. Kiss. *Ever.*

He nuzzles his nose against my cheek and kisses my lower jawline. "We should get back. I'd hate for Principal McCauley to ban us from auditions because we got caught cutting." Then he whispers, "Can't miss you showing up for yourself."

Theoretically, I know the only approval that matters is my own, but damn if Cris doesn't make me feel seen and important and worthy. That's enough to make me want to be the person Cris sees.

So here goes nothing.

TRACK 9
SHE/HER/HERS

My world is somehow both hazier *and* sharper after the kiss.

Sunnyside's hallways don't seem to exist; they dissolved, and now I float through wide-open spaces, unrestricted. I remember my first time in an airplane with Mom, staring out the window at a horizon that, high above the clouds, seemed endless. Infinite blue skies. Freedom. This is a little bit like that.

Until I get to the auditorium long after school ends and suddenly everything becomes *too real*. I plop down on the floor, under a big yellow poster board announcing the musical auditions in thick black Sharpie, my backpack in my lap. I reach inside the large zippered pouch to touch the lucky heels Monroe gave me and silently run through my audition song.

My phone buzzes.

MONROE: At Exile now. Be back to help you get ready.
ME: Don't be late plz 🙏 🫣 😥
ME: Btw I'm dying rn
MONROE: . . .

MONROE: STOP THAT

MONROE: YOU WILL CRUSH IT!

I respond with a crying emoji because that's productive.

"Carey?" Phoebe Wright stands at the end of the hallway in front of the double doors that lead to a parking lot. She's bathed in the warm orange glow of the setting sun streaming through the glass behind her.

Great. I don't know why I didn't factor her into any of my nightmare audition scenarios last night. She's been on *actual* Broadway in ensembles since we were in elementary school and last year had an actual lead role in *Riverdale: The Musical.* Rumor has it she turned down a role in *Hamilton* so she could finish high school. If she's auditioning for Elphaba, which of course she is, there's no way I stand a chance.

As she walks toward me, her long, tight curls bounce. "'Ello, Gov'nuh!" She says in a weird British accent. She must register the confusion on my face because she looks down at the floor. "Sorry, I do this thing where I talk in fake accents when I'm nervous." She clears her throat and takes a deep breath. "Can I join?"

I motion to the space next to me and shuffle over a bit, even though there's already plenty of floor space.

"You get nervous?"

She sits cross-legged beside me. "Are you kidding? Every single audition scares the shit outta me." She wrings her hands, then stretches her fingers. I never thought of Phoebe as having anxieties. She always seems so confident, like being talented at everything is as natural to her as breathing. "You wanna know a

83

trick? Every time I go out for a part, I don't take it seriously. I get there early, center myself, and go in with the mindset that it'll probably be a no because I can't tell you how many rejections I've heard. Like, it's depressing."

"Really?" I assumed Phoebe got every part she went out for. "You're next-level amazing."

Her cheeks swell with a smile. "Thanks. I know I'm good. But the industry is picky and racist. Especially when it comes to Black girls." She shifts her weight to get comfortable. "How come I've never seen you audition for anything?"

"I don't really want to act, so plays aren't my thing."

"And musicals?"

"Same thing. But a friend"—I cringe at calling Cris a friend, but I don't know how to refer to him; it's not like we've had the Talk yet. It's only been a week and one life-altering kiss— "convinced me to try out."

"Cris?"

"Yeah, how'd you know?"

"Word travels fast. You two are in the latest *Sunnyside Upended!*" She pulls out her phone, swipes a few times, and hands it to me. Unlike the school newspaper, *Sunnyside Up!*, *Sunnyside Upended!* is unsanctioned by the school and consists of Fake News "alternative opinion" pieces meant to cause drama mixed in with anonymous rumor mill gossip that anyone can post. The school has tried to shut it down but can't figure out who runs it; all anyone knows for certain are the select group of students who routinely write "articles" for it. I try my best to ignore its existence entirely.

I swallow hard, reading: "Rumor Has It: A Guitar Hero on

the DL is hooking up with our resident genderqueer Sunnysider. But one of them has skeletons in their closet . . ."

My body shivers. Skeletons? "All press is good press?" I croak.

She leans in. I don't think I've ever been this close to her before. Her dark brown skin looks so smooth and blemish-free. I'm jealous. "You two are adorable."

"Thanks." I drop my face so she won't see my red cheeks.

"Don't let *this* get to you." She wiggles her phone screen, and I resist the urge to grab it and stare at the text. She reaches into her bag and grabs a warm bottle of water, and I notice a hot pink–yellow-and-blue enamel pin fastened to the inside flap so that only she can see it. I immediately recognize it as the pansexual flag and smile. Guilt smacks my gut because I've resented Phoebe for her confidence and talent. I envied her. So I put her in this little box. It's time to let her out.

"So, you're a singer?" she asks. "What do you sing?"

"Power ballads. The kind you'd sing in a big stadium. Spotlight on me and only me. Thousands of people screaming my name," I confess, almost breathless.

"Like Sam Smith?"

I clear my throat. "Sam is such an inspiration. I love that they're genderqueer too. But, um . . ." I play with the zipper on my backpack. "I mean like Mariah."

I brace myself for her rejection, but her lips curl into a bright smile.

"Well, hot dog!"

I stifle a laugh. Monroe was right: between this and the strange fake accents, Phoebe *is* fucking weird.

"I expect a backstage pass when you're famous. Though, I gotta say, if you want to be a diva like Mariah, you better stop apologizing for being fabulous. Stick with me. I got you."

"Codswallop!" I respond, in my best over-the-top British accent.

She sucks in a breath and holds it in before saying, "You know that means 'nonsense,' right?"

I shrink, but she bursts into a hearty belly laugh so loud it infects me, too.

I try to conjure up some British phrases from my time binging *Fleabag* or *The Crown* and land on, "I'm positively *gutted*!"

She roars even louder.

When we calm down, she says, "You're hilarious."

"Me?"

"Seriously! I have to bite my lips in English class when you thoroughly read Max like a book. It's college-level reading. He deserves it, too. Everyone thinks so."

I blush from the compliment and hide my face from her. "I wish that were true."

"The world is moving on without people like him, and he's not exactly running to catch up. He's trying to stop it." She swipes through her phone again. "I'm assuming you didn't see Max's Alt-Op-Ed in *Sunnyside Upended!* either." She hands me her phone again.

"Max can write?" I say, reading the headline of his article: "Which Lucky Girl Will Be My Date to Senior Prom? Taking Applications Is the New Promposal."

"To be fair, it's basically one giant caveman grunt."

"Don't you mean cave drawing?" I ask.

"Cave drawings are intricate, advanced forms of storytelling and record keeping. I wouldn't compare the two."

I read Max's first paragraph:

> The closer we get to senior prom, the more the halls of Sunnyside buzz with rumors of who will ask who to prom and how they'll do it. Last year's most controversial promposal involved sparklers that set off the fire alarms in the science wing. Not surprisingly, Principal McCauley has placed restrictions on this year's senior class promposals. I say we do away with the promposal all together. Why is it the guy's responsibility to put himself out there and risk rejection? Last year, I spent ages coming up with the perfect plan to ask out a girl, crafting *her* fairy-tale promposal. But that didn't matter. She had no appreciation for the time and care I put into thinking about her and rejected me. She said she liked someone else. My feelings didn't matter. This year, I'm rejecting the nice-guy promposal and all the self-important girls who overlook us and taking applications: Ladies, I'm single.

I involuntarily retch. After everything he's put me through, he has the audacity to call himself a *nice guy*? "He's awful. This is so sexist. Fucking neckbeard."

She waves her hand and lets out a howl. "What's up with that? Shave, white boy!"

"He's happy he can grow any facial hair. Ya know, because

he's a *man*," I say. "I feel bad for the girl he asked to prom last year. Any idea who she is?"

"Nope, but I'd love to buy her a coffee. Give her a medal," she says. "Ugh, I don't even know why I read this trash." She tosses her phone into her bag.

Now that she mentions it, I'm wondering the same thing. I shift uncomfortably. "Why do you?"

"The way I see it, I need to know what I'm up against. I know what it's like to be the subject of Sunnyside gossip," she says, her voice getting lower. I try to think about the last time I heard anything bad about her and come up short. Maybe I haven't been paying enough attention. "It's self-inflicted pain to read it, trust me." She clenches her fist. "I hate that I feel like I constantly have to be on guard, but knowing what they're saying at least allows me the chance to protect myself."

"Sounds complicated." I want to ask her how that equates to her protecting herself, because to me, it sounds like yet another way to expose my vulnerabilities. Instead, I whisper, "But I know how you feel." I shift my weight and grab at my backpack, pulling it closer like a blanket, and the sparkly red heels almost slide out. I zip my bag before she sees them. "You've totally got Elphaba," I say, changing the subject.

"Elphaba?" She furrows her brow and frowns. "I don't want Elphaba. I'm going out for Glinda."

"Glinda?"

She must see the shock on my face because she shifts her entire body to face me. "Hell, yeah. Elphaba may technically be the lead, but Glinda is the real star. Also, I'm not painting myself green for each performance. I swear, if I see one more Black actress in greenface, I *will* scream. So, if this musical is gonna happen with me in it, it's gonna have a Black Glinda."

My relief is replaced with the desire to yell, "YAASSS! I love that!" I promptly tell her about wanting to play Elphaba, which unravels into my entire life story, minus the super depressing stuff because the mood has been upended enough already.

She smiles and the yellow specks in her brown eyes reflect the light. "I always knew there was more to you, Carey Parker. It's nice to *finally* meet you." She pauses. "A genderqueer Elphaba and a Black Glinda. That'll turn heads. I love it."

"You think?"

"Are you kidding? This'll make history! At least at Sunnyside."

Her words flood me with hope.

I unzip my backpack and my heels gleam under the fluorescent light. "They're my good luck charm."

Her brow furrows, and I nod my head, signaling that it's okay for her to touch them. Carefully, as if they're irreplaceable museum artifacts, she reaches in and guides them out, and though it feels like she's turning my skin inside out, I have to remind myself that, as Dr. Potter says, it's okay to let myself be vulnerable. "These are so cute! I can totally picture little Carey sashaying across the carpet in these. You should do your project for Mr. Kelly's class on these shoes."

I exhale in relief. "You think? I hadn't thought of that."

"A good luck charm can absolutely equate to a security blanket."

"That's kind of perfect," I say. "Maybe I'll write a song to go with it."

"You write songs?"

I nod hesitantly, hearing Mr. Jackson's words in the back of my head. "I don't know if my writing is any good, but I hear melodies in my head and write to that."

"I'm seeing a video essay of you in red heels, singing an original song." She sits up a little straighter. "Show me what you got?"

Normally, I'd run away screaming before letting someone who isn't Mr. Kelly see my scratch lyrics, but I'm oddly comfortable enough with Phoebe that I reach into my bag and hand her my notebook without hesitation. "I have something I wrote for Kelly's class. Oh! And my mom has home videos of me wearing these shoes and singing songs when I was, like, seven. I can probably splice them into the project."

"That would be amazing!" Her eyes scan my notebook. "These lyrics are so raw. But it's just a few lines." Her voice drifts away, and she starts to hum a new melody. "I can hear the rhythm," she sings before abruptly stopping. "You have to finish it."

Phoebe and I huddle together as other students show up to audition, our ideas buzzing in the air, isolating us and protecting me from feeling nervous. At one point, she takes my phone, plugs her number in, and sends herself a text of nothing but crown emojis. "Now that you're my new best friend, I have some ground rules. No texts before homeroom, no—"

Mr. Kelly rounds the corner with a tall, voluptuous woman in pink glasses, with long, pin-straight dark brown hair who dwarfs him as they walk side by side. She holds herself with such poise it makes me sit up straighter. This must be his friend who works on Broadway.

Phoebe hands back my phone and we sit up straight to listen.

Mr. Kelly whistles and everyone goes silent. "First off, thank you all for showing up for auditions! Whatever happens, you're all fearless and courageous, and I'm inspired by you." He looks directly at me, and my cheeks heat. "As you know, this year, we're lucky enough to be putting on *Wicked*, an incredible show with a lot of moving parts, which is why we have Ms. Diaz." He points to the woman next to him. "She's a stage manager on Broadway and my best friend. She's graciously offered to volunteer her time to help put this together."

"Please, call me Rachel. None of this Ms. Diaz stuff, I'm not my mother," Rachel says, enunciating each syllable to perfection. "Shawn—err, Mr. Kelly and I went to school here at Sunnyside, and I was always part of the shows, both onstage with the cast and backstage with the crew, so it's cool to be here. I'm excited to see what you got."

"Don't be nervous," Mr. Kelly adds. "We're not going to Simon Cowell you."

He pauses for laughs, but nobody does. Someone shouts, "Who?" and Mr. Kelly puts his head in his hands and mumbles, "I'm so old."

Rachel clears her throat and elbows him. It's clear this is a routine for them, that they've known each other a long, long time. "We want to see the best of you. Final cast announcements will be posted Friday." There's something regal about her. The way she stands with such authority. I'm girl-crushing.

"We're going to hand out random numbers to everyone who signed up, and you'll go onstage in groups of four," Mr. Kelly explains. "I'm going to ask all the Elphabas to line up over here." He points to the far end of the hallway. "Glindas over there, Fiyeros here, and everyone else at the other end of the hallway."

Phoebe grabs my hand, squeezes it, and we part, filing into our respective lines. She's first in hers and first to get a numbered card, of course, but I hang back and wait so I'm at the back of the Elphaba line. Mr. Kelly hands me a card with a seven on it; underneath is a time: 6:30 p.m. He pats my shoulder with a nonverbal good luck. I lock eyes with Phoebe, and she flashes her card, also a seven. The universe is keeping us together.

I text Monroe my audition time.

MONROE: Perfect. On my way.

Cris dashes down the hallway. He grabs a number and stands with the rest of the Fiyeros. He catches me staring and puffs out his chest like a superhero, hands on his hips, then nods for me to do the same. When I do, he makes a quick heart with his fingers and I blush.

"Break a leg, everyone!" Rachel exclaims as Mr. Kelly opens the doors to the auditorium. Everyone files in noisily, chatting about nothing and everything, from squeals over the latest BTS single to rumors about random parties this weekend.

I tune out the chatter.

I have to.

The lush background vocals of "Everything Fades Away," a Mariah B-side from the *Music Box* album, play in my head, and I'm hoping my heart rate will steady. But it doesn't, because in an hour and a half, these people are going to hear me sing for the first time.

Fuck. My palms are clammy.

I look for the exits.

I can't do this.

What did I get myself into?

TRACK 10
SHE/HER/HERS

MONROE: I'm here. Girls' room next to the auditorium.

Makeup is strewn all over the white porcelain sinks. Black garment bags hang on the doors to the stalls.

Monroe wraps her aqua hair in a messy bun. "I brought my team," she says, gesturing toward Joey, whose arms are folded as she flashes me an over-the-top, toothy smile. "Let's get started. We don't have much time." Monroe instructs me to wash my face with a fancy scrub that smells like eucalyptus and lavender. She doesn't wait for me to dry off before examining my face; water drips down my neck and under my shirt. She blots my skin with a towel and begins with the foundation. "Jo, can you be *extremely careful* and take the jacket out of that bag over there? Do not let it touch anything in here. I don't know the last time this place got a good bleaching. Then get out the shoes. Carey, did you bring whatever you're wearing for pants?" Monroe death grips my face with one hand as she delicately applies a light layer of foundation with the other.

"In my bag," I say, trying not to move my lips.

"No way!" Joey exclaims. "Are these the shoes Carey used to steal from you?" She pulls out my lucky sparkly red heels.

Monroe cackles like a witch. "Of course you brought them."

"I remember the day Carey wouldn't take them off. It was after Mom painted our faces. Carey insisted on being a princess, and somehow that meant getting butterflies all over his face," Joey says, then flinches. She quickly corrects herself. "*Her.* Sorry."

I nod, accepting her apology. She didn't do it maliciously. "Butterflies are Mariah's official logo. She's royalty, so . . ."

Like always, Monroe makes a fake vomit noise at the mention of Mariah.

"You were a tiger, right, Jo?" I ask, remembering the bright orange, yellow, and brown stripes on her cheeks. Joey had climbed a tree in their backyard and perched on a wide limb like a jungle cat. She patiently showed me how to get up, too, talking me through which branches to grab hold of. She was always blazing paths and pulling me up alongside of her. "And Roe was a—"

"A slug. Yes, we all remember that." Monroe had to go to a birthday party afterward, and her mom didn't want to clean her entire face, so she drew two tiny green antennae on Monroe's forehead while Joey and I got to paint our full faces. Monroe had never looked so miserable to be left out. She'd made up a sad little song about being a slug.

Without looking at each other, Joey and I start singing: "I'm Roey the Slug, I'm a really big bug, and nobody wants to give me a hug."

Monroe rolls her eyes, but I can tell she's holding back.

"Shit, how did it end?" I ask, and Joey stares at me, her eyes searching for the words.

Monroe huffs before providing the finale. "Because nobody likes a sluuuuug!"

"That needs to be your audition song, Car," Joey says warmly.

"Okay, I need you all to shush." Monroe applies lime-green eye shadow. When she's done, she takes a step back and admires her artistry. "Not gonna lie, I'm amazing!" She motions for Joey to bring her the jacket. "I need the pièce de résistance!"

I slip my arms into the snug fabric and slide my feet into the red heels. I stand a little straighter. I feel complete. Monroe grabs my arms and turns me toward the mirror. I love the person staring back at me: the green around my eyes is vicious, and my body is draped in drama. This is the Carey Parker that little me wished to be. It's pure euphoria.

"No crying!" Monroe shouts. "I didn't have time to get waterproof mascara."

"Your phone is buzzing." Joey hands it to me.

PHOEBE: Your bf is about to audition. Our group is on standby. Where r u?
ME: OMW! Tell him to look stage left.

"I gotta get out there," I say.

Monroe and Joey fold me into a hug sandwich. "You got this," Monroe says.

I breathe a sigh of relief. Maybe I do.

My heels *click-clack* on the linoleum floors as I race back to catch Cris's audition. I quietly open the door to the auditorium to him onstage singing Queen's "I Want to Break Free," the song he overheard *me* singing at Exile. Now I totally get what people mean when they say they have butterflies, because my chest and stomach flutter, and I feel so light I'm certain I could fly. No wonder he wanted me to watch. He's a rock god, and his charm pulls me toward him like an invisible lasso. He's wearing a button-down shirt that's open a bit at the top, and I have to remind myself to breathe.

Everyone in the theater is on the edge of their seats as his voice wraps around them. When he's done, he looks stage left and makes eye contact with me. He smiles. I want to run and give him a hug, but that would be unprofessional.

I clutch my heart and mouth, *"Amazing."*

He blushes, and a goofy boyish grin beams across his face.

Our shared reverie is broken when Mr. Kelly thanks Cris for his audition, then shouts, "Group seven!"

Cris walks toward me and I hug him. "You were incredible!"

"Break a leg," he whispers.

Careful not to let the audience see me, I wait at the edge of the curtain. Phoebe is on the opposite side of the stage, and when she sees me, her face lights up. She gives me a thumbs-up.

"Glinda first," Rachel announces.

Phoebe saunters onstage. "Phoebe Wright, I'm auditioning for Glinda the Good Witch, and to show my range, I'll be singing 'Popular.'"

A bold choice, no doubt, but one that will undoubtedly cement her being cast. I've heard Phoebe sing before, and she has an incredible voice, but I wouldn't call it bubbly like Kristin

Chenoweth's, the original Glinda. But when she starts, everyone in the auditorium is captivated. She glides across the stage, pretending it's dressed, and miming as if there are props. Her voice is crystal clear, but a bit more nasal than normal to fit the role. People in the audience laugh on cue with the jokes in the song, and thank God we're going out for different parts, otherwise I would've bolted already. When she finishes, the entire auditorium breaks into raucous applause. Every girl who has or will audition for Glinda must be slinking down in their seats.

Mr. Kelly is still applauding when Rachel yells out, "Thank you," as if she had been stranded in a desert and Phoebe is a truckload of ice-cold water. Then she asks the next "Elphaba" to take center stage.

I wobble forward on jellied legs, catching Phoebe's eye, and she lifts her chin, signaling for me to stand up tall, go out with confidence. She's right.

This is it.

My moment.

I already have everything I need.

The time for merely existing is over. It's time to live.

I inhale, closing my eyes.

I tune out everything around me until I hear only my own breathing.

Inhale.

Exhale.

I wonder if this is how birds feel just before they leave their nests for the first time, not knowing if they'll spread their wings and fly or fall to the ground. A part of me wants to stay in my nest a little while longer, to be sure I'm ready. But the only way to fly is to try.

I find my place center stage and squint through the lights. I clear my throat. "I'm Carey Parker, and I'll be auditioning for Elphaba."

"You know that part is a mezzo-soprano, yes?" Rachel asks. Subtext: This is a girl part.

"You're in luck! I'm a mezzo-soprano," I say.

"Don't you mean countertenor?"

"I *mean* mezzo-soprano." There's no malice in my voice. I expected this to happen. When I told Coach Trevisani I was genderqueer, he said my range made me a mezzo-soprano. Maybe that was his way of saying, "I'm cool with who you are." It meant everything, but I'm not about to get into that with a virtual stranger.

My eyes adjust to the harsh spotlights as Mr. Kelly leans in and whispers something to her, and her eyes widen with realization. "What will you be singing for us?" she asks.

"Lady Gaga's 'I'll Never Love Again.'" For Grams.

There are audible gasps, a few quiet chuckles, but I block them out. I look for Cris, but I can't find him, which is probably for the best.

I adjust the microphone, steady myself, and begin the first verse, softly. At the pre-chorus, I get louder, my voice building until my emotion explodes with the chorus. As I belt out the words, my confidence ignites, which I haven't felt in a long time. The powerful lyrics trigger my tear ducts, and I'm still singing, but the words become a beautiful release.

When I finish, it takes all my energy not to collapse on the stage.

The auditorium is silent; everyone collectively holds their breath. My ears pound. My heartbeat thump, thump, thumps. And then.

Explosive applause. Hoots and hollers and it's all . . .

For me.

I take a quick bow and make my way toward the side of the stage. Once I'm in the shadows, I can finally breathe normally.

Cris runs up beside me and twirls me into his arms. "That was *incredible*! Holy fuck! How do you feel?"

"Like I'm flying."

TRACK 11
SHE/HER/HERS

Early Friday morning, right before winter break, Mr. Kelly posts the *Wicked* cast list on the main office's bulletin board.

It's not like it is on TV or in the movies, with all the eager wannabes standing on tippy toes, crushing the shoulders of whoever is in front of them so they can see their names written big and bold next to a gold star sticker. In real life, nobody gets to school much before homeroom. I'm the only one here.

I can't look yet.

Phoebe bounces down the hallway, hopscotching from tile to tile. "You ready?"

"Nope."

Her confidence melts, and her entire body shivers. "Same. I'm a *bloody* wreck." Her fake British flares.

"You're a shoo-in."

"The second you think you're better than everyone else, you've already lost. We're all vulnerable." She's speaking directly to my neuroses.

"I hate feeling vulnerable."

"Get used to it. You're a *vocalist*, girl, an artiste!" she says. "And a damn talented one."

My cheeks heat, and I look to the floor. She grabs my chin gingerly and tips up my head so I'm forced to look at her.

"You gotta stop this," she says.

"What?"

"Trying to make yourself disappear."

"I'm not—"

"From one invisible person to another—we can hide from the world, but not from each other." She locks her arm with mine.

What does she mean when she calls herself invisible? Phoebe Wright is many things—Broadway star at seventeen, student body president, smartest person in class, larger-than-life—but *invisible* is not a word I'd use to describe her.

"Time to rip off the Band-Aid."

"We have to wait for Cris." I look down the hallway, hoping he'll round the corner.

She glances at her naked wrist and taps a phantom watch.

"Five minutes?"

We pace back and forth, and Phoebe stares at her phone impatiently.

My phone buzzes:

CRIS: running late . . . don't wait for me babe

He called me "babe"! Now nervousness over the cast list is competing with my excitement and anxiety over his text.

As I'm about to tell Phoebe, she says, "I can't wait for that boy," and makes her way toward the board. She barely takes a glance before shrieking. "Carey! *Look!*"

SUNNYSIDE HIGH *WICKED* CAST, IN ORDER OF APPEARANCE:

GALINDA/GLINDA | Phoebe Wright
THE WIZARD OF OZ | Dana Palmer
MADAME MORRIBLE | Danielle Glimmer
ELPHABA | Carey Parker
DOCTOR DILLAMOND | Adam Chang
FIYERO | Cris Kostas
NESSAROSE | Blanca Rodriguez
BOQ | Damon Miles

There it is.

My name.

It must be a mistake.

Phoebe is jumping up and down beside me.

I read the list over and over again.

Elphaba. Carey Parker.

My eyes scan for imperfections or smudges or, I don't know, some other sign that someone erased the real Elphaba and wrote my name as a joke.

Elphaba. Carey Parker.

Phoebe touches my arm. Her brows are furrowed with concern. "Carey, you okay? You look whiter than usual?"

"I can't . . . I can't believe it."

Her face relaxes into a grin. "Believe it. You're a star." She pulls me into the warmest hug, but I'm too shocked to reciprocate. My arms dangle at my sides, and when she lets go, I race to the only all-gender bathroom in the school.

I lean against the cool porcelain sink. The whole school, my whole world, is about to hear me, see me—the real me—onstage for the first time. When I'm sure I won't topple over, I reach into my backpack and pull out my lucky ruby red slippers and think about all the times I wore them as a kid, clicking my heels and believing in magic.

I look up at my reflection.

Same rust-red hair.

Same freckled face.

Same ice-blue eyes.

Same cheekbones and nose as Mom.

Completely different Carey Parker.

I fumble with my phone and call Cris.

"Carey?" His voice is creamy peanut butter on chocolate ice cream during a heat wave.

I try to speak but nothing comes out.

"Is everything okay?" There are a few soft knocks on the door. "It's me. Let me in."

I barely get out a, "Come in," before the knob turns and I see his magnetic smile. He wraps me in his arms, and I lose myself in the crook of his neck.

"How'd you know where I was?" My words are muffled.

He kisses my forehead. "Phoebe. Congratulations, by the way. You deserve this."

"So do you," I say, congratulating him back. "It doesn't feel real."

He pulls back. "It *is* real."

"You mean I'm not dreaming?"

He smirks. "Shut up." He pecks my lips. "How's that for real?"

I lick my lips. The shock from getting the part dulls, but it still tugs at me. "Now what?"

"The sky's the limit."

TRACK 12

THEY/THEM/THEIR

The tangy aroma of tomato sauce and fresh basil permeates the air as Mom readies homemade lasagna. Mom wanted me to invite my friends, including Cris—gulp—for a celebratory "Congrats Carey" dinner, but the thought of being the center of attention like that gives me hives, so I convinced her to make it a Christmas party.

The kitchen is a thousand degrees hotter than the rest of the apartment, so I fling open windows to let in an icy breeze.

Mom's looking a hot mess with crusty red splatters on her black turtleneck sweater because she refuses to wear an apron. "Carey, I need you to clean up the living room and run a comb through your grandmother's hair. And don't make her look like the Grinch!"

"But it's Christmas!" Last year I styled Grams's hair into a point at the top of her head, and it swooped downward in one big curl. At the time, Grams still had the wherewithal to give me the dirtiest look, followed by a knowing smile, which of course made me laugh.

"Carey Parker!" Mom full-names me. She's not in the mood for my shit tonight.

After I make Grams look totally un-Grinch-like and tidy up the living room, there's a knock on the door.

Monroe is in the hallway; her leather snakeskin boot taps anxiously on the wood floor. Her face is blotchy and red. "I fucking hate Christmas. Exile is a nightmare. Customer lines out the door! Fucking capitalism and consumer greed." She shoves a tray of vegan, gluten-free black bean brownies into my hands. "Merry Christmas, best fwiend!"

I lead Monroe into the kitchen, and Mom nearly jumps over the counter to give her a hug. "Where's my Joey?"

"Sportsball practice. She'll be here soon," Monroe explains.

Mom clutches her hands to her chest in relief. Then she tells me to keep stirring the pot of extra sauce while she goes to get dressed before everyone else arrives.

"Can we dig into your brownies now?" I ask once Mom is out of earshot.

"Works for me. They're way healthier than anything we normally eat. Remember our sleepovers?"

"You mean when my mom bought us each our own gallon of ice cream and bag of chips, and we'd binge-watch a million movies all night? We should totally do that again. Though Jo probably wouldn't go for it."

"I see what you're trying to do," she says. "We've been over this, Carey. I don't want to get involved. She's my sister. You're my best friend. No." She picks at her cuticles.

"It seems like things are getting better between us," I offer.

"Car, she's always gonna be there for you, but . . ." Monroe exhales so loudly it's like all the air rushes out of her body. She cuts into the brownies and pulls out two squares, one for each of us. "She's hurt."

"*She's* hurt?"

"See, this is exactly what I didn't want to do." Monroe puts her brownie on the counter and folds her arms. "I've got my damn FIT interview after New Year's that I have to prepare for, my job is killing me, I'm up all night making costumes for the musical. I have problems too, Carey." Her voice is heavy, tired.

"You're my best friend, and I keep putting you in the middle instead of dealing with Joey. I'm sorry." I scoot closer and put my arm around her. "I haven't been asking you about you. I'm awful."

She squeezes my arm. "You're not awful." She looks into my eyes. "Just a bit self-focused. I get it. You've been through a lot. I'm only saying it'd be nice if you'd ask me what's going on with *me*." She shoves the brownie into her mouth.

Guilt tugs at the corners of my eyes. Monroe is my best friend, and I'm dangerously close to fucking things up with her too. I have to listen to her. "You're right. I'm a horrible friend."

She shakes her head. "There you go, making it about you again."

Crap. I totally *am* fucking this up. "Let me try again. What's going on with you?"

She sighs again. "The more I think about FIT and Exile and that stupid boy who won't grow the balls to ask me out, the more I want to shut myself off from everything."

"Boy? The manager dude?"

"Thom." She pronounces the *Th* and looks at me sheepishly,

blushing. "He's so adorable. And fucking frustrating. I throw out all the signs, and he flirts and then . . . nothing. I've tried asking him out, but he doesn't get that that's what I'm doing. It's like he's an actual idiot. An idiot I want to kiss," she says, chocolate coating her teeth.

"We need a frienaissance. Take a night and de-stress and watch movies, or do whatever you want, before your interview. We can talk about this boy. Or not."

Monroe leans into me. "I really need that."

"And I'll talk to Joey. I just wish I knew what I did wrong."

"You are so incredibly dense," she says matter-of-factly. "I'm only saying this once, so *listen*. She was totally in love with you. You kissed her the night before prom, and then you came out the next day. How do you think that made her feel?"

Joey was in love with me? Monroe's words smack me across the face. Holy shit. When I came out, *she lost me*, the idea of me and her together. The night before junior prom washes over me like ice cold water in the middle of a steaming hot shower.

Monroe had been passed out asleep on the floor of my bedroom, and Joey and I were in my bed watching *Mean Girls*. Joey started to cry, saying something about senior year being our last year together before college. She was scared about everything changing. And I hugged her, but it lingered a bit too long. There was, like, all this tension between us that I'd never felt before. I was drawn to her, and in that moment, it felt right, like her lips were all I needed. So, we kissed.

She moved closer to me, and her legs tangled in mine. And I freaked out. I told her we should stop because Monroe was *right there*. I knew I'd made a mistake the second our lips touched.

I loved Joey, in ways I will probably never fully understand, but I could never be what Joey needs in that way. We cuddled the rest of the night.

And then prom happened.

There's a tightness in my chest and a dull throbbing in my temples.

"Fuck." This is what Dr. Potter was talking about; I wasn't thinking about Joey. I never *actually* thought about Joey's feelings. "I have to make this right."

Monroe cracks her knuckles; it sounds like carrots snapping in half. "Good. In other news, tell me all about this boy, Cris."

He's an entire symphony. "I hear music when he's around."

"Oh, you're so screwed," Monroe says.

"We both are." I'm about to tell her more when I get a text from Cris telling me he just parked out front.

I flash my phone screen to Monroe, and she immediately yells to Mom, "Carey's boyfriend is here!"

I elbow her. "He's not my boyfriend! But he did call me 'babe,' so . . ."

"Sounds like he is to me," Monroe says.

Mom slides into the kitchen, freshly dressed from her shower. "Boyfriend? I thought you were taking things slow!"

"He's not my boyfriend, *shush*," I hiss, as I hear the large front door to the building slam shut, signaling that Cris is making his way up the one flight of stairs to our apartment. My stomach twists. "We haven't had that conversation yet."

"Have you kissed him?" Mom asks.

"Mom!"

"I'm your mother, I can ask these questions."

"They totally have," Monroe adds.

Mom makes this weird squealing noise, and I fear we're about to have one of our Gilmore Gays sessions—she loves that old show—but there's no time for that.

"I don't know what it all means yet. So . . . be cool?"

Mom doesn't let up so easily. "What are his intentions?" She motions for me to get out of the way of the saucepot. She thrusts the wooden spoon filled with steaming sauce toward my mouth, which I happily, but hastily taste test.

My lips smack. "Amazing! But Mom, seriously, be cool, *please*." She makes a long humming sound, which means, *don't tell me what to do*. Then I add, "You too, Roe."

Their collective gaze weighs on me as I walk out of the kitchen. My worlds are about to collide. I resist the urge to blurt a random Mariah Carey fact, like how she wrote "All I Want for Christmas Is You" in 1994, and it's the most popular holiday song of all time, managing to become her nineteenth *Billboard* Hot 100 number one twenty-five years later, in 2019. The thought is enough to calm me down.

I open the door to find Cris nervously pacing the hallway with a bouquet of pink stargazer lilies. "The dude at the flower shop told me they represent prosperity. Thought it was appropriate." He flashes a smile that makes my knees weak. I check behind me to make sure Mom and Monroe aren't lurking like creepers before leaning in to him and his lips. He nibbles my bottom lip, then licks his. "Marinara?"

I exhale. I am *so* screwed.

After introductions, where Mom totally nudges me in the ribs in a way-to-go move that makes me slightly uncomfortable, she sits Cris at the breakfast counter next to Monroe and gives him a small plate with a plump, sauce-smothered meatball and instructs him to eat.

"This is delicious!" he says as he stuffs his face. I love the way he eats, like he hasn't in days and every meal might be his last. "Is there mint in here?"

"*Fresh* mint. It's my mother's secret recipe," Mom says. "So, Cris is short for . . ."

Here come a million questions.

"Crisanto, actually," he says proudly. "It's Filipino. Mom was from the Philippines, Dad is Greek."

"Was?" she asks.

I cringe. Mom always picks up on the details.

Cris's shoulders droop, and his head hangs low. "She passed a few years ago."

Mom reaches across the counter and takes his hand. He smiles tightly, then carefully retracts his hand, asking where the bathroom is.

When Cris is out of sight, I say, "Mom, can you not?"

"I didn't know!" She fidgets nervously with her fingers. "Go check on him."

I knock on the bathroom door and whisper his name. When he opens it, he forces a smile that quivers at the corners of his mouth. I slip in, close the door behind me, and pull him close. His body is rigid against mine, like he's trying not to cry. I rub his back until his muscles relax and his breathing returns to normal. I pull back to get a good look at his face.

But then he leans in and kisses me with such intensity it takes the wind out of me. It's a voracious hunger I haven't experienced before. He walks me backward until I'm pressed against the bathroom wall.

Cris's lips move to my neck; his fingers tangle with the fabric of my drapey black cardigan until it lifts, exposing bare skin. My body shudders.

Though I want him, *really* want him, my mom and best friend are too close for comfort. "Cris, stop."

His entire body goes limp. His head falls onto my shoulder, tears flowing like a waterfall, upper body heaving.

"Today is the anniversary of, um, when my mom . . ." I've never seen pain like this before. The dark brown of his eyes begs me to take away his hurt. "I went to the hospital and she actually looked pretty good, you know? She was smiling and talking about how, no matter what, she was coming home for Christmas." There's a quiet river of tears streaming down his cheeks. "She was pretty weak because of the chemo, but she hugged me so tight. She said, 'I'm so proud of you, and I'll always be with you.'" He's quiet for a moment. "The next morning, Dad got the phone call. I wasn't planning on saying anything tonight. I was actually doing pretty good today. I managed to avoid my dad, who takes the day off work to lock himself in his room and cry."

There's nothing for me to say. How can you comfort someone who lost their mom? I can't fathom. There's a part in *Wicked* where Elphaba doesn't know what to do to save Fiyero's life, so she tries all these incantations and spells. Everything she says and does amounts to nothing. I want to cast a spell and take away his tears, numb him to this, but I can't. So I put my arm around him, hoping he feels safe with me.

"You know what's really hard?" he asks. "My dad is great,

but I feel alone a lot. My mom's family all live in California. You know how many Filipino people live in Sunnyside? You're looking at him." He holds on a little tighter. "I want to feel connected to my mom. And my dad likes to shut himself off from talking to me about her, especially today."

"I don't know what it's like to be Filipino, but I want to know all the things that make up who you are," I whisper.

He doesn't respond and I worry that maybe it wasn't the right thing to say.

After a few minutes of comfortable silence, he chuckles. "Your mom probably thinks I'm unstable."

"She's pushy. I'll talk to her."

He shifts his weight off me. "I like her. She reminds me of my mom." His voice is full again, but he doesn't let himself break this time. "I had this whole plan for tonight that had nothing to do with having a meltdown in your bathroom over my mom." He struggles to laugh. "I was going to ask if we could officially be official, but fuck, that sounds so corny." He grabs my hand and intertwines his fingers with mine. His smile twitches like a fading neon light.

I like him so much it scares me. "Try me."

He gets down on one knee on the tile floor and holds out his hand. "Carey Parker, would you be my . . ." His eyebrows scrunch. "I'm sorry, I don't know the term to use for someone who is genderqueer. Boyfriend? Girlfriend? Special friend?"

"Ew! Special friend?" I laugh.

"Lover?"

"Okay, Taylor Swift." I motion for him to stand up. "In a support group I used to go to at the local LGBTQ center, a lot of people used 'partner.' I don't know how I feel about that, but it's better than special friend or lover."

"Howdy, partner!" His deep voice makes for a great Southern drawl.

I retch. "Hearing that out loud is not cute."

He laughs. "How about I call you my boo?" His eyes widen and his mouth drops. "Wait, I got it. My boo-friend."

"Boo-friend?" It's weird, yet so right. "I love it."

"Is it cool if you call me your boyfriend?" he asks.

"No, you're my special friend," I say, wagging my finger at him, and he laughs. Maybe I can't take away his pain, but I can make him smile.

Maybe that matters more.

He kisses me. It's gentle. A promise. "Can I ask you something else?"

"You're pushing your luck." I bite my lip playfully.

"Coach Trevisani asked how many tickets I'd need for the winter showcase yesterday. I said two. One for my dad, and one for you. If you'd like to come."

"To Carnegie Hall?" I ask, thinking how strange it'd be to see Coach Trevisani again after I dropped off the face of the earth.

"If it's awkward . . . feel free to say no."

"No," I say quickly. Then I laugh. "Of course, I'll go, stupid."

He wraps his arms around me. "The day is turning around."

I kiss him this time. I never want it to end.

When we emerge from the bathroom, Joey has arrived, and she and Monroe are digging into Mom's saucepot, scooping up meatballs like raccoons in a trashcan. Their parents sit at the breakfast counter eating chips and dip while talking to Mom about work. Their mom is short, like Monroe, and if it weren't for Monroe's ever-changing hair color and diamond-studded nose piercing, they'd look identical. Their dad is pure Joey— tall, ashy blond, broad shoulders, sportsball running through his veins.

"There they are!" Mom exclaims. "I want to make a toast to my incredible child. Carey, can you wheel Grams in here?"

Grams is slumped over in her wheelchair, staring blankly at the television screen in the living room. I kneel in front of her, and her eyeballs dart around their sockets until they focus on me. She moves her lips like she wants to say something. I kiss her forehead, and she stops stirring.

"Come on, Grams, let's join the party."

As I wheel Grams into the kitchen, Monroe slips out to get Phoebe, who has just arrived. Everyone in the kitchen sort of stops and smiles at Grams like she's a newborn, waving at her like they're about to say, "You're such a pretty little girl" or "goo goo, gaa gaa." I wonder what it must be like for her, if the real Grams is trapped inside this shell of her body, wanting to say something sarcastic and humorous, the way only Grams knew how, but unable to. Instead, she takes turns looking everyone up and down, then holds her hand out to Cris, who takes it hesitantly. She gently brings it to her cheek and holds it there.

Cris looks like he's scared to move or breathe. "It's nice to meet you."

When Phoebe peeks her head into my kitchen, she doesn't

skip a beat, introducing herself to everyone and commanding all the attention in the room.

Mom puts her arm around Phoebe. "Phoebe has been over every day since auditions, making Carey practice because she knew Carey would get the part." There are tears in Mom's eyes. "You've helped bring music back to this house."

Phoebe blushes. "We've almost nailed 'Defying Gravity.'"

"I haven't hit that high note at the very end of the song yet," I say. Our voices blend brilliantly, with Phoebe's strong, complex range melting into my bombastic belting soprano, creating an aural root beer float: bubbly, sweet, creamy, and rich.

"You can do it. I've heard you," Cris says.

"That's what I keep telling them," Phoebe adds.

Then Grams chimes in with a jagged, "D-d-d-don't cry," aimed at Mom. This, of course, makes Mom actually cry.

Mom kisses Grams on her forehead. "Don't worry, Ma, I'm happy. Now that everyone's here, a toast!" She grabs the bottles of champagne from the fridge and plastic flutes she found at the dollar store. "I figure you all can have a little champagne. It won't hurt." She does a little dance like Amy Poehler's character in *Mean Girls* and says, "I'm a cool mom," which makes me bury my head in my cardigan. She pours and passes the glasses and says, "I want to say how proud I am of Carey, that they will be sharing their gift with the world. RoeRoe, we're all so excited for the costumes. They're going to be spectacular."

Monroe snuggles up against Mom.

"JoJo," Mom continues. "We can't wait to see you play in the last Hoop-Off game before college. And Cris and Phoebe, welcome to our crazy chosen family. You kids are all doing amazing things. You only have a few more months left in high school, so enjoy every single moment! Cheers!"

At the same time, with the same fervor, everyone yells, "Cheers!"

Mom looks to me as if she wants to pass the proverbial microphone, but I don't know what to say that she hasn't already. I'm feeling a million different emotions at once. There's a warmth in this kitchen emanating off the love in the oven crafted by Mom, inspired by Grams, as I'm surrounded by my best friends, new friends, Cris. Happiness like I haven't felt in a long time, maybe ever, lodges in my throat. Mom reaches out and places her hand on mine, and almost instinctively, everyone inches a bit closer to me.

"All right, that's enough of this," Mom says. "I'm starving." She begins passing out plates and fills them up one by one, and soon, nobody is talking because they're busy stuffing their faces. I can tell when people are full by the rising volume of chatter that takes the place of scraping forks (and the occasional moan of satisfaction).

While everyone is distracted, I seize a moment with Joey.

"Hey, Jo. Everything okay?"

She bites the corner of her lip the way she does before a big game. Or when she wants to tell me something. "All good."

Something's up with her, and for once, I don't think it has anything to do with us. "Thanks for coming."

She arches her eyebrows. "Why wouldn't I?"

I resist the urge to call out our mutual stalemate. No need to cause a scene. I count to five before responding to calm my nerves. "No reason. Do you think we can hang over the break, just the two of us? To talk?"

She takes a moment to respond, her gray-blue eyes never leaving mine. "I'd like that." She pauses. "I'm really proud of you, Carey. I hope you know that."

"I do now."

Then she leans in, close enough that nobody else can hear. "Just be careful. With Cris."

My heartbeat quickens. "What do you mean?"

"I know you're happy, so I'm trying not to judge him," she says. "But don't you think it's weird that—"

"That what?" I cut her off angrily. "That he's into me?" I try not to get loud, but I can't help it. Is she serious right now?

"No, Carey, I didn't mean—"

"Whatever, Jo." I stand and shove the chair out from under me. "I can't deal with this right now."

"Carey," she pleads, but I don't want to hear it. Monroe, Phoebe, and Cris, who were staring at us, look at each other awkwardly, unsure what to do.

"Party's over," I mutter. "Merry fucking Christmas."

TRACK 13
THEY/THEM/THEIR

Cris tag teams the dishes with Mom while I get Grams ready for bed. I kiss her good night, then plop down on a stool at the breakfast counter. I rest my head on the cool Formica.

"You tired?" Mom asks, but she doesn't wait for an answer. "I'm going to bed. Don't be loud, please." She kisses my forehead. "I hope you had a good night, but I really hope you can work things out with Joey." She places a hand on Cris's shoulder as she leaves and says quietly, "Maybe you can talk to them. Thank you for helping with the dishes."

"I love your mom," he says once she's out of earshot.

"She loves you." I wonder if his mom would have liked me.

"I should go, too, though," Cris says.

"No, don't," I say quickly. Joey's words are swirling in my head: *Be careful*. There's a pang in my stomach that wasn't there before, and he can't leave while I still feel like this. "I was thinking we could watch a movie."

He flashes another goofy smile. "I'd love that."

My bedroom is a cool gray with a slate accent wall. White picture frames, all the same size, hung at the same height, wrap around the room. Each holds a picture of one of my heroes: Lady Gaga, Whitney Houston, Freddie Mercury, Sam Smith, and way too many (or not enough?) vintage Mariah. There's a nook at the far end of the room that's been padded with acoustic foam to make it look like a recording studio that also has a record player and shelves of neatly stacked records. Mom got me a small pleather loveseat from a consignment shop in town to complete the look.

He asks permission to sit on my bed. I used to have fantasies about being in my bed with boys, but I never spent much time thinking of what the moment would feel like in real life. It's terrifying and exhilarating, my heart racing, my muscles wanting to pull him closer as he slips off his Converse, but my head is telling me to relax. He pulls a pillow under his head and stretches his limbs so that a small patch of his belly peeks out from under his shirt. I have to look away because all I want to do is get on top of him and kiss him, a feeling I'm wholly unfamiliar with. It's making me forget to breathe.

"Can I ask you a question?" he says, and I gesture for him to ask whatever he wants. "What's the deal with you and Joey?"

"The deal?"

"I'm not blind. The tension is *real*."

"We have a lot of history. I don't know how we got here." I stare at the wall behind him, thinking about everything that has gone down between me and Joey and everything she still doesn't know about me. I turn away. I close my eyes and picture Joey in her emerald-green dress at junior prom, standing alone, waiting for me. She's saying something, but I can't hear her. All I can hear is my own heartbeat.

I want to tell Cris everything. That I'm fragile, a house that endured an earthquake and is still rebuilding its foundation. That I want him to be a person I can trust, but that Joey's warning has me on edge.

He pokes my arm. "Where do you go when you go dark?"

I take a deep breath. "Can I trust you?"

"Of course you can, boo-friend." Our shared gaze doesn't break until I bury my head in his chest. He holds me tight, the way Mom used to when I would cry.

I tell him what neither Monroe nor Joey knows about me. "Last year, I wanted to die." He doesn't pull away. "When Junior year started I was so fucked up I couldn't see straight. It was before I came out. My dysphoria got so bad that, some days, I made myself throw up so Mom would let me stay home from school. Nobody knew. Except Grams. I could talk to her. And she caught me trying on one of her old fancy dresses." I pause, remembering how the fabric felt against my skin. "She kept them in the back of her closet. She was forgetful then, but her Alzheimer's hadn't gotten that bad yet. She suggested we go to the mall, and she'd help me try on clothes that fit the person I knew I was on the inside."

"That's amazing," he says. "I wish I could've known her like that."

I smile. "She would've loved you the way she loved perusing the aisles for a fabulous new caftan, a Golden Girl hunting for a bargain."

"A what girl?" he asks.

"*The Golden Girls*. It's an old eighties sitcom we binged together. It's the best."

"Noted." Something tells me he's actually going to make it a point to watch.

"Anyway, we spent hours trying on clothes at the mall, and it was the first time that I felt like I could breathe. I was just so happy, and Grams didn't give a shit who was watching. But—" My voice trails off. "I wish I'd been paying more attention to her, because I turned around and she must've forgotten where she was and wandered off and—"

"What happened?"

"I stepped out of the dressing room after trying on this incredible black sequined dress, but Grams wasn't waiting for me. She was gone. She'd started wandering the store and got lost. I didn't think about how I was still in that fucking dress! I had to find her. I took off running, yelling her name, searching for her behind the racks. I wasn't paying attention to anything else around me, so I didn't see Max following me, recording everything."

"Fuck," Cris mutters.

"When I saw him, my body went numb. I couldn't move. Like if I stood still, he'd disappear. But he didn't. I asked him to stop recording me, but he laughed. I went to grab his phone, but he shoved me, and I tripped on that fucking sequined train. He took another picture of me and bolted. I collapsed. Sobbed on the floor. The store manager found me after finding Grams.

"That was the night I told Mom I wanted to find a therapist. I didn't tell her what had happened at the mall, just that it felt like Earth's gravity was slamming me to the ground every single day, and I needed someone to talk to. She was skeptical because, at the time, she thought 'therapists are for crazy people.' But I'd been Googling for LGBTQ-friendly therapists for months and had Dr. Potter all picked out. Mom must've seen how much pain I was in, because she agreed.

"The next day at school was quiet. Max did nothing, said nothing. The photos weren't plastered all over the walls at school or passed around in text chains or on Instagram or Snapchat. Nothing. He kept looking at me in disgust, which made my stomach curdle, but that was it. On one hand, it was a relief. On the other hand, I knew it was a matter of time until he blabbed my secret.

"I started going to Dr. Potter and worked with her for long time. I didn't have the words to express who I was inside, but going to her office made me feel safe, at least for an hour a week.

"Fast forward to Sunnyside's promposal season. Joey and I were eating lunch, and she asked me to go with her. I was so happy—and relieved. I'd wanted to ask her, because she was my best friend. I knew we'd have the best time together. We spent the entire period planning and coordinating.

"Later that day, I was in the locker room after gym, waiting in the far corner until all the boys showered, changed, and left before doing the same." I don't tell him how deeply uncomfortable it always made me to have to be in that locker room at all. Some things are too vulnerable to reveal. "When I'd finished showering, I draped a towel around my waist and another around my shoulders and tiptoed to my locker to change. But when I opened it, there was nothing there. My clothes were gone."

I shudder at the memory. "Someone coughed behind me. I turned, and it was Max. He had this demonic grin I'll never forget.

"I told him to give me back my clothes, but he said, 'Shut up' and . . ." I don't want to repeat the horrible queerphobic slurs, but I do, and Cris winces. He grabs my hand, his own palms sweaty, and squeezes.

"I told him to fuck himself. Then he took out his phone and showed me the video and picture from the mall. 'You want everyone in school to see this?'

"Everything went cold, my entire body shuddered, as the air in the locker room grew thinner. I tried to breathe, but my head was so fuzzy, and I forgot how.

"I didn't know what he was going to do to me, and it was all I could do to keep myself upright, not to pass out from the fear. I had to figure out how to get away.

"He wanted to know what girls liked about me. He said, 'You're no man.' His jaw pulsated with anger, and his words punched me right in the gut. I became dysphoric, wanting to crawl out of my skin and to get away from him. And myself.

"I begged him to leave me alone, but he wouldn't budge.

"'Tell me, Parker,' he insisted.

"I didn't know what he wanted me to say. I couldn't process anything. I just wanted to escape. I may be taller than Max, but his presence was bigger than me. If I tried to run, I knew he'd catch me.

"He cleared his throat and started to walk around me. I closed my eyes, braced myself for whatever was going to come next. Then he said: 'I try so hard with the cunts at this school.

None of them want a nice guy like me. I work and I work and I work. I spent months on a promposal for the girl of my dreams. How could she resist?' Then he stopped. 'But she said no. What the fuck is wrong with me, huh?' I could almost taste his Dorito breath, he was so close to me, and it soured my stomach. Then he said he realized it was me, not him.

"He kept saying, 'I'm a man. A real man. And you?' He grabbed the towel around my waist.

"I'd never felt more exposed. I started to cry and asked him to give back my clothes, but all he did was laugh and took another picture on his phone. '*Click-click*,' he taunted.

"I don't know what came over me, but I lunged at him, which was a mistake because he nailed me right in the balls. I doubled over and fell to the ground."

I'm practically in tears as I share this with Cris. "And you know what he did? He laughed. 'You thought you could take me?' he said. 'You just made yourself a lifelong enemy, Parker. Better watch your back.' Then I heard the door to the locker room creak open, and he yelled, 'Good luck getting your clothes back.'

"I laid my head on the wet tile floor. The locker room smelled like sweat. There were cracks in the dirty grout, and I lay there, staring at them until I thought I heard someone come in. I managed to find random clothes in the gym's lost and found bin. I didn't even care about skipping the rest of the day. I walked home in a daze.

"I felt nothing. Not sadness, not anger, not pain. I felt like I *was* nothing. Like I would never be anything, and there was no song I could ever sing that would bring me back to life."

I exhale slowly. "I never told anybody about that, besides Dr. Potter."

Cris has been holding my hand and squeezes it softly. "I'm so sorry, Carey."

"A few weeks later, Mom and I went to visit my Uncle Mike, who is a doctor, and I stole a bottle of painkillers he had in his medicine cabinet from an old sports injury. The day I was going to take them, I stared at the white label on that orange bottle for hours. I tried to imagine what it would feel like to swallow them all, to lie down on my bed and slip my headphones on and listen to something ethereal, soothing, one last crescendo before I faded out."

The pain and shame I'd felt flows through my body afresh, coursing through my veins and into my heart until it hurts to breathe.

"I don't remember why I decided not to swallow the pills I stole, but I was lying on top of my bed, listening to Mariah's 'Close My Eyes' and clutching the bottle, when a thought drifted into my head like a falling leaf: *I don't want to die.*

"So, I sent the text that saved my life. 'Mom, I need help.'"

———

Cris holds me tight until we fall asleep, fully clothed, our limbs entwined. I'm safe in his arms as he snore-growls like a small dog.

I wake up as the sun begins to creep over the mountains beyond the Hudson. While he sleeps, I send Dr. Potter a text; she gives her patients a special number in case we're ever in a bind and need to talk. It's a courtesy, a safety net, and I don't use it unless it's important.

ME: I told Cris about my ideations last night

While I wait for her to answer, I take out the notebook I use to write all my lyrics. It has the poem I submitted to Mr. Kelly a few weeks ago:

> *I've been too*
> *Scared to die,*
> *But afraid to live.*
> *I have to try,*
> *to forgive myself.*

I change up some of the wording and add two lines to the end:

> *I've been too*
> *Scared to live*
> *Scared to die*
> *To forgive myself*
> *I have to try*
> *One day I'll be stronger.*
> *Maybe I already am.*

I've been afraid to sing in public because of rejection, because I didn't think that anyone would see me the way I see myself.

My silence has been about self-preservation, but I didn't need to protect myself from the people who love me. I needed to let them in.

As Cris snores, I write another verse. Or maybe it's a chorus. I don't quite know what it is, but I hear the melody in my head and the words pour out.

> *You want me to believe*
> *I'm not good enough,*
> *But you won't*
> *Ever get the best of me*
> *Because my voice is*
> *the one thing*
> *You can never take from me*

I start to hum as I write, hearing plunking piano keys, sparse at first, then a full band with strings and horns and booming baselines. As I orchestrate in my head, my phone vibrates.

DR. POTTER: Are you okay? How do you feel?

ME: Safe 😊

ME: I'm ready to confront what I've been running from

DR. POTTER: That's great, Carey! If you need to see me this week, let me know and I'll come in to the office.

ME: I should be good. I'll see you after the New Year

DR. POTTER: Remember: You already have everything you need.

I lock my phone and stare at the digital clock on its face. *Shit!* I have to get Cris out before Mom wakes up. She trusts me, but I don't think she'd be happy about our impromptu sleepover. I shake him until his eyes peek out from behind his lids. He jolts up, asking if I'm okay. I tell him we have to leave before Mom catches us, so we quickly tiptoe out of the apartment and walk to the diner down the street for breakfast.

"Thank you for trusting me with your story," he says as he dips a piece of French toast into a pool of sugary, sticky syrup.

"Thanks for listening. Nobody knows but Mom, Dr. Potter, and Mr. Kelly. Definitely not Monroe and Joey." When I came out to Mom in Dr. Potter's office afterward, it felt like a weight had lifted off my shoulders, but Dr. Potter suggested a retreat specifically for kids who suffer from suicidal ideations. Mom called the principal and told her we'd had a family emergency, and Uncle Mike helped us pay for it. I think he felt guilty for leaving his pills accessible in his house. I didn't tell Monroe and Joey why I was out of school because Mom told their mom some sort of lie and they bought it.

"Why didn't you tell Monroe and Joey?" he asks.

I shrug. "Didn't want to worry them." I pause. If I'm being honest with Cris, I *have* to go all in. "I also didn't want them to judge me or feel sorry for me. And I'd have to come out to them. I wasn't ready." Joey tugs at my thoughts. "I think part of why I resent Joey is that she doesn't know what I've been through. I know it's not her fault, but ever since I came out to her, she's pulled away, so I haven't felt like it was safe to tell her or Monroe."

Cris nods. "I get that. I didn't tell anyone when my mom was sick. I didn't want fake sympathy." He tools a bite of cinnamon-battered bread around his plate, his fork scraping the ceramic. "I always knew Max was space junk, but I never thought he was actually evil." His voice is a strange mix of sadness and shock. "I knew his older sister pretty well." He takes a deep breath and looks away like there's more to that than he's willing to say. "We were close. When I'd go over to their house, he kept to himself. Stayed in his room a lot. Real quiet. I guess looking back, he talked to his sister like she was garbage, but I thought that was a sibling thing."

"What did he do?" I ask, trying to wrap my head around the idea of Cris being friendly with anyone associated with Max.

He tells me some of the things he heard, and I involuntarily recoil. "There was always, like, disgust on his face when he looked at his sister."

I spear a hunk of Belgian waffle. "You still close with her?"

"Not . . . really. She went to college and . . ." He takes another bite of French toast. "How come you chose to tell me what happened before you told Monroe or Joey?"

"We don't have a lifetime of tangled history. And I trust you."

After a few seconds of silence, he whispers, "I hope I'm worthy."

There's something cloudy in his eyes now that makes me hesitate. Could Joey be right in her warning? Cris hasn't given me a reason to doubt him, and regardless, I'm relieved that someone knows what I went through last year. I flash him a smile. "Same."

TRACK 14
HE/HIM/HIS

Sunnyside High's Winter B-ball Hoop-Off is a yearly event on the Saturday before Christmas that rivals the homecoming football game at any other school. Girls' basketball is pretty much the only sport at Sunnyside worth community-wide celebration. There have been five girls in the last eight years who graduated and went on to the WNBA after college, and Joey will undoubtedly be the next.

The pep rally in the gym is teeming with people, everyone wearing some version of our school colors, purple and white. I'm in a Monroe Cooper original, an eighties-inspired iridescent purple cropped bomber jacket with bunched sleeves. My version of school spirit.

Cris and I find Monroe and Phoebe on the bleachers before the principal announces the marching band. Mom sits with the Coopers a few rows down.

"Yaaas, bitch, work!" Monroe yells, snapping her fingers and bobbing her head.

"You really can't pull that off, Monroe," Phoebe says.

"Just . . . no." She turns to me, "Carey, serving looks! Giving me life! But before y'all get cozy, Principal McCauley wants to talk to us."

"Me?" I point to myself as the band marches across the shiny basketball court, the flag twirlers tossing their glittery batons in the air in a sparkling display of agility.

Phoebe grabs my hand and pulls me toward Principal McCauley, who is standing with Mr. Kelly on the side of the gym.

"Carey, Phoebe. Thanks for taking a few minutes," she says. "Congratulations on the spring musical!"

"I've never heard voices like theirs before," Mr. Kelly adds.

Our principal nods like a politician. "I would love it if we could surprise the gymnasium with a bit of an introduction to our theater stars. What do you say?"

"Do you have anything you think you can perform?" Mr. Kelly asks.

I want to say no because I'm not ready to sing in front of the entire community, but Phoebe totally ruins it. "Absolutely! Carey and I have been working on 'Defying Gravity' and we're pretty fantastic."

I shoot her an are-you-kidding-me death glare.

"Oh, perfect!" Principal McCauley says. She's not one for big shows of emotion, so when she pitches her voice, she means business. "Do you think you could do it a cappella? I know it's last minute and all."

"We have an instrumental recording we've been using to practice." Phoebe takes out her phone, finds the song, and hands it to Mr. Kelly. "If you can plug it into the speakers, we'll be good to go."

"Wonderful! Do you think twenty minutes gives you enough time to prep?" The way she asks is less of a question and more of a statement. She's gifted us a mere twenty minutes to run lyrics and for me to prepare to hit that high note at the end. *Is it too late to ask for a gift receipt?*

Mr. Kelly walks us to the nearby exit, then hangs back to talk to me. "Sorry about this, but Principal McCauley insisted, though I told her it may not be appropriate, given the suddenness of the request."

"It's fine." I shove my shaking hands into the pockets of my white acid-washed skinny jeans. "I'll be yet another punchline in the next *Sunnyside Upended!* No big deal."

"Carey, remember what I said to you a few weeks ago?" he asks.

I stare at him blankly.

"Be the diva you wish to see in the world," he repeats. "You said you want to be like the greats. What makes someone like Mariah Carey a diva?"

Ask me a question about Mariah, and I can talk for hours. "Mariah is unapologetic about who she is. She doesn't take herself too seriously, but she presents herself to the world authentically. She's silly and weird and super feminine and vulnerable if you really listen to the lyrics of the songs she writes—which, by the way, unless it's a cover, are all of them. Eighteen of her nineteen *Billboard* Hot 100 number one hits were written by *her.* Her talent for singing and songwriting speaks for itself. Even though some people think she's a fake. But she's so real it hurts." I take a deep breath. "I want to feel like that. I don't want to hide."

"Right. Mariah Carey doesn't hide. She turns her pain into power," Mr. Kelly says, and suddenly it all clicks. My dream is not just about wanting to be a diva or a singer. It's about being true to who I am and how I see myself, regardless of what others see.

"Thank you, Mr. Kelly," I say before directing us to a nearby classroom to practice.

We run through the song twice. Both times, I flub the fucking high note. When the dance team is halfway through their performance, Mr. Kelly emerges to give us our five-minute warning. We're next.

My palms are sweaty.

I steady my breathing.

I can do this. I can do this.

A roaring applause fades with Principal McCauley's voice on the microphone: "Before we get to the main event, we have one more surprise for you! The stars of the upcoming spring musical, *Wicked*, are going to perform for us. Please welcome to the stage, Carey Parker and Phoebe Wright!"

There's a tap on my shoulder, and when I turn around, my breath catches in my throat. Max. I can't get a word out before Phoebe jumps to my defense.

"Get the fuck away, mouth breather," she snaps.

"I heard a rumor you two would be performing today." He smiles. It's unnerving. How they hell did he hear about it before we did? "Just wanted to wish you good luck, Parker. We'll be watching."

We?

Phoebe grabs my hand and we stride out to center court. "You okay?" she whispers. I hear clapping, but it's far away, somewhere behind the beat of my own heart.

What would Mariah Carey do? She'd go out onstage and belt her heart out. And if something were to go wrong, she'd smile through it.

I got this. I already have everything I need.

I nod to her and signal Mr. Kelly to start the track.

Phoebe-as-Glinda chastises me-as-Elphaba to stay calm, and everyone goes wild because Phoebe Wright is a damn superstar.

A surge of energy rushes through my veins. When I open my mouth to sing, I become Elphaba. I don't look at the crowd, I give everything I have to Phoebe, feeding off her performance. As we reach the middle of the song, our harmonies reach the rafters, lifting my spirit off the ground, and as I belt the climax, I truly feel as if all the gravity in the room is gone, and I'm soaring high above the crowd.

I hit the high note at the end.

My vocal cords throb from the strain.

When I open my eyes, all I hear are deafening screams.

My heart pounds.

"CAREY! PHOEBE! CAREY! PHOEBE!"

Mom jumps up and down from her place in the bleachers, tears of joy streaming down her cheeks.

"CAREY! PHOEBE! CAREY! PHOEBE!"

"Give it up for Carey and Phoebe!" Principal McCauley announces, her voice booming with pride. "The spring musical is shaping up to be our best yet, Falcons! But we still have a basketball season to own, am I right?" The crowd's cheers shift from our names to "FALCONS, FALCONS, FALCONS!" as Principal McCauley introduces the team one by one, ending with star player Joey Cooper, who runs over to me, grabs my hand and lifts it into the air in a championship wave, which makes the entire gym erupt in applause. She gives me a hug and runs to the center of the court.

Phoebe and I run past Mr. Kelly, who gives us a double thumbs-up, out the doors and into the empty hallway.

She jumps into my arms. "That was incredible, Carey! Holy shit! I knew practicing would pay off!"

Cris and Monroe barrel through the doors a few seconds later and jump on us.

Monroe says, "I'm at a loss for words."

"That's a first," I say with a smile.

"You performed magic," Monroe says.

I turn to Cris. "How'd I do?"

"Is that really a question?" Cris rolls his eyes before pulling me into the deepest kiss ever. Like, tongue-in-mouth, hands-grasping-at-back, chest-to-chest kiss that makes me dizzier than singing under a white-hot spotlight ever could.

When we pull away, I hear a cough, and a disgruntled voice says, "Excuse me?"

Cris's hands go limp, and he distances himself from me.

A tall blond girl I vaguely recognize who graduated last June walks toward us. Courtney *Something*. Max is behind her, smirking. My gaze shifts back and forth between them until it clicks: Courtney *McKagan*. Max's sister, the sister Cris is supposedly friends with.

"Courtney!" Cris seems unable to form words. "What're you doing here?" He steps toward her.

"You've been ignoring me for weeks! I just got home for

winter break, and I figured you'd be here. I didn't think you'd be doing . . . *this*!" The way she says "this" makes me feel like I'm a dirty little secret.

Courtney was never Cris's friend. She was—*is?*—his girl-friend. That's why Cris was acting weird at breakfast, almost bewildered by the truth about what Max did to me. Or maybe he was overacting and already knew what Max had done.

Monroe and Phoebe stand off to the side, watching a car accident they can't stop from happening.

"What's going on?" I ask.

"Stay out of this, sidepiece," Courtney hisses. "And while you're at it, stop making out with *my* boyfriend."

"Didn't Cris tell you?" Max asks. "He's dating my sister."

Cris's face is drenched in guilt.

"You have anything to say, Cris?" Courtney asks. Then she turns to Max. "Did you know about this?"

"Cris?" I plead, but the damage is done. Not only did he lie to me, he conveniently forgot to mention his connection to my tormentor.

"Right. Fuck all of you." She gives Cris the finger, then directs it at her own brother, before storming out of the building.

"Courtney, wait!" Cris shouts after her. She doesn't turn. He looks at me, pleading with his eyes, and I nod at him to go after her.

What hurts the most is that he does.

Without a word to me, he chases after *her*, each step deepening the cracks in my heart.

Max lets out a loud breath. "Wow, that was super awkward."

I turn to him. "Why'd you do that?"

"Sounds like a question for Cris," Max says. "I'm gonna go watch the game."

Max practically skips away from the wreckage as I bleed out all over the floor.

TRACK 15
HE/HIM/HIS

Twenty-three missed calls from: Cris Kostas

CRIS: carey, plz pick up!

CRIS: PLEASE! plz plz plz!

CRIS: i'm so so so sorry

CRIS: if you would pick up i could explain

CRIS: i meant to hurt you

CRIS: omg I meant i never***^ meant to hurt you!

CRIS: i understand if you never want to see me or talk to me again

CRIS: i'm such an idiot

CRIS: i know you probably don't believe me, but i was starting to fall in love with you. i mean, i am, not "was," and i should've told you about courtney. i told her it was over so many times. it's BEEN over since she left for college, but she won't accept that. i know you don't have any reason to trust me, but i'm telling the truth.

CRIS: i want to be with you, boo-friend

CRIS: courtney means nothing. i made it clear to her tonight.

ME: Please leave me the fuck alone.

TRACK 16

HE/HIM/HIS

I refuse to think about Cris. I repeat this to myself until it becomes a harsh, angry song about how men are trash, something akin to a snappy Lizzo bop, or maybe a moodier jam like Mariah's "GTFO."

When that doesn't work, I allow myself to cry until my tear ducts are empty.

The thought that Cris loves me is too much to bear on top of how I feel about him. Was everything a lie? If he dated Courtney, Max's sister, was there a chance he knew what Max did to me last year? Max could've pulled Cris aside at their house to show him the video of me at the mall or the naked photo in the locker room. Would he have kept that secret? I'm so fucking pissed: I feel betrayed, lied to. In my mind, Cris has been recast as a bystander all those times Max targeted me. Mom tries to play devil's advocate, but I'm not ready to hear that Cris didn't know about Max. It's easier to hate him this way.

Cris texts me again, but I don't bother to look. I fling my phone across the room as my bedroom door opens.

"Mom, I just wanna be alone," I whimper.

"Not Mom," Joey says, ducking in case of more crossfire. She tucks her hands into the big pocket of her navy hoodie with a basketball embroidered on the chest. Her frizzy blond hair is tied in a messy ponytail.

I try to say something, but the words lodge in my throat. I practically leap off the bed and pull her into a hug. She hugs me back, so hard that we both start crying.

"I'm so sorry." I don't know what she's apologizing for, being standoffish for the last six months or for what happened between me and Cris, but I don't care.

"No, I'm sorry," I say. "I should have listened to you."

We pull away from each other at the same time.

"I was worried you wouldn't want to see me," she says.

"You're the only person I want to see right now."

She smiles, but I know that this isn't a magical fix to our friendship. There's a lot we're both not saying. I'm not sure if I'm emotionally ready to deal with our fractured friendship, but I can't keep running from her.

"I need to get out of this room. You wanna go to the park by the river and talk?"

———————

There's an icy chill in the air. The park is filled with families because Sunnyside Village holds nothing back during the holidays; every year, Santa's workshop throws up on Main Street. Thousands of twinkling lights are wrapped around the barren trees that line the river, red and green wreaths are hung on streetlamps, and every park attendant and police officer dons a fluffy Santa hat, like an insane little town from a Hallmark Channel movie. The one thing that remains untouched is Cris's willow tree.

Despite our emotional reunion in my bedroom, Joey is so far away from me as we walk that there might as well be an entire planet between us.

"Sometimes I can't wait to leave for college," she says, leading us to a bench by the river. "Then I come down here and it's like so much of my life is wrapped up in this place. In you."

"You won't miss me." I smirk, only half kidding.

Her head whips toward me. "Don't do that."

"Do what?"

"You know I'll miss you," she says. "Just because things have been awkward doesn't mean I don't love you or won't miss you next year. You mean more to me than that."

"I haven't felt that from you in a long time."

"Are you really that clueless?" she snaps, turning her body toward the water so I can't see her face. She wipes her cheek with the sleeve of her hoodie. "*You* kissed *me* the night before junior prom. When you saw me in my dress the next day, *you* told *me* I took your breath away. I *thought* you liked me. Did you ever like me like that, or were you just being cruel?" Her voice is thin, like one more word will break it.

I remember that day, seeing her and wanting to cry because I loved her, really loved her, but not *that* way. "For the longest time, I was convinced you were my soul mate. That night when we kissed, it wasn't a joke. I wasn't playing any games. I *wanted* to kiss you." I dip my head in my hands. I feel like I'm hurting her all over again. "After it happened, I knew I'd made a mistake. Because I finally figured out I didn't feel *that* way. I didn't want to hurt you. I promise. Last year was really rough, and I was still working through a lot of shit."

Her voice is quiet. "You really hurt me."

"I know. I own that. And I'm sorry." My voice breaks.

"I need you to know that I'm fine with who you are. No, not fine, *beyond happy* for you. Proud of you that you can be honest about who you are. And I love you. So much. It was never, *ever* about your identity. It's just . . ." She pauses. "Why couldn't you tell me the truth? Why did the entire school have to find out *before* me?"

A breath I deliberately trapped in for far too long finally escapes my lips. "Fuck." I never looked at it like that. She deserves to know all that happened. Cris can't be the only one. Not anymore.

"Remember when I missed school for a couple of weeks last year?" My words, like my hands, are shaky. "I wanted to kill myself . . ." I don't think she exhales until I finish telling her everything.

"Carey . . ." Tears pool in the corners of her eyes. "Why didn't you tell me?" She pulls at her fingers frenetically.

"I didn't tell *anybody*. Except Mr. Kelly. Dr. Potter thought that I should have someone I could go to at school if I ever have those thoughts again.

"I got through the rest of the school year pretty much unscathed. Max left me alone. Until prom. He overheard something you said to Roe about us kissing, and he cornered me in the bathroom. He threatened to send the video and pictures he took of me to you, and then to the entire school. I didn't know what to do. Roe was waiting for me when I came out of the bathroom, and I told her what Max was doing. I had to come out to her. I didn't tell her about my ideations or anything, but she said we needed to stand up to him. I decided that if I came out, he wouldn't have all that power over me. So I got up onstage and grabbed the mic from the DJ and . . . I'm sorry I didn't tell you first. I was scared."

She grabs my hand. "Don't ever apologize for doing what you needed to. Or for who you are. Ever." She swallows hard and wipes tears out of her eyes. "It was amazing that everyone applauded in support of you." Her voice gets low. "*I'm* sorry you had to go through all that with Max and come out before you were ready."

"I *was* ready. Maybe not in that exact moment, but I needed to say it."

"Fucking Max. I hate him for taking so much from you," she says, and I nod in agreement. "And I hate that I made you feel more alone. I was so focused on how *I* felt."

"*I* didn't give *you* a chance, Jo."

"We both suck." She lays her head on my shoulder. "I would've beaten his ass." Then she picks her head up. "Wait, what happened to the pictures?"

"Monroe. After I came out, she cornered Max, shoved him up against the wall, and told him to delete the pictures or she'd report him for intent to distribute child pornography. I was sixteen, after all."

"She really should be a lawyer," Joey says. "Fuck, Carey. I didn't know *any* of this. Monroe never said a word."

"There's a lot we haven't said to each other," I say. "I didn't

146

want to lose you, but I never thought about it from your point of view."

She sighs. "I had my heart broken that night. I liked you in ways that you couldn't reciprocate. I know that now. But it was like the weight of the world was lifted off your shoulders. I'm glad you're being true to you. It's been hard to be around you because I can't be *with* you. I felt like I couldn't tell you, so I couldn't fix *us*." She holds tight to me and for the first time I think we're actually okay instead of playing at being okay. "I'm sorry I wasn't there for you, even before prom."

"I was in a dark place. But you *were* there for me. You and Roe were everything. We hung out every day and talked on the phone every night." It's hard to explain what suicidal ideations feel like to someone who doesn't know what they're like; it's heavier than depression, which I still experience often, so I try this: "A few years ago, I had surgery for a stomach hernia— remember that?—and the surgeons pumped my chest full of air during the procedure. My chest was in constant pain for days from both the air and the surgery. I remember crying out of desperation because it felt so tight. Then, over time, the pain became less and less until one day I woke up and it was gone. Now, I can't remember what it really felt like. Wanting to die is a memory I can describe, but not one I feel anymore, thanks to Dr. Potter and a lot of figuring out how to work through my feelings. I take it day by day. I may not see my future clearly, but I know one is there. Like a tree during the winter that *will* blossom in the spring. And that means I have the chance to fix what's broken." I knock my shoulder into hers.

She knocks back. "You're stuck with me, best friend." She stands up and extends her hand. "It's time for nachos. And Lizzo. And filling each other in on the last six months because we've been tiptoeing around the important stuff and that's not best-frienderly." When Joey gets excited, she goes full-on breathless Monroe.

I take her hand and she yanks my lanky ass off the bench. "Abso-fucking-lutely! But first, I have to know: How'd *you* know Cris wasn't to be trusted?"

"I know you don't read *Sunnyside Upended!*" she starts. "But there was an op-ed written by Max . . ."

"I saw that! Phoebe showed it to me—HOLY SHIT was that about *you*?"

Her lips purse. "Disgusting. Do you know what he did for his promposal? He broke into my locker and left a kid-sized basketball with '*Prom, Love Max*' written on it. And he waited in the hallway after practice for me to find it. When I opened my locker, he was behind me with flowers decorated to look like little basketballs." She lowers her head. "It was sweet, and I tried to turn him down nicely. I told him I was already going with you. I didn't know he was basically blackmailing you. I didn't know he'd do what he did to you."

"It's not your fault. Holy fuck, I can't believe I never knew this. Did you tell Roe?"

"No!" she says quickly. "It's embarrassing. Max is the last person I'd ever date. He's such a sexist ass. If I told Roe, she'd never let me—or him—live it down. And I didn't want to draw any attention to either of us."

"What does this have to do with Cris, though?" I ask.

"I knew Cris used to date his sister, Courtney." She locks arms with me as we walk toward Main Street. "Courtney was on the basketball team. We weren't friends, so it's not like we talked after she graduated. I figured they'd broken up when she left. But when Roe told me that you were dating Cris, and that Max got sent to McCauley's office for bullying you, I was worried what you might not know about Cris's dating history would hurt you. I didn't have a real reason not to trust him, just my gut." She stops walking and turns to look at me. "You deserve more."

The problem is that I thought I knew what *more* meant with Cris.

I don't say anything, and we keep walking.

"Roe is on the warpath. If she sees Cris, she'll rip out his throat."

"He was too good to be true," I say through gritted teeth.

"Maybe. You know what isn't too good to be true? Nachos."

I wish gooey cheese, crispy tortilla chips, and spicy jalapeños were enough to heal me. But Joey is, and that's all that matters right now. "Last one back to the car buys the first plate."

"You're on," she says, taking off toward the car like the Flash.

TRACK 17

HE/HIM/HIS

A new year = a new Carey.

Well, almost.

Joey has a basketball game on New Year's Eve day, which isn't technically a new year, but it is a great reprieve from thinking about Cris and the fact that not only am I pissed off and sad, I also have to share a number of scenes with him in musical rehearsals next week.

So, I guess I'm still on my Cris-obsessed bullshit. But I try not to let my thoughts dwell on him as I watch Joey glide across the court with ease and precision. We've been spending a lot of time together; the more we hang out, the more we fall back into our rhythm, the more we repair the damage we've done to each other. Cheering her on from the stands, being there to support her, makes me feel a little less incomplete.

After the game, Joey and I meet up with Monroe and Phoebe at Exile Café. Phoebe has been helping me work on my video project for Mr. Kelly's class, and she had the idea for me to sing the song I've been writing during the open mic tonight. Phoebe's friend, Isaiah Walker, is playing too, and he agreed to play guitar behind me while she records me singing in the *Wicked* heels to use as my video's "thesis statement."

"You nervous?" Joey asks as we make our way to a small round table at the back of the café.

"Not at all." I puff out my chest like Superman, a gesture I hope will eradicate any residual fear. But the image of Cris doing the same before auditions a few weeks ago makes the pose feel heavy.

"Why should you be?" Phoebe asks, nursing a cappuccino topped with chocolate dust.

Monroe already ordered me a hot tea with lemon and honey, which she passes to me, and a vanilla cream latte for Joey.

"It's only one song," I add, playing with my blue bracelet.

"What're you singing?" Joey takes a gulp of her latte, which gives her a thick frothy mustache.

"Something I've been working on for a long time," I say.

"A Carey Parker original?" Monroe squeals. "This is a first." She turns to Phoebe. "You know, Carey is our unofficial third twin and we have yet to read any writing or hear any of his songs, though he's been writing them since we were kids."

"Third twin?" Phoebe repeats.

"Just go with it," I whisper. "I haven't written in a long time. But I've picked it up again recently. I've been inspired." I look at Joey but think about Cris.

Monroe leans in and whispers, "I'm on the lookout for Cris. I swear if that boy shows up, I will bodycheck a bitch." She clenches her fist.

"Have you seen him?" Phoebe asks me.

"Nope." Cris has kept his physical distance, but he texts and calls nonstop. Part of me wants to hear his voice, see what he has to say.

Monroe clears her throat. "You're conveniently leaving out the part where you made Joey and I drive by Cris's house the other night."

Phoebe's eyes widen. "Where was I, and why wasn't I invited?"

"Don't worry," Joey says. "You didn't miss anything. We literally sat in the car and watched Cris through the window." She shudders. "It was creepy, but also sad."

"This is character assasintion," I say.

"So no epic showdown? Or grand love declarations?" Phoebe asks. "Lame sauce."

"Don't encourage that," Monroe says. "He deserves better."

I'm imagining Cris walking in right now: He would stand at the counter, order a coffee, and then turn to see me sitting with my friends. Over the speakers, Mariah's "Heartbreaker" would start playing, and the chatter in the busy café would cease. Everyone would get up and start dancing in an epic choreographed flash mob. Monroe, Phoebe, and Joey would crowd around me and say, in cheesy music video dialogue, that I'm "so much better than him" before I, a sad, jilted Mariah, would sing about how badly Cris broke my heart but how I can't stop thinking about him.

Phoebe snaps her fingers in my face before I get to the part in my daydream when I fight a doppelgänger of myself in the bathroom. "So, Isaiah, my friend from church who's playing tonight, is very cute. My mom has been trying to set me up with him for, like, ever, but he's very, very gay. I'm just saying, no time like the present to move on."

I shake my head. "I'm not ready for that."

"Rebound!" Phoebe urges.

"He's doing me a favor by letting me sing with him," I say.

"I am so ready to hear you sing," Monroe interjects, probably sensing my discomfort with this conversation. She positions her chair at the perfect angle to view the performance area. "Your mom would love this. We should call her."

"She'd be so embarrassing," I say.

Joey flails her arms, "Oh, Carey, my baby!"

Monroe joins her, clapping, and dabbing at her eyes with a napkin.

"Y'all are vicious," Phoebe says.

"They're not wrong." I take a swig of my tea. "I love her, but she's *that* mom."

Thom, Monroe's flannel-clad manager-slash-crushboy comes over to us holding a box wrapped in silver paper with a big purple bow. The way he looks at Monroe, with sad puppy dog eyes, makes it clear he has it bad for her. He's kind of adorable.

Thom stands over us awkwardly, and Monroe rolls her eyes. "I told you I'm not working tonight. I need a night off, with my friends, like a normal human."

He blushes beneath his lumberjack beard. "Actually, I was told to give this to Carey." He hands me the box and shifts his weight from foot to foot for a moment until slowly backing away. When Monroe waves at him, he almost trips over a nearby chair.

"Wow," Joey starts, "Thom is crushing extra hard today."

"He finally asked me out last night." Monroe moves in closer and her voice gets all high as she starts to giggle. I've rarely heard her giggle. Is she malfunctioning?

"He *what?*" Phoebe, Joey, and I say, almost in unison.

"After we sorta, maybe, made out in the storeroom."

Joey punches her sister in the upper arm. "Why didn't you tell me?"

Monroe lifts her coffee to her lips as if she's trying to hide behind it. Her words bubble up behind the liquid as she mumbles something that sounds like, "*I dunno I kinda like him leave me alone.*" Her eyes dart among all three of us.

"Isn't he a little old . . . ?" Phoebe begins.

"He's only two years older than us. He's in college," Monroe insists, then expertly redirects everyone's attention. "Who's that from, Carey?"

"Cris has been sending me a gift every day since Christmas Eve," I say. "To apologize."

"That boy doesn't know when to quit." Phoebe takes the box and inspects it by shaking it. "Feels light. You get anything good at least?"

"They're all little things, nothing major." What I don't tell them is that all his gifts made me swoon. A soft, cuddly teddy bear? How adorable is that? I used to dream that a boy would give me stupid little gifts like that. I tear open the paper, saving the bow because, *hello*, it's gorgeous.

Inside the box are two envelopes, one small and skinny, another greeting card–size, which I open first. It's handmade, with two genderless people outlined in black, holding hands. One is colored in with purple, white, and green—the colors of the genderqueer flag. The other is colored in with purple, blue, and pink—the colors of the bisexual flag. Inside is a note from Cris.

Carey,
You have every right never to talk to me again. I wouldn't blame you. I should have been completely honest with you about everything. I was wrong. What's worse is that I hurt you, and I'll probably never have the chance to make things right. I'll have to live with that.

I know we'll see each other at rehearsals soon, so if we can't be together, hopefully we can still be together onstage. I'll settle for just being around you. I want you to know how much you inspire me. I've never met anybody like you, and I know we only had a little time together, but you shifted something in me.

I hope you like my last gift. Take whomever you want, but I hope you choose me. I'll wait outside the venue for you.
Love,
Cris

I'm so fixated on the word "love" that I almost forget about the skinny envelope. Inside are two tickets to the Mariah Carey tour at Radio City Music Hall at the end of January.

It takes every muscle in my body not to jump onto the table and scream so loud you would think Mariah herself was in Exile Café. I told Cris I could never afford a Mariah show, not with Mom stretched so thin with Grams, so I've had to settle for watching grainy, shaky secondhand recordings of her shows on YouTube.

I can't believe he did this.

Joey and Phoebe grab the card and read it together, following it with a collective, long and drawn out, "Awwwww!"

Monroe takes it from them, reads it, and snarls. She makes as if she's going to rip it, but Joey grabs it first.

"He has a girlfriend. *Had*." As I correct myself, I realize I don't know the whole story. "He didn't tell me anything about her, like that she was related to Max. Even after I told him that Max was my nemesis."

"People make mistakes." Joey's eyes say, *You make mistakes too. You're not perfect.* "Is there a chance he didn't know about you and Max?"

"Oh, shut up, Jo," Monroe pipes in. "I never trusted him." She sucks at her teeth.

"Maybe," I respond to Joey. "I haven't talked to him since the Hoop-Off, so I don't know." I sigh and gently place my forehead on the tabletop. I miss him. "He *was* a *really* great kisser."

"Who was a really great kisser?" The chair next to me screeches as it slides against the floor.

"Izi!" Phoebe squeals, jumping into the very sturdy arms of the stranger who's joined our table. I recognize him from the posters in the front windows; his muscles bulge out of his tight black tee. He's taller and thicker than his picture on the poster, but it's like he's airbrushed in real life—no man looks like Isaiah Walker in real life except, apparently, Isaiah Walker. I immediately feel inferior sitting next to him. "Friends, this is Isaiah Walker. Izi, these are my Sunnyside people." He shakes everyone's hands. "And this is Carey!"

Isaiah zeros in on me, and I notice him staring at my

bracelet. He smiles and something catches in the back of my throat. "Nice to finally meet you. Phoebe never stops talking about you. I love what you're wearing!" He points to the lush, drapey, bloodred cape Monroe made me for Christmas.

"Wait until you see the heels," I add.

He bites his lip and tilts his head. "About this song. I have my stuff in the back room if you wanna jam before we go on. This way I can get a feel for it."

Joey is hanging on his every word, nearly drooling. Monroe elbows her and says, "He's gay. Close your mouth."

Phoebe nods for me to go, like, *Get the fuck to the back room and play with the hot boy who wants to put music to your words.*

I follow Isaiah through Exile Records to the back room. It's super small, only enough room for the two of us. It's dark, dingy, and stinks of must. It must double as the break room, because there's a small, rusted table littered with music and guitar magazines, an ashtray piled Rocky Mountain high with ashes like dirty snow. Next to the table is a mini fridge with a slight stench of rotting meat. There are autographed posters of local bands like Filthy & Gorgeous, The Original Dolls, and The Menstrual Cycles haphazardly hung on the walls, and in between are stickers of prominent nineties bands like No Doubt and Sublime amid more obscure names like the Exploding Hearts and the Soda Pop Kids. I'd need some rubber gloves, a bottle of Clorox, and at least one reference to Mariah Carey or any other diva, living or dead, in order to feel a bit more at ease.

"It's kinda gross in here, I know," he remarks. "The walls are painted with STDs."

Holy crap his eyes are mesmerizing. *Must look away.* But can't.

"Phoebe says you have an incredible voice. I'm glad she's made some friends at your school," he says. "I've known her for a long time and she's always been a loner."

"Really? She's so . . ."

"Loud? Friendly? Larger-than-life?" he finishes.

"Exactly."

"People think that the Phoebes of the world aren't alone because they're so out there. Shows you how little people know."

"I was one of those people," I admit.

"Most are." He puts his phone on the table and sets his guitar on his lap. "Tell me a bit about your song. Because I can riff off any melody." He offers me a stool.

I pull a piece of paper from my pocket with the lyrics I wrote to "I'm Ready" and hand them to him. I start humming the melody and Isaiah mirrors it on his guitar. We run through it a few times.

"I think I got the basic melody," he says. "Let's run through, full throttle."

I prop up my phone to video record the session so I can hear what it sounds like after. After a few bars, I sing:

Spotlight on, am I ready?
The world a stage, waiting for me
But the darkness creeps in, slowly
Devouring the light until I

Stay inside the lines
And play the role assigned

I've been too
Scared to live
Scared to die
To forgive myself
I have to try
One day I'll be stronger
Maybe I already am

I wonder if I'll ever fly
The open air calls out to me
But I get tangled in branches
Too afraid to spread my wings and
Take that first leap
What if I fall?

No longer
Scared to live
I want to try to
Be true to me
It's time to fly
One day I'll soar higher
Maybe it's time

You want me to believe
I'm not good enough

But you won't
Ever get the best of me
Because my voice is
the one thing
You can never take from me

One day I'll be louder
Maybe I'm ready

I'm ready

I'll scream out loud
I'm done apologizing
For wanting to shine
For wanting to fly
For being myself
No day like today
I'm ready

"That was . . . incredible," Isaiah says. "You got some song-writing chops. And that voice!" Isaiah sits back and rests his arms behind his head. "That was better than sex."

My entire body tenses, and heat flushes my face.

Isaiah checks his buzzing phone. "There's a guy here I used to jam with. You'll like him. He's cool. You have to play that song for him. I hope you don't mind, I asked him to back me up on keyboards." Once he's done texting his friend, his attention returns to me. "Where did that come from? Those lyrics, I mean. There's a story there," he says, leaning in closer.

"There's a lot of story there," I say, not wanting to get too specific.

"Well, it got to me. It was beautiful." His brown eyes are beacons drawing me in. "Phoebe tells me you're single."

Damn, he doesn't waste time. Neither do the goose bumps rising to the surface of my skin.

"Recently." I linger on the word longer than I should, but I want to make sure that Isaiah knows I'm not looking for anything. Especially when I can't stop thinking about Cris despite how hard I've been trying. Something tells me Isaiah has had more experience with this stuff than I have. "How do you know if someone is being honest? I really liked this guy, but he withheld pretty important stuff from me. I don't know if I can trust him."

He laughs awkwardly, an I-know-because-I've-been-there sort of laugh. "That's the thing. You don't. Trust is built little by little, over time. For it to work, he has to deserve a chance, and you have to be open to giving him one."

"How do you know so much?"

"Got my heart ripped out of my chest too many times. Pro-tip? You have to kiss the wrong boys before you find the right ones."

"Maybe I *just* need to kiss some wrong boys," I mutter, and he smirks.

Maybe it's the dim lighting or that we're all alone and it feels easy, but I'm moving toward him and he moves toward me, and it's like I have zero control of my body as my arms reach around the back of Isaiah's head and he wraps his arms around my back and pulls me toward him—and holy shit, this is actually happening. It's tender but with just enough force to catch me off guard. When he pulls back, I work to catch my breath.

"Why'd you stop?" I ask.

He blinks a few times and looks as surprised as me. "Wanted to check this was okay."

I slide my buzzing phone out of my pocket and see a missed call from Mom. She can wait. Isaiah's full lips make me forget about all the other shit. My fingers pull at the back of his head. "Don't worry," I say. "I don't know what *you're* doing, but *I'm* kissing the wrong boy."

He barely gets out a "nice" before his lips are on mine again. I've never experienced something that felt so right, yet so incredibly wrong at the same time. I've never kissed somebody I don't have feelings for. His lips become more aggressive, his tongue delicately dancing with mine, and I get so completely lost in his touch that I don't register the knocks on the storeroom door or see it opening.

Isaiah chuckles as he backs away. I lick my lips. He tastes like mint ChapStick.

Then I hear a voice that shatters my bliss. "Isaiah? *Carey?*"

Cris. He doesn't give me a chance to register what's happening before he bows out of the storeroom.

I close my eyes and lightly bang the back of my head against the wall.

"*That's* the right boy?" Isaiah asks. "Of course, he is." Isaiah grabs hold of me. "What're you doing? Cris is good people. They don't make 'em like Cris. I've known him a long time. Whatever he did, I guarantee he didn't mean to hurt you. Go after him!"

That's all I need to hear. I lurch toward the door, when my

phone vibrates again. I fumble with it, and it falls to the ground, but I don't stop. I'll get it later. Cris is running for the exit and I have to catch him.

Isaiah shouts something after me, but I ignore him.

"Cris, wait!" I'm yelling like a crazy person. Seeing Cris speed walk past strangers in winter coats browsing the record selection is like living a rom-com movie scene where the idiot main character, a lovesick fool with blinders and a penchant for ruining absolutely everything, lets the love of their life walk away, and the audience is all, "Go after him!" But those movies are so predictable, and it'll take another hour of sappy montages before the main character gets their shit together.

But not me. Not tonight. I can't let Cris go. Not without explaining myself to him.

I push past bodies blocking my path and chase after him.

He doesn't turn around. "Leave me alone, Carey." He races out of Exile and down the street, nearly tripping over his feet on the curb.

"No." I grab the sleeve of his wool jacket. His head turns toward me, and it's like he looks right through me.

"What do you want from me?" he yells. Passersby stop on the sidewalk and stare at us. He's breathing so hard that hot air streams from his nostrils. "You ignored me for the last two weeks. You wouldn't hear me out long enough to tell you *my* story. You assumed the worst."

"You could've texted it," I say, trying to deescalate.

That fails spectacularly. Cris goes berserk. "YOU MEAN WHEN I TEXTED YOU EVERY DAY, ALL DAY, AND YOU IGNORED ME? You wouldn't hear me out. While I've been trying to win you back, you're making out with Isaiah Walker in a storage closet. I'm a fucking idiot."

"It's not like that, I—"

"You what?" he cuts me off. "You don't get to keep me here. You don't get to keep me period. Not now. Maybe . . ." He hesitates. "Maybe not ever."

There are so many things between us that've gone unsaid. He didn't tell me the full truth about Courtney. I don't tell him that I don't care that he has an ex-girlfriend, that the betrayal was who that ex is related to *and* that he didn't tell me. He doesn't apologize for chasing after her at the Hoop-Off game instead of staying with me. I don't tell him that Isaiah meant nothing, that he—Cris—makes me feel alive and special and that I should've heard him out. I don't tell him that I may have overreacted.

We *are* the rom-com clichés I hate.

Isaiah has followed us from Exile, and in between our shared, deliberate silence, he hands me my phone. He quietly apologizes to Cris and walks back inside the record store, throwing his hands in the air like he is tired of *our* drama. Asshole.

Cris grunts. "I'm done."

"Wait." I stare at my phone. There are ten missed calls, and a text, all from Mom.

MOM: 911. CALL ME. GRAMS IN THE HOSPITAL.

TRACK 18

HE/HIM/HIS

Cris doesn't say anything as he drives me to the hospital. I call Mom, but I'm not processing anything she's saying. Cris grabs hold of my hand as she talks. My fingers wiggle free of his grip. All I care about is seeing Grams. I can't breathe until I know she's alive.

At the hospital, he walks me inside to the elevators, and we ride to the fourth floor. "Do you need me to stay?" he asks, eyes puffy.

The elevator doors open and we walk out.

I shrug, and he pulls me into a hug. But he's the one who is shaking.

"You can go."

"I can stay," he offers again, his voice cracking.

"You don't have to." It looks like he's going to respond, but I cut him off. "Thanks for driving me. I'm sorry for everything."

He doesn't say another word. He turns toward the elevator but pauses like he's going to look back, and I want him to so badly, because then maybe it means we could be okay, that he knows I was stupid for freaking out without hearing his story and that I never should have made out with Isaiah. But he doesn't. The automatic doors open; he steps inside and disappears behind them.

I drag my feet to Grams's room. Two nurses wheel in cots for Mom and me to spend the night. I thank them, never taking my eyes off Grams.

The Alzheimer's corridor of the hospital is a portrait of neglected souls filled with elderly patients. Some of them pace back and forth, muttering small nothings to nobody. Some are mentally paralyzed, frozen in chairs inside their rooms, unable to say anything at all. I imagine their doors are open with the hopes that someone will come in and claim them or just sit with them. The hospital air makes me lightheaded, almost nauseous, and the steady *beep-beep-beep* of the machines that track Grams's heartbeat makes me uneasy, like any second those beeps could stop.

I sit in the chair next to her bed opposite Mom and lay my head on Grams's lap. Grams gently runs her fingers through my hair as she wheezes. It grows louder by the second until it's all I hear, the sound of the beeping machines replaced with the sounds of her struggling to breathe.

The doctor says that Grams has forgotten how to properly swallow food, and that bits of food have been collecting in her lungs for who knows how long. We hadn't noticed it because it happened over time as she ate. Eventually it developed into a small cough, then a larger cough, and since she can't vocalize her pain, she wasn't able to tell us that something was wrong. So we couldn't have known before tonight, when Mom said Grams stopped breathing and turned blue.

Grams can't say anything, but her eyes dart around the room, in a panicked, *Don't leave me here.*

The only way I know how to calm her is by singing, so that's what I do.

I sing through my tears.

I sing as the nurses pop their heads in to listen.

I sing when the nurses quietly say, "Happy New Year!"

I sing until we both fall asleep, hoping that when I wake up, she does too.

TRACK 19

THEY/THEM/THEIR

A sliver of sunlight creeps through the blinds. My eyes flutter open, and for a split second, I forget where I am. The *beep-beep-beep*s are an instant reminder. I straighten up. A pain shoots up my back from being slumped in the chair next to Grams's hospital bed. Mom is fast asleep on one of the cots. A nurse with blond hair pulled back in a tight ponytail checks Grams's vitals, and Grams's eyes are still wide open in silent panic.

I grab her hand. "Shhh, Grams. It's okay. We're here."

"She had a restless night, huh?" the nurse asks.

My temples throb. "I slept for an hour total."

"You giving them trouble, Rosemary?" The nurse's voice is kind, playful, and it makes me hate her for talking to Grams like she knows her. "Your friend didn't get any sleep either," she says to me.

"Friend?"

"Yeah, the cute one with the messy hair and glasses. Cris, I think. He's been in the unit's waiting room all night. Just left. He wanted to make sure you were okay but didn't want to come in. Said you two were in some sort of fight. He cares about you, that one."

"He said all that?" I thought Cris left. He *stayed*. My breath catches in my throat.

"I have a way of making people talk," she says. "It's my nurse superpower. If you ask me, I don't know what happened with you two kids, but someone who sleeps in a hospital waiting room all night because they're worried about you, is not someone you let get away."

Grams squeezes my hand in agreement.

As the nurse moves around the bed, I let go of Grams's hand so that she can continue her morning vitals.

I search the chair for my phone and find it wedged underneath the cushion. I thumb through the pictures I've taken with Cris: after *Wicked* auditions, when he smashed his cheek to mine and stuck out his tongue, pride in his face after watching me sing; during our Arcadia date after he kicked my ass in Skee-Ball; our last selfie at the Hoop-Off game, where we cheesed for the camera against a backdrop of hundreds of Sunnysiders. I study the candids I took of him onstage at his audition, shooting a ball up the Skee-Ball ramp, sipping coffee while deep in thought at the park overlooking the Hudson River. The Cris in these pictures would never hurt me. Is it possible that this Cris and the Cris who kept vital information from me are the same Cris? Is the Cris I constructed only a fairy tale, and the reality is more complicated than I expected? Can the two versions coexist?

For the first time, I decide to open all my unread texts from Cris. There are dozens of "I'm sorry" messages and teary-eyed emojis and pleas for me to listen to him. Nothing that explains the

Courtney–Max situation, but I'm starting to think that maybe I should've let him explain it to me instead of icing him out.

As I scroll through his texts, I find a video he sent me on Christmas morning. I wait until the nurse is out of the room to press play.

Cris, in a black tank top that accentuates his muscular upper arms, sits on the floor of what must be his bedroom. I haven't been inside his house, but there's a mattress with a blue down comforter in the background, and I make out a framed picture of him and his mom on the nightstand beside it. He's holding his guitar with one hand and fiddling with the positioning of his phone with the other.

"Testing, testing." He flashes his goofy smile. "Hi, Carey. I know there's a chance you won't see or play this, but I thought, why not give this a shot." He plucks the strings on his guitar and I immediately recognize the melody. "This song is for you. It's my favorite Mariah song, and the lyrics convey a lot of what I'm feeling right now. Merry Christmas." He sings a moody, stripped-down version of Mariah's "8th Grade," a song from her fifteenth studio album, *Caution*, my second favorite next to 1997's *Butterfly*. The lyrics detail a story of first love, how she wants to be her crush's entire world, but she knows she's not. She asks the object of her affection to put himself into her shoes and to look at their relationship from her point of view: What if he had her, and then suddenly she was gone from his life? What does it feel like when your entire world just . . . ends?

As I listen to Cris sing against the backdrop of beeping hospital machines, I can't help but think, "A little bit like this."

TRACK 20
THEY/THEM/THEIR

I try to stop myself from yawning. That's a total fail. My body is too tired from spending the last few days and nights of winter break at the hospital, so I let it happen, right in the middle of rehearsal, and it's way louder than I anticipated. Everyone stops and stares. Phoebe nudges me in the ribs.

"What? It's not like I'm onstage," I whisper as another, smaller yawn escapes my lips. "*My bad.*"

Cris leans forward and glares at me, *through* me. We're currently at a stalemate; neither of us has approached the other. I've wanted to, but I'm emotionally and physically exhausted. Mom caught me rewatching the video he made for me and asked me why I wasn't calling him. Dr. Potter thinks I'm being stubborn. She thinks I need to talk to him so we can each explain how we feel. That sounds so fucking rational, right? But Grams needs all my energy. I don't have the space to process my very complicated feelings for Cris. Not now. That makes my heart hurt more because I think, through all this, I love him.

I love him. It's an admission that sucks the air from my lungs.

I gasp, making everyone look at me again. Phoebe nudges me harder. I might as well crawl under the damn seats and disappear.

Mr. Kelly and Rachel stand on the stage, addressing the entire cast. Rachel glares at me and puffs her cheeks like a blowfish. I slink down in my seat. We've been rehearsing the opening number, "No One Mourns the Wicked," which I'm not in, and let's just say it hasn't been cute. More like a massacre of the music. The tech crew, which has been working since before break on building the set in the art rooms, peers out from behind the curtains as Rachel yammers on about hitting marks and remembering cues and the importance of rehearsing the songs when we're home so when we come in, we know the lyrics. I focus on the stage crew's T-shirts and paint- and varnish-splattered jeans as they traipse around the stage, pretending to measure random things and look up at light fixtures so that they're not obviously gawking.

Rachel holds her clipboard and pen, looking like she's trying to choose her words carefully. "Okay, Phoebe, you're hitting all the right notes, but I need every other person on that stage matching Glinda's energy." She looks to Mr. Kelly for backup, and he nods.

She goes on. "Citizens of Oz, the Wicked Witch is—presumably—dead. Not *you*. You all are very much alive. And you're supposed to be happy about that. Right now, you're acting like a bunch of sad, tired zombies. We've run through this number every day for a week, and it's actually gotten worse."

The cast stares with blank eyes.

"Are you hearing anything I'm saying?"

A few heads give ambling nods, but she might as well be talking to a group of sedated puppies because none of them seem to get it. She puts her clipboard down and makes her way to the center of the stage. "Here's what I want to see from you. Follow my lead. Don't do, just watch." Rachel runs through the number with Phoebe, flawlessly playing everyone who isn't Glinda.

I can't keep my eyes off Cris. Halfway through, he stands up from the audience and walks toward the exit. I quietly tiptoe after him. He sits on a large boulder outside the main entrance of the school. I don't say anything, but I know he sees me.

"It's finally getting cold," he says. "Happy January."

I shove my hands in my pockets, searching for warmth. "Weather small talk . . . nice."

He propels himself off the rock and pushes past me back inside.

"Cris, wait . . ."

He stops walking and turns. "For what, Carey? It's clear we're not gonna work. I've apologized a million times. You've never responded. I took you to the hospital. I've been waiting for you to—" I want to move toward him, but I'm afraid that if I do, he'll run again. "I wanna get this off my chest. I felt something with you that I've never felt before with anyone. *Anyone.* I made a mistake. It was fucked up. But I'm not gonna apologize again if you won't talk to me."

All I keep thinking is, *We can fix this. I need you.* But I can't get the words out.

"It's *you* who wasn't ready. I don't care that you kissed Isaiah. Isaiah kisses everyone. *I've* kissed Isaiah. I feel like the worst person in the world for hurting you, but I'm hurting too. I didn't know how you'd react if I told you I dated Max's sister. I didn't want to cause you more pain, or make you doubt me. But you didn't even try to hear me out. And that night at the hospital . . . I hadn't been there since my mom. I'm still feeling pretty fucked up about that, and I just wanna get through this musical." He takes a few steps toward the door but stops when his hand touches the silver handles. His shoulders rise like he's taking a deep breath, then he disappears inside.

Minutes pass before I follow him in.

"Excuse me, Mr. Parker," Mr. Jackson says, walking down the hall like he's on a mission to destroy me. "It's past school hours. What're you doing here?"

"I'm at rehearsals. For the musical."

Mr. Jackson looks me up and down. "Let's go, Parker."

"What? Where?" What's he going to do? Make me sit in his office and write, "I will not fight with my pseudo ex-non-boyfriend outside school" five hundred times until my fingers blister?

"Principal McCauley's office." He walks toward me, but I duck him.

"For what? I did nothing wrong. I have to get back to the auditorium for rehearsal." It takes all of me not to tell him to go fuck himself.

"You shouldn't be here unattended. Who knows what trouble you're getting into." He looks toward the door of the auditorium like Cris's afterimage is still there. He stands over me. He smells like mold and cigars.

"I'm. In. The. Show!" I wriggle out from his grasp.

"I heard rumors. How about we go in together, and I can see for myself."

"Fine." What more am I supposed to say?

Rachel immediately spots me. "Carey, our star! We've been looking for you." She waves her arms, beckoning me to the stage. "I want to take a look at act 2, scene 7. Give our Glinda a break for a bit."

Mr. Kelly gets out of his seat when he spots Mr. Jackson walking behind me like I'm his prisoner. "Everything okay?" His gaze bounces back and forth between Mr. Jackson and me.

"Kelly? I didn't know you were in charge of the play."

"*Musical*, not play, and I've mentioned it at every single departmental meeting this year," Mr. Kelly says matter-of-factly.

"*He* is in the play?" Mr. Jackson points to me, and his pronoun use makes me wince.

"Yes." Mr. Kelly looks to my wrist. "*They* are in the *musical. They* are our star."

Mr. Jackson mumbles something unintelligible and looks around. Everyone is watching us. "Mind if I watch?"

Mr. Kelly looks to me for approval. I roll my eyes and shrug. What am I supposed to say, no?

"Elphaba, Fiyero, take your places," Rachel commands. "Have you both gone over this scene yet? I want to run through the song a few times, and then we'll worry about stage directions and all that."

I'm so unnerved by Mr. Jackson that I have no idea what scene Rachel is talking about. Phoebe hands me my copy of the script, and, *of course*, it's "As Long As You're Mine," which is essentially a soft-core sex scene sans sex, sub magic. This is what I've been dreading since the demise of my whatevership with Cris, and now Mr. Fucking Jackson is watching our first run-through.

The piano starts and Cris's body is turned from mine. The heat rises in my chest. I love him and hate him at the same time. I miss my cue and try to catch up, but my voice is squeaking out the words I know by heart but now feel like distant memories buried beneath the weight of Cris's disdain.

Mr. Jackson chuckles as he leans back in his seat. He props his feet up on the arm rest of the seat in front of him.

Rachel cuts the music. "What's wrong, Carey?"

Cris is looking at me now. He mouths, *Let's just do this.*

"I'm not feeling very passionate right now," I say.

Rachel gets up. "I actually think the key to this scene isn't passion. It's that Elphaba has finally found someone who truly sees her for the first time. Is that something you can relate to, Carey?"

The memory of the night Cris and I spent in my bedroom floods me. The feeling of being wrapped up in him, his arms holding on to me like he was afraid to let me go. As long as he belonged to me, and me to him, we would be okay. I didn't think to prepare for the moment he would let go.

"Actually, yes." I pull Cris aside. He gnaws on his lip as his gaze avoids mine. "I know you don't want to talk to me, but I have to get this out. Listen to the words of the song instead of just singing them with me. You wanna know how I feel? This is it."

I walk back to center stage. The pianist bangs on the keys.

This time, I won't avoid Cris.

I'll sing *to* him, hoping he'll see me the way he saw me before. I need him to.

An urgent sadness pours out of my mouth and drowns the stage as I tell him that as long as he's mine, nothing else matters.

There's a gritty anger in his voice, and he holds back at first.

We circle each other on the stage like hungry lions. My voice swirls with his in harmony. He can't look away from me. The crescendo lassos us together as he grabs me and pulls me toward him so hard that I nearly fall, but he catches me. Our voices rise at the climax, and by the end, I'm breathless, not because it's a hard song, but because of the way Cris is holding on to me, like he's afraid to let me go. When we finish, he kisses me. There's rage behind it but also desire. I match it, and our bodies are closer than they've ever been—until I realize that we're in front of an auditorium of people.

I pull back. Cris bites his lip.

Phoebe whoops and hollers. But she's the only one.

A few people are videoing us.

Rachel clears her throat, and it's like a car engine backfiring. "That was, um, a choice! Maybe for the show a little less tongue, or no tongue at all. But the song? Perfection."

"Is this a joke?" Mr. Jackson is on his feet. "Seems like you're trying to push some sort of agenda here, Kelly."

"Excuse me?" Mr. Kelly rises to meet him.

"You think *this* is appropriate?" He gestures toward Cris and I. "Two *boys* kissing onstage like that? Singing about holding each other in that way? This is wildly unsuitable for our students."

Cris moves in front of me, like he's trying to shield me from Jackson's words. I grab on to his arm for support, and somehow our hands find each other.

"First of all, that's offensive," Mr. Kelly says. "The identities of my cast have no bearing on their talents or the show we're putting on."

Mr. Jackson crosses his arms and puffs out his chest again. This must be some sort of alpha thing, like two animals challenging each other. "Your judgment is clouded, Kelly, because you're a . . ."

"I'm a *what*? Gay? Yes, and that has no bearing on my work as a teacher or director."

How dare Mr. Jackson! His implications are repulsive. Mr. Kelly is the most respected teacher in the entire school. And I'm not being biased. He's won teaching awards two years in a row, and he's been here only four years. He was hired when I was a freshman, and I remember hearing about the awesome gay eleventh- and twelfth-grade English teacher. I made it my mission to be in his classes. Mr. Jackson, on the other hand, has the worst reputation in the entire school among students. All he does is patrol the hallways, sneering at us, doling out detentions, and basically being a Dementor.

"With all due respect, Mr. Jackson," Mr. Kelly says through gritted teeth. His fingers fiddle with the pleat of his sport jacket. "This isn't an English department activity, so I appreciate the feedback, but this conversation is inappropriate and offensive."

The entire cast watches the showdown intently.

He blinks at Mr. Kelly in disbelief. "You really believe this filth is appropriate subject matter? Don't forget you're up for tenure this year," Jackson threatens. "Exposing our students to this sort of degradation is—"

"Please, stop." Mr. Kelly's volume is dialed up to the max. "It's a musical about friendship and standing up for what you believe in."

Rachel hops off the stage and moves toward her friend. Without saying a word, she places her hand on his back, and Mr. Kelly slowly regains his composure. "It's best you leave. We have a lot of ground to cover in today's rehearsal. I have a duty to these kids."

"Yes, a duty you're not fulfilling." Mr. Jackson stuffs his hands into his pockets and heads up the aisle and out the door, letting it slam behind him.

"I'm sorry you all had to witness that," Mr. Kelly begins. "I know word travels fast around Sunnyside, but let's call this auditorium Vegas. What happens here, stays here." His hands are now visibly trembling.

"Mr. Kelly, that's insane," Phoebe says. "That was the most blatantly homophobic thing I've ever seen."

Chatter explodes across the auditorium.

I'm frozen in place. I haven't moved from Cris's side.

Cris squeezes my hand so tight it feels like my fingers have fused together. I face him, and he looks like he's about to be sick.

Mr. Kelly is still talking, but we're not listening. I try to get Cris's attention, snapping my fingers and lightly tapping his color-drained cheeks until his eyes drift slowly toward me. All he does is shake his head before letting go of my hand and walking slowly offstage.

"Cris!" I follow him backstage. In a quiet corner, he slides to the floor and starts hyperventilating into one of the velvet purple curtains hanging from the rafters. All I can do is rub his back and say, "I know" over and over again, hoping that maybe it'll make us both feel better, though I know it won't.

When his breathing slows and the color returns to his cheeks, he says, "Did that really happen? It's like Jackson doesn't think we're human." There's not much I can say to comfort him, because, quite frankly, there's nothing anybody could say to comfort me right now. Being close to Cris helps though. "He can't get away with that."

"What can we do?" I stop rubbing his back and sit down cross-legged on the floor in front of him.

"Complain? There's gotta be someone who'll listen! Principal McCauley, maybe."

"Is it worth it? Will anything change?"

"Really, Carey?" He sits up a little straighter and glares at me. "Nothing ever happens if nobody takes action. I—" He stops midthought. "Never mind."

"No, say what's on your mind."

He takes a second to compose himself before carefully choosing his words. "A teacher like him shouldn't have a job. We're out. What about the others in the room who aren't?"

"Are there people in the musical who aren't out?" My mind races, thinking of who it could be.

"I don't know. But that's exactly the point. Nobody knew I was bisexual until I let people know. I read somewhere that one out of ten people are questioning either their sexual identities or gender identities." He reaches a hand toward the stage. "How many people are in this room right now? More than twenty.

That means—statistically speaking—maybe two other people could be trying to figure out who they are. And that's, like, a super conservative guess." His face carries so much pain. I remember the day at Arcadia when he told me about his own coming out. "Even if there's nobody in *this* room questioning or in the closet or whatever, that's *one* room. What about all the classrooms that homophobe walks into? What about you?"

"Me?" My temples throb. I hate that this happened. I hate that Cris is upset. I hate that I'm using every muscle in my body to keep myself upright, to stop myself from shaking so that I can be strong for Cris, who looks like he's about to shatter.

"I can't stop thinking about how you almost, you know. You're stronger now, you're so strong." He grabs my hand and kisses the squishy space between my thumb and pointer finger. "But you weren't always, and what about the next kid suffering in silence?"

"You're right. We'll go tomorrow. Principal McCauley has to help," I say, mostly to convince myself that something positive can come out of this afternoon's experience. I have to believe in the system.

"Promise?" he asks.

"Promise."

TRACK 21

THEY/THEM/THEIR

Mr. Jackson said gay people shouldn't be allowed in schools!

Mr. Kelly attacked Mr. Jackson at musical rehearsal!

Mr. Kelly is getting fired for pushing a gay agenda!

Carey and Cris Kostas had sex onstage in front of the whole school!

Word now travels at warp speed thanks to *Sunnyside Upended!* rumors. Mr. Kelly's plea at rehearsal yesterday did absolutely nothing to stop the entire school from talking about what happened, though the finer details—and truth—have become distorted.

"What the hell?" Cris snatches an empty lunch tray with such anger that the entire stack almost topples. "I knew everyone gossiped, but this is ridiculous. I just read on that alt-garbage

Upended! that you ripped my shirt off during rehearsal and Mr. Kelly recorded it on his phone."

I can't help but laugh. "What kind of gay porn telephone is happening here?" I grab a carton of French fries and block Cris from grabbing his own. "We'll share."

"Watch yourself," he warns. "Just because we're sharing fries doesn't mean I'm gonna let you rip this shirt." He pinches the fabric of his vintage David Bowie concert tee from Goodwill; it's a little tattered, with a few moth-bitten holes that I can't stop thinking about sticking my fingers inside to feel his skin. I'm a total creeper, I know, but holy shit, he looks so sexy and grungy.

"Is that an invitation?" I ask as we find a spot in a deserted hallway.

"We should probably talk about everything," he says.

"Do we have to? Can't we get through the day, week, month, spring musical first?"

"Are you trying to be adorable?" he asks. "Your distraction is almost working." He reaches for one of my fries. We ate a lot of fries last night at the diner after rehearsal as we hashed out our plan for today; it was the first night since Grams went into the hospital that I didn't see her, but Mom said it was just more of the same, and she encouraged me to take the night off. Cris and I emailed Principal McCauley and set up a meeting with her for the last ten minutes of our lunch period today. Phoebe is ducking out of class early to join us, and we're supposed to be going over exactly what we're going to say. But right now I just want to flirt because it's way more fun than thinking about this meeting, which makes my insides twist until I'm on the brink of a full-on vomit attack.

"We didn't talk about our kiss yesterday."

I try to be sly: "Which one?" When he dropped me off after the diner, he went to give me a hug, and our noses grazed. Before I knew it, we were full on making out again.

"Any and all kisses need to stop."

Pretty sure my *heart* just stopped. I try to swallow but can't. There's a hollow ringing in my ears, and I'm being so dramatic, but it's like he told me Mariah Carey had died.

"Why?" My question comes out a little more breathy than I would've preferred.

"We haven't talked about *why* we stopped kissing each other in the first place. I still have a lot of feelings about what went down with us. Maybe you do too, I don't know. And with the Mr. Jackson stuff now, it's too complicated to sort out all at the same time. I think we should be friends." He bites another fry and chews. "For now." His phone alarm goes off. "Fuck, we gotta meet Phoebe." He stands up and pulls me up with him.

Phoebe is waiting in front of Principal McCauley's office with a grimace. "Max is in with Principal McCauley. With his parents. He said Mr. Kelly is going down."

"What does that mean?" I look to Cris for answers. Out of the three of us, Cris knows Max and his family the best.

"I don't know," Cris says. "I spent a lot of time at Courtney's house when we were dating, but never with her parents. What I do know is that she's the progressive misfit. They're all pretty conservative. She used to fight with them all the time. I don't think they liked that she was dating a bisexual Filipino. They're more the 'we think the Confederate flag is an American symbol' type. Hashtag white pride."

Phoebe rolls her eyes. "Of course, they are." She lowers her voice. "Max also said other parents are going to complain. About *Carey.*"

"Carey who?" I ask. "Carey me?"

Cris puts his hand on my back.

"They want you out of the musical," she says, but then emphatically adds, "but that is not gonna happen. I promise. I will quit the show."

"No, you won't," I say. "I won't let you."

"And I won't let you be kicked out," Phoebe says.

"Same." Cris holds out his hand. Phoebe and I reach for an "all in," and pull up just as Max and his parents exit Principal McCauley's office. Max's parents don't look anything like Max: His father has a neatly trimmed beard and seems like a Wall Street type. His mom, on the other hand, is meek and a bit mousy. She makes sure to stand behind him, to look to him for direction on where to walk. I wonder what else she needs permission for.

Max smirks as he passes us but doesn't say a word.

Principal McCauley waves us in and offers us seats around the circular conference table by her desk. "I understand that our meeting is in reference to something that happened at the musical rehearsal yesterday." She sits and folds her hands together on top of the shiny red wood. "I've heard the rumors, and I've also heard about the incident from both Mr. Kelly and Mr. Jackson."

"Incident?" Phoebe asks. "No disrespect Principal McCauley, but that makes it sound harmless."

"Trust me when I say that I take what happened very

seriously," Principal McCauley responds. "As you can see, there's a lot going on at the moment."

"Like Max's parents complaining about me?" I ask.

"There have been . . . *concerns*, yes." She's trying to be judicious, but I see through that.

The muscles in Cris's jaw pulsate. "Carey is being targeted because of who they are. That's the only real *concern*."

"Targeted?" she asks.

"Yes," Cris says, getting to his feet in frustration. "Everyone knows it." He takes a deep breath, then sits down again.

Her lips go tight, but then she calmly asks, "Have there been threats? Physical harm?"

Cris and I exchange knowing glances.

I can't tell her how Max assaulted me. I won't relive that out loud.

Phoebe answers for me. "I've been in class with Max when he's said some repulsive things to Carey. And I've seen him being sent down to your office for bullying other kids. Doesn't that qualify?"

Cris chimes in as well: "Mr. Jackson's behavior toward us is completely discriminatory." He tells her about what happened at lunch last month, and the three of us take turns telling stories from his classes and what we've either experienced or heard around school. "And what happened yesterday, with Mr. Jackson going after Mr. Kelly because Mr. Kelly is gay and Mr. Jackson thinks he cast Carey in the musical for some agenda, well, that's completely wrong. He has a pattern of being homophobic and we won't stand for it." Cris licks his dry lips and hides his shaking hands under the desk.

Principal McCauley sits back in her chair and lets her glasses fall to the tip of her nose. "I have heard some of these *rumors*." She's choosing her words carefully.

"They're not *rumors*," I say, my temper flaring. "You don't know what we've had to endure at this school."

"Is the entire school acting this way?" she asks, knowing we couldn't possibly say yes to that.

"N-no," I stutter. Cris bites his lip as the color drains from his face; we exchange glances, and I know what he's thinking because I'm thinking it too: This is blatant denial. No, *erasure*. The school is downplaying the queerphobic garbage that goes on beneath the surface when nobody is looking. Just because students aren't holding Gay Is Not Okay signs doesn't mean that queerphobia doesn't exist. For every few fist bumps of solidarity, there's an under-the-breath "no homo" comment or snicker when someone like Max says something gross. McCauley seems to think "safe enough" is fine. But it's not. "That's not the point."

The bell for the next period rings from the speaker in the corner of her office. "I get it," she says, pushing herself up from her chair. "This is a delicate situation. I appreciate you meeting with me. If anything else comes up, please come see me."

The three of us leave, not knowing what happened.

"I'm gonna try to reach out to Courtney again. See if she can help us," Cris says, and I know that now is not the time to feel jealous, but fuck. I hate that he's going to talk to her. "I'll see y'all at rehearsal." Cris shakes his head as he walks away.

Phoebe puts her arm around me. "How do you feel?"

"Worse, somehow?" I say. "In so many ways."

"I know," she says. "This school is seriously fucked up. *Less* discrimination is not acceptable. There needs to be *zero* discrimination."

"I wish everyone thought that," I say.

"I can't wait to see the look on Max's face when you show your video project today in class," Phoebe says.

After I had to rush out of Exile, I didn't get a video of me singing my song in front of a crowd. But I used the practice video in the storeroom with Isaiah instead, and Phoebe helped me edit it so that it looked intentional. The dark, grainy quality of the taping actually looked pretty cool once she had the idea to make it black and white.

I shudder thinking about how Max will react.

She lets go of my arm as we arrive at Mr. Kelly's room.

"All right, settle down," Mr. Kelly shouts over the chatter at the sound of the final bell.

"Hey, Mr. Kelly, is it true you slashed Mr. Jackson's tires?" One of Max's friends shouts out from the back row the second he sees me. Max swivels around to high-five him.

"That's enough," Mr. Kelly says. "We're here to learn."

"I heard a theory Holden Caulfield was gay!" Max calls out. "What do you know about *that*, Mr. K?"

"Max, one more word, and you'll be in detention after school," Mr. Kelly states, drawing out his words so they're sure to lodge themselves in Max's ears. "Carey, you ready to show your video project to the class?"

"It's now or never." I log into my email and pull up the video from my drive. Mr. Kelly turns off the lights, and the black-and-white video montage featuring home movies of me in the glittery slippers, the only element that's in color, plays over my voice explaining their significance: "For me, the shoes were how I expressed my gender identity. When I wore the shoes, I felt alive, like a part of me that had been sleeping was awake. It didn't need to make sense to anybody else, it made perfect sense to me. When the world told me I was wrong, all I had to do was slip on those shoes and everything felt right." The video leads into the footage from Exile's storeroom, and the classroom is silent as I sing my original song, "I'm Ready." At the end, there's a shot of me hanging up the slippers, which are shown in all their Technicolor glory, on a hook in the back of my locker, explaining that I keep them with me at school for luck as I prep for the musical.

When it's over, everyone claps, except Phoebe, who screams out a booming, "Yass!"

"That was great, Carey! Does anyone have any questions before we discuss the significance of Carey's—"

Max interrupts. "Look, Mr. Kelly, this project seems cool and all, but why are we constantly talking about gay stuff in class? What kind of *agenda* is this?"

My teeth grind when he says "agenda."

"Mr. Kelly," Phoebe starts. "Max is being so offensive."

"Why does Carey always enlist girls to fight *his* battles?" Max says, with a laugh.

Max using the incorrect pronoun is like adding lighter fluid to the low-roaring fire that's been burning in my belly for days. Usually I can ignore people using the wrong pronouns, but I can't stop my anger from exploding like wildfire.

"CAN EVERYONE STOP MISGENDERING ME!" I'm panting.

"Yes, Max, please use Carey's correct pronouns," Mr. Kelly says calmly.

"What's the big deal? Why does it matter? This is English class," Max says. "You seem to be the only teacher around here who uses class time to talk about totally irrelevant stuff, and my dad says that it's impeding *my* education."

The class erupts in conversation. It's impossible to sift through all the low rumbles, but I hear a couple of people say that Max needs to shut up. You'd think it'd give me a little solace, but nope. Max knows how to hollow me out like a jack-o'-lantern. I try to sing Mariah's "Looking In" silently to myself, imagining myself alone on a stage with a microphone, singing a cappella. Mr. Kelly is talking, but I don't hear him. Instead, the lyrics—about how people look at her like she has everything but her insecurities paralyze her, and that maybe she'll always feel like an outsider but she'll protect herself from anyone who seeks to take advantage—soothe me until I can focus.

Mr. Kelly looks shaken as he takes control of the chatter. "Proper language is essential in the English classroom. What we talk about in discussion is connected to the words we study on the page, and vice versa. We're not simply learning about literary devices, we're learning how stories and writers shape our world-views. We're learning to tap into those stories to make sense of the world. And from that, we're learning how to communicate and interact with our communities."

Max laughs. "Is that on the final? Because I only want to pass. All this stuff feels like an agenda."

I clench my fists.

Mr. Kelly sighs. "Maybe we should table this conversation."

"To intentionally misgender someone is a direct attack," Phoebe interrupts, her voice growing louder with every syllable. "I'm so tired of every teacher silencing these types of conversations. Even you, Mr. Kelly—no offense."

"Don't apologize," Mr. Kelly says. "It's true, the school administration does encourage us to shy away from these types of discussions."

"Discussing liberal propaganda is *not* your job," Max says. "This isn't Gay Studies."

"Max, Principal McCauley's office, immediately." Mr. Kelly isn't fucking around this time. The vein in his neck is throbbing.

Max stands up. "You're silencing me. Everyone always silences me. My voice matters too, you know."

Phoebe rolls her eyes. "He's about to All Lives Matter this, isn't he?"

"I'm so tired of girls and wannabe girls shutting me down," Max says. But he doesn't move. "Just like my fucking sister."

"I had your sister in class, Max," Mr. Kelly says. "*She* was an *exceptional* student."

The class goes silent from everything Mr. Kelly doesn't say.

I turn to look at Max and his face is bright red, his lips pursed in anger.

Mr. Kelly repeats, "Please report to the principal's office. Now."

Max heads toward the door. "I don't get how I'm always the bad guy." As he storms away, he sticks out his middle finger and flips off the entire class.

Everyone gasps. Mr. Kelly struggles to wrangle our attentions again after that. "Okay, class, let's get back on track."

Yeah. That isn't happening.

Mr. Kelly brings his hands to his lips like a megaphone and starts yelling for order. "Listen up, we're not going to discuss Carey's project. After Max's outburst, I don't think it's fair to Carey. So, we're going to move on to . . ." He checks his roster on his iPad. "Blanca Rodriguez."

As Blanca moves to the front of the room to set up her project, I look out the window. A light flurry of snowflakes swirls past. The sky is a dull gray, hazy over the Hudson River in the distance, which usually means the snowfall is about to get intense.

A small bird with light blue feathers on its back and a rust-colored belly flies to the windowsill, a small red berry in its mouth. It hops on the ledge a few times and cocks its head. I stretch my neck, and from this angle, I can see a hole in the brick façade, big enough for the small bird. Tufts of grass peek out. I wonder if it has a family in there to protect, to keep fed during the long winter ahead.

It's starting to snow harder now, the flakes bigger and denser. It must be so cold.

With one great thrust, the bird propels upward and disappears into the opening. Even birds know when to retreat.

Suddenly, Principal McCauley's voice pours out of the loudspeaker. "Attention, Sunnyside students. Due to inclement weather, the school will be closing immediately. All winter sports and after-school activities are hereby canceled."

I ignore Mr. Kelly calling after me and book it out of the classroom.

The kids in the hallway crowd in around me. All I want to do is get the fuck out of here.

I get to my locker and immediately notice the lock is broken. I unhook the dangling piece and stare at it in my palm, my whole body frozen in place, afraid to open the door. Who did this? It couldn't have been an accident.

I look around. No other lockers are damaged.

This was targeted.

This is about me.

Phoebe comes up behind me. "Hey, since there's no rehearsal tonight, wanna walk down to Exile? Hang out?"

All I want to do is retreat. "I have a doctor's appointment later. M-maybe next time." My voice shreds like cheap fabric.

"What's wrong?" She looks down at my hand. "What happened to your lock?"

I shake my head, unable to speak.

"Want me to open your locker?" she asks, and I nod. "I'm sure it's fine, Car. Who would break into your locker?" She pulls the door open slowly at first, in case anything is rigged to jump out or leak out—clearly we've both seen too many teen horror movies.

Nothing happens.

So she opens it the rest of the way.

It's empty, except for the books I always keep there and the pictures I have taped to the inside. No, wait. There used to be a picture of me and Joey, but it's gone.

Phoebe sticks her face inside. "All clear. See? Told ya."

When she pulls away, it dawns on me what else is missing.

"My lucky ruby red slippers," I whisper. "They're gone."

Phoebe's eyes go wide. Then her phone buzzes. She takes it out. "It's just a *Sunnyside Upended!* message." Then her face goes pale as she reads.

Everyone's phones buzz and the hallway becomes a beehive of digital activity. One by one, heads turn from their phone screens to me. I hear the climactic whistle notes from Mariah's "Emotions," but they're not coming from the school's speaker system—the music's coming from everyone's phones. I'm pretty much convinced this is some sort of fever dream.

Except it's not.

Because people are laughing.

Phoebe starts yelling, "Shut the fuck up, this isn't funny!"

I make a grab for Phoebe's phone, but she yanks her hand away.

Monroe and Joey burst through the crowd toward us.

"We were coming to find you to drive home when—" Joey begins.

"I'll fucking kill him," Monroe growls.

"What the fuck is going on?" I yell, catching them off guard. It breaks Phoebe's concentration for long enough that I'm able to grab her phone to see why everyone is laughing.

My hand shakes as the video Max took of me in the black gown at the mall plays. It's a short loop, about ten seconds of me grasping for his phone and falling to the ground, ripping the dress. It's set to Mariah's "Emotions."

Fucking Max. He broke into my locker. He stole a picture of me and Joey and my lucky slippers. He used my queen, Mariah, as a way to hurt me. He sent this video into *Sunnyside Upended!*

194

I thought Monroe had him delete everything on his phone at prom. He must have had it backed up. If he kept this, what else does he have on me still?

I have to get the fuck out of here.

I push people out of my way, trying to tune out their laughter and calls of concern.

My heartbeat races.

Fast.

Too fast.

I try to sing to myself to calm down, but the melodies clash together, and I can't remember a single word. I search for a random fact about Mariah, but it's as if everything I know about her has been deleted. My mind blanks before the panic sets in.

I burst through the front doors of the school out into the snowstorm. I need to get as far away from this school as I can.

Then I'm going to scream until my lungs bleed.

TRACK 22

THEY/THEM/THEIR

Dr. Potter says, "Tell me what's going on," in a soothing voice that blends with the whir of the ambiance machine in the corner. What she's *really* saying is, *"What happened? Because you look a fresh mess. Your body is so tense it might as well be made out of cement, and your resting bitch face is out of control."*

Maybe I'm projecting.

I don't want to answer her. Half out of fear that I'll cry, and half out of fear that once I start talking, I'll go wild. I'm an unstoppable forest fire of emotions: one ember is all it will take to ignite a blaze that not even Dr. Potter will be able to put out.

"Do you want to talk about what happened today at school?"

I avoid eye contact.

"Your mom called and filled me in, a bit. Let's start there."

Of course she did. When Monroe and Joey couldn't find me after school, they called Mom, who promptly freaked out. Now that Monroe and Joey know about my ideations, they watch me like mama birds do their chicks. It makes me feel safe and suffocated all at once.

I grit my teeth. "I'm tired."

She leans back in her black leather office chair and rests her hands on her stomach. She's waiting for me to talk.

I glance out the window. The snow has turned to rain. My gaze fixates on the passing cars, one after another after another, blurs of color sliding across pavement. Raindrops *tap-tap-tap* haphazardly on the sill, lulling me into a trance.

"Did you know that Mariah's nickname in high school was Mirage? She always cut class because she was determined to be a famous singer. Her classmates thought she was a mirage, a figment of their imagination, an afterimage. Isn't that funny? I never thought of myself as a mirage, more like the invisible person. For a while, I wasn't. I thought I might finally belong at school. But Max—what he did . . ." I choke out everything that's happened over the last few days. "We tried to tell Principal McCauley that the school felt unsafe after Mr. Jackson's tirade, but she didn't listen."

"Who is we?" Dr. Potter asks.

"Phoebe and Cris. And me."

"What did she say?"

"She made it seem like it was all in my head. Downplayed it like, no big deal, whatever. But this? Today? That can't be in my head, right?"

"It's not." Dr. Potter pushes her glasses up the bridge of her nose. "That's a form of microaggression."

"Exactly. But how can I prove that? She made me feel like I'm in the wrong for being targeted, you know?"

"How did seeing that video make you feel?" Dr. Potter asks, circling back to Max.

"Embarrassed. Everyone was laughing at me. It made me feel violated all over again." I take a deep breath. "Why does Max keep doing this to me? And before you ask, yes, I'm sure it was Max. He's the only one with the video. Mr. Kelly sent him to the principal's office, and he broke into my locker, stole my lucky ruby red slippers, a picture of Joey and me, and released the video. It's like he did it as a threat or something." I'm breathing heavily now, but it's not a panic attack.

No.

This is *anger.*

Scorched-earth-level anger.

I continue. "But fuck that, and fuck him. I'm not going backward. I can't. It's just—how do I not let them get the best of me?"

"What would Mariah do?"

"She's way too blessed to be stressed," I say with a chuckle, but Dr. Potter doesn't laugh. She's serious. I take a moment to reply. "I'm sure she internalizes some of the hate that's out there. She was diagnosed with bipolar disorder in 2001, but didn't come out publicly about that until 2018. That's seventeen years of suffering in silence as people called her eccentric and out of touch."

"What do you think she does to get through the hard days and negativity?"

"She channels her raw experiences and feelings into her music."

"What does it feel like when you connect with a song? When you perform?"

"When I'm singing or onstage, it's like nothing else matters."

She clears her throat. "Why give the Maxes and the Jacksons of the world so much power over you?" She waits. "Does the rest of the school's seeing that video mean they are now against you? Do you give them that power over you?"

I shrug, honestly unsure of the answer.

"Did Max steal the best of you along with your shoes?"

I fiddle with a thick rubbery leaf of the jade plant on the table next to me. "I didn't have my lucky slippers until *after* I decided to audition. They were a gift from Monroe. I would've sung without them. It's not like I was thinking about them or wearing them during the audition or at the B-ball Hoop-Off game performance." I go quiet because I hear the voice of younger Carey in my head, crying because those shoes made them feel whole, and now they're gone. "But little Carey . . ." I start to feel the rising tension in my cheeks, around my eyes. I'm trying to fight off the tears, but I can't. "Little Carey just wanted to feel loved."

"Who do you think denied little Carey love?"

There's only one real answer, the only one that matters. "Me."

She nods, her eyes watery. "I think it's time you let little Carey off the hook. They're tired. They've been through enough. They need *you* to love them. Remember when I told you that you already have everything you need? Little Carey is such an important piece to that puzzle. You have to remember to love Little Carey."

"This isn't about the shoes," I mutter. "Or the video."

"You're right. This is not about the shoes or the video. This is about what you deny yourself."

"Love."

Dr. Potter lets me sit with that for a few minutes. "What can you do to love little Carey?"

"Stand up for myself?" It comes out like a question.

She stands. "Don't let what happened today have power over you." She urges me to stand and take a Superman pose. "Take your power back."

"How?" I pose with my hands on my hips and puff out my chest.

"The world is your stage, Carey. And right now, the spotlight is on you."

I mull over what Dr. Potter said with Mom on the drive home.

The world is your stage.

The spotlight is on you.

"What do you think she meant by that?" Mom asks, trying to suppress a yawn after a long day by Grams's side.

I know, but I'm afraid to say it out loud. So I shrug and stare out the window.

Once home, we collapse on the couch. It's eerily quiet without Grams here.

"I can't cower," I finally say.

"Divas make their voices heard," Mom says. "Trust me, that principal already heard an earful from me today. And she will again tomorrow. Maybe I'll call Max's parents too."

"I don't think that'll do any good. I saw them the other day. His mom reminds me of a commander's wife from *The Handmaid's Tale*."

"Oh, we need to finish watching that, don't we?" Mom reaches for the Apple TV remote and swipes until she lands on the remaining episodes of the last season. She holds her arm out for me, and I sidle up next to her. She presses play.

"Thanks for standing up for me," I say.

"Always," she says, giving me a squeeze.

As we watch the horrors unfold on-screen, my mind is spinning with Dr. Potter's words. I can't let Max get away with what he did. While I have no concrete way to prove my locker, the video was him. I don't have to let him win. I *can* fight this.

I *must* push back. But how?

The next afternoon, I stride down the hallways of Sunnyside High in my Elphaba heels with my head held high. Everyone takes notice now. I suppress the urge to look around, to take stock of their faces, but I know that if I linger too long, I'll interpret even the slightest of smirks as judgment. I keep my head up, eyeline just above everyone else's.

I hear Mr. Kelly's voice from behind say my name. When I turn to see him, the loudspeakers boom and crackle. "Carey Parker, please report to Principal McCauley's office. Carey Parker to Principal McCauley's office. Thank you."

"I was looking for you," he says. I register the lack of surprise on his face. He knew this was coming. "Come on, I'll walk you."

As we enter the main office, Max is leaning against the wall, a grimy look on his face, smirking like he knows what's about to happen. What did he do now?

Principal McCauley meets us at the door to her office.

"Mr. Kelly, I don't remember asking you to be here," she says as her round glasses fall to the tip of her nose.

"I'm here for Carey," Mr. Kelly says. He points to Mr. Jackson, who sits at her conference table. "If he gets to be here, then Carey deserves to have someone on their side." All color has drained from his face. He turns to me. "If you want, I can call your mom."

"Please," I say.

He calls, but Mom doesn't pick up the phone.

Mr. Jackson taps his fingers on the table.

"I couldn't get ahold of your mom, Carey, but I left a message for her to call back Principal McCauley," Mr. Kelly explains.

"I want Mr. Kelly here," I say quickly.

Mr. Jackson rolls his eyes. "There's obviously some kind of *agenda* here, McCauley, and I want answers." His voice slices.

"Patrick, please, some decorum," she demands. "Carey please have a seat. We've gotten more . . . complaints about your involvement with the spring musical." She folds her hands as she sits at the head of the table.

"How many?" Mr. Kelly asks.

"A few parents have expressed their concern at having Carey play a female lead. Some were of the opinion that their girls were passed over in favor of an ideological crusade."

Is she serious?

"Why does a vocal minority get to dictate the musical's

casting? It's not like parents determine the varsity sports teams' rosters," Mr. Kelly says. "Besides, Carey out-sung them all."

Anger bubbles in my throat. "No disrespect, but this is all very offensive. You used to be an English teacher, right, Principal McCauley? While I don't identify as male, you *do* know that men used to perform all the roles in Shakespeare's plays, including the female characters, right? Gender has always been performative, but patriarchal society has us believe it's strictly binary to keep anyone who isn't a cis man from gaining any sort of power or voice. A few weeks ago, at the Hoop-Off, you seemed perfectly fine with my role in the show when you asked me to sing without notice. Now, because a few parents and Mr. Jackson, who has repeatedly misgendered me and disrespected my identity, have complained, you're choosing their side?"

"This is insane, McCauley," Mr. Jackson says. "We can't let this emotionally disturbed *boy* confuse our other students."

I try not to scream when he calls me a *boy* so deliberately, but I want to. So fucking bad.

"Patrick, please," Principal McCauley says, holding up her hand. She turns back to me. "I respect your identity, Carey—"

I cut her off. "Do you? Because you haven't stood up for me or done anything about what Max did to me yesterday. I know my mom called you about the video."

She clears her throat. "That is a separate issue, one that we are investigating internally. Since the *Sunnyside Upended!* is not school sanctioned, our resources are limited, and as that post was anonymous, and could have been sent in off campus, it's hard to—"

"I know who it was! It was Max."

"Defamation!" Mr. Jackson cries.

Principal McCauley puts her hand in the air to silence Mr. Jackson. "Believe me, Carey, I want to get to the bottom of what happened. I want to help you. But there are procedures we need to follow. We will discuss that further at another time. For now, let's get back to why you're here. The musical. While you're correct on your knowledge of Shakespeare, the reality is that Mr. Kelly's casting choice sends a message to the student body, a message that may seem admirable in theory, but one that some parents aren't comfortable with. And after a lot of consideration, I've asked Mr. Kelly and Ms. Diaz to recast the role of Elphaba and move you to another role within the musical. We still want you in the production. And I believe this is a fair compromise."

Mr. Jackson grins so wide he might as well get up and do a dance on the table.

I want to ask how many complaints she received. I want to ask why she's letting queerphobia win. But I'm too shocked to open my mouth, and it feels like my body is shrinking so that soon, no one will be able to see me anymore.

Mr. Kelly exhales so hard, I worry he might pass out. "I was under the impression that this was an ongoing discussion, that nothing was final yet."

"Take a seat, Kelly," Mr. Jackson says. "You don't want to ruffle any feathers with tenure on the horizon."

"Is that a threat?" Mr. Kelly asks.

"Gentlemen, please. *Decorum.* This is not the time or the place," Principal McCauley says calmly, the way Dr. Potter changes the pitch of her voice when she wants to ease my nerves.

The intercom on her desk beeps, and a voice on the other end alerts Principal McCauley that she has an urgent call. "Excuse me for one moment, please."

I turn back to Mr. Kelly, who whispers, "We'll fight this. I promise."

Pressing a finger to the hold button on her office phone, she dismisses Mr. Jackson, who happily struts out. He is convinced he has won, isn't he? Disgust sloshes around my belly like sour milk.

"Carey, your mother is on the line."

She tries to excuse Mr. Kelly, but I ask him to stay.

"It's about your grandmother," Principal McCauley says, and hands me the phone.

Mom's word are waterlogged as she tells me that Grams has taken a turn for the worse. The doctors predict she has only a few hours left, a day at most. I hand Mr. Kelly the phone. I feel numb as Mr. Kelly places his hand on my shoulder.

I look out the window.

No rain.

No sun.

Just a blanket of white clouds stretched across the sky, a layer of dull nothingness.

Mr. Kelly says something, but I don't hear a word.

The entire world has been drained of all sound, all music, and all that's left is a deafening silence.

TRACK 23
THEY/THEM/THEIR

Mr. Kelly offers to drive me to the hospital. Mom gives him and Principal McCauley her permission over the phone. I lean my head against the icy cold window and watch the dead, barren trees whiz by, a blur of browns and grays.

"I'm sorry." My voice is thick.

"For what?" Mr. Kelly asks.

"For dragging you into all this."

"Never apologize for being exactly who you are," he says gently.

He pulls into the hospital parking lot, and I stare up the side of the tall, glass building. My brain is telling my arm to unbuckle my seatbelt and open the door, but my arm isn't listening. If I get out, it's real, Grams will die. If I stay in his car, Grams is still alive. I can't control anything that happens once I go inside. This realization crumbles my resolve. I lean forward and dry heave. I'm not crying, but my entire body is shaking uncontrollably; I want to so badly, but nothing is coming out.

"Take all the time you need," Mr. Kelly says, putting a hand on my back.

I don't remember walking into the hospital or taking the elevator up to the fourth floor, but somehow I'm at Grams's bedside, holding her frail, cold hand, beside Mom and Uncle Mike.

Grams eyes are open, but she's not focusing on any of us. Her breathing is labored, and when she inhales and exhales, she gurgles and sputters. It's the sound of a child sucking every last drop from a juice box. The nurses call it the "death rattle."

Mom and Uncle Mike take turns telling stories about Grams from when she was younger, about how full of life she was with her jet-black bob and the tight dresses that accentuated her hourglass body. How anywhere they went, Grams had to sing. One time, when they were kids, she took them to the Bronx Zoo, and at the gorilla exhibit, all the children waited impatiently by the glass, pounding it and yelling, but the gorillas hid. Then Grams started singing Lena Horne's "Don't Take Your Love From Me," and all the children stopped and listened, and by the end of the song, the gorillas had emerged and were listening to Grams too.

"It was incredible," Mom says.

"I would've loved to have seen that," I say. "I remember sitting on her ugly green couch with the gold stitching—remember that?" Uncle Mike and Mom laugh. "I would lay my head on her lap and she'd sing Doris Day's 'Secret Love.' I used to wait for the bridge when her voice would go up an octave and she'd belt out the line that ends with 'daffodils.' She always stopped, winked, and I'd laugh so hard I felt like I was gonna pass out.

I was totally convinced 'daffodils' was a word she'd made up, so one day I asked her what it meant."

I turn to Grams, and she's staring at me now. I struggle to remember what she looked like back then because this version of her, the one where her skin looks waxy and her hair is stark white and dry, isn't the Grams I want to remember.

Mom grabs my hand. "You look exhausted, baby. Why don't you take a nap." She points to an empty cot.

"We could be in for a long night," Uncle Mike adds.

"Is she in pain?" I ask.

"The nurses say no, but . . ." Mom stops as Grams gurgles so loudly it jostles every bone in my body. "I don't want to see her in this state anymore. This is no way to live." She leans in and kisses her mother on the forehead. "I love you, Mom."

I don't want to let go of Grams's hand, but they're right. It could be a long night, and it's been a horrible day already.

I kiss her cheek and whisper, "It's okay, Grams. You can let go."

Her thumb presses into my hand, and it's all I can do to keep from bursting out into tears. I can't be here. Every single muscle is telling me to run out of this hospital, but Grams is telling me to stay.

So I stay.

I lie down on the cot and close my eyes. I hum quietly to myself to drown out the sounds of her struggling to breathe. Eventually, my body relaxes, and I drift into the darkness. In the distance, a beautiful young woman dances on a stage, a single spotlight shining down on her raven-black hair that falls gently on her shoulders. Her rose-tinged lips mouth words I can't hear.

Then, in the middle of a song, she stops and looks through the crowd at me. In an instant, it's just the two of us. The crowd is gone.

She gently cups my chin and kisses my cheek and says, "I'm okay."

I tell her that I love her. She opens her arms and they become the wings of a bird.

All I can do is watch as she flies away.

TRACK 24
THEY/THEM/THEIR

I brace myself against the lectern at Grams's church and try to ignore the mild discomfort I feel being here at all. Grams loved going to church, and she tried to get me to come too, but I never felt included by the priest or his sermons. But the priest came to visit Grams every week to sit with her and pray once it got too difficult for her to travel; last week, he told me how much she used to brag about me. She loved this place, so the least I can do is be here for her now, to honor her the way she would want me to.

My hands smooth out the fabric of my all-black velvet suit with the red floral lapel, Grams's favorite color. Everyone is waiting for me to say something, but the words aren't coming out. Each time I try to speak, my body starts to rattle. I try focusing on someone in the crowd, Phoebe or Cris, but they're sitting next to each other and Cris's puffy, red eyes make me cry all over again. Monroe and Joey look at each other, and without hesitation, they walk up to the podium and stand on either side of me.

"I can read for you," Monroe says. "If you want."

My lips quiver and I nod. Joey grabs my hand and I lean on her as Monroe begins to read from my notes:

Grams,

Remember what you used to say to me after we'd had a great day of lunch and a movie or singing together or when I would watch you cook, wondering how it was possible you put so much heart into your dishes? You would turn to me, grab my hand, and say, "Don't forget me when I'm gone, you hear?"

I used to say, "Shut up, I could never forget you."

Then you'd say, "You better not. I'll haunt you." And you'd squeeze my hand and smile, and we'd laugh. Then you'd get serious and tell me, "One day, I won't be around, Carey. But I'll always be with you."

I never imagined there would come a day when I wouldn't come home and smell your meatballs with the fresh mint and your tangy sauce, or when you wouldn't make me my favorite French toast, again with fresh mint, in the morning. You passed down your love of mint to me. How is it possible you won't sing to me again? Or that you won't be here to see me onstage at Madison Square Garden one day? Now you live only in my memory, and though your mind wasn't around for the better part of the last few years, living without you is still a hard concept to grasp.

My earliest memories are of you singing. I will

never forget the sound of your voice: the timbre,
so buttery and rich, and the sweet intensity in
every song you sang, like each word had some
special meaning that only you were aware of. You
taught me how to sing with my soul.

I miss the sound of your voice. I miss your
hearty, witchy cackle. I miss the way you used to tell
me you loved me, as if I were the only person in the
entire world. I miss the way you cheered for me when
I would sing silly little songs I'd made up as I stood on
the couch, like it was a stage, one I was honored to
share with you. Life was so much simpler back then,
when laying my head in your lap could solve every
problem; back when the thought of not having you
around never crossed my mind; back when you said a
daffodil could be anything I imagined it to be.

I wish you could be here for when the world
finally hears me.

I won't forget you. I promise. You will always be
with me.

Monroe finishes and she and Joey hug me so tightly that I
don't want to break free for fear I might completely crumble.

But I have to let go.

As they walk back to the pews, I look to Mom and Uncle
Mike and motion for them to join me. Together, we sing one last
song for Grams.

There have never been this many people in our tiny apartment. If Grams were here, she'd love making herself the center of attention, singing and dancing as everyone clapped to the beat—and hate the mess of it, going around to clean up spills with an old dish rag while muttering about how "people are such slobs."

I keep ducking hollow "I'm sorry for your loss" platitudes. Can't people come up with something new to say?

"When my mom died, everyone apologized to me, too," Cris says. "It's the worst."

Monroe, Joey, and Phoebe stand awkwardly around me, as if they're protecting me, not quite sure what to say themselves, so they continue to stuff their faces with store-bought hors d'oeuvres and dipping sauces. Mom didn't have the strength to cook, and I can practically hear Grams's under-the-breath remarks about *that*.

"Can we go to my room?" I wave my hands around. "*This* is too much."

On our way, a nice older woman Grams used to play bingo with stops me. She speaks in broken English, dipping into Italian when she doesn't know the right words to say. She gives me a sloppy wet kiss and pinches my cheeks before I'm able to break away. When I walk into the bedroom, Cris, Joey, Monroe, and Phoebe are huddled together, talking in hushed voices.

"Now's not the time," Monroe hisses, motioning for them to be quiet.

"Not the time for what?" I ask.

"Nothing. We should talk about happy things," Joey says, and Phoebe elbows her in the ribs. "What? We should."

"The three of them"—Phoebe gestures—"think you shouldn't know what's been happening at school."

"We think it's too much right now," Joey says, elbowing Phoebe back.

"What's happening at school?" I haven't thought about Max or Mr. Jackson or getting booted from the musical in days, my anger replaced with grief and the systematic monotony of funeral arrangements and eulogy writing and sitting through two wake services. If anything, I'm numb to it all.

"Mr. Kelly is out," Phoebe says.

I frown. "What? What does that mean, *out*?"

Phoebe's jaw jerks like she bit down on something cold. "Carey, he's no longer directing the musical."

"Who is?" Nobody says anything. "Come on, guys, please. My grams just died. You owe me the truth." I figure if I have to grieve, I might as well get some benefit from it.

Cris cracks a smile. "Nice."

Monroe's head snaps toward him, like, *how dare you speak?* Joey raises her eyebrows; we're thinking the same thing: Monroe is a dog with a bone, and she isn't going to let go of what Cris did to me so easily.

Phoebe glares at him. "Mr. Jackson."

"Fuck! I saw Mr. Kelly last night at one of the wake services. He didn't tell me."

"You think he'd tell you that news at your grandma's wake?" Monroe asks.

"Fair. What's the rest of the cast saying? Is Rachel still helping direct?" I ask.

"She's still there, but *e-ver-y-one* is pissed about Mr. Kelly,"

Cris says. He looks to Phoebe and she nods, so he keeps going. "There's talk about all of us quitting."

"Now *that*'s insanity," I say. "You can't quit!"

"Why not?" Phoebe asks. "You're the second most talented vocalist at Sunnyside—behind me, of course—and what they're doing to you and Mr. Kelly is beyond discrimination. This is the time to stand up and take action."

"After you were kicked out, the rumors have been crazy." Cris adds, "A lot of people I've been talking to think it's not right what McCauley and Jackson did to you."

I look to Joey and Monroe. "Really?"

They both nod. "There was this weird energy shift," Monroe says. "After Max sent out that video and word spread about how Jackson behaved at that rehearsal, it's all anyone can talk about. And for once, it's not all made-up gossip. People are mad, and it's sticking."

"Do people think Max was responsible for the video?" I ask.

"He laughs about it all the time," Joey says. "I almost punched him yesterday."

"But she has a scholarship to a D1 school to worry about." Monroe rolls her eyes at Joey's caution.

"There's no concrete proof," Joey corrects. "Yet."

I don't know if it's incompetence or ignorance from the school administration, but the more I learn about the utter lack of action from Principal McCauley, even after I told her it was Max, the more adrenaline rushes through my veins. "So, what do we do?" I ask.

A smile spreads across Phoebe's face. "So glad you asked. I don't think there's anything we can do about Max. But . . ."

She pulls a folded piece of paper from the pocket of her black dress and hands it to me. It's a petition to get Mr. Kelly reinstated as director of the show. She hands me another piece of a paper. "We also want to get you back as Elphaba. This hinges on you. You're at the center of it all."

"I don't know . . ." I feel the fatigue not only from Grams's sickness and funeral, but from fighting Max and Mr. Jackson, in my bones. I *want* to push back, to hold them both accountable and to fight for Mr. Kelly. But . . .

All I wanted was to be onstage. To sing. Not lead a whole freaking movement. "I feel like I'm the reason this is happening. I'm the problem." My mind drifts to Mr. Kelly, and I know what I *need* to do.

Joey grabs my arms. "This school is protecting bigots who can't do their jobs, like Mr. Jackson, and persecuting great teachers, like Mr. Kelly, who are actually making a difference in our lives, and you, because you're brave enough to live in your truth. That scares them." She holds my gaze. "You're not a problem to be solved. You did nothing wrong."

"They have to know we won't be pushed around," Cris says. "McCauley doesn't believe that what happened with Jackson actually happened. It doesn't matter that Phoebe and I complained, or that Mr. Kelly put his career on the line to tell the truth."

My chest swells with confidence. They're all not only here *for* me, they want to fight *with* me because they believe *in* me. I mutter, "Fuck yeah."

"Does that mean you're in?" Monroe asks.

I remember what Dr. Potter said last week about using my

spotlight *and* voice. If my friends are willing to fight for me, I should be willing to fight for myself, right? I've spent the better part of my life afraid of this moment, the moment when I have to stand up for who I am. And now that it's here, I'm not scared. I'm pissed.

I've read about members of the LGBTQ+ community fighting for their rights, for equality, for the ability to just be. Where would I be if it weren't for brave transgender women like Marsha P. Johnson, who was one of the leaders of the Stonewall Riots? What if she backed down or did nothing? What if there was no March on Washington in 1987 to demand more research and response to the AIDS crisis, which was killing tens of thousands of queer people? What if James Obergefell didn't take his case to the United States Supreme Court when his partner was terminally ill, yet Obergefell's name wouldn't be allowed on his partner's death certificate because of the ban on same-sex marriage?

I'm not saying I'm the next great activist, but I'm a proud genderqueer person, and I refuse to leave Sunnyside High another empty quote in a yearbook. Not when hidden LGBTQ kids are probably watching me, listening to the rumors, bearing witness to horrible people like Mr. Jackson, who would rather see us as silent, second-class citizens hiding rather than out and proud and equal. I can't back down. I won't. Not now, not ever. Grams always said that the world should hear me, and there's more than one way to use my voice.

I put my hand on my hip. "I was in *before* you all started pitching me." They stare at me, stunned; Cris smirks with pride. "I can't turn my back or pretend what's happening is fine. I'm done living in fear." I take a deep breath. "But we need to do *way* more than petition."

Phoebe, ever ready, waves us all in closer. "Gather round. I have a plan."

TRACK 25
THEY/THEM/THEIR

Phoebe, in a form-fitted Rosie the Riveter sweater and red head-band that tucks her curls back from her face, opens the front door of her ranch overlooking the Hudson River. Cris, Monroe, Joey, and I are greeted with the deliciously sweet smell of nut-meg and hot maple syrup. "I hope you're hungry, because my mom is making waffles."

Cris breathes in deep and sniffs his way inside like a cartoon bloodhound. "I don't know your mom yet, but I love her."

"Suck up," Monroe whispers loudly; Joey coughs to mask Monroe's contempt.

Phoebe leads us through an expansive foyer and past a living room to the kitchen, where her mom is whipping batter in a large metal bowl.

When she sees us, she beams, places the bowl on the coun-ter, and takes us all into one big hug. "I'm so happy you kids are here! I'll be out of your way in a moment. Have one more batch to make." She points to a stack of white dishes, a pile of forks, and an array of butters, margarines, and syrups next to a mound of fresh waffles. "Help yourselves!"

Phoebe points to one of the tubs of butter. "That's Mama's homemade honey lavender butter, and that's blueberry syrup. I swear you'll never have a better waffling experience."

I hang back to talk to Phoebe's mom while everyone attacks the waffles.

"It's a shame what's happening, Carey. I'm proud to see all of y'all fighting back." Ms. Wright points to the bowl of batter and orders me to whip. We wait for the blue light on the waffle iron to flash before she takes the bowl from me and pours it onto the hot iron. It spreads out and bubbles before she closes the lid and flips it over. "Did Phoebe ever mention her uncle?" I shake my head no. "My brother was the sunshine and the breeze and everything pure in this world."

The machine beeps and she takes out the waffle and pours the last of the batter in. Phoebe, Cris, Joey, and Monroe are eating, but they've also stopped to listen.

"He was not much older than Phoebe when he enlisted in the army. He was stationed in Iraq for two tours. This was during the Don't Ask, Don't Tell days, and he fell in love with another soldier." Ms. Wright shakes her head and takes out the last waffle and plops it on the plate with the rest of the stack. "I remember him calling me up and telling me about a man who made him smile." She runs water into the dirty bowl and steadies herself on the counter for a second before continuing. "Someone caught them together, and they were *both* dishonorably discharged, left with no money or job prospects, their military careers over. Two weeks after he returned home, my brother's boyfriend took his life. The shame they both felt." Her eyes are teary. Phoebe walks over to her mother and wraps her arms around her. "My brother wasn't allowed at the funeral. He was *broken* by that." She can't choke out the rest, but she doesn't need to. "For what? Why?"

I'll never know what Phoebe's uncle went through, but I feel a kinship. He was trapped by rules created by a system designed to punish people like him. People like me. Hearing her uncle's story makes me feel closer to Phoebe. It also makes me even more sure that we need to fight back against what is happening at Sunnyside.

"Mama became an activist, leading rallies against Don't Ask, Don't Tell," Phoebe says. "I remember going to protests as a kid. I didn't know what was happening, but I knew it was important."

"My baby was raised to do what's right," Ms. Wright says, wiping the tears from her eyes. "And *that*'s why I tell my brother's story."

"Phoebe Is Always (W)right," I say, repeating her student body president slogan.

"I like you." Ms. Wright makes her own plate of waffles. "If you need me, I'll be in the living room. Just shout."

"Thanks, Mama," Phoebe says. "Okay, let's get to work. I know Cris has to leave soon, so—"

Monroe groans. "The world doesn't need to revolve around one person's schedule."

Joey nudges her. "Be nice!"

Cris rolls his eyes and stuffs the last of his waffle into his mouth.

"You have to leave?" I ask him.

"Yeah," Cris responds, mouth still full. "Remember the Carnegie Hall showcase? It's this coming week. I have to practice."

Oh, fuck. I completely forgot. Cris got me a ticket. But we're not together anymore. I wonder if he wants or expects me to go. Last week, before Grams died and I was booted from the musical, Cris said he just wanted to be friends, and friends want friends to see them perform, right? Though I'm pretty certain he only got me a ticket because we were dating, which I very much wish was still our current reality. Cris has been at my house every day since Grams passed, and not a moment has gone by that I've felt like he hasn't been there for me. If it's possible, I love him more now. So much that I want to cry because he's right in front of me but just out of reach. I have to tell him how I feel.

"Can I talk to you for a second?" When we're out of earshot of the others, I say, "I don't want to be someone who is afraid to say what I need to say. I know we decided we're only friends and that's fine. But I really need you to know how much I appreciate you being there for me the last few days, you know, with Grams and stuff."

"It's nothing," Cris says. He looks like he wants to say something else, but before he can, I hug him, so tightly that I hope we fuse together. I smell his neck, inhaling his coconut shampoo, and I don't want to let him go.

He clears his throat. "We should, uh, get back," he says and pulls away. He walks back to the table before I can say anything else.

My stomach drops. How is it possible that I keep blowing it with him so hard?

"You coming?" Phoebe asks, waving me over.

The kitchen table is hidden beneath poster board, markers, scrap paper, Phoebe's laptop, and everything I didn't say to Cris.

"First things first, we have to set a goal." Phoebe sets her fingers to the keyboard, ready to type.

"Carey reinstated in the musical," Monroe says.

"Mr. Kelly back as director," I add.

Phoebe types as we talk.

Cris sits back, not saying anything or looking at anybody.

"Mr. Jackson fired," Joey says with anger.

"This is all great," Monroe says, "but we also need a policy change at the school level or else something like this can and *will* happen again."

"Roe's right. Getting back into the musical would be great, but that's not really why I'm doing this. I don't want someone else to go through this. Maybe we demand some sort of anti-discrimination policy?"

Phoebe types and clicks, squinting her eyes at her screen. "Sunnyside's website has a link to the official school Code of Conduct." We gather around her as she pulls up the link.

"This is all about students," Phoebe says. "Absolutely nothing about teachers."

"At least the dress code policy has been updated," Monroe says. "Small victories?"

"Sexism solved," Phoebe jokes. "Good on that!" She throws Monroe a fist bump.

"I can show a little thigh for the boys." I kick my leg in the air like a Rockette. "They wouldn't be ready!"

"Can we concentrate?" Cris shifts awkwardly.

"Did he really just?" Monroe snipes.

Cris's gaze snaps toward Monroe. "Is there a problem, Roe?"

"*Mon*roe," she corrects, "and yes."

I reach over and put a hand on her arm, but she swats it away. "Come with me." We walk to the living room, and I whisper, "What's your deal?"

"Nothing." Her voice is ice. "Except, why does Cris think he can come in here like he's part of the group after what he did to you? I don't trust him, Carey. I know you said you're over it and that you love him and blah, blah, blah, but neither of you actually talked about what happened, right?" I nod in confirmation. "You've been through enough, and I'll be damned if I'm going to watch you get your heart broken on top of all that."

"I get why you're concerned, but I'm fine," I say. "You don't need to protect me from Cris."

Monroe inhales deeply. "I hope you're right." She raises her eyebrows and turns on her heel to the kitchen.

"We should demand a no-tolerance policy in the Code of Conduct that mandates all teachers respect the identities of their students," Phoebe says. "This way, it's clear this movement goes beyond wanting basic respect from students like Max, and also applies to teachers."

"We can call it the No Jackson Law of Common Human Decency," Cris says, his voice still tight from his passive aggressive battle with Monroe.

Phoebe laughs. "I like that."

"So, we have four goals," Monroe reiterates, running her hands through her freshly bleached platinum-blond hair. She refuses to look at Cris. "How're we gonna accomplish everything?"

"Petitions for Carey and Mr. Kelly," Phoebe says. "Maybe one to get Jackson fired?"

"And then what?" I ask. "What do we do with the petitions if we somehow get enough people to sign them? It doesn't guarantee that anything actually changes. My mom looked into it. It's not common—or easy—for a tenured teacher to be fired."

Ms. Wright peeks her head in. "Sorry to overhear, but coming for coffee. It's not common, but it's not impossible for a tenured teacher to be fired. You have to get on the school board meeting agenda." She pours a fresh mug of coffee.

"How do we do that?" Joey asks.

Phoebe smiles. "It would be really helpful if we knew a parent on the school board, huh? Oh wait, I have that covered."

"Would you do that for us, Ms. Wright?" Cris asks.

"Absolutely," Ms. Wright says. "What can you accomplish by Thursday?"

"That's five days away!" I say.

"Better get to work," Ms. Wright says. "I'll take care of getting your time slot. You'll need a parent advocate though, because students aren't allowed to speak without one anymore, thanks to one Miss Monroe Cooper."

Monroe blushes.

"After Monroe stormed the school board with demands to change the dress code, the board became stricter with the community participation rules so that students—"

"Would be silenced," Phoebe cuts her mom off.

Ms. Wright laughs. "That's the unofficial party line." She digs into a drawer in the built-in desk on the other side of the kitchen and pulls out a thick, bound manuscript. She tosses it onto the counter, and it lands with a thud. *"Officially*, the New York State School Board Association rules decree that it's up to the discretion of the body to allow students to speak. There is no requirement that school boards allow members of the public to speak, and that includes students. The board also has the ability to restrict speech that could create privacy issues, and that includes the discussion of a specific student without a parent advocate for that student. The board is adamant about following proper public forum decorum."

"'Public forum decorum'?" Joey repeats. "Sounds like a shitty Dr. Seuss book."

I nod in agreement. "Decorum is another form of the binary. You're either respectful and quiet or unruly. It's time to shatter that. And Mom will do anything to help."

"Our parents will too," Monroe says.

Joey's brow furrows. "What will a school board meeting do, though?"

"Principal McCauley will be there, as will most of the prominent members of the town. Trust me, you'll make big waves." Ms. Wright takes a sip from her mug. "Parent voices go a long way. And this is about ensuring school grounds are safe, equitable spaces."

"That's good," I say, writing down that talking point for Mom. "What if we get all the signatures we need and rock this meeting, and it still goes ignored?"

"We need to make waves *before* the meeting. *Fast*," Cris says. "Then the school board will have to take us seriously."

"Word is gonna travel fast about the petitions," Monroe says.

"That's not enough." Cris looks to Phoebe. "Phoebe and I were talking. We think the cast needs to boycott the musical."

Phoebe looks to her mom, who gives her a proud smile. "I've been having private conversations with Rachel Diaz, and she said that would get a lot of attention. She has an in with *Broad-wayWorld*, and she thinks one of their writers would do a piece about this if we can pull it off. With her name attached to it, it's pretty much a guarantee."

"We also need social media awareness," I say. "We each have a few hundred followers, and so do most people at Sunnyside, so we can get the story trending locally. Then we need some outlets to pick up our posts on *their* social media."

"Ahem. I have a few thousand followers." Phoebe playfully wags her tongue.

"We also need news exposure," Monroe adds. "And a hashtag."

"Oh, I've thought about this." Cris grabs a piece of a paper and writes out two hashtags: "#SingForEquality" and "#LetCareySing."

"Hmm. Those are *kind of* brilliant," Monroe concedes.

"I don't wanna be a hashtag," I say. "What about '#WeWillNotBeSilenced'?"

"That's good! But it's broad. And every movement needs a face. Your voice is the one that started this," Phoebe says. "There's power in your name. It humanizes the cause."

I know she's right. I have to squash the little voice inside my head that says, *You're not important enough to lead them.* Ms. Wright nods her head and sips from her mug.

"You're right." I take a deep breath. "Let's do it."

"Good. Then we'll put the hashtags on top of the petition papers and ask everyone who signs to post and tweet their support for Carey."

"Is that it?" Joey asks.

"Hell, no! We have to protest. Mom told me the school board can't fire Jackson or reinstate Mr. Kelly or Carey right away, if at all, unless we make a lot of noise," Phoebe says. "That's why, when we get back to school on Monday, we have to hit the ground running. Every single student at Sunnyside has to know that we're planning to protest."

"Even the assbags who laughed at Max's video of me?" I ask.

Everyone goes silent.

Monroe puts her hand on my arm. "Carey, you've been absent, so you wouldn't know, but nobody is laughing. Maybe a few people, but they suck. Most are pretty angry at whoever did it."

"*Max,*" I correct.

"Right," Monroe says. "Except we have no proof it was him. Beyond him laughing about it and not outright denying it was him. Plausible deniability."

Then Phoebe pipes in. "Don't worry, I got people on that."

"People?" Cris asks.

Ms. Wright laughs. "My daughter has her ways. And with all of you working together like some fierce fivesome, I'd be scared if I were Principal McCauley. Don't tell her I said that, though."

"The Fierce Five?" Joey says. "I like that."

I'm only slightly comforted by these new revelations. I doubt anyone can find proof that connects Max to the video. But that's not why we're here.

"When do we plan to protest?" I ask. "After the school board meeting. Like, Friday?"

"No . . ." Joey thinks out loud. "It should be the day *of* the school board meeting. Friday, too, if they don't meet our demands."

"Maximum exposure *and* leverage," Phoebe agrees. "So, we have the petitions, the cast walkout—which Cris and I will make happen Tuesday—the protest and school board meeting on Thursday, and then a contingent protest on Friday, if our demands aren't met. And we'll start fires on social media."

"How're we getting signatures before Thursday's meeting?" I ask.

"There's a drug awareness assembly on Monday," Phoebe says. "It'll be perfect. The whole school will be there. If the five of us break up, we can cover most of the student body before it begins. But Carey, you shouldn't have the petition with your name on it. For PR reasons. We'll handle that one."

PR reasons? Where did Phoebe Wright come from? She's such a damn boss.

"This is so awesome!" Joey jumps to her feet, punching the air.

Once we figure out the logistics, dates, and locations, we get to work making signs for the school board meeting and protest. Monroe designs and colors a sign with various queer flags—pride, genderqueer, transgender, bisexual, lesbian—and "#Sing-ForEquality" in bold black letters. I use glue and glitter to craft my sign, Fabulous Genderqueer Diva! Joey's has the words Rise

Up! in rainbow letters, but Phoebe makes my favorite sign. It's simple, but so effective: Respect My Existence or Expect My Resistance. We also make a few with only the hashtags on them, and a couple of full-color ones that say, Fire Jackson and Reinstate Kelly.

Before Cris leaves for his Carnegie Hall practice, he makes two signs that say, If God Hates LGBTQ PPL, Why Are We So Cute? and Don't Erase My (Bi)dentity with "#LetCareySing" on the bottom. When he's done, I follow him to the door.

He's wrapping a scarf around his neck when he says, "We did good today."

"Thanks for everything." I start to lean in for a hug but remember our awkwardness from earlier. It yanks me back by an invisible rope. At the same time, he tries to react and reach out for a hug, but neither of us seems to be able to meet in the middle. This is *so* fucking weird. My shoulders slump. "Um, good luck at rehearsal. Or practice. Whatever. Tell Coach I said hey."

Tell Coach I said hey? I hate myself. Why is this so hard?

"You should stop by the studio sometime," Cris says.

I perk up. That sounds like a clear invitation. Is this him leaving the door open to an us? Maybe I've been reading him wrong, and he *is* still interested in me?

Then he says, "He'd love to see you. Maybe you can come back for lessons."

My heart drops. Coach wants me there, not him.

"I told him what's been going on, and he said no matter what happens, the one thing they can't take away from you is your voice. He'd be proud."

Cris leaves, but his words linger.

They can't take my voice from me. It reminds me of Mariah's self-appointed theme song, "Can't Take That Away" from her 1999 album *Rainbow*. She wrote it during a contentious battle with her record label, who was working to undermine her success. She knew that, no matter what anyone tried to do to her or say about her, there was something beautiful and resilient inside her that nobody could take.

The words I wrote for "I'm Ready," about how no one can take away my ability to sing, flood me. I can't believe I didn't see the parallels before. When Mr. Jackson told me my creative short story for class was inappropriate, tried to separate me and Cris at lunch, or got me removed from the musical, I let him. Every time Max McKagan tried to publicly shame me, I let him burrow inside my head and make me feel like I didn't matter. For a long time, I allowed them to take pieces of me. Little by little.

I'm stronger than that. I have to be.

Back in the kitchen, I take a piece of blank poster board and write, My Voice? #CantTakeThatAwayFromMe.

I step back and survey my work, my friends' work.

The Fierce Five. We *are* fierce.

I hear Grams's voice: "Give 'em hell, kid."

Though I'm scared, I'm not afraid.

I'm ready.

TRACK 26

THEY/THEM/THEIR

Phase one is underway minutes before the drug awareness assembly begins. I haven't been in the auditorium since getting booted from the musical; it feels like I'm trespassing.

That only energizes me.

Phoebe hands out clipboards with pens tied to them with double-knotted rainbow strings. "Remember the script we agreed on last night." She hands out small index cards. "In case you forget, Carey wrote out each one."

"How're we gonna tackle this space?" Cris asks.

Monroe leans into Joey's ear, and I hear her mumble, "He's good at juggling more than one person at a time."

Joey rams her elbow into her sister's ribs, and Monroe gasps.

"There are two orchestra sections, which are the largest. I'm thinking one of us on each of those, with one person working the center aisle to help," Phoebe says. "And two people in the mezzanine sections."

Joey and I volunteer to be in the back, so Phoebe, Cris, and Monroe tackle the front. We get into position and sweat beads my brow. Then, like a dam breaking, students flood in through all the doors. Phoebe wastes no time hitting up the incoming students, who crowd around her to hear what she's saying.

Here goes nothing.

"Hi, I'm Carey Parker, and I am petitioning to get Mr. Kelly reinstated as spring musical director. Mr. Kelly was the victim of a homophobic tirade by Mr. Jackson and has since been unceremoniously kicked out as director due to a discriminatory campaign by Mr. Jackson and Principal McCauley. Please sign our petition, which will be presented to Principal McCauley, the superintendent of the Sunnyside school system, and the school board this Thursday. Show the school that you're against discrimination and stand with equality."

Student after student signs; there are a few who decline because they don't want their name out there. I find it super difficult not to roll my eyes so hard they'll pop out of their sockets because it's the same students who post nearly naked selfies on Instagram, yet are afraid to sign a petition for a good cause. Right.

Monroe delivers her script across aisles like a sermon. People clamor to sign her clipboard.

Mr. Jackson beelines toward her.

"Roe, heads up!" Cris shouts.

Monroe instinctively grabs the clipboard before Mr. Jackson can reach it and books it to the other side of the room.

I have almost two full pages of signatures as everyone settles into their seats. I work on a collection of nearby teachers; every single one signs the one for Mr. Kelly, but none touch Mr. Jackson's, politely declining with fear in their eyes.

As the assembly starts, the Fierce Five sneak out and meet in the girl's bathroom.

Monroe and Joey do tallies for all the petitions.

"Grand total: A pretty dismal 97 signatures for 'Fire Mr. Jackson,' a pretty awesome 213 signatures for 'Reinstate Mr. Kelly,' and a whopping 250 signatures for '#LetCareySing,'" Monroe exclaims, holding up the loose pages and waving them around like a trophy. "Not bad for what, like, ten minutes worth of work?"

I wipe sweat from my brow. Ten minutes? Felt more like a very frantic five seconds.

"It's a good start," Phoebe says. "But we have work to do before Thursday."

"A lot of people wouldn't sign the Jackson petition," Monroe says. "His students are afraid he'll find out and retaliate."

"Can't say I'm surprised," Cris says. "When I had him for class, I complained because when we were studying 'The Yellow Wallpaper,' he said women write with less potency than men."

Phoebe clenches her fists. "We *all* know what he meant by that."

"I went to the douche who was principal before McCauley, and he was like, 'Duly noted,' and that was it. Jackson found out I complained, and he made my life miserable. He tore up an essay I had to handwrite because my laptop died and my mom . . ." Pain is etched on the skin around Cris's eyes.

I grab his hand, but he wriggles free. I change the subject. "We need at least two-thirds of the student body to sign each petition, right? I did the math. There are five hundred forty-three students in school, so we need at least three hundred sixty-four students on each petition. And that's just for them to take us seriously."

"Good thing we're going to get more than that on each petition." Cris flashes a confident smile and my chest aches.

"This is a good start, though, right?" Joey asks.

"Absolutely!" Phoebe says. "I'm gonna confirm with Rachel that her *BroadwayWorld* reporter friend is coming tomorrow for the boycott."

"That's definitely happening?" I ask.

Cris nods in affirmation. "I got the ball rolling."

"We need to keep getting signatures." Monroe passes out more sheets to everyone. "Everywhere you go in this godforsaken place, get a signature."

"Aye, aye, Captain." I salute her.

Joey stuffs hers in her backpack. "I'll bring 'em to basketball practice. The boys' team is in the gym at the same time, so I should be able to lock them down." She turns to Monroe. "We have to go."

"Go?" I ask.

"I have my interview with FIT today, remember?" Monroe runs her fingers through another new dye job, a brilliant swirl of purples, greens, and blues that looks like a photograph of a distant galaxy.

"I wish I could be there to cheer you on," I say.

"I'm putting on a fashion show inspired by you. You *will* be there," Monroe says.

The four of us crowd around her and hug her tightly, wishing her luck.

With a salute, she marches away with confidence. Right

before she rounds the corner, she turns and does a running man dance.

She's going to crush it.

In every class, I pass around the petitions. Some teachers are hesitant when they find out what I'm doing, but most tell me to make it quick. I garner a few more signatures here and there, but not nearly enough to make a dent. As I walk into Mr. Kelly's class, everyone is chattering so loudly it feels like being inside an aviary.

Phoebe is staring at her phone, and when she notices me, she beckons me over. "Carey, you *have* to see this!" She turns the screen around and then slowly swivels it back toward her, my eyes following it like a lure until we're shoulder to shoulder. She presses pause on a dark video that I can't quite make out. "So, you know how the weekly *Sunnyside Up! Report* is sent to the whole school every Tuesday morning? Someone sent it out early. Like, way early. And look at the headline story." She swipes out of the video, into her email, and points to the screen.

Is Sunnyside High Covering Up for Homophobic Teachers?

"Oh shit," I gasp. I need to resubscribe so I get these alerts.

"It's a piece written by an anonymous student who must be in the musical, because they were there when Mr. Jackson went off. They talk about what happened to you and Cris, and it mentions us canvasing at today's assembly. There are pictures of us with the clipboards in the crowd. And look! There's a video." She presses play. The clip starts in the middle of "As Long As You're Mine" and ends long after the cheers, just as Mr. Jackson goes off. "Sucks that it cuts off there, right?"

"Hold on," I say, replaying the video clip. "Look. When Mr. Jackson starts talking, it swivels around to him, so you kind of see his misshapen body. It's a sliver, a ghost, but it's there. I bet there's more to the video."

I look up to find Blanca Rodriguez staring at us, but she turns away when our gazes meet.

Phoebe plays it again and again. "Who was sitting on that side of the auditorium?"

"Whoever wrote the article, obviously."

Phoebe glares at me with a thank-you-Captain-Obvious. "Who's on the newspaper and does musicals?"

Before I can answer, Mr. Kelly ambles into the room and everyone goes silent. I slink back to my desk and wait with the rest of the class for him to begin. But he doesn't. Not right away. His face is sunken and unshaven, like he hasn't slept in days.

"Turn to page 87 in your textbook and read the poem by Warsan Shire. Then answer the critical thinking questions. If you finish early, sit quietly."

Phoebe raises her hand. "Mr. Kelly, I'm supposed to present my project today."

"Not today, Ms. Wright."

"We're not studying poetry, Kelly," Max says, launching a stink bomb of pizza breath down my neck.

Mr. Kelly doesn't bother to look up. "Then do homework for another class. Or leave."

"So, I can . . . walk out?" Max asks, rising to his feet.

"Be my guest," Mr. Kelly says. "But if you do, don't think you're coming back. You'll be graded accordingly." I've never heard such irritation from Mr. Kelly before. Max sits slowly and nobody makes a sound until the bell rings. Not even Max has the gall to push Mr. Kelly further than normal today.

Phoebe and I wait for everyone to leave the classroom after the bell before approaching his desk. When he looks up, Mr. Kelly shakes his head. "It's been a long year," he says.

"It's the second week of January," I say.

"I'm guessing you saw the *Sunnyside Up! Report*," Phoebe says.

He nods, unfazed. "Principal McCauley and Mr. Jackson are not happy about what you're up to."

"Do you want us to stop?" I ask.

He raises his eyebrows. "Did I say that? What they're doing to me has nothing to do with what you are doing to call them out. I'm proud of you. I can't say much, but you have people talking. Important people." He stands up and softly pushes his classroom door so that it's almost closed, but still slightly ajar.

"Ms. Wright," he continues. "A few weeks ago you asked why we were still talking about Holden Caulfield's hat. Perhaps it's those moments when we lose our quote-unquote security blankets and see the world for what it truly is that dictates what we're made of. Do we choose to take the world at face value, accept the phoniness? Or do we push back, try to create a better reality? Holden is one very narrow, very angsty teenage view of the world, which holds some truth but is also very pessimistic. He made up his mind about the world at sixteen. That's the tragedy of Holden Caulfield." He folds his hands, allowing his lesson to sink in.

Phoebe makes a *hmm* sound and takes out her phone, opens her notes app, and jots something down I can't read. "Can I write about this? Extra credit?"

Typical Phoebe.

Mr. Kelly laughs and nods, and as he does, something clicks for me.

"Holden may have given his hat to his sister to protect her, but there's no way to truly shield someone from the horrors that wait beyond the carousel," I say.

Mr. Kelly's eyes are heavy with sadness. "That's the hardest part of my job. To know that students come and go and I can't protect them beyond my classroom."

I touch my green-and-purple bracelet.

I tell him he can relax, that he's done his job. He's protected me. *All* of us.

It's time for us to push back. To create that better reality.

——————

Mom pulls up in front of Sunnyside and honks her horn in rapid-fire succession. She waves me over hurriedly.

"Mom, relax," I say, hopping into the passenger seat.

"You looked cold, waiting out there like that. Look at your nose. So red!" She places her warm palm on my frigid face.

"Can you just drive?" I slink down low enough that nobody can see me. Thankfully it's late. Pretty much nobody is left at school except people without their own cars, like me. With Monroe and Joey in the city for Monroe's FIT interview, I have to fend for myself. It's strange for Mom to pick me up from school, but after Grams died, she vowed to scale back work to spend more time with me.

"So, guess who I was on the phone with?" She smirks like she can't wait for me to figure out her secret. I have a gut feeling it's Monroe and Joey's mom.

"Did she get in?" My heart beats a little faster. "She got in, didn't she? Hold on, let me check my phone." I yank my phone out of my backpack and see seven texts from Monroe, all sent a couple of minutes ago:

MONROE: Hello, hi, hey, guess what?
MONROE: HELLOOOOOOO GUESS WHAT????
MONROE: I
MONROE: GOT
MONROE: INTO
MONROE: WAIT FOR IT . . .
MONROE: FIT, BITCH!
MONROE: ON THE SPOT ACCEPTANCE. I AM THAT GOOD.

"SHE GOT IN!" I shout, clutching my phone to my chest.

We both scream until the volume inside the car is too much for either of us. I swipe until I find the perfect song on my phone: Mariah's "Fantasy." It's our go-to for every celebratory moment. We sing along, full-throated, Mom attempting to hit the high notes and failing. She's no Grams.

Halfway through, I lower the volume. "I want to do

something for her. She deserves a celebration tonight." After everything Monroe has done for me, it's the least I can do.

"They'll probably be home in an hour. What did you have in mind?" Mom asks.

"An hour?" I brainstorm with Mom. An hour is enough time to order food from Monroe's favorite vegetarian restaurant on Main Street, pick it up, and get to the Coopers' house. Since they never lock their side door, we'll be able to get inside. There's even a pharmacy next to the restaurant that sells balloons. I'll enlist Phoebe to grab Monroe's manager-nemesis-turned-pseudo-maybe-boyfriend Thom from Exile, too. Phoebe is really convincing, so there's no way he can say no to her. "Think we can do it?"

Mom takes a deep breath. "You're asking for a lot these days. First you want me to be your parent advocate at the board meeting, now this . . ." She smirks. "I'm kidding, baby. Of course we can do this."

"Oh, she's full of jokes since Grams died," I deadpan.

"Better than tears." She's not wrong.

With no time to spare, we set out on our mission.

There are exactly five minutes between Mom and I, Phoebe, and Thom arriving at the Coopers' and their car pulling into the driveway. My feet tap-tap-tap against their kitchen floor so rapidly that I'm sure I could take flight.

The second the doorknob turns and we see Monroe, we yell, "Congratulations!" I press play on my Beats Pill. Monroe's favorite song, Lady Gaga's "Marry the Night" starts playing, and Monroe starts scream-singing, her eyes beaming. I race toward her, and she flies into my arms. Together, we do Monroe's version of dancing: jumping up and down, limbs flailing. Joey does her signature move, the shopping cart. I can't imagine what this looks like to Phoebe, who shakes her head at us, and Thom, who looks slightly horrified.

Soon, Mom and the Cooper parents are dancing with us, so we drag Phoebe and Thom onto the kitchen floor and turn up the volume as high as it can possibly go.

It feels *so* good to know that, despite all the horrible shit, there can still be moments of pure joy.

TRACK 27

THEY/THEM/THEIR

PHOEBE: Meet me in the library. I solved the mystery of
the video.

Phoebe is with Monroe, Joey, and Cris, sitting around a desktop computer in the library. A copy of last year's yearbook sits open in front of them. Phoebe waves me over. The *Sunnyside Up! Report* is open in multiple tabs on the browser.

"After I left the Coopers' last night, I did some digging," Phoebe begins.

"You were all together last night?" Cris asks.

This is awkward. I didn't invite him because Monroe isn't Cris's biggest fan. It would've been odd if he were there.

"Cool. Thanks for the invite," Cris adds coldly when nobody responds.

"My fault," Monroe says. "It was a small family thing."

Cris looks to Phoebe, and he opens his mouth, probably to ask why Phoebe was included, but decides not to say anything. I avoid his gaze.

"Anyway," Phoebe continues, pointing to the screen. "I bet our mystery writer is behind some of the really controversial posts because they always write under Anonymous." She flips through the browser and points to some of the headlines: **Sunnyside's Undocumented Families Being Unfairly Targeted**; **Sunnyside's Dress Code Is Hypocrisy at Its Finest**; and **Sunnyside High Cancels Secret Visit from Planned Parenthood After Parent Complaints: Here's What You Need to Know**.

"This person is a national treasure and should be protected at all costs," Monroe says.

"I'm pretty sure it's Blanca Rodriguez," Phoebe says. "She's the only one who is on both the newspaper and in the musical. *And* she's credited as a head staff writer but has zero bylines. And since we weren't rehearsing any scenes with her character the day Jackson went atomic, she would have been in the audience."

"Woah," I say.

"That's not all. Guess who is the faculty advisor of the newspaper?" Phoebe says.

Monroe smirks because she's clearly figured it out already.

"Who?" Cris asks.

"Mr. Kelly," Phoebe answers. "Which means he gives the go-ahead for any article that gets sent out in the weekly report."

Mind: blown. No wonder he's looking rough. He's working to disrupt the corrupted system from within.

"Do you think Blanca will be open to talking to us?" Joey asks.

"Only to Carey." Phoebe passes around a text message chain between her and Blanca. "I messaged her this morning. She wouldn't say if there was more to the video, though."

Cris looks at me, urging me to accept.

"Text her and tell her I want to talk," I say.

While we wait for her response, Phoebe continues. "That's not all. Look what Blanca sent me." She maximizes a different tab. "Up until last year, the *Sunnyside Upended!* had been called 'Hallway Gossip' and was part of the newspaper."

"I remember that," Joey says, and I look sideways at her. "What? It was entertaining!"

Phoebe shows us an article from the *Sunnyside Up! Report* dated a year ago: *Sunnyside Up*'s 'Hallway Gossip' Shut Down. "The article says the original 'Hallway Gossip' section could no longer independently corroborate unsubstantiated rumors. It got out of hand when a series of mean-spirited tips, specifically targeting junior girls, were accidentally sent out. The administration responded by immediately pulling 'Hallway Gossip.'"

Knowing Mr. Kelly, I bet he feels like he *has* to shoulder all the blame for the creation of *Upended!* given how it emerged from the death of a section in his school paper. Fuck.

"I was one of the girls," Joey mutters, and anger at Max hits the back of my throat like bile, remembering what Joey told me about Max's promposal last year.

Phoebe continues, "*Sunnyside Upended!* launched after prom last year, supposedly unaffiliated with Sunnyside High, yet it's literally only gossip about Sunnysiders." Excitement brightens her face as she connects the dots for us. "Guess who used to work for the newspaper but quit after 'Hallway Gossip' was discontinued?"

I don't have to think about it. "Max McKagan."

"*Ding-ding-ding,*" Phoebe says. "I don't have any proof that he's behind *Sunnyside Upended!* or that he's the one who sent out that video of you at the mall, Carey. And I bet he won't post anything about you for a while to keep a low profile after that. Still, the coincidences are too much to be coincidences."

Joey grunts. "Of course, he's behind it all. The horrible rumors directed at junior girls on 'Hallway Gossip' were posted after I turned down his promposal." She slams her fist on the desk and a librarian shushes her.

My body slumps down in my chair. "Why come after me? What did I ever do to him?"

"Does his motivation matter?" Monroe asks.

I want to say no, but the question nags at me.

Phoebe's phone buzzes. "It's Blanca. She said that you two have the same lunch period. Where's a good place to meet?"

"Mr. Kelly's room," I relay. "That's the safest place I know."

The bell for homeroom rings. Phoebe assures us everything is set for the walkout during musical rehearsal, and that Rachel was able to get her reporter friend to take the train up from the city for the exclusive. Our plans are coming together, but we don't get far. Over the loudspeaker, Principal McCauley announces, "Carey Parker, Phoebe Wright, Cris Kostas, Monroe Cooper, and Joanna Cooper, please report to the principal's office *immediately.*"

Fuck. They're on to us.

TRACK 28

THEY/THEM/THEIR

One by one, we're called into Principal McCauley's office.

Joey's first, and she's practically sweating through her shirt.

"What're they doing?" Cris asks.

"Divide and conquer. Clearly McCauley's not happy with what we're doing." I fill them in on what Mr. Kelly told Phoebe and me yesterday.

"They're trying to split us up," Phoebe whispers. "She's gonna try to threaten us so that we stop. We have to stick together." She looks around to make sure McCauley's secretary isn't looking. When the coast is clear, she tiptoes over and presses her ear to the solid wood door.

"Anything?" Monroe asks, but Phoebe shushes her.

After a few moments of straining, Phoebe says, "Nothing. Hope Joey doesn't cave."

"Ugh," Monroe sighs. "I love my sister, but she hates being cornered."

The door opens and a shook Joey, lips tight and bone white, walks over and slumps down in the seat next to me.

"Ms. Wright, come in." Principal McCauley closes the door behind them.

"What happened, Jo?" Monroe asks.

"She threatened to suspend me." Joey shakes her head. "She wanted to know who came up with the idea for the petitions. She knows about the school board meeting." Her head droops to the floor. "She said that if I didn't cooperate, my division one basketball days would be over."

I sigh. Joey shouldn't risk everything she's worked for, for me, for this cause. Joey has been training to play in the WNBA. She's always at a practice, a tournament, sleepaway training camp, or with a professional trainer. She made the high school varsity team in eighth grade. She can't risk all that work. I won't let her.

"They can't do that," Cris says. "It's, like, our right to free speech."

Monroe side-eyes him. "The administration can do whatever they want. We have no rights. We're wards of the school system. And our parents give their consent by sending us here."

"*American Horror Story: The Corrupt School System*," Cris says.

My fists clench-unclench-clench-unclench. I need to squash the voices in my head telling me we're all fucked. I resist the urge to tell Joey that Mariah Carey went to beauty school before she was famous. She racked up five hundred hours before she was discovered and became the biggest-selling female artist of all time. So maybe there's still hope for us. But I'm not sure if a panic-induced Mariah joke would help.

Joey leans over and touches my arm. "I said any school that

doesn't want me because I stand up for what I believe in is [
school I want to play for."

"You did?" I'm ashamed for doubting her.

"There are more important things than basketball."
looks to Cris and Monroe. "We have to stick together or
Besides, I signed a morality clause when I committed, and
isn't sticking to my morals, I don't know what is."

"I'm proud of you, sis." Monroe reaches across my la
grabs her knee. "She'll probably pull the same shit wi
and FIT."

"Gah," Cris says, exasperated, knocking the back of hi
against the wall.

McCauley saves me for last.

As I walk into her office, she graciously offers me
before taking one herself.

"I'll stand." I won't give in to her fear tactics. "Pri
McCauley, you're not gonna get me to turn on my friends.
all due respect, it's pretty despicable that you're trying to p
a known bigot by silencing us when we're speaking up a
clear injustice." I pause to gather my thoughts and center n
"Can I ask you a question?"

"Go ahead," she says.

My palms are sweaty. "Do you know what it's like to
Do you know what it's like to cry yourself to sleep becaus
don't fit into the boxes everyone else seems to fill so nicely?
you ever thought about . . ." I pause as the corners of m
begin to burn and I quickly wipe away a stray tear. "About ;
ways you could take your own life because you feel like
wrong, like God or whoever you believe in made a mistak

you know what that's like? There could be a whole school of good, supportive people, but it only takes *one* Max or *one* Mr. Jackson to harness all your fears and make you feel unsafe. It doesn't matter how much quote-unquote progress we've made when there are still real threats to queer people. We are students in this school, your school, who you're supposed to protect. Instead, Mr. Jackson, who says the most hurtful things, is the one you're protecting. What is your job, Principal McCauley? To give Mr. Jackson a platform, or to listen to your students?" There's more that I want to say, but my entire body is shaking.

Principal McCauley is quiet for a moment. "Are you finished?"

I nod, but my mouth says, "Mr. Kelly is the best thing that's happened to this school. He's saved me. Our petitions are as much for him as they are for me and students like me who are too afraid to speak out. Have you ever spoken out against something you knew was wrong? I'm human, just like you, just like Mr. Jackson. I should be treated like one."

Principal McCauley stands and walks to the door. She summons the rest of the Fierce Five inside, then shuts the door again. She walks around the room with her hands behind her back. "Carey gave me a lot to think about. The superintendent is not happy with what is transpiring, between your rallying students at the assembly and that stunt in the school newspaper. And I have to show that I'm holding people accountable for their actions." She takes a deep breath. "So, you all will be suspended for the rest of today, and tomorrow."

"You're taking *us* out of school? Interrupting *our* learning?" Monroe balks.

"My hands are tied. It's not up to me, unfortunately." Principal McCauley's gaze is stoic, but her lip twitches. She doesn't want to do this. "You can come back to school Thursday, so that you're able to attend the school board meeting. You'll also need at least one other adult to represent you at the school board meeting, besides Ms. Wright's mother. Though I'm guessing by Ms. Parker's incessant calls, it'll be her." A hint of a smile creeps across her lips. She walks to the window overlooking the courtyard. The dry, dead grass is brown, each blade frosted over with icy dew. "I suspect the entire school is gossiping about why you've been called to my office. Perfect fodder for the spread of discord, if you have the right . . ." She pauses. "*Opportunity*. I may have forgotten something in my car. Perhaps I'll take a walk *outside*, so I'm not able to observe any potential disruptions in the hallway." She opens the door to her office and ushers everyone out but me. "For the record, Carey, you're much braver than you realize." She grabs her coat and walks toward the exit.

"What did she mean by that? If we have the right *opportunity*? Why do we care that she's going outside?" Joey says, looking down the empty hallway.

"She was telling us to make noise," I say, extending my elbows for Phoebe and Cris to link arms with me. "Follow my lead." Joey links arms with Phoebe, and Monroe links up to Joey. Together we stand across the hall in solidarity. I close my eyes and yell, "WE WILL NOT BE SILENCED!"

The Fierce Five, in locked arms and step, start down the hallway, chanting until students peek their heads out of classroom doors, many recording us on their phones. Some teachers, visibly irritated by the disturbance, try to shut their doors, but that doesn't stop the students inside from watching from the windows. Other teachers, the cool ones like Mr. Kelly, salute us with head nods and proud smiles.

I spot Blanca Rodriguez and motion for her to join us. She squeezes past her math teacher to get in front of us and records us, making sure to pan to all sides to take in the students swelling in doorways. As we march out of Sunnyside High, our chants fill the air:

"LET CAREY SING!"

"LET CAREY SING!"

"LET CAREY SING!"

TRACK 29

THEY/THEM/THEIR

"That was awesome!" Blanca Rodriguez ties her long, shiny black hair into a loose ponytail that falls to the middle of her back. "I streamed that to TikTok and posted to Twitter and views are spiking!"

Thom brings her over a small white plate with a warm banana and pineapple macadamia nut muffin. Monroe tells him to pull up a chair. He does. Exile is dead this early, which works out because Cris declares it our de facto headquarters.

"That's incredible." I'm a bit nervous and shaky, but quickly add, "Thanks! We wouldn't have gotten as much traction if you hadn't written that article," hoping to get Blanca to admit it out loud.

Monroe, Joey, and Cris lean in to hear her answer.

She licks her dry lips and reaches into her pocket for some ChapStick. "Someone had to do something. Mr. Jackson has gotten away with such horrible stuff."

"So, it *is* you who writes all those articles?" I ask.

She puckers. Then shrugs demurely in confirmation.

"How'd you get Mr. Kelly to agree to run that?" Phoebe asks.

"Easy. If it's anonymous and the issue goes out earlier than it's supposed to, he can claim he didn't see it," she explains. "I went to him with a story when they initially booted him as director. He said no. It wasn't until he found out what you guys were up to that he agreed. I swear, I wasn't looking for a story when I started recording you at rehearsal. Honestly, I was so moved by your voices, but then Jackson started going off . . ."

She pulls out her phone and swipes to the full video, handing it to us to play.

"This'll be enough to get Principal McCauley to believe us," Joey says. "Right?"

"It's not *only* her we need to convince," I say.

Cris coughs and rolls his eyes. "Everyone knows Jackson's a homophobic dick, but nobody has evidence he can't refute. *This* is our smoking gun."

Monroe side-eyes Cris. "Do you have to use a gun metaphor?"

"Leave him alone, Roe," I say.

Monroe gives me a witchy death glare. She forces a fake smile at Cris.

"I don't need you to stick up for me," Cris mumbles, before turning to Monroe. "What *is* your problem with me, by the way?"

"Besides"—she motions her hands in circles in front of Cris—"you in general?"

"Holy tension, Batman," Blanca says. "A divided house cannot win."

"She's right," I say. "Please."

"Tell *your* friend to lay off," Cris demands.

Monroe is a rattlesnake ready to strike its prey. Nobody moves or breathes. I can't defend Monroe without alienating Cris, and if I defend Cris, I risk a fight with Monroe. There is no easy out.

Monroe purses her lips. "*I'm* fine."

Cris backs away and crosses his arms. "I'm *fine*." He gnaws at his lip, clearly *not* fine.

"Can we get back to the plan?" Phoebe asks.

"Yeah, one sec," I say. "Cris, I want to show you something." I nod toward the record stacks in the shop. He reluctantly stands.

Phoebe's eyes go wide at my departure. "Okay, we'll continue without you."

"Be right back!" I say.

"Blanca, I heard you know someone into hacking . . ." Phoebe's voice fades as Cris and I enter into the record shop.

Cris rocks back on his heels. "I don't know what her problem is." His lip quivers.

"It's me," I say. "She's territorial. A dog with a bone, and all that." I chuckle to lighten the mood.

It doesn't work.

He eyes the stacks. Sitting on top of the nearest pile is a vinyl of Sam Smith's album *Love Goes*, a masterclass in queer heartbreak. His fingers graze the plastic covering. "You wanna know why I came up to you that day?" he asks. "It wasn't because I was some big Sam Smith fan. I barely knew any of their music. I approached you because when I'd see you around school or town or at Coach's studio, I would feel less alone, less . . . lost. *Felt*."

I want to tell him that I'm right here, I understand, but the air around us is dense with everything unsaid between us. And with everything going on, it feels like the wrong time to tell him that I love him, that when he's around, I never feel panicky because he's music to me. Even if I could somehow say exactly what I feel, he doesn't give me the chance.

"I believe in what we're doing, Carey, and I'll fight till the end. But *this* is too hard. I'm tired of people leaving me behind." He takes off toward the café before I can tell him that I'll never leave him.

I sigh and follow him, my feet dragging my heavy heart.

Blanca says, "I'm in" to whatever Phoebe requested.

"Perfect," she says, giving me a look that says, *I'll fill you in later.* I'm too distracted by Cris to pry. "Back to the task at hand."

"How else can I help?" Blanca asks. "I had Jackson in ninth grade. I asked him if we were reading any Latinx writers, and he laughed in my face and told me their work is not traditional literary canon."

"What does that mean?" I ask.

Monroe purses her lips. "Traditional literary canon equals white and male."

Phoebe nods, impressed with Monroe.

"Jackson is awful. I want to help get him out. This school needs a lesson in respecting identity," Blanca says. "I'm sending you all a copy of the full video. Get this out on social media *today.*" She grabs Phoebe's laptop and searches the hashtag "#LetCareySing" and spins the screen around for us to see. "Look, half the school is already tweeting about the march using the hashtag."

"Holy shit." I point at the laptop to candids of our march. "Look at the pictures!"

Cris sits up straighter but avoids looking at me. "If we spam our feeds with the real video, we might actually gain some attention."

"Exactly," Blanca says. "I'm going to lead the walkout from the musical today after school, since you've all been suspended." She glances at the time on her phone. "I have to get back to school before they notice I've cut and I'm barred from rehearsal. But don't worry, I'm gonna FaceTime Phoebe so you can watch it live."

"We need someone to stream the walkout, too," Monroe adds.

"I'm on it," Blanca says, and Monroe looks mildly impressed.

Phoebe places both arms on the table like she's commander in chief of an army. "Can you bring the cast back here after the walkout?"

"Absolutely." Blanca slings her bag over her shoulder. "Wish me luck!"

"Mr. Kelly will be here. Tell them that," I blurt without thinking about how I could possibly make that happen.

When Blanca leaves, they all look to me, confused.

How do I reach out to him now that I'm suspended? "I'll figure it out."

The next few hours are spent furiously tweeting about systemic discrimination, and the protection afforded to teachers who hide behind tenure. Each of us composes our own threaded story, making sure to include all the hashtags and attach the full video of Mr. Jackson's rant to every tweet. One by one, our classmates start retweeting and engaging with us, and before we know it, more and more random people join in. Some people quote-tweet me *and* tag various celebrities and activists.

Phoebe, Cris, and Joey work on cold-calling local newspapers as I watch my notifications triple in numbers. I do a quick search for Mr. Kelly and find his profile on Twitter. He barely posts, but since I have no idea where he lives, the only option I have is to send him a direct message and hope he sees it.

@CareyParker: Hi Mr. Kelly! I'm sure you've heard I was suspended today with my friends. We're working on getting our story out there. We were able to get a full video of Jackson's tirade. It's getting good exposure. I probably should have told you this sooner, but I want to thank you for everything you've taught me. You were there for me and understood things about me that nobody else did. You're the definition of a great teacher. And we still have so much more left to learn from you. Don't give up. Phoebe, Cris, Monroe, Joey, and I are holding a pre-protest meeting at Exile Records Café today after school. Please come. We'd love to see you.

Monroe calls me over to the record shop once I'm done. "What was that about earlier?"

"What?" I ask.

"Taking Cris's side over mine." She folds her hands in front of her chest. "Are you two together again?" This isn't playful Monroe. This is impatient Monroe, which always makes me slightly uneasy because it means her volcanic temper can erupt any second.

"No. I—"

"He's not right for you. There's something about him I'm

not buying. His whole wounded-musician-who-used-to-date-Max's-sister thing. I don't trust him." She's immovable. "He lied to you. That's not okay in my book. And I don't know why you can't see that."

She's gone all mama bear. Except I'm not her cub, and I don't need her protection. "Cris made a stupid mistake and lied by omission. Yes, it was hurtful. But I never gave him the chance to explain, either. That's my fault. Roe, I really fucked things up with him." I try to explain it, but I'm walking a tightrope between my sisterhood with Monroe and the potential relationship I could have with Cris, and I don't like it. So I show her the video of him singing Mariah's "8th Grade," hoping she sees the Cris I see. When it's done, I add, "He was probably scared to tell me about his connection to Max."

"Do you know that?" she asks. "I'm watching out for you."

A wave of anger rushes over me, and I can't control my tongue. "I don't need you to." I glance over at her flannel-clad make-out buddy behind the register, and he waves awkwardly, so I wave back, but it reads like a passive-aggressive effort. "You're dating your boss. Because that's a healthy decision. I don't get involved with your love life, stay out of mine."

"Right. Excuse me while I do just that." She storms over to Thom, slides next to him, and wraps an arm around his waist.

Joey comes up behind me. "What the hell was that?"

I methodically massage my temples. "Doing what I do best. Making a mess."

TRACK 30
THEY/THEM/THEIR

"Musical rehearsals should be starting in three, two, one . . ." I stare at my phone as the digital clock turns from 3:59 p.m. to 4:00 p.m., bracing myself on a café table.

Minutes later, Blanca FaceTimes us from the auditorium. She's standing next to Rachel, who waves excitedly like a mom.

"The cast is primed and ready to go, as soon as Jackson gets here," Blanca says.

Phoebe shakes her head. "He's always late."

"Because he doesn't care," Cris adds.

Rachel pops her head back into the frame. "So, you know, my friend, the reporter from *BroadwayWorld*, is here. He's interviewing some of the cast members. Blanca already gave him the gist of the story and sent him a link to the anonymous"—she offers a thumbs-up—"*Sunnyside Up!* article."

"I gave him a great quote," Blanca shares.

"I'll be filming everything," Rachel adds. "I'm not an employee here, so they can't fire me!" She's a true ride-or-die for Mr. Kelly.

"Oh! Jackson's here. See you soon!" Blanca must've hit the flip-screen button, because she disappears and suddenly we're able to see the auditorium. Mr. Jackson books it down the aisle. He positions himself center stage and starts to talk.

The video wobbles.

"It's come to my attention that there's a petition going around school to get me fired," Mr. Jackson begins. "This is a total witch hunt."

Blanca interrupts him. "Witch hunts were the patriarchy's way of using the guise of religion to permanently silence women who dared to be different. This isn't a witch hunt, this is a response to years of your blatant discrimination, and we won't fall for your false victimhood. This is what justice looks like! Let Carey sing!"

I punch the air. *Fuck yes, Blanca!*

His jaw tightens and he sneers. "I will not tolerate these outbursts. I *will* have resp—"

"Let Carey sing!" another person shouts.

The view blurs as Blanca stands. "We will not be silenced!" Blanca yells so loud that the speakers on Phoebe's phone make a piercing screech. She shouts, "We will not be silenced!" over and over until the rest of the *Wicked* cast and tech crew join her. Leading the charge, Blanca heads into the aisle with her fist in the air. She must be walking backward because we're able to see everyone in the production following her, screaming, "We will not be silenced!"

Mr. Jackson stays by the stage, hurling idle threats.

Nobody listens. This is what unity looks like.

Once outside, Blanca's face returns to the screen. "Carey, say something to everyone." Blanca barely gives me time to think before turning the screen so that everyone in the cast can see me, but they are still shouting. "Everyone be quiet! Carey wants to say something!"

Everyone cheers for me.

WhatthehellamIdoing?

WhatdoIsay?

Phoebe elbows me. "It's another stage."

Words dislodge from my brain as I stand, hoping to channel Blanca's energy.

"For too long, we've sat by while ignorance grew unchallenged at *our* school. A piece of salacious gossip here, a *Sunnyside Upended!* blast there. Staying quiet when someone says something blatantly discriminatory in the hallway. We need to hold ourselves to the high standards we want our teachers to meet. How many of you have been victim of or witnessed a snide remark or an outright violation of our personhood, our right to exist, by a tenured teacher?" A wave of hands fly up. "There shouldn't be any hands! Enough is enough! I am not the first victim of queerphobia at Sunnyside, and I won't be the last, unless we stand together. Sunnyside is *our school.* This isn't only about me getting kicked out of the show, or Mr. Kelly being unfairly targeted by the administration. This is about how *our school* is letting this happen, and probably has for decades. *Our school* is protecting the Mr. Jacksons of the world. If one person is discriminated against, we're all at risk! We *cannot* be silenced! Come to Exile Records and let's take action!"

They start to chant again before the screen goes black. Call ended.

Joey wipes a tear from her cheek. "Shit. That was good."

I look over at Monroe, who watches us from the counter, cozied up to Thom, clearly still stewing. I wish she were next to me so I could share this with her.

"Good?" Cris launches himself from his chair. "That was incredible!" He begins pacing, then stops in front of me. He takes my face in his hands and smooches me like a cartoon character. Still, it sends chills through my entire body.

"What was that?" I ask Cris.

Phoebe mumbles something that sounds like, "I'm going over there," and drags Joey with her.

Cris is jittery from the rush of my speech, but he sobers quickly. "What?"

"You kissed me," I say. "I thought we were done with that."

He blinks.

"You can't say we have to stop kissing, then kiss me, then say *this* is too much, and then kiss me again. It's not fair. I—"

"You what?" he asks, cutting me off.

This is not how I want to tell him that I love him.

We stare at each other, silent stalemates.

The doors of Exile Records burst open, and Blanca leads the Sunnyside cast of *Wicked* into the store, shouting, "Carey! Carey! Carey!"

Thom's face is shell-shocked as he watches dozens of new bodies storm the aisles. He and Monroe work quickly to accommodate the new crowd by moving furniture before whizzing to the counter together to take orders and make fresh coffee to pass out. Guilt arrests me as I watch him. I've been so wrapped up in the whole Cris saga that it dawns on me that I haven't bothered to get to know Thom. All I know about him is that he's nice, seems genuine, and uses his managerial power to allow us use of Exile *and* give us free coffee. And I selfishly, stupidly threw their new relationship in Monroe's face earlier. I have to make an effort.

Blanca bounds over to me. "How amazing is this?"

"I can't believe *everyone* walked out," I say, mentally counting heads. The tech crew, the band, every cast member is here.

Blanca leans in. "I didn't want to say this earlier, in front of everyone, but . . ." Her gaze drops to the floor, and she whispers, "I'm a lesbian. Nobody knows. *Especially* not my family. I keep to myself a lot, and seeing you around school and stuff is just . . ." She dives in for a quick hug. "I feel seen."

I squeeze her tightly. "Same."

When she lets go, I climb onto a nearby chair. "Thanks for coming, everyone! It couldn't have been easy to walk out on the musical, and I'm so grateful for your support. But the fight isn't over. And, uh . . ." I lose my train of thought because Mr. Kelly pushes open the door. He sees me and cracks a proud smile. I stretch out my hand and point. "Everyone, *our* director, Mr. Kelly!"

Heads turn toward him, but nobody shouts. Instead, they clap. It's slow and steady at first, a show of appreciation and respect, but it intensifies, punctuated by hollers and whistles. Mr. Kelly's cheeks go red, and his eyes are wet.

Cris grabs a chair for Mr. Kelly and slides it next to mine. As he walks toward us, someone shouts, "We love you, Mr. Kelly!"

He's more put together than he looked yesterday, his face

clean-shaven, the bags under his eyes only slightly weighted. He hugs Rachel before standing on the empty chair and motions for the crowd to quiet down, the same way he does when he's at the front of his classroom.

"I tried to think of what to say on my way here, and this is what I came up with: I remember when I was in high school. Let's hear it for the Sunnyside Falcons!" Rachel whoops. "There were two out kids at the time. I was *not* one of them. It didn't matter that there weren't rumors spread about them, because the locker room was filled with words like 'fag' and phrases like 'no homo,' even seventeen years ago. Still, it always stuck with me that those two kids were brave enough to be who they were without apologies. I wish I were brave back then. That's why I admire people like Carey Parker." He turns to me. "They've taught me so much about being brave, and the cost of cowardice. I don't have to explain my casting choices to you all, because you've heard Carey's incredible voice, and they were the best person for the role, hands down. But this isn't about a role. This isn't about me, either. This is about justice. This is about your education. This is about making Sunnyside High a safe space for all to learn!"

Clapping thunders around us.

"I stand with Carey. I stand for what's right! I admire each and every one of you for doing the same. This is the real world. Classrooms are meant to prepare you for life beyond school, but books and stories can only take you so far. Use your voices. Take this energy with you into the world. When you're eighteen, you'll be able to vote in elections and effect real, tangible change. Now, and even then, this is your power. Use it." Mr. Kelly hops down off the chair and joins the rest of the crowd, right in front next to Blanca. He leads the next chant: "Let Carey sing!"

The applause nourishes me as Mr. Kelly passes the torch back to me.

Once the noise simmers, I say, "None of this would have been possible without Blanca Rodriguez, Joey and Monroe Cooper, and Cris Kostas. They inspire me in ways I can't begin to tell you. And give it up for Exile Records, especially Thom, who's behind the counter."

Thom waves sheepishly. "You're always welcome in Exile."

Mr. Kelly stifles a laugh. He mumbles, "The irony."

Monroe's eyes soften and she mouths a thank-you.

"But I wouldn't be here if it weren't for Phoebe Wright." I hold out my hand to help Phoebe up next to me. "She's been instrumental in organizing everything. I can't take credit for this movement. So, if you're shouting for me, you better screech louder than Christina Aguilera for Phoebe!"

We laud her like the queen she is.

"We will not be silenced!" she shouts, pumping her fist in the air. "Our work is far from over. We need your help." Rogue voices simmer as she speaks. "We need you to retweet and tweet about this as much as possible between now and Thursday. Thursday at ten a.m., right before the end of third period, we're holding a student walkout. Time to disrupt as much of the school day as possible, so dress warm and bring snacks!" She pauses for mild laughs. "Each one of you can help by spreading the word, since we're suspended. After the walkout and protest Thursday, we go to the school board meeting with our parents to present our demands. We need the protest to continue outside town hall. Make signs. Chant. Stand up against this injustice. If our goals aren't met by Friday, we make a silent human chain in front of the school. We need every Sunnyside student to help. Will you get your friends to join us? What do you say? Are you with us?"

Deafening cheers squash any remaining doubts.

TRACK 31
THEY/THEM/THEIR

At home, Mom prepares a feast of artisanal grilled cheese sandwiches with brie, sundried tomatoes, fresh mint, and fig jam, with a side of homemade sweet potato chips. Mom is nailing the food game lately, so when I called her after the rally and told her I was inviting my friends back, she said she would supply the sustenance. Once she finishes preparing the meal, she says a quick prayer to Grams; does the sign of the Father, Son, and the Holy Ghost; and blows a kiss at the sky. I look up too, hoping Grams is watching, wherever she is.

Just as I stuff the biggest chunk of sandwich into my mouth, Monroe sidles up to me.

"Hi, best fwiend," she says.

I try to say, "Hi, best fwiend" back, but it comes out sounding more like "Ha bosh fwah," and we both laugh, which causes me to choke.

"Thanks for inviting Thom too," she says, waving over at him. He smiles cheekily. "I'm officially done holding a grudge." She leans in close.

I swallow as quickly as I can and say, "Sorry for what I said."

"Same. I'll try to be nice to Cris. He's not . . . *horrible*." She bites her lip.

As everyone continues to stuff their faces, Mom wanders into the living room. I follow and plop down next to her. "How's my food?"

"Orgasmic," I say, immediately regretting my word choice.

"Excuse me?" she says. "How would you know? Oh God, do we need to have *the talk*?"

I want to run far, far away from this conversation. "No, no, Mom, shit. No."

She smiles. "Relax. I'd be more nervous if there weren't a giant chasm between you and Cris. The tension is, as the kids say, *real*." Mom stretches her feet up on the coffee table. "It's nice to have life in this apartment again. Though it would've been nice if you told me you were suspended instead of getting a call from the principal." Her tone changes, becoming more serious.

I brace myself. "Sorry, Mom, I—"

"Sorry nothing. I went off on her. I said, 'How dare you discriminate against my child after everything that's happened to them?' I'm not happy you were suspended, but I'm proud of you for standing up for yourself. You have one life." She wraps her arms around me and squeezes like she used to when I was young. "You need to live it freely."

It's nice to have her hold me tightly again. It's like she's been afraid I was fragile and would crumble in her arms. Sometimes I am. Maybe I had to break to learn how to become stronger.

"Thank you," I whisper, squeezing her back.

"You never have to thank me, baby." She kisses my forehead,

and I rest my head on her shoulder. "I'm ready to give that McCauley a piece of my mind. The bigger question is, are you ready for what's about to happen?"

I swallow hard. "I don't think so," I confess.

"That's okay. I don't think one is ever ready for something like this. You have to follow your gut and your heart." She wriggles her arm out from under me and pushes me away. "Go hang with your friends. I'm gonna rest my eyes for a minute."

As I head back into the kitchen, I think about how grateful I am for Mom, how she's always been exactly what I needed.

Everyone is too tired to drive home, so I arm them with enough blankets and pillows to turn the living room into a giant slumber party. It doesn't take long before light snores, mostly from Thom and Monroe, and heavy breathing fills the space.

I tiptoe to my room, leaving the door slightly ajar behind me.

As I change into comfy pajamas, there's a soft knock on the doorframe.

Cris leans against the wall. "I should head home."

"It's late. Just sleep here." My face blushes. "Not *here*. I mean, out there."

"I don't know. I need to get a good night's sleep," he says. "Especially tonight."

I open the door wider so Cris can come into my room. "Why tonight?"

His eyes widen, then his head droops toward the floor. "Tomorrow night is the Carnegie Hall showcase."

I gasp. *Fuck.* I can't believe I forgot. Cris got me a ticket and asked me to come. I had totally forgotten with everything else that has been going on.

His hands are in his pockets and he rocks on the balls of his feet by my desk. He's studying the corkboard above my laptop, his gaze lingering on the Mariah Carey concert tickets he sent me for Christmas tacked there. Does he remember what he wrote in that card? That he'd be waiting for me outside Radio City, hoping I'd show up? Or is he thinking about that night at Exile when he caught me in the storeroom with Isaiah. I don't want to be the person he remembers for kissing another boy, who didn't listen when he begged to be heard. I want to go back to that day in the park, beneath the willow tree, when he made me feel like Cinderella, when he felt safe enough to open up to me. Is it too late for that? Is it too late for me to say that I want to go to Carnegie Hall to hear him perform? Does he want that? I wish I could read him. The fact that I can't and that I'm over-analyzing everything makes me seethe with anger. Is this what love is, being driven absolutely mad from uncertainty?

"Why'd you kiss me?" I blurt.

He turns toward me. "Because I wanted to. Because you inspired me. The bigger question is why did you kiss me back?" He stands before me.

Do I tell him that I love him, or is that selfish because I know he doesn't feel the same way and telling him is nothing more than getting it off my chest?

Or do I break my own heart and just let him go?

TRACK 32

HE/HIM/HIS

"Carey, wake up!" Someone shakes my body until my eyes flutter open. I struggle to focus, and for a second, my mind tricks me into thinking that Cris fell asleep next to me. Because last night, when his lips were inches from mine, I told him exactly how I felt and then kissed him. We fell onto my bed, ripping off each other's clothes and exploring each other's body. Except reality hits. None of that happened. I said nothing, and he went home.

I rub the sleep from my eyes. "What happened?"

Joey's frazzled blond hair comes into focus. She pulls my arms until I'm sitting up.

"We're famous!" she shouts. "Well, technically, *you*'re famous."

"What?" I grab my blue bracelet and slip the green, purple, and white one off my wrist.

She hops onto my bed and sits cross-legged. "Look at your notifications!"

I unlock my phone. A little red bubble pops up: twenty

thousand notifications. Tweets from celebrities and regular people all around the country, and about that in new followers. I scroll through my feed. It's all thanks to one quote-tweet from trans talk show host and actress Shirley Gaines, from an article written about us on *The BuzzWord*, the most popular website for viral content. The article compiled all our tweets and quotes from the *BroadwayWorld* article, which went live last night, and features excerpts of my, Phoebe's, and Mr. Kelly's speeches, as well as quotes from Blanca and others in the show about Mr. Jackson. I reread Shirley Gaines's tweet over and over again:

@THESHIRLEYGAINES: This is an incredible group of students from New York fighting against anti-LGBTQ+ bias. Would love to have you on my show, @CareyParker! #GenderqueerIsBeautiful #SingForEquality #LetCareySing

From there, other major news outlets, out celebrities, and famous political commentators and activists picked it up, tweeting things like:

Our school systems are supposed to be places where students of all identities should feel safe to learn. This is a moral failing. I believe we can do better, and expect better from our teachers. @CareyParker

Protests planned by Sunnyside HS in Sunnyside, NY, for Thursday and Friday after teacher goes on homophobic

tirade. I see you, @PhoebeWright @CareyParker!
#SingForEquality #LetCareySing

It breaks my heart to see the blatant discrimination in
our schools, especially toward nonbinary or gender
nonconforming students, but I'm hopeful for change when I
see young people standing up for what's right. Never back
down @CareyParker. #SingForEquality #LetCareySing

I'm busy retweeting and responding when Phoebe and Monroe bust into my room holding their phones.

"Where's Blanca and Thom?" I ask.

"Blanca had to get home. She said something about a top-secret mission," Monroe says, eyeing Phoebe, who coughs. "Thom had to get to the shop. But not before Momma Parker made them both take a freshly baked muffin."

"She's so extra," I say.

"She's the best," Monroe says.

"Very true." I flash them my phone. "This response is insane."

Phoebe takes a deep breath. "There's no backing down now."

I look around my room at my friends. No matter what happens next, this is exactly where we all need to be. "Never. This isn't about going viral or whatever."

I type one more tweet:

@CAREYPARKER: If anyone is in the Sunnyside area
tomorrow at 10am, come to the high school w/signs. If
you can't make it during the day, come to SS Town Hall

at 7pm. Our work is far from over #WeWillNotBeSilenced
#SingForEquality #LetCareySing #LGBTQEquality

"All right, let's not waste time." I say, pinning that tweet to my page. "We have to make sure everything is set for tomorrow."

"We have the whole day," Phoebe says.

"Actually, there's something I need to do tonight."

MONROE: Are you sure you wanna do this, Carey?

JOEY: roe you are the wurst

MONROE: The würst? Am I a sausage, fräulein?

ME: Lmao

JOEY: what?

MONROE: OMG HOW ARE WE RELATED? It's "worst" not "wurst." Wurst is a sausage. I worry for you.

JOEY: thank god you proofread my essays #twinning

ME **sends selfie in front of Carnegie Hall with a frowning face**

ME: Neither of you is helping me right now

JOEY: omg have the best time! are you gonna tell cris how you feel?

MONROE: There's still time to catch the next train home

JOEY: don't listen to her carey. tell him how you feel.

JOEY: don't take him for granite. i know he loves you the way you love him.

JOEY: i've been there i know the look

MONROE: IT'S "GRANTED." TAKE HIM FOR GRANTED. HOLY SHIT.

JOEY: you love me 🤪

ME: Lmao omg I'm crying 🤣

ME: He doesn't know I'm coming. We didn't leave things so great last night, so 😬

ME: Wish me luck. Love y'all.

MONROE: You got this! Love you!

It's always colder in the city than it is in Sunnyside. Maybe it's all the concrete and steel and breezeways and the fact that, despite all the bodies in constant motion, it always feels like you're alone in a crowd.

I'm on the corner of Fifty-Seventh and Seventh, staring up at the Carnegie Hall marquee, wondering what the hell I'm doing here. I study the poster of Coach Trevisani's students behind the glass. Cris is featured prominently. I wonder where I would've been placed.

"You okay?" Mom asks, emerging from the ticket booth inside.

"Why wouldn't I be?" I ask.

"Because you could've been onstage," she says. "And Cris doesn't know you're here."

"Jeez, Mom."

A gust of wind blows down the street and she shivers, then arches an eyebrow. "So, here's the deal, kid. Cris *did* leave a ticket for you at will call." She hands it to me. "However, in case you didn't want to sit next to Cris's father, since that might be awkward given all that's happened, I managed to score two tickets in the nosebleeds."

I let out a sigh of relief and shove the ticket Cris reserved for me deep into my jacket pocket. "Thanks for coming with me."

"What kind of parent takes their suspended child to the city for a show?" She playfully knocks into me.

"A good one. It's a nice break from all the protest planning."

"How'd it go today?" she asks, holding the door open for me.

"It's crazy how much it's picking up speed." I start to tell her about how the word is spreading online, and how newspapers were contacting me and Phoebe all day, but I'm sidetracked by the sight of my old vocal coach, mingling with rich-looking people in elegant winter coats. I desperately don't want to be seen.

Mom turns, and the second she sees him, she waves him over. "Will! Will Trevisani!"

"I hate you," I sigh.

He makes his way toward us.

"Stop avoiding," she whispers before turning her attention to Coach Trevisani. "Carnegie Hall? This is big-time!"

"Mariella Parker? I thought that was you!" Coach Trevisani is tall and broad-shouldered, a giant of a man with a deep operatic voice. "I—Carey?" He blinks a few times and does that cheesy motion where he pretends to rub his eyes to get a better view. He gives Mom a hug, then asks if it's okay to hug me. "It's been far too long. I'm so happy to see you here."

"We almost didn't come," Mom says.

"We're here to see Cris," I add quickly.

He smiles the way a proud papa might. "That kid doesn't shut up about you. He's constantly going on and on about Carey

Parker this, Carey Parker that. He spent all afternoon telling the other performers what's going on at Sunnyside. I'm sorry about all that." He offers a sympathetic nod. "But I'm impressed with your determination. That's how you make a difference."

"That's what I say," Mom agrees.

"You know, Carey, I can probably squeeze you into the lineup for a song," he offers.

"Oh, really!" Mom exclaims. "Carey, that would be so cool!"

It would be incredible to sing onstage at Carnegie Hall, but I shake my head. "No, that's not why I'm here. I'm here for Cris." I don't want to distract Cris or make him think I came here for anything other than to see him shine. He deserves the spotlight. "He's worked hard. But, if it's okay with Mom, I'd like to restart voice lessons again."

Mom nods enthusiastically.

"I'd like that very much," Coach Trevisani says as someone I don't know comes to tell him that he's needed backstage. He excuses himself, but not before telling Mom he looks forward to seeing her after the show to talk more.

Mom and I follow the crowd inside, and she locks her arm with mine. "I'm proud of you. Grams would be too. I know you felt like you had to quit your dreams because you didn't feel like people would allow you to be who you are." She stops. Her voice grows quiet, trembling. "I couldn't protect you from that. I'm glad you found your voice again."

I sigh. "So much time feels wasted."

"Nothing is wasted when you're taking care of yourself." She starts up again. "It'll be good to see Coach again." Something tells me she's talking about her, not me.

"Next time, can you not flirt so hard?" I add.

"He wasn't wearing a ring. That's all I'm saying."

"Ugh, Mom, gross," I say. But I want my mom to find her happiness too.

When the lights dim and the performances begin, I know one day, I'll be on that stage. It doesn't matter how long it takes me to get there, or that I'm not onstage now. What matters is that I'm finding my way out of the darkness and toward that spotlight, and that my dreams and I are worth fighting for.

Cris is one of the last singers to grace the stage. The stage is blanketed in darkness, save for a sliver of light in the center, highlighting a wooden stool, a piano, and a guitar. He steps up to the microphone and says, "I'm Crisanto Kostas, and tonight, I've prepared a collection of songs that represents who I am at this exact moment." He picks up his guitar and positions himself on the stool. "This is for you, Mom." He plucks at the strings and begins a gritty, heavy version of Tears for Fears's "Everybody Wants to Rule the World."

I reach for Mom's hand, who cries silently as he sings about nothing lasting forever.

When he's done, he walks over to the piano, and his fingers run wild across the keys.

"I didn't know he played piano," Mom whispers.

He plays Troye Sivan's "Postcard," a song about someone being completely undone by their lover, and how they can't sleep until they've gotten over everything that happened between them. Nearing the emotional bridge, he chokes up, singing about being pulled in, then pushed away. Then his booming voice builds to a crescendo and crashes into earth-shattering silence before a choir comes onstage to join him for the final chorus. As he belts, it's like the audience takes a collective breath and holds it until he finishes. Every note breaks and mends my heart, and I replay it in my mind over and over again, long after the show ends.

TRACK 33

THEY/THEM/THEIR

It's 9:53 a.m. on Thursday.

T-minus seven minutes until the walkout.

My body is in math class, which is weird after being suspended because it feels like I never left, even though so much changed in the days since. I have no idea what my teacher is talking about. She could be speaking complete gibberish, which, let's be honest, math definitely is, but my mind is in another galaxy. I didn't sleep at all last night, unable to stop thinking about Cris's performance and how I hated myself for escaping after the show without seeing Cris or letting him know that I was there. When we got home, Mom distracted me by putting on Mariah Carey's so-bad-it's-good film *Glitter*. Now, all I can think about is the scene where her DJ boyfriend asks her to show him what she's made of, and she effortlessly belts out fire over an eighties-inspired Jamaican dance track.

At 9:59 a.m., I brace myself, fiddling with my green-white-and-purple bracelet.

The alarm on my phone goes off at exactly 10 a.m. Everyone looks at me.

It's now or never. Time to show them all what I'm made of.

My legs shake as I stand.

The teacher says something to me that sounds like, "Please take your seat," but my pulse is racing, so she sounds super far away.

I hope the others are doing this and I'm not the only one.

A rhythmic pulsing in my head thumps in time with my beating heart.

Here goes nothing.

"We will not be silenced!" I yell the signal phrase over and over again, and I hear Monroe in the room across the hall doing the same.

At first, nobody moves. Then Toni Wallace, a short, pale girl with plump red cheeks; a Mohawk; and a necklace made of tiny sugar skulls rises to her feet and throws her fist in the air, syncing her voice with my chant: "We will not be silenced!"

Our teacher is frozen in place, watching as all her students stand in unison. For a second, we lock eyes, and she gives me a nod of approval, but then I open the door.

The hallway is filling with students, all shouting, "We will not be silenced!"

I lock arms with Monroe, and we lead the march toward the main office. We open every classroom door along the way, motioning for any student still sitting to join us. The older teachers yell for us to get back to our classes, threatening detention, suspension. One says we'll be expelled, but the younger teachers don't interfere. Some even join in, in support.

Monroe shouts, "They can't expel all of us!"

This encourages anyone still sitting to jump up and join in.

Security guards won't let us out the front doors, so we lead everyone into the main office, filling every available inch, our shouts swelling, echoing. More security guards arrive. The secretaries rise to their feet, unsure of what to do. Some dude picks up a chair outside McCauley's office and hoists it over his head. Behind him, another rips the large poster announcing the spring musical off the corkboard and holds it high in the air while shouting, "Let Carey sing!"

Principal McCauley emerges from her office. "Everyone, please get back to your classrooms immediately!"

A voice I can't place shouts, "Hell, no, we won't go!" and with that, the chants switch. The energy becomes chaotic. There's a push in the crowd, the way concertgoers in mosh pits push their way toward the front of the stage.

This was not supposed to happen. When we planned out all the possible scenarios, we were confident we'd be able to get everyone outside quickly. We weren't supposed to stop in the main office. We don't have a contingency.

We don't have a contingency.

Fuck!

It's getting harder to breathe. The near pandemonium feels insurmountable.

Panic sets in as clumps of students activate their mob mentalities, leveling up like this is all some sort of video game and not real life.

Monroe grabs my sleeve. "We have to get everyone out before people wreck the office."

"I'm trying!" Except I'm not.

The heat in the room rises. My classmates are all yelling my name and pumping their fists in the air. All of a sudden, it's as if someone pressed a mute button, because I can't hear them, I can only see angry faces, the scared looks of the teachers on the fringes, the secretaries perched on their desks, recording everything on their phones; the movements the crowd collectively makes toward the security guards at the door.

Then it hits me: if the guards moved, we could all leave and this would be fine.

There would be no rising tensions.

No yelling.

No pushing.

They've trapped us, cornered us, and it's only making it worse.

I am the leader.

They're all here because of me.

This is my responsibility. I won't let this turn. I *will* get us out of here.

Bodies push.

The crowd swells, rising and falling like waves crashing on the shore.

Sweat drips down the back of my neck as I thrust toward the guards.

I wave my arms and shout, "Please, be peaceful everyone!"

Nobody hears me.

Principal McCauley places her pointer finger and thumb in her mouth and blows a whistle so loud it causes nearby students to wince in pain. "All you, Parker."

"Security guards, let us pass! We will leave the building and keep it civil." I turn to McCauley, and she waves to the guards to let us pass.

"Please make your way to the front courtyard!" I yell. I turn back to thank Principal McCauley, but she's shepherding students to ensure they all get out safely.

Monroe wastes no time herding everyone outside. I take a look around the office. Aside from a few chairs getting pushed about and the poster for the musical, nothing is damaged. I wait for the end of the line to join back in.

Blanca, who is walking next to Phoebe, has her phone in the air, recording everything. When she sees me, she turns the phone on herself. "Here's Carey Parker, the person leading the charge! I'm livestreaming. We already have thirty thousand viewers!"

I grab her phone and look directly into the camera. "We will not be silenced!"

As we walk, Blanca hands her phone to Phoebe and motions for her to go on ahead. Then Blanca whips out the petitions. "Before we go outside, I wanted to give you an update. I got a lot of signatures yesterday. Musical peeps are working on getting more today, too."

"You think we'll have enough for the school board meeting tonight?" I ask.

"More than enough. So far, the only people who won't sign are Max and his friends. And the Conservative Values Club." She makes a face like she's vomiting.

"I'm shocked," I deadpan.

"Also," she says, hesitating for a moment. "I found something you should see." She takes an iPad out of her bag and hands it to me. "Phoebe asked me to look into *Sunnyside Upended!* to see if I could trace who is responsible for it. My older brother is kind of a hacker genius, and he was able to break through the firewalls and encryption."

My heart beats fast. "Did you get proof that Max is behind it?"

"Not specifically by *name*. But we did find the email linked to the site's creator, and the origin of the video." She points to the screen. "MM8152004@email.com."

"MM? Like Max McKagan?"

Her eyes widen. "I checked, and the numbers are his birthday. My brother did more digging and found that address linked to a Tumblr account called TheLoneliestChad."

She swipes open the Tumblr app. It's filled with content about how lonely the writer is, mixed in with long-winded anti-women posts about being rejected, bone-chilling diatribes on how the "gay agenda" is ruining his chances at finding a girlfriend, and reblogged links to really dark memes and fringe extremist websites. She scrolls down until she gets to the very first post, dated more than five years earlier. There's a picture of a very young-looking kid who I would recognize anywhere: Max. "Guess he forgot about that."

"What do we do with this?" I ask her.

"Up to you. I'm ready to turn this information over to Principal McCauley. Just give me the word."

"I have to think about it." Now that Blanca has confirmed what I already knew to be true, there's something really sad about Max. I don't feel any sympathy for him, and I don't understand him, but it's clear to me he's not stable. Maybe he's even in pain. He's a twenty-first-century Holden Caulfield, a remnant of 1950s male identity left to fester and toxify, and *Sunnyside Upended!* is his red hunting cap. Max has caused me an incredible amount of pain, but the point is to stop it, and to do that, I need irrefutable proof. I need him to admit to it, to stop hiding behind his anonymous gossip machine.

Blanca bites her lip. "It's up to you, but Max shouldn't get to keep making you—or anyone else—feel unsafe."

"I know." I hand her iPad back to her.

"Oh, and you'll never guess what else I found . . ."

Joey bursts through the doors, "What the hell, Car? We're all waiting for you!"

"Go," Blanca says. "We'll talk later."

I make a mental note to revise our name from the Fierce Five to the Savage Six. Blanca is badass.

It's cold and the sun is shining, so it takes a few seconds for my eyes to adjust. There's a sea of puffy jacket–clad people, floating heads with knitted winter hats in all colors. The crowd extends past the front of the courtyard into the parking lot. Cris, Monroe, and Joey hand out signs while Phoebe stands on a platform that Monroe borrowed from Exile Records. Thom and other Exile employees I recognize are setting up a table with donated pastries and giant thermoses of hot coffee to keep us fueled. Behind the hundreds of Sunnyside students, I spot dozens of people from around our small town. Beyond the chanting and people waving the two-finger peace sign, there's a kinetic synergy in the air. It fills me with a sense of camaraderie, pulling me toward the crowd.

I've spent most of my life hiding, and looking around now, I realize that I'm not afraid anymore. It's a curious feeling to see hundreds of people all standing beside you, fighting for you, for change, for a future you belong to.

I belong.

Police cars zip up the hill and double-park crookedly in front of the school. Cops in riot gear step out of their vehicles, forming a perimeter around the protestors. Seems a bit much, until I see Principal McCauley making her way toward them; she must have called them. The officers stand with their arms crossed, talking to each other, with just enough oomph in their stance to say, *Keep it peaceful.*

Phoebe keeps her gaze on the officers and grabs my hand, helping me onto the platform. She hands me a microphone, and the crowd starts chanting, "Let Carey sing!" I raise my eyebrows to ask her if she's okay, and she looks back at the cops, then gives a small nod.

Without any music, before the noise dies down, I close my eyes and let this feeling of joy and fear drive the notes that come out of my mouth. I sing P!nk's "Wild Hearts Can't Be Broken," a song she wrote about rallying and fighting for women's equality. What she says in that song is everything I could possibly think to say to this crowd: No matter what happens, we won't stop until we get what we demand, that our collective spirit cannot be broken, that we are strong and will not be broken.

I am not broken. Maybe I never was.

When I'm done, I hop off the platform and head into the crowd, side by side with my fellow students who have put their education on the line for me, and Sunnyside residents taking time out of their busy workdays to come to the high school and demand the system do better with me.

The wind is icy, and our breath swirls above us like mini smokestacks, but I don't feel the cold at all. Maybe it's the adrenaline, but I'm restless. I want to talk to people. Strangers pat me on the back and tell me they're with me.

"Thanks for organizing this," a freshman girl says. "I came out last summer, and I was so excited to start high school, and . . ." She looks down. "Then I heard about what happened at the rehearsal and it made me scared again. Especially because I'll have Jackson next year."

Another woman says, "My cousin is gay and lives in Alabama. When he came out to his immediate family, they kicked him out. I haven't heard from him in a year." She has tears in her eyes.

Toward the back, an older man stops me to tell me that I have a beautiful voice. "You remind me of my sister. She's trans. I saw your story on the news last night, and I felt like I had to be here. For her. This is my first time at something like this."

Story after story of relatives and friends, friends of friends, and acquaintances in the workplace pour out of people's mouths. We're united by the stories we share. I drink it in, fully aware that, a few months ago, I wouldn't have had the courage to show up here, especially not for myself.

Vans from major news networks pull into the Sunnyside lot. They unload cameras on tripods, and reporters stand near the front line, with Phoebe, Cris, Monroe, Joey, Blanca, and the backdrop of protestors behind them.

Meanwhile, one by one, our peers step to the microphone to share stories about Mr. Jackson and the state of Sunnyside, with its toxic, gossipy underbelly, and impassioned speeches about gender equality. More people show up: kids from neighboring towns, Zipcars full of millennials from New York City with painted signs. The camerapersons record all of it.

I move to the fringes of the crowd to catch my breath when my phone rings. It's Mom. She's no doubt streaming it online while at work. The service is shitty, so I lose her. I walk deeper into the parking lot, between cars and away from protestors, and try to call back, but it doesn't go through.

A tap-tap-tap on my shoulder stops me. I turn and am face-to-face with Max and his melty-faced goons.

"What do you want, Max? I'm surprised you're here."

"Your protest is a Get Out of Class Free card, Mariah."

I can't help but snort. "You do realize this is a pro-LGBTQ rally, right? So, you being here means you support what we're fighting for."

"He's not a queer," one of Max's friends with a patchy mustache says.

"First off, you don't get to use that term, especially when you position it as an insult. Also, you don't have to be queer to be here. Look around you."

Max grinds his teeth.

"What're you gonna do, Max? You've lost. If you all wanna still be homophobic fuckbags while the rest of humanity progresses, fine, but you're missing out on a lot." I don't have it in me anymore to deal with him.

"Where're you going?" He follows me, and I make the

mistake of turning around again. His friends follow behind him. He bumps his chest against mine, like a scare tactic from a cheesy eighties movie where the bullies have mullets.

"You're pathetic. I feel sorry for you, Max. You're not worth any more of my breaths."

As I start to walk away, he says, "Better not turn your back, Mariah." Then pokes me in the back and whispers, "*Click-click.*"

I turn and see his right hand fixed not in the shape of a camera, but a gun. "Is that a threat? Moving on from blackmail and physical assault? What's next?" This is my chance to get him to admit to being behind everything. "I know who you are, *TheLoneliestChad.*"

His face drains of all color.

I'm in control now. I won't let him scare me anymore. "I see you exactly for who you are: a scared, lonely person who would rather hurt others than fix yourself. Look around, Max." I point toward the crowd. Phoebe is leading them in song. "All these people are here for me. Who's here for you?"

He puffs out his chest, clenches his fist, and barrels toward me.

I hold out my hands to stop him, but his weight bends my wrist back. I slam my chest into his, and he propels backward into the arms of his goons.

He dives toward me, and I fall to the ground.

Crashing to the pavement, I'm instantly transported back to that day in the locker room. He stands over me, between my legs, and lifts his foot like he's about to stomp or kick me.

There's no time to think.

With every ounce of strength I have, I slam my leg into his, his body tumbling backward.

One of his idiot friends yells, "Fight!"

I scramble to my feet.

His friends back away. Max looks after them, betrayed.

Someone from the crowd is running toward us.

Max stumbles to his feet, sneers, and shouts, "Fuck you! You think you won? There's more where the video came from. Don't think I won't post what I have. Don't think I won't go after your little group of freaks, too."

There it is. A confession.

He must register what he said because he wastes no time lunging at me again.

I close my eyes and brace for the impact, but there's nothing.

Max yelps.

I open my eyes. The random person who ran over has grabbed Max and holds his arms back.

"What do you want to do?" the man pinning Max's arms asks. "The police are here. I heard everything. Just say the word."

"Carey, please, don't," Max pleads. I've never heard him call me by name before.

"Why shouldn't I?" I ask. "After everything you've done to me?"

He doesn't say anything. Not one fucking word. But he's practically shaking, though I can't tell if it's from anger or fear. Either way, that is not my problem.

"C'mon, Parker, don't be like *that*," one of Max's friends says.

My face scrunches in disgust. It's not my job to have sympathy for someone who enacts violence against another person. It's not up to me to fix him or talk to him. I'm so tired of having to compromise myself to make other people comfortable. I'm not doing it anymore, definitely not with Max.

What's crystal clear is that Max isn't going to stop, and standing by and doing nothing is not acceptable. Maybe it never was, but I thought in the past that if I left him alone, he'd leave me alone too, which is naïve because it's the same as pretending the problem doesn't exist.

I have to find Blanca. We have to share the information about Max's Tumblr.

"Keep him here," I say, keeping the other details to myself. "I'll be back, um . . ."

"Matt," the man says. "Name's Matt. You got it, boss."

I keep to the perimeter to get to where the police are standing, near the microphone where Cris is singing a Hurts song called "Beautiful Ones."

There's a line of teachers standing outside the main office, Mr. Kelly in the middle. He gives me a thumbs-up, then puts his hand over his heart.

I squint but don't see Blanca anywhere.

The news crew is interviewing Phoebe as I walk past.

She grabs my jacket and pulls me into the shot.

"This is Carey Parker. The reason we're here," Phoebe says.

"Have you seen Blanca?" I whisper under my breath to her.

"We're on TV right now," she says through a toothy smile.

"Make sure to cut that out," says the reporter, who I recognize as Janet Storm. Grams used to watch her every night at six p.m. without fail. She's wearing what looks like an expensive suit underneath a thick winter jacket. "I was asking Phoebe about why you're organizing and what you hope to get out of these demonstrations. Are you interested in telling the world your story? The segment will air tonight at six."

I can't see Matt or Max and his friends from here. My stomach twists in nervous anticipation. But I can make time. Especially to be on the news. There'd be no way Principal McCauley and the school board could ignore our demands then, right?

"What are your pronouns, Carey?" Janet asks.

"They, them, please," I say, and she nods in affirmation.

The cameraman points to Janet. "I'm here with Carey Parker, the student who started it all when they were cast as Elphaba in their school production of *Wicked*, a role historically played by a female-identified actor. Carey identifies as genderqueer. What was the response you received once the role was announced publicly?"

"Well, Janet, the response was really positive." I talk about the standing ovation at the Hoop-Off performance and how, for a hot minute, I actually felt safe at Sunnyside.

"One question our viewers have is whether or not you are taking this too far," Janet says.

"This?" I ask through clenched teeth. Phoebe's grip on my arm tightens.

"The protest. Is *this* really necessary?" Janet thrusts the microphone toward me.

"I think that's a biased question. It's our right to protest against injustices; it's what the United States of America stands for. I shouldn't have to feel unsafe or unwelcome in the school I go to every day because a teacher has incorrect views about queer people. Teachers like that shouldn't be bankrolled by the school. My mom, a hard-working single mother, is a taxpayer, and her voice deserves to be heard too. So do the voices of the actual students." I motion for the camera to pan for a view of the crowd. "Clearly they have something to say. This isn't the first incident, and we're hoping to put an end to them because no student deserves to be in an environment where they feel unsafe. So no, I don't think we've gone too far. I don't think we've gone far enough."

Janet turns back to the camera. "You heard it here, folks. Carey Parker of Sunnyside High School is fired up and demands action. They—"

I interrupt her. "It's not just me. Other students have had similar experiences with this teacher. Other teachers have dealt with this discrimination too." I hope Mr. Kelly can hear me. "We're standing up for both students and teachers. As students, we value our education. But if the administration is intent on protecting one teacher over protecting their students against hateful speech, then the school is not doing its job. We want accountability and transparency. So, if you'll excuse me, I have a protest to get back to."

And I walk out of the camera's frame.

I don't get far when, without warning, a crackling explosion rings out over the crowd, almost like a single firework.

My heart stops as panic seizes the crowd and someone in the distance yells, "Run!"

TRACK 34
THEY/THEM/THEIR

Fear coils around me like a snake, suffocating me.

Blurred figures run, flail, shout. Images of everyone in my class at Sunnyside and all the beautiful people I've met today flash in my mind like the snapshot reels in a vintage viewfinder.

My chest heaves and I get dizzy as I search for Phoebe, Monroe, Joey, or Cris, but I can't see them. If something happens to any of them, I'll never forgive myself. Tears form as I think of all the new memories we might never create, the chances we might not get to take.

I don't believe in prayer, but I find myself praying for all of us.

Police officers spring into action, systematically searching the crowd for the source, for a literal smoking gun or blood, or worse.

This is all my fault, this is all my fault, this is all my fault.

Nobody would be here if it weren't for me.

I can't breathe.

I don't know how long we're on the ground, maybe hours, maybe seconds, before Mr. Kelly comes toward me, crouching like a human shield.

No, he's shaking us, instructing us to stand up.

Using a megaphone, an officer says, "Please do not panic. Shots not fired. I repeat, false alarm. No shots fired."

Mr. Kelly's voice finally reaches my ears. "Carey, it's okay."

My legs are jelly.

"What happened?" I ask.

"Carey!" Joey screams, running toward us, Monroe and Phoebe in tow.

They grab on to me, pulling me into a hug, our heads resting on one another's shoulders. I close my eyes and hold tightly. I tell them I love them. We stick together, until we feel safe enough to peel away.

When my eyes flutter open, I see Cris standing alone, trembling.

I run to him and wrap my arms around him. He holds on to me like he'll never let go. My hug matches the power of his. It seems like a stupid time to tell him that I love him, that I came to see him at Carnegie Hall, and that he fundamentally changed my life the day he came up to me in Exile, but I don't want him to think that the idea of dying has anything to do with my sudden declaration of love. So I say nothing. Again.

"What happened?" I ask Mr. Kelly again.

"A car backfired." Mr. Kelly points to a group of officers questioning someone.

Max.

"I bet he *made* his car backfire," I mutter.

"I don't think Max would be that stupid," Mr. Kelly says frankly. "It's a crime to yell fire in a crowded theater."

"He knew what he was doing." I tell them about what Max did in the parking lot. "He knew how to disrupt the protest." I point to the news camera. "Look. It's probably all over TV and social media."

"He keeps getting away with everything because nobody catches him," Cris says.

Joey's fists clench. I can tell she wants to tackle Max on the spot.

"I have a feeling that's about to change," I say, spotting Blanca in the crowd. I wave her over. She explains the connections between *Sunnyside Upended!* and Max's secret Tumblr page, and when I add in Max's parking lot confession, Mr. Kelly agrees we have to go to the police.

"Excuse me, officers," I say, my voice clear and steady as I walk over to the police, who are speaking with Max. "Max pretended to have a gun when he attacked me earlier today. There's more . . ." Then I tell them *everything*, the video of me he posted online, the threats he made when he assaulted me in the locker room and at prom, the attack in the parking lot. I don't leave anything out.

When I finish, Joey steps forward to add her story about the promposal rejection and how he came after her through the "Hallway Gossip" posts. Mr. Kelly confirms that Max's posts were the reason that section of the *Sunnyside Up! Report* was shut down. Blanca does her best to connect the rest of the dots.

Monroe tells the officers about how Max threatened me at junior prom; I'm grateful to her for speaking for me.

Cris tells them that Max used to threaten Courtney, his own sister, with violence when she would say anything to challenge him.

Phoebe tells the officers about how Max has verbally attacked me in Mr. Kelly's class, which Mr. Kelly confirms.

Matt, the man who helped me when Max attacked me earlier, walks up. "I saw him threaten Carey earlier." He points to the spot in the parking lot.

Max's friends turn on him, corroborating that Max pantomimed a gun.

"Son," an officer says, looking at Max with stern disappointment. "Is all this true?"

Max looks like he wants to whip out a nasty comment but hesitates—then admits he made the car backfire because he thought it would be funny. He doesn't say a word about anything else.

Max's friends slowly back away toward the student lot and hop into an old, blue Toyota with a Confederate flag bumper sticker. I watch out of the corner of my eye as they peel off down the road.

"It's illegal to cause a public panic for no reason," the officer says, reaching behind his back for a pair of handcuffs while another radios the station with an update. "What you did was purposely negligent and intended to scare people, which could have led to serious injuries." Then he turns to me. "You should head down to the station with a parent to file a police report."

I nod. I wish Mom were here because she would know what to do.

I want Max to stop harassing me. I need it to end.

The officer reads Max his rights and helps him into the back of a police car. Then he says, "So you know, he most likely will post bail." After seeing Max's father in person last week, it's clear what he means: They have money. Power. Influence. Max will probably be back in school next week.

The cop car pulls out of the school lot, and Max's face in the window gets farther and farther away. I may never fully feel safe, but I'll be damned if I roll over this time.

TRACK 35
THEY/THEM/THEIR

Wrangling a crowd after a car backfires is like herding hundreds of kittens.

Not only are our bodies exhausted from being outside all day, chilled to the bone, but we have to push past the fear and panic caused by Max.

Those who stay are committed to the fight. A good mix of students, parents, and randoms march with us down the windy road from the high school to Main Street. We wave our signs at passing cars, who honk, some out of frustration and instigation as they scream through open windows for us to "get the fuck out of the street," but some cheer us on.

Behind me bodies swallow up the sidewalk as far back as I can see.

Phoebe and Blanca are deep in conversation in front of me. Joey pumps her fists in the air next to me, and Monroe and Cris walk together behind us until we reach town hall. Monroe nods to me warmly, and my heart skips seeing them make an effort with each other. I guess a near-death experience can bring frenemies together.

Mom waits on the steps with the Coopers and Phoebe's mom. Her maroon pantsuit and gray paisley silk scarf tied loosely around her neck is absolutely everything. Fortune 500-realness! Her eyes bug out when she gets a look at the crowd. "Good thing I ordered food. You can thank Grams's priest, who reached out and wanted to help."

Grams's priest? Damn. Was not expecting that.

Mom directs the foot traffic to a delivery van from a local deli in town that makes the best hot sandwiches. A few men in white chef uniforms pass out foil-wrapped deliciousness to people in the crowd, who swarm them.

I tackle her with a hug, and she kisses the top of my head. "I'm so glad you're safe. I wish I could've gotten out of work to be there. I hadn't heard what that *boy*"—I can tell she wants to use another word for Max—"did at the protest until Phoebe's mother called me."

I tell her there's more to the story than that, and we'll have to file a report or press charges. We agree to talk about it later. Max is the last thing on my mind. The appeal to the school board has to be priority right now.

"You ready for this?"

"God, no. You know I hate public speaking. My back is sweating." She turns around. "Can you tell?"

"You look beautiful, Mom."

"I don't know when you grew up into this person you are today, but I have never been prouder of you." She gives me a wet kiss on the cheek, which I promptly wipe away. "Remember when we used to listen to Mariah's 'Butterfly' and you would ask me why I would cry? I'd tell you I missed your father. The truth is that I worried about when you'd emerge from the chrysalis you created to protect yourself and fly away from me. I wanted to keep you safe, but I knew I couldn't do so forever. One day, you would become the butterfly you were always meant to be."

I fight back tears.

"You're looking a little pale," she adds. "Did you put on any foundation today?"

"Mom!"

"Wait, there's lipstick on your cheek." She wets her thumb and presses it into my skin. "Okay, ready to fly?"

Town hall is overflowing with parents and community members who fall silent when we enter the meeting room. Most of the protestors stay outside to make as much noise as possible. We take our seats closest to the front. Phoebe's mom takes her place with the school board at the front of the room, a few seats down from Principal McCauley. There are journalists with pens and pads against the back wall. Good. I hope they get everything.

The school board president is a stuffy old white man with a mustache and glazed-over eyes. "Today, our very town was turned upside-down by student activists who are here tonight to talk to the school board. We're tabling regular business to address the protests. Are there any parents who would like to speak on behalf of the disruption?"

I nudge Mom.

She stands. "Yes, I'm here for that agenda item. May I approach the bench?"

"Ma'am, this isn't a courtroom, do what you want," he says.

Mom takes the petitions from Blanca. Together with the Coopers, she walks to the microphone in the center of the room. Mom bends closer to the mic than necessary, so there's some feedback as she introduces herself.

She clears her throat. "My child is genderqueer." There are murmurs throughout the room. She takes a deep breath. "Many of you in the room are parents too, and I imagine you want the best for your children and love them just as fiercely as I love mine. We can love our kids unconditionally, but we can't shield them from the hatred in others' hearts. What happens when the hate lives inside a teacher responsible for educating our children? My child has been a victim of hatred and blatant discrimination at Sunnyside High, most of it coming from a teacher *you* employ. Why do we have teachers who think it's okay to target students, single them out, and berate them?" She holds up the petitions. "I have here three petitions, each with nearly four hundred signatures from the students of Sunnyside to reinstate Shawn Kelly as director of the musical, my child as the lead in the musical, and to fire Patrick Jackson, the teacher responsible for this horrible injustice."

Principal McCauley raises her hand, and the school board president recognizes her. She clears her throat. "I have tried to explain this to Mrs. Parker."

"Ms.," Mom corrects.

"*Ms.* Parker. I do not have the power to simply fire a teacher. We have committees that review such things. And a committee will review the teacher in question and the accusations against him. Those are matters that cannot be discussed publicly. The teacher in question has the right to defend himself."

Mom scans the room. "I don't see him here tonight."

Principal McCauley commands the room. "There is an internal investigation. The teacher in question elected not to be here tonight. He was told a union representative could attend on his behalf, but again, he elected not to involve the union, despite my encouragement to do so."

Her *encouragement*? I swallow a groan of disgust.

"Nice to know he's taking this process seriously," Mom says, speaking out of turn. "Do you see how this is a problem?"

Voices erupt from the crowd, and the board president pounds his gavel for order. Mom apologizes, and he recognizes Principal McCauley, who sternly says, "I cannot comment."

Mom raises her hand to speak and once she's given permission, her voice is louder and stronger. "I understand that you can't comment. But while you're upholding the confidentiality of this teacher, how do you think your students feel about that silence? Isn't it possible they might feel their concerns are being ignored?"

"Emotions are clearly high. Let me see those petitions." The school board president flips through them so quickly it's impossible for him to digest the significant amount of signatures on each. He passes them to the folks on either side of him. "Is that all?"

"As a parent, I demand there be an antidiscrimination policy at Sunnyside for the teachers to adhere to. It shouldn't be just for the students. Our teachers need to be setting examples, being inclusive in the classroom, and not targeting students based on their identities. Over the last week, I've been in contact with many of the district's parents, and we are ready to put forward a motion.

"It's also come to my attention that there were only six parents who complained about my child being cast in the musical. Six. Out of nearly one thousand parents who have high school–age children. If you go on Facebook to the Sunnyside High Parent group, practically all the posts are in support of Carey and Mr. Kelly," Mom says, power threading her words. I didn't even know such a group existed. *Go, Mom!* "As taxpayers and parents, *we* deserve to be heard *now*."

"We'll get to that in a second. First, a question. Do you honestly believe it was okay for these students, *your* child, to miss a day of school to *protest*?" he asks.

Mr. Kelly stands up. "That's exactly what education is all about, sir. Shawn Kelly, member of the English Department at Sunnyside High. An education is not about performing well on standardized tests. It's not about reading *Catcher in the Rye* or whether you know how to dissect a frog. It's about learning how to think. It's about cultivating their passions so that they can make a better world for us. We're exposing them to the world and helping them figure out how to process information. My job is to prepare them for their lives. These kids inspire me every day with their knowledge and bravery, and quite frankly, *we* could stand to learn a lot from listening to what they have to say at these demonstrations."

"That's a lovely sentiment," the school board president says.

I lean toward Phoebe and Blanca and whisper, "We need to show him the video of Jackson going off."

Blanca gets out her phone, but Phoebe puts her hand on Blanca's. "Not yet."

"It's not a sentiment," Mr. Kelly rebuts. "There's substantial evidence that corroborates the fact that treating students with respect in regard to their identity, whether that be the simple act of acknowledging and using the correct pronouns or including those identities in the curriculum, boosts student success. Not just for gay, trans, or nonbinary students, for *all* students. This is about allowing every student full participation in the education process. Isn't that your job to oversee as a body, Mr. President?"

Mom steps in. "I agree with Mr. Kelly, who, by the way, is a brilliant educator and has been an incredible resource for Carey. My mother, Carey's grandmother, used to demonstrate for women's rights in the seventies and eighties, when she was supposed to be nothing but a housewife. She used to say to me all the time, 'You better give those bastards hell!' Imagine where we'd be if someone told her to sit down and shut up, which is essentially what you're doing when you ask me if I'm okay with my child taking part in a peaceful protest."

Other parents, including Monroe and Joey's, stand up to speak, sharing their opinions with the school board. Nearly every parent in the room has something positive to say in support of me and defense of Mr. Kelly. There are a few, though, who express concerns with the nature of the protests, who have trouble with certain teachers' "agendas."

After listening quietly to everyone's testimonies, the school board president huddles with the rest of the board, including Principal McCauley. After minutes that feel more like hours, he says, "Thank you all for your candor. However, the teacher in question isn't here to defend himself, and I can assure you all that the appropriate committees are investigating these claims. Beyond that, I don't think the school board is in any position to give in to the *other* demands. Is this correct, Principal McCauley?"

My teeth set. I brace myself for the worst.

Principal McCauley stands and smooths her skirt. "I cannot comment on the ongoing investigation into the accusations against the teacher in question. However, the spring musical is one of the most beloved traditions in the Sunnyside community. We have seen the outpour from the community on this matter, and we want to make this a production for *all*. We are prepared to let Carey back in the musical, in the role they earned on the sole basis of their talent." She looks to me for acknowledgment, but I wait; I want to exhale, but I feel there's a giant "but" coming next, so I hold my breath as she continues, "We are also prepared to reinstate Shawn Kelly as musical director. Patrick Jackson will remain as codirector."

"Are you kidding?" I jump to my feet. "The whole point was to *remove* Mr. Jackson."

The school board president bangs a gavel on his desk. "I appreciate your enthusiasm, but that is all that can be done on the matter during this meeting."

"You're okay with this teacher intentionally harming our students?" Mom asks.

"Has this teacher harmed any student, McCauley?" he asks.

"Not that I'm aware of," she says. "Not *physically*."

I hold up my phone and press play on the video of Mr. Jackson's tirade at the *Wicked* rehearsal for the entire room. It's so quiet, like everyone is holding their breath.

Seems like you're trying to push some sort of agenda here, Kelly.

Two boys kissing *onstage like that? This is wildly unsuitable for our students.*

You really believe this filth is appropriate subject matter? Exposing our students to this sort of degradation . . .

When it finishes, I look directly into the eyes of the school board president. "You're saying I have to endure *that*? That's only what's been caught on camera. Ask Principal McCauley if there have been complaints about Mr. Jackson."

"Have there been additional complaints?" he asks Principal McCauley.

"That information is privileged," she says, her voice cracking.

Privileged my ass.

"Do you believe Patrick Jackson is a physical danger to students?" he asks.

She looks at me, then back to him. "I do not, no."

"Physical danger isn't the only danger a student can be put in!" Cheers and sharp shouts of support boom from behind me.

The school board president angrily bangs his gavel and demands order. Once the dust settles and the sounds of silence weigh down on the room, he checks his watch and says, "I'm afraid our hands are tied. At least until the proper investigations are concluded. That's all the time we have for tonight." He asks for a motion to adjourn, which is given and seconded. His wooden gavel pounds the desk once more.

That's it.

Meeting over.

We're stuck with Mr. Jackson.

TRACK 36
THEY/THEM/THEIR

Can I really go back to the musical with Mr. Jackson at the helm?

No. *I won't.*

After everything I've been through with him and Max, how far I've come, I refuse.

The icy chill outside town hall barely registers, at least not while the foghorn inside my head blares: *We failed, we failed,* I *failed.*

I fixate on the vacuous blackness of the night sky and wish it would swallow me so I could disappear. Do I give up?

Cris clenches his jaw. His eyes meet mine and his stare says everything I'm thinking: This can't be the end. Our pain has to amount to more than a few days of online viral buzz.

He looks away, then huffs. I follow his line of sight to a blue Toyota parked on a side street. Max's friends. He blazes past me.

"Where're you going?" I yell after him, but he doesn't stop.

Phoebe grabs on to me. "Tweet exactly what I say." She

stands on the town hall steps overlooking the crowd and shouts, "They're not prepared to give us what we deserve, so tomorrow morning at six a.m., we picket the school. We'll link up peacefully in front of the school! Nobody gets in until our demands are met!"

I don't have the heart to tell her it won't work. Principal McCauley and the school board president made it clear tonight that our rallies won't impact anything. But I tweet her call to action, word for word.

There's a hesitancy from nearly everyone who remains; slumped shoulders and disinterested half glances confirm what I already knew. Together, as a unit, we look strong, but one poke with a stick and our strength can crack like the thin layer of ice that floats on the Hudson.

Phoebe waits for me to step up, but I'm overwhelmed.

"Phoebe's right," I yell, my voice shaking. "I, *we*, can't be complacent. This fight isn't over." I flash my phone toward the crowd. "Everyone spread the word about tomorrow! They may not fire him, but that doesn't mean we can't show him exactly what we think of him."

Someone starts to clap in support, and slowly, everyone follows.

Until a scream shatters the fragile air around me.

"Somebody help! Please!"

I pan the area for the source of the scream. On the side street, the taillights of what looks like a blue Toyota flare a hellish red, and the engine revs. Its headlights flood the street, illuminating the darkened storefronts, as it takes off. The blood in my veins runs cold.

Blanca, who had been standing under a streetlamp, breaks into a run.

I trap a breath and follow her toward a circle of bodies on the sidewalk. I push through them. Cris lies on the ground, crumpled in the fetal position, blood dripping from his nose, clutching a dislocated shoulder that juts out like a broken action figure's. His glasses are shattered next to him.

"Call 9-1-1!" I hear myself yell. It's hard to tell if I'm awake or dreaming. I wedge myself next to his body as incoming sirens wail the saddest song I've ever heard.

TRACK 37

THEY/THEM/THEIR

Paramedics hoist Cris onto a stretcher.

I pick up Cris's glasses and pocket them.

An officer, the same as earlier, questions Blanca, who holds Phoebe's hand.

Joey, Monroe, and Mom don't leave my side, and I won't leave Cris's. I hold his good hand as the paramedics temporarily sling the other.

Police pivot toward Cris and bombard him with questions. He tries to recount what happened, but his sentences are minced, and I can't make sense of what he's saying. The voices around us seem far away, muffled, and my head spins as I try to intervene on his behalf, but I don't even know what happened, so it's not helpful.

Mom, who is on the phone with Cris's dad, pulls rank and stops the questioning so we can get some air. "Let Cris breathe," I think she says.

I want to breathe for him, to absorb some of his pain, but I can't. The only thing I can control is not letting go of his hand until an ER doctor separates us at the hospital.

As we wait . . .

For an update on Cris.

For a reason as to why this happened.

For something that would make sense of this fucked-up situation.

Why would someone attack Cris? Who would attack him?

Cris definitely saw the blue Toyota and took off in that direction.

It had to be Max. Or his friends. I'm not sure who that car actually belongs to, but I don't care. He was involved somehow. I know it. I swallow memories of him attacking me in the locker room, but his face pushes up like food poisoning. I run to the bathroom and vomit.

Mom holds me as I stare at the taupe floral wallpaper in the waiting room. I don't cry, because I can't. I don't blink, because I don't feel alive. I try to fixate on something, anything but the incessant flashing of red and white ambulance lights. I failed him. Again.

Cris's ER doctor walks by us with a cup of coffee.

I rush after him. "Is he okay?"

"Excuse me?" the ER doctor asks.

"Cris Kostas. He was admitted earlier. Cute. Dislocated shoulder."

He chuckles. "I can't give out private patient information unless you're family."

"Please, doctor," Mom begs, exhaustion in her voice after

hours of waiting. "Cris is like family. We just want to know he'll be okay."

He nods. "He's out of surgery, and he's doing well." It sounds like he's used to giving bad news. He doesn't bat an eyelash. "It could have been much worse. I'm afraid there's nothing more I can say, but his father is in with him if you want more information."

"Thank God," Mom says.

I rush to the nearest garbage can and hurl more bile into the black bag. Mom's hands rub concentric circles across my back as she tries to tell me he's okay, that everything's okay.

I wish I could believe her.

My heart thumps rapidly against my chest as I wait in the hallway outside Cris's room, about to meet his dad for the first time ever. I hate that this is the way I'm meeting him. Mom tells me to breathe, but I think I've forgotten how.

His dad doesn't look anything like his son, except for his lips, which are full and totally Cris. The exhaustion in his eyes tells stories of the terror he must've felt when he got the call about Cris tonight. "He's sleeping. It'll be a while before he's up for visitors."

"Will he be okay?" I ask.

Cris's dad nods and tries to smile.

"Thank you. I'll be praying for sweet Cris," Mom says, tears of relief in her eyes.

I peer past them, into Cris's room. His eyes are closed; the sound of the *beep-beep-beep*ing machines is unnerving. It's impossible not to think about Grams as I stare at the IV drips he's hooked up to.

As I turn back to them, Cris's father puts a hand on my shoulder. "My son says you're pretty special. He talks about you all the time." He blinks away tears.

The thought of Cris talking to his dad about me makes being here harder to deal with. They don't talk much, and the few words they've exchanged lately have been about me?

"He's more important to me than I know how to explain." I wish I could tell Cris that.

"He needs you to show up for him now."

Guilt floods me. But it's more than guilt, it's a cold sadness, a realization that I haven't been the person Cris deserves to have as a friend, let alone to love. If I were in his shoes, what would I think about me? He's been fighting for me, but I haven't fought for him. I've been too afraid to share my true feelings. I wish I could wave my Mariah hand and all the hard bullshit we've been through would vanish and we would be back at Arcadia playing *Mario Kart*, eating French fries, and kissing between the machines. When we were *us*.

But that's impossible. I can't go backward. "I will," I whisper. I reach into my pocket and hand over Cris's glasses.

As we say our goodbyes, he says, "Be the person my son thinks you are."

TRACK 38
WE/US/OUR

Zero. Hours. Of. Sleep.

Mom and I spent all night driving in circles around town, listening to Mariah Carey's entire catalogue because neither of us can stomach the idea of going home after leaving the hospital. We end up at the riverfront park, our car facing the willow tree where Cris and I had our first date. How appropriate.

The digital clock on the dash is getting closer to six a.m. as the last song on the *Glitter* album ends. I skip past *Charm-bracelet* and go right to *The Emancipation of Mimi*, the greatest comeback album of all time, and drown my sorrows in "We Belong Together."

"You don't have to go to school today," Mom says. "You can call out sick. We can stay home, watch old movies."

I fiddle with my blue bracelet, tightening it and loosening it. "That's not an option."

"Good." She tries to smile. "Just checking."

"Ya know," I say, turning down the volume as Mariah

launches into the first chorus, "It doesn't seem fair. Having to keep fighting like this."

"I know, baby. Teachers like Mr. Jackson shouldn't exist in the first place."

While Mom's right, I'm not talking about Mr. Jackson. "It shouldn't be this hard with Cris, right?"

She laughs. "Hard? Life with your ass of a father was hard. What you and Cris are going through right now is hard because *you're* making it that way."

"Ouch." My leg bounces restlessly. "Do you think it's fair what Cris's dad said to me? That I need to be the person Cris thinks I am?"

"I don't know if I'm the best person to ask. I am a bit biased. You *did* come out of me."

I involuntarily retch. "*Mom.* Gross. Be honest."

"What do you say every time we watch a romantic comedy and the two main characters can't seem to get it together?" she asks.

"That there would be no movie if they told each other the truth." I roll my eyes. "Our situation is more complicated than that."

Mom purses her lips. "Is it, though? You seem to go out of your way not to tell him how you feel. How's that working out for you?"

"I do *not* do that."

"Carnegie Hall?" she asks as Mariah belts the final chorus of "We Belong Together." I turn up the volume until the track fades. Mom places her hand on mine. "Show him how you feel. You'll regret the chances you never take. Grams taught me that."

"You're right." In a perfect world, Cris and his dad would come over for dinner, and they'd laugh with Mom and me, and

I'd get to know his dad and Cris would get to know Mom. I make mental notes of all the ways I want to know Cris, if I get another chance to.

"I know." She presses the ignition button and the car engine roars. "It's almost six. You have a protest to lead."

My head rests against the cold window as we drive up Main Street toward the school. "What if nobody shows up today? How do we come back from last night?"

"If Mariah made it through *Glitter* to make the biggest comeback in music history," she says, "so can you."

"Bring on the comeback."

The road to Sunnyside High has bumper-to-bumper traffic. There isn't usually anyone here this early, but once news got out about the Jackson "ruling" and what happened to Cris, people from all over the area are showing up. There are far more demonstrators gathering at the school today, including well-intentioned folks passing around donuts and hot coffee. Mr. Kelly and Rachel direct groups of people with new Justice for Cris signs written in thick letters. There's a space by the front entrance where Cris's picture is propped up on a stand, surrounded by lit candles and mini pride flags. My throat tightens and I'm grateful that Cris will get the chance to see what people have done to show their support for him, to stand in solidarity with *us*.

News reporters are off to the side, filming preliminary footage for their respective broadcasts. Next to one of the news vans, Janet Storm is deep in conversation with Blanca. I wonder what they're discussing.

"Who did all this?" I ask Phoebe, Monroe, and Joey. This a lot more than we'd initially planned for this morning.

"We did," Monroe says. "Stayed up all night."

"You?" I knock shoulders with Monroe. "You like him, don't you?"

"Shut up. Don't make it a thing." Monroe is quiet for a moment. "How is he?"

"I think he'll be okay."

"Will *you*?" Monroe asks.

I shrug. "I have to be. I owe it to Cris."

"People are awaiting direction about forming a human chain." Monroe motions for me to get up on a nearby low concrete wall.

Phoebe, who gnaws at her nails, notices my hesitation. "You okay, Gov'nuh?"

"I'm scared. I don't want to let anyone down. What if *all this* was for nothing, and Mr. Kelly and the rest of us are *forced* to work with Jackson? And we're right back where we started. Except now Cris is in the hospital," I whisper.

"Change doesn't happen overnight." Phoebe tucks stray hair under her pink wool pussy hat. "I don't have to tell you that this is the most action this white-bread town has ever seen. Probably will ever. Nobody expects Sunnyside to start a revolution. But we have a chance to make a real difference. Look around." She motions toward the people, all anxiously waiting direction, anger in their eyes as they whisper about Cris and the attack. "The police here are *on your side*. Some of us wouldn't be that lucky." Her gaze holds mine and I hear everything she doesn't say. "You only fail if you fail to use this privilege."

"Thank you for putting that into perspective for me."

"I'm here all week," she says.

I hop up on the wall and shout, "Justice! Equality! Fairness! These are our demands. We're not asking for more than to be treated with the same respect and decency as everyone else. Bigotry at this school left to fester by those who are supposed to teach us how to respect others has led to Cris Kostas being attacked last night in an act of hate. We cannot let this go. This is about not letting hate win. The love I've experienced the last few days from all of you has been inspiring, and through this experience I've realized just how much power there is in the collective. The administration knows that. So do those who oppose us, who use hate as a weapon." I try to make eye contact with every single person I can see. "I am a person. Cris is a person. We deserve respect. Not tolerance. *Respect*. That's what we're fighting for. Principal McCauley, we will link arms and make a human chain until Mr. Jackson is gone." I make it a point not to specify whether I mean gone from the show or gone from the school. "Do this for Cris! No screaming, no fighting. Every student, parent, and stranger link arms. Stand together."

And we do.

I link with Mr. Kelly and Blanca, and they each link to someone else until dozens upon dozens of people become a barricade to Sunnyside High.

We stand strong.

We show solidarity.

We are united.

The first cars arrive in the faculty lot, followed by yellow school buses and media vans. Teachers and secretaries and custodians mill around the front of the school, searching for an opening. They don't cross the picket line.

"Shawn," one of the math teachers says pointedly. "What are you doing?"

"What I was hired to do: standing up for our students," Mr. Kelly says. "Care to join?"

Principal McCauley paces.

"If we won't fight for our students, what are we doing here?" He asks.

The math teacher nods in agreement. Mr. Kelly unlinks his other arm and pulls her into the fold. Soon, more teachers ask to join, until only a small fraction stand before us, refusing out of solidarity with Mr. Jackson.

Students wander off their buses and try to break the chain, wriggle between bodies, but to no avail. Our instructions were clear: nobody gets through.

"Join us," I urge, my voice steady.

Some kids drop their bags and link up. Others walk off in small groups. I try not to dwell on those who choose to walk away, because when I look to either side of me, the chain is getting tighter. There's a pit in my stomach because there will always be people who don't believe in fighting for what's right, and that sucks.

Jerks with anti-LGBT signs march to our picket line and shout that we're corrupting the minds of young students, or that we should go to hell. The juxtaposition of our silence against their appalling words is startling, and Janet Storm and the other news reporters are drinking in all this compelling footage.

Their venom intensifies as they try to break the teachers

through our line, shoving their hands between us, prying our bodies apart like they're using the Jaws of Life. My hands become clammy. I try to think of a Mariah fact, or sing one of her songs to myself, but nothing is working. I sweat through my mittens. Then, Cris's Carnegie Hall performance flashes in my mind. He was so exposed, honest, vulnerable on that stage, and I felt such admiration, something I've only felt watching Grams sing. My breathing steadies and my resolve renews. I mentally transfer this strength to everyone in the chain, which is needed as more counter-protestors roll up.

My muscles ache, but I don't let go—and neither does anybody else. They scream at us and tell us we're anti-American, anti-God, anti–freedom of speech. Anti-, anti-, anti-.

We say nothing.

We stay quiet.

We are immovable.

An adult I don't recognize spits in Mr. Kelly's face. He remains steady. He tells me he can handle it, but if any of us is touched, he'll go wild and definitely lose his job.

"Why don't they just go home?" Phoebe asks.

"Unfortunately, they have as much right to be here as we do." Mr. Kelly sucks in a breath when a visibly irritated Mr. Jackson gets out of a parked Dodge. "Stay strong."

My chest heaves.

My body trembles.

My grip loosens.

Both Mr. Kelly and Blanca have enough strength to support me. Each squeeze tighter, reinforcing the chain.

"I got you," Blanca says. "You trust me?"

"Of course."

"Okay. I'm letting go for a second. Don't freak out." When I release her hand, she yanks her phone out of her pocket, dials an unknown number, and says, "He's here. Yeah. Okay." When she's done, she turns off her phone and sticks it back in her pocket.

"What was that?' I ask.

Mr. Jackson cranes his neck, looking for an opening, when he spots us.

"You'll see," she says.

Mr. Jackson stops in front of us. "Kelly, I should've known you'd be here. Let me through." His hot breath spirals in thick clouds between him and Mr. Kelly.

"No," Mr. Kelly says.

Janet Storm and her news crew quickly make their way to us. She nods at Blanca.

Mr. Jackson doesn't flinch at the sight of the reporters. He's so confident in his own righteousness that he smiles like a cartoon villain, the corners of his lips curling. "If you value your job, I'd suggest you let me do mine."

"This *is* my job." Mr. Kelly looks to me. "I'm protecting these kids."

Mr. Jackson's nostrils flare. "From what?"

"From people like you who call themselves educators."

Mr. Jackson clenches his teeth. "That's enough!" He's so loud that everybody around us—in the chain and outside it, including Principal McCauley, the police, and the other news crews—takes notice. "This circus has gone on long enough."

Mr. Jackson clasps his hands together and points them

between me and Mr. Kelly. He dives forward, trying to pry our bodies apart. Mr. Kelly locks his arm with mine, pulling me close to him, and I try my best to match his strength. Janet Storm motions for the camera to move in closer.

The force of Mr. Jackson's body against our arms is too great. Our human chain bends inward, and with it, my arm. I'll have to let go to prevent my arm from breaking. Searing pain shoots up to my shoulder and through my body until I can no longer stand it.

"Please," I yelp. "Stop! You're hurting me."

"Patrick!" Principal McCauley yells, dashing over to the commotion. "Take your hands off the student. Now. This is absolutely unacceptable."

Mr. Jackson backs off, huffing and puffing. He's trying to regain his composure when he turns and there's a camera in his face.

Janet Storm thrusts the microphone at him. "Do you have comments about the student-led protests?"

"Do you see what's happening here? They're trying to prevent me from entering my workplace and doing my job. This school is hell-bent on forcing this agenda down our throats, to the detriment of other students' education."

"What is your response to the petitions signed by students, parents, and members of the community to have you removed?" Janet asks.

Mr. Jackson looks directly at me. "The school will be hearing from my lawyer."

"Do you think it's appropriate to harm a student?" she asks, holding the microphone back toward him.

"I didn't harm anyone. I was *trying* to get to my office." Mr. Jackson's face is emotionless now.

"Yes, you did hurt me," I say, trying my best not to focus on the throbbing pain.

"This student is claiming otherwise," Janet says.

"This student claims a lot of things," Mr. Jackson replies coldly.

"Can you comment about the most recent allegations against you?" Janet asks.

Principal McCauley's head cocks toward Janet.

Blanca squeezes my hand.

Mr. Jackson scowls incredulously.

"Early yesterday morning, our team was sent detailed evidence that you've been teaching without the appropriate credentials for the better part of the last thirty years. This calls into question the very system of protections in place for someone without the proper accreditation versus the students who are most at risk and in need of protection."

Principal McCauley lets out a breathless, "What?"

"Fake news!" Mr. Jackson shouts.

But Janet has the documentation. She quickly passes copies to both Mr. Jackson and Principal McCauley. "It took us until this morning to independently verify this information, but it is, in fact, true. This is the original scanned paperwork Sunnyside has on file for Patrick Jackson, and according to New York State law, he does not have the proper credentials to teach in the first place. He never passed the certification test."

Blanca holds her breath as Principal McCauley examines the evidence.

Monroe, who is linked to the other side of Blanca, lets out a "Holy shit!" She shouts to the rest of the chain, practically loud enough for the neighboring town to hear: "Mr. Jackson isn't certified to teach!"

Mr. Jackson crinkles the papers in his grip.

Janet slides the microphone back to him. "Any comment?"

"Get this camera out of my face, bitch." With a swift motion, Mr. Jackson slaps the mic out of her hand and lunges for the cameraman, pushing him to the side as well. Then he turns his attention to Mr. Kelly. "You did this."

Before Mr. Jackson can reach Mr. Kelly, the police are already springing into action, racing toward Mr. Jackson and restraining him. The same officer from yesterday, who arrested Max and responded to Cris's assault, handcuffs him.

"Officer, he attacked me, Janet, her cameraman, and tried to go after Mr. Kelly," I say.

"I can confirm." Principal McCauley finally steps up, dropping the poised politician act. "He's assaulting not only the students, but other faculty. And he's trespassing. He's not a credentialed teacher and he's trying to get into the school."

"You can't do this," Mr. Jackson pleads, shoving the officer away.

"I didn't do this. You did. It's time to stop playing the victim, Patrick," Principal McCauley says.

Monroe, Joey, Phoebe, and Mom, who are linked to the other side of Blanca, start chanting, "Take him away! We want justice!"

Like wildfire, it catches on until the whole chain, Mr. Kelly included, is yelling:

"JUSTICE!"

"JUSTICE!"

"JUSTICE!"

The officer tells Mr. Jackson they're taking him in for physically assaulting a minor and an officer, and reads him his rights. "This isn't over!"

This time, we drown him out.

Every single news crew captures Mr. Jackson getting into the back of a police car, our collective voices triumphant.

As the police car with Jackson drives away to the cheers of the crowd, a familiar face emerges from the parking lot. She has long blond hair under a fuzzy wool hat. For a second, I assume she's a random person here to offer support. When she waves to me, it registers.

That's Courtney McKagan, Cris's ex and Max's sister.

TRACK 39

HE/HIM/HIS

"What is she doing here?" Joey hisses.

My lips are dry from the cold. "I don't know."

Our human chain is starting to break up under the assumption that we won. Janet Storm is making the rounds, interviewing additional students and teachers so that when she breaks this story, it's a blockbuster.

Courtney is hesitant, fiddling with her gloved hands, clearly unsure if she wants to join us or not. My instincts tell me she didn't come here to fight.

"I'm gonna go talk to her," I say.

"Seriously?" Monroe starts. "She's Max's sister. You really think she's not gonna try to talk you out of pressing charges?"

I turn and find Mom. "What should I do?" I ask her.

"What's in your heart?" Mom asks, and I conjure Cris.

"She's probably hurting. Cris is in the hospital. Her brother is . . . well, you know. If she were here to spit on my face or break the chain, she would've done that already," I say. "Jo, you know her from the basketball team. Is she like that?"

Joey doesn't hesitate. "No. But . . ."

"Thanks." I hug Joey and whisper, "I'll be fine."

"Love you, Car," Joey says, the way she used to when we were young, encouraging me to climb trees and making sure I didn't fall flat on my ass.

I count the steps, seventy-eight in total, it takes to get to Courtney. We face each other awkwardly, neither of us sure who should make the first move.

"Hey. I wondered if we'd meet again." That comes out sounding like a cheesy one-liner in a superhero movie face-off, so I add, "After the Hoop-Off disaster, I mean."

Her smile is timid as she extends her hand.

I don't offer mine. "What're you doing here?"

"My brother—"

"If you're here to plead his case or try to get me not to press charges, you can go home. He's not worth my forgiveness or pity or whatever." I can barely get out the words because my heart is raging against my ribcage.

"Carey, I'm not here for that. I just wanna say . . . I'm sorry."

Huh? I was not expecting that. I exhale like a deflating balloon.

"I don't expect you to believe me or feel bad for Max, because I don't, not after what he did to me at the game in December or all he's done to you and Cris." She barely chokes out his name. She blinks away tears. "Max grew up with our dad treating women like objects. He uses religion to justify his hatred of LGBTQ people. I've tried to get through to Max, but . . ." She shakes her head in failure. "Anyway, I didn't come here to get you not to go to the police. It's the opposite. Max told me what his friends did to Cris last night."

"His friends?" I eye her up and down. "You sure it wasn't him?"

She shakes her head. "He was home, grounded after my parents had to pick him up from the police station. It *was* his friends. He told the police that when they showed up at our house this morning to question him about what happened to Cris. And he had the texts from them to prove it."

"You believe him?" My voice is shaking.

"I was home last night too." Her lips tremble. "I loved Cris. He's the best person I know."

"That doesn't make Cris magically better," I say. "What do you want from me?"

"Nothing. I hate everything my brother has done to you. I feel . . . guilty. I know this doesn't make anything better, but I'm on your side, and I'll do what I can to make it right."

I don't know what to do with this information. It sounds like she's looking for absolution, which I'm not here to give her. Do I feel pity for everything she has had to endure at home? Yes. But I'm still going to file a report and press charges. I have to protect myself and keep this from happening to others. That's more important.

"I also wanted to tell you that Cris really was broken up with me when I saw you two together at the game. For what it's worth, he ended things at Thanksgiving. He'd been trying to for months."

"We broke up." There's a dull pain in my chest when I say that out loud.

"I know," she says.

"Wait—how?"

"Cris and I talk. I still want him in my life, even if I can't be with him. He's my friend, and he's had enough people leave him."

"I love him," I blurt.

Her smile says she knows this already. "You should tell him that."

The nerve! I try my best to channel a zen Dr. Potter but fail miserably; she notices me avoiding eye contact and shifting leg to leg nervously and finally says, "Take care of him?"

"I will," I say without hesitation.

She waits for me to say goodbye or hug her or something, but *girl*, that's asking far too much. Max has chipped away at me for too long; I'll be damned if I'm going to give anyone in his family more of myself.

"Oh, before I go." She reaches into her satchel and pulls out the ruby red slippers that Max stole from my locker.

"Keep 'em," I say. "Or give them back to Max since he wanted them badly enough to steal them." I don't need them to be confident in who I am anymore. Maybe I never have. "He also took a picture of me and Joey."

"I didn't see that," she says.

"Of course not."

"Sorry."

"Me too." I thank her for coming and make my way back to my friends.

"How'd that go?" Joey asks.

"I'm good." I don't tell them what Courtney said; hers is not my story to tell, and there's been far too much gossip around Sunnyside High.

"Ahem." Principal McCauley clears her throat. "Can I have a word with you, Carey?"

Janet Storm hovers nearby and motions for the cameraman to capture our interaction.

Principal McCauley says, "You haven't felt safe in your school. You have my word that there will be a thorough investigation into Mr. Jackson. I will ensure that a zero-tolerance discrimination policy is front and center at the next board meeting, though after your mother's and Mr. Kelly's stellar performances last night"—she looks to both of them and smiles,—"it's already on the agenda. It needs a majority approval to pass, which I have no doubt it will get. The rest of the board will be hearing from me regularly until it comes up for a vote." Her voice is more natural than I've ever heard it. "Let me not mince my words here: I'm sorry, Carey."

"Thank you." What else is there to say? I can't tell if she's paying us lip service because Janet Storm and the cameras are pointed directly at us, or if she's genuinely going to implement change. Time will tell, and I say as much, out loud, so that everyone, including Janet Storm, hears.

Principal McCauley uses a megaphone to say, "Everyone, please report to your homerooms and await further instruction on the schedule for the rest of the day."

Once the cameras stop rolling and Principal McCauley begins herding everyone inside, Phoebe says, "Makes you wonder." She eyes the police officers politely clearing the area after our peaceful protest. "Would this have happened if Blanca and her brother hadn't hacked into the school's servers and found out about Jackson's credentials? Would we have seen justice?"

Mr. Jackson became his own downfall. And it wasn't from what he did to me or Mr. Kelly or any other student over the course of his tenure at Sunnyside, but a technicality, and that hangs over us like storm clouds.

We all look at each other, knowing the answer to Phoebe's question.

TRACK 40
HE/HIM/HIS

ME: Turn on the news!

ME: Jackson's out, officially. This is wild.

ME: I wish you were here to experience this with us.

ME: You were on my mind all day . . .

ME: HOLY SHIT! The BuzzWord just DMed me. They want to do a profile on me and you and the rest of the Savage Six!

ME: (That's my new nickname for us + Blanca, who is fucking badass btw.)

ME: How are you feeling? Sleeping or singing to the nurses? lol

ME: We have so much to catch up on. I'd love to come see you. Let me know if that's ok. Monroe wants to come too ha

CRIS: thanks but i'm not rly up for it

CRIS: i'm getting out monday i think. back to school next week probably

CRIS: congrats on the win. you deserve it

TRACK 41

SHE/HER/HERS

Mr. Kelly instructs me to stand onstage behind the curtain. Cloaked in darkness, I hold on to the velvet fabric and relish the first few minutes of quiet I've had in weeks. I wonder if Mariah has moments of stillness, or if her days are filled with constant motion, endless interview requests, and the constant gnawing feeling that she always has to perform. Does she ever get a moment to just *be*?

These moments of stasis are few, but rejuvenating.

I quickly send a message to Cris:

ME: I know you're not coming home until tomorrow, but can I see you tonight?

"We have a lot of ground to cover if we're going to make our March twenty-sixth opening, especially since we lost rehearsal time," Mr. Kelly announces. "We'll rebound. But first, without further ado, please welcome back to the stage, my Elphaba and yours, Carey Parker!"

Applause fills the auditorium. It might as well be Madison Square Garden. I apply a light layer of ChapStick, smack my lips, throw open the curtain, and step out into the stage lights.

To a standing ovation.

To whistles from the tech crew, Monroe, and the rest of the designers.

To cheers from the choir and Rachel.

To stomping from Phoebe and Blanca in the front row.

It grows and someone starts chanting:

"LET CAREY SING!"

"LET CAREY SING!"

I'm so full it's like my body is floating.

Mr. Kelly hands me the microphone.

The screams grow louder until I clear my throat.

"All I ever wanted was to belong." I take a breath and remember what Dr. Potter told me last night in an impromptu session. This week may be hard with rehearsals, but it's okay to celebrate, to revel in this victory, even if it feels foreign to me. "I know Mr. Kelly wants to jump into rehearsals, but I want to invite everyone to a special little celebration-slash-thank-you I'm hosting at Exile Records Café afterward."

Mr. Kelly motions for me to take a bow.

"LET CAREY SING!" Joey chants.

"LET CAREY SING!"

Rachel shuffles over to me and hands me the script. "How's act one, scene three?"

I smile because it's "The Wizard and I," my favorite song in the entire *Wicked* musical, and I've practiced it alone in my bedroom every morning since I got the part. The morning Grams was rushed to the hospital, I sang it for her as I made her breakfast for the last time. I'd bounced around the kitchen, pretending to be Elphaba daydreaming about meeting the Wizard of Oz. I'd always connected with the lyrics—about Elphaba finally finding someone who would accept her for exactly who she is; the Wizard would look past the things she hated about herself, her green skin and talent for wielding magic, and see her as worthy—but it's not until this moment, as I stand under the stage lights and belt out the song, that I realize Grams was this version of the Wizard of Oz. She was the first person who truly saw me, who taught me not to operate within other people's limits.

Tears stream down my face as I sing the last verse, where Elphaba envisions her dreams coming true because I know now that everything I'll ever need or want can never come from a spotlight or a stage or even a theater full of friends, but from how I see myself.

The applause is just icing.

———

Mom hangs pride flags of every stripe throughout Exile Café, courtesy of Thom, who lets us use the space free of charge. *Again.* He's definitely a keeper.

The entire cast and crew of *Wicked* arrives to an elaborate homemade buffet of Mom's signature dishes, from Grams's mint-laced meatballs to a tray of lasagna with pasta from scratch. There's enough to feed an army.

Table by table, I make it a point to sit down and talk with everyone. Most of the cast and crew have been virtual strangers to me, perhaps because I kept to myself. Though I've known most of them since kindergarten, it's like I'm meeting them for the first time.

After making my rounds, I check to see if Cris has responded to my message.

Nothing.

I wander back to the record stacks, thumbing through vinyls, hoping if I touch the right one, Cris will magically appear, like a genie in a bottle.

My fingers land on Troye Sivan's *Bloom*, and Cris singing "Postcard" at Carnegie Hall is all I hear. The way the lyrics beg his love not to give up on him makes me appreciate this post-protest haze, and as strong as I am now, I don't feel finished, like someone paused my song just before the climactic final verse.

Giggling distracts me. I peek around the corner, and Blanca and Phoebe are standing close, their hands entwined. Phoebe leans in for a kiss.

"Whoa," I say.

They jump away from each other but relax when they see me.

"You scared the fuck outta me." Blanca moves back toward Phoebe.

"When did this happen?" I ask, grinning.

"Lots of late nights and longing stares." Phoebe shrugs, a smirk creeping across her face. "No need to make it a thing."

It's a *major* thing! Little by little, we keep finding each other.

I hug them both. "I love y'all."

Phoebe slaps my back. "You too."

Blanca's phone buzzes. "Oh my God! The *BuzzWord* article is live!" She points to the byline where her name sits next to the main writer. "This is honestly the best thing that could have happened."

When they reached out wanting to do a profile on us, I figured I might as well leverage it as much as I could. It only seemed right that Blanca help write about what happened and get a proper signal boost.

"Are you bummed that you're not profiled too?" Phoebe asks Blanca.

"Hell no!" Blanca says. "I'd much rather be behind the scenes. Now I have an *actual* byline in an *actual* article on an *actual* worldwide, well-known website."

I read the opening:

What began as an anonymous article published in an online high school newspaper after a teacher went on a queerphobic tirade against two out students and an out teacher turned into a multiday, multilocation protest. Organized by a group of students who gained nationwide attention, the protests culminated in a bombshell revelation that the accused teacher, Patrick Jackson, did not have the proper New York State credentials to teach.

This brave show of democracy in action was streamed live on Twitter from beginning to end and united a small community in demanding antidiscrimination policies for its LGBTQ+ public school students. *The BuzzWord* got to know the five individuals at the center of this small-town protest that went viral and captured the attention of the nation.

"This is fucking cool," I say.

"I love how your profile lays out your story, Carey," Phoebe says. "How you describe what it means to be genderqueer, the importance of your pronouns—you've really found your voice. I love this line." She points to Blanca's screen: It's unfair that politics seeks to politicize my identity because this is my life, and I'm not up for debate.

"My favorite part is this." Blanca points to the next paragraph: Mariah's music has saved me, made me feel less alone. Without her music to guide me, I doubt I'd be here right now. I am a lamb for life. Thank you, Mariah, for everything. [Editor's Note: A "lamb" is what Mariah affectionately calls her most ardent of fans.]

Blanca smiles. "Do you know how much we had to edit out of the interview? The first draft was basically a Mariah testimonial."

"If the crown fits." I place an imaginary crown on my head and Phoebe bows.

Mom peeks around the stacks. "There you are! We've been looking for you. They got the sound all set up for you. You ready?"

I hop to my feet. "Absolutely."

Phoebe and Blanca follow me back to the café and sit next to Mr. Kelly and Rachel. Mom sits down next to Monroe and Joey and their parents, directly in front of me, as I planned. Dr. Potter sits in the back, incognito of course; I'm happy she accepted my invitation. Coach Trevisani, whom I reached out to after the protest dust settled, is at a keyboard he brought to back me up. He nods, ready.

Inhale.

Exhale.

"Good evening, everyone." I tighten the pink bracelet around my wrist. "Thanks for coming out tonight. It kind of feels like I've been doing a Thank You tour the last few days"—that garners laughter from the crowd—"and my heart is so full that I doubt I'll ever stop saying 'thank you.' But there are two people in particular that I—" I make the mistake of looking directly at Monroe and Joey. Tension tugs at my jaw, and my voice fills with emotion. "Monroe and Joey, you are everything to me." I make a heart with my fingers and place it to my chest. "I wrote this for you. It's still a work in progress, but isn't everything? It's called, 'Some Things Last.'"

Coach Trevisani helped me arrange it based on a melody in Mariah's "Always Be My Baby." He graces the keys, and the music speaks for me.

> *They say there's no way*
> *That we'll ever survive*
> *Cause time has a way of*
> *Making people say goodbye*
> *But I want you to know*

That whatever comes next
We can make it together
I'll always be right by your side

You are the best part of me and
If our paths diverge eventually
There's one thing I know, some things last forever
And I hope you know
Our memories are treasures I hold
I'll take with me wherever I go
If there's one thing I know, we will last forever

When we were younger
We were invincible
Climbing trees hand in hand and
Building our memories
But sometimes trees fall
To make room for new roots
That doesn't change us
We have each other to help us grow

Coach Trevisani plays chords that soar around me as I launch into the bridge of the song. His voice backs me up, effortlessly harmonizing with mine. With his vocals, I'm able to scat and riff once we get to the final chorus, feeling the words and using every note to convey my sincerity to Monroe and Joey.

After a splashy finish only Mariah could appreciate, where I swerve away from the microphone and look to the heavens,

Monroe and Joey jump to their feet and storm the small stage, wrapping their arms around me.

"It was the best way I knew how to share everything I couldn't say," I whisper.

"We know," they say in tandem, squeezing me tightly.

After a few more songs, I drag Phoebe up to sing with me, and then it's time to help Thom clean up and kick everyone out. Thom tosses Monroe a broom, and she scoffs at him, commenting about his gendered action. He almost takes it back before reminding her she's technically on the clock, and sweeping the floors is part of her job. She salutes him like he's a drill sergeant.

"Bummer Cris didn't show." Monroe rides the broom around me in circles like a witch.

"I didn't expect him to." She arches her eyebrows. "He's done so much for me and look where it got him. In the hospital. I don't blame him for wanting to stay away."

"You know he doesn't want you out of his life, right?" Blanca interrupts. "Eavesdropping is my forte."

"I don't know," Monroe says. "He seems pretty standoffish."

"Trust me," Blanca says. "He's got it bad, my sources confirm."

I laugh. "I don't blame him for keeping his distance. I have to figure out a way to show him that I'm not going anywhere."

That's it! I have to *show* him that I love him. Words aren't enough. Maybe they never were. His dad and everyone else have been right: It's my turn to show up for him.

"Roe, you mind if I borrow your car?"

She sniffs my breath. "Sober?"

"Shut up," I say.

"Jo, where are my keys?" Monroe yells across the store to Joey, who is helping Mom clear empty trays of food. "Carey is about to go declare her love for Cris."

Joey pouts and says, "Aww," before tossing me the keys to Monroe's car. "Don't fuck this one up."

No pressure.

I pace back and forth on his lawn, fighting the urge to run. I found an instrumental treatment of Troye Sivan's "Postcard" online, which I've been listening to while learning the lyrics since that night at Carnegie Hall. Cris sent me a video of him playing a Mariah song, so I'm going to serenade him with Troye Sivan on his front lawn. This is either going to be cinematic AF, or I'm going to crash and burn.

I hop up and down, shaking off my nerves before pressing play on my phone so the song streams to Monroe's car stereo. It's loud enough to wake Grams.

I sing, hoping he'll hear me, *really* hear me.

Cris peers through the front window. At least, I think it's him. It's a skinny shadow, and his dad is a massive Greek marble statue, so it isn't Mr. Kostas.

No one comes outside.

The buildup to the final chorus is way too loud, and neighbors open their doors to yell at me. Mr. Kostas opens their front door and stares me down. He's scarier in the moonlight than he was in the safety of the hospital.

"Carey? Turn that shit off. You're pissing off my neighbors."

I fumble with my phone, but it's cold outside, so it's not registering my touch. I bolt to the car and turn off the ignition.

"My bad, Mr. Kostas."

"It's late." Mr. Kostas's voice is harder without the music to soften it.

I see Cris's silhouette in the window. "Is Cris here?"

His dad crosses his arms; his stare peels me apart layer by layer until I'm nothing but bleeding organs on the ground. "He's asleep. Not in the mood for visitors."

"Right." I bend down and pick up a box I brought with me. "When he's up, can you tell Cris that I'm sorry for everything? I should've listened to him and believed him. I fucked up. I was hurt and scared and a million other things. Tell him I was at Carnegie Hall and cried after watching him sing 'Postcard.' Tell him that I . . ." I almost say *love him*, but that seems awkward to say to his dad. "I know 'sorry' is a stupid word that means nothing without action, but if he gives me another chance, I'll never stop showing him that I mean it."

"Is that all?" Monotone syllables wrapped in skepticism. Cool.

"Please give this to him. They're tickets to the Mariah Carey show. Tell him *I'll* be waiting for *him* outside the entrance to Radio City." If he doesn't show, I'll have my answer. And if he doesn't want to see the show *with* me, he'll have to tell me as much, but at least he'll get the chance to see her.

"Didn't *he* get them for *you*?"

I nod. "I wouldn't be able to enjoy the concert if he weren't there with me. He's what I want, not Mariah." I say a secret prayer to Queen Mariah not to smite me for that.

"Carey," he says as I turn back toward the car. "Thank you for what you did for my boy. The picket line."

"Don't thank me, Mr. Kostas. I'm the one who should be thanking him. He saved me. In more ways than I can count."

The front door shuts. Cris's shadow moves away from the window.

My heart is racing as I hop back into the car.

I can't believe I just did that!

Who even am I?

My breathing steadies until I'm able to pick up my phone without shaking. There's a random Twitter DM notification. There have been hundreds of DMs over the last week, and I usually wait until right before bed to answer them—assuming they're not the "you're going to hell" kind, which comes along with the territory—but this one makes me stop in my tracks.

@NICKD_TEAM_MC: Hi Carey! I'm on Mariah Carey's team & passed along the BuzzWord article on you to MC. She was incredibly moved by your story and would love to offer you and your friends backstage meet and greet passes and tickets to her upcoming Radio City show. What you do say?

I read it ten times before committing to an ear-piercing Mariah-esque whistle scream.

TRACK 42

THEY/THEM/THEIR

I'm way too anxious to function, so Monroe styles me in skinny black pants with an attached angular skirt and a fabulous primary color sequin bomber jacket, a couture outfit she made for her showcase interview at FIT.

"If you spill anything on this or tear it, I'll rip your throat out," she says.

"I can't have it?"

"Sweetie, no." But Monroe's reluctant eyeroll means she'll totally give it to me.

Phoebe does my makeup: a touch of highlighter on my cheeks, a subtle yellow eye shadow, and deep blue nails.

"Will Cris mind us tagging along?" Joey asks.

"If he shows. I haven't heard from him since the epic disaster known as Front Yard–gate, so it'll probably be us." I pucker my lips. "It's too bad Blanca couldn't come."

"Couldn't get out of her cousin's quinceañera," Phoebe says. "I'm bummed."

"You couldn't snag an invite?" Joey asks.

Phoebe holds up her hand and shakes her head. "It is *way* too soon for Meet the Entire Damn Family."

"You know, the more I watch all of you, the happier I am to be in a relationship with me, myself, and I," Joey says confidently.

"Until you see those fine college boys next year," Phoebe says.

Joey shrugs. I'm looking forward to weekend-long getaways to see her next year while I figure out how to make my diva dreams come true. Mariah worked as a backup singer when she was my age and recorded demos for her debut album, which she released at twenty. If she can make it happen, so can I.

I drink in my reflection in the floor-length mirror, appreciating what little curves and muscle tone I have on my lanky body. "I'm feeling myself tonight."

"Good because we have a train to catch," Monroe says. "And if you want to buy him flowers from the place next to Exile, we need to leave like five minutes ago."

The entire train ride to Grand Central is like a crash course in my neuroses. I oscillate back and forth between repeating Dr. Potter's "I already have everything I need" and the urge to declare complete devastation if Cris doesn't show up. The reality, though, is that after everything I've been through this past year, hell, this past month, I know that my self-worth isn't wrapped up in Cris or anyone else for that matter. My life won't be over. I love him, it'll take time to recover from him, but that's the point: there's always time to recover.

Each step on the walk to Radio City is heavy. Monroe, Joey, and Phoebe try to distract me by dancing around random pedestrians and singing parodies of *Wicked* songs, but I'm barely paying attention. Because as we draw closer, there he is, on the corner of Fiftieth and Sixth, right in front of the Radio City Music Hall marquee.

"Scatter," I whisper to the girls, and they duck down Fiftieth.

He straightens his coat to hide his sling, and when he smiles, everything I had planned to say disappears from my mind.

"You came to Carnegie Hall." His glasses have new lenses, but the frames are still cracked, bound together by black electrical tape. How fucking adorable is that?

"I went to Carnegie Hall," I confirm.

"Why didn't you tell me?" There's a breathlessness about him.

My mouth is dry, and he opens his to say something, but I cut him off. "I thought you were done with *us*. I didn't want to lose you as a friend, so I never told you that I'm pretty sure I've fallen in love with you. You're the first thing I think about in the morning and the last thing I think about at night, and when we're not together I want to be with you. This last week apart has been horrible and—"

"Whoa, whoa, slow down. You're starting to sound like Monroe," he says.

I shove the flowers toward his good hand. "These are for you. The girl from the shop said they're a symbol of humility and devotion. They're strong and beautiful, like you."

He places his hand on mine. "These remind me—"

I cut him off. "Of the flowers you got me. I like a good layer of symbolism. Mr. Kelly would be proud."

"Ahh, so Mr. Kelly *is* my competition," he jokes.

I want to jump into his good arm but would probably refracture his rib, so I start to tell him to shut up, but he kisses me.

When we pull away, he says, "I pulled away when I knew you were trying to get closer. I didn't want to get hurt. I had fallen so hard it scared me." His eyes are an ocean, and I'm hopelessly, helplessly lost at sea. "I, uh . . ."

"What?"

"Right after the school board meeting, one of Max's friends tweeted this." He pulls out his phone and plays the video of me that Max sent out in *Sunnyside Upended!* but a photo of Mr. Jackson is superimposed in the frame, doctored to make it look like he pushed me to the ground. The word "OWNED" flashes on the screen at the end.

"I've seen that. I fucking hate people. *That's* why you took off?"

"I saw them parked across the street, laughing at us. I just wanted to talk, try to get through to them. I swear I wasn't planning on pulling the first punch, but—"

I cut him off. "*You* punched first?"

He bows his head in shame. "I was pissed. I'm sorry."

"Don't be."

"You're not mad?" he asks.

"I super hate violence. But it's a little hot that you did that for me." I move in closer. "That was a joke. Kind of." I smile. "The best we can do for each other is to be better. No more punching assholes. Promise?"

"Promise." He kisses me again, this time with his entire body pressed against mine. He winces in pain. "I'm still pretty bruised." He kisses the tip of my nose. "So, you *think* you love me?"

"Maybe," I say playfully.

Cris raises an eyebrow, and it simultaneously drives me crazy and makes me want to kiss him. "Well, I love you, *and* you drive me mad." He kisses the space on my hand between my thumb and index finger. "Be my boo-friend?" He stares into my eyes. His breath is ragged, and his lips move closer to mine. There's a slow magnetic pull between us, and it's impossible to resist as his lips graze mine, so softly, so gently that I melt into him.

Monroe coughs. "Can y'all get a room?"

"Oh God, you're here to finish me off, aren't you?" Cris says.

"Am I allowed to laugh at that?" I ask.

"I'd be disappointed if you didn't." Cris's good hand clasps mine. "But seriously, what are you doing here, Roe?"

"Apparently seeing Mariah Carey fo' free!" she says. "Y'all can come out now, Cris and Carey are back together." She makes a vomiting noise.

As Joey and Phoebe round the corner and yell, "Surprise!" I fill in Cris about the DM from the guy on Mariah's team.

"No fucking way," he says.

"He's way less angry than I would be if a bunch of randoms crashed my date." Phoebe gives Cris a high-five.

"Yeah, we can totally head home if you want to be alone," Joey says.

"Speak for yourself." Monroe punches her sister's arm. "I dyed my hair rainbow for this shit. I don't like Mariah, but legends appreciate legends."

Cris laughs. "Nah, there's plenty of time to be alone."

I blush.

"Very TMI," Joey says.

"It's nice to be around friends. But . . ." Cris yanks the original tickets from his pocket. "Fuck, what about these tickets I paid for?"

"I was hoping you'd ask," I say. "I've got two buyers lined up. Thought it was only fair you get paid back."

"How'd you know I'd be here?" Cris asks.

"I didn't, but they wouldn't have cared if it didn't work out." I take out my phone, send a quick text, and show Cris.

ME: Cris showed up! 🖤 You and Coach T. still at dinner?

MOM: 😊

MOM: We'll be there soon, with money for Cris

"Coach T.?" Cris scrunches his forehead. "As in, our vocal coach, Coach T.?"

"The very one. They've been texting since we saw you perform at Carnegie," I say.

"She deserves to be happy," Joey says. "In case anyone is keeping score, I'm the only single one here, and I gotta be honest. I love it. If I've learned anything this past year, it's that I'm a badass, and I'm stronger on my own."

We pull Joey into the center of a group hug, and it works until she Hulks out and shoves us off her. Passersby look on in shock as we die laughing on the sidewalk.

At the ticket window, we leave the tickets for Mom and Coach T. and we're greeted by a tall man with a headset who introduces himself as Nick D. He's carrying an iPad and a cellphone. "Nice to meet you, Carey. Your story really inspired all of us. Especially Mariah."

Mariah knows who I am.

This is not real.

"This is the part when I realize I'm dreaming, right?" I say, breathless.

"Afraid not. You'll have a meet and greet with her after the show," Nick D. continues. "That's when you'll get a backstage tour and get to walk on the Radio City stage. Mariah thought you would enjoy that."

I'm speechless. Literally. No. Words.

Cris snaps his fingers, but I'm too far gone. "That means they're psyched," Cris says for me, and I nod like a robot.

"You'll be watching the show from the front row," Nick D. adds. "Hang out in your seats after the encore, and I'll be out to get you."

Front. Row.

For Mariah. *Freaking.* Carey.

No big deal.

Except.

VERY FREAKING BIG DEAL!

"Awesome," I choke out. "Awesome."

The lobby of Radio City is an art deco dream sequence. Everyone is an extra in an elaborate Broadway-style stage production just for us, dancing around us under looming crystal chandeliers. It's like when Elphaba and Glinda go to the Emerald City for the first time in Act I, Scene 14 of *Wicked*, as they sing "One Short Day," except instead of waiting for the Wizard to see us, we're waiting for Mariah Carey. Which is way better.

The lights dim and a neon *MC* lights up the hall. Mom and Coach Trevisani text us from the second mezzanine once the show starts. They can see my sequin jacket next to the stage. Cris holds me for support as Mariah rises from beneath the stage in a floor-length, skintight pink sequined gown. Nothing else matters as Mariah belts through her setlist. And I'm right there alongside her! During "My All," she looks right at me and winks, and chills arrest me as I feel Grams's presence.

Her encore is a one-two punch of "We Belong Together" and "Hero," but it's the outro, a little-known bonus track called "Runway" that lifts me off the ground. It's a song about rising above people's expectations, because in order to become your best self, you have to stay true to yourself and choose love. She sings about shaking off any fears that haunt you so you can finally know what it feels like to fly. New favorite song, for sure.

I'm floored. Done. Mop me up because I'm but a puddle.

I'm still high as fuck after the show ends, unable to focus on my friends' conversation as we wait for the meet and greet. When the auditorium is nearly empty and Nick D. returns, he says, "Mariah saw a video of you singing and wants to invite you to sing for her onstage." I nearly pass out.

"Mariah wants *me* to sing? Now?" I look to my friends, hoping they snap me out of what I'm convinced is a daydream.

It has to be, right?

"Can I get on the piano?" Cris asks, and suddenly the here and now all comes into sharp focus.

I follow the markers on the black stage, little strips of masking tape pressed to the dark floorboards. I see Mariah's initials in certain spots, and those of her backup dancers. At the front, hidden from the audience, is a setlist taped to the stage. I fight the urge to reach down and stash it in my pocket as a souvenir.

My heart thuds against the inside of my chest as I slowly lift my head toward the thousands of empty seats that fan out from the stage. The grandiosity of the hall, the way the great stage is fixed in the center of it all like a setting sun, the projected pink and purple butterflies that fly majestically across the walls, all bring to life a magic I didn't think existed. Even with the house lights on, without the smoke and mirrors of the elaborate neon *MC* sign and stage lights, it's like I've found exactly where I belong.

I want to breathe, or blink. I'm afraid that if I do, all this will somehow vanish.

No. It won't vanish. This is real.

This spotlight belongs to me.

I grab hold of Mariah's diamond-studded mic and exhale, hearing my breath through the powerful speakers. My lungs fill and expand, bigger, deeper, wider, as I steady my feet on the stage.

Like Mariah would to her band, I nod to Cris, and he knows what song to play. He tickles the keys, and I close my eyes and sing, not for Mariah or Cris or my friends, but for me. Because I can. Because I deserve this moment. Nothing and nobody can take this feeling away from me, and I hold it tight to my chest.

So I sing.

And I keep singing every day thereafter until opening night of *Wicked*: at home for Mom, in the car with Cris, as I walk through the halls of Sunnyside High, every time I step onto the auditorium stage for musical rehearsals. I never hold back. Every time I open my mouth, I give it everything I have. Because everyone is counting on me. Because *I'm* counting on me. Especially on opening night, which is oversold.

Opening night is oversold! It still feels like a fever dream that the entire town and then some has come to see my debut.

I'm not scared. Not even a bit.

Backstage is organized chaos, according to Rachel. Bodies dash from one side of the stage to the other for last-minute fittings and run-throughs and staging. Blanca practices deep-breathing exercises. There's a faint smell of wet paint. Monroe runs a lint roller over my witchy black ensemble before taking off in a panic, shouting incoherently about someone wearing the wrong costume.

I peek out from behind the curtain. In the front row, Joey sits with Mom, Coach Trevisani, Dr. Potter, the Coopers, Phoebe's mom, and Cris's dad. I imagine Grams is there too. I *know* she is as the curtains rise and the orchestra swells.

I hear her voice saying, *"Give 'em hell, kid."*

Phoebe glides across the stage in a blinding blue gown covered in rhinestones. As she sings, the audience is no longer spectators, but citizens of Oz.

Cris gently pecks my lips so as not to smear my makeup. "Break a leg."

Purposely shutting everyone out but Mr. Kelly, I wait for my cue. He points to me. I run to the center of the stage and the applause is so loud I have to wait for it to die down before I say my first lines. This is nothing compared to being onstage at Radio City.

My eyes are wide open. I got this.

Love pours from my lips, flooding the auditorium and illuminating every dark corner of the theater.

No longer caged, I'm sprouting wings and defying gravity.

The walls of the auditorium fall away, and the world opens up to me.

I'm free.

A NOTE FROM THE AUTHOR

Around the age of fifteen, I started suffering from suicidal ideations because I knew I was different. As a young child, I didn't have the words, yet I always knew on some level that I was queer. I suffered in silence for the better part of a decade, always putting on a happy face when I was around family or friends, while inside, I bled, hoping that one day there would be an end to all the pain I felt. There were many nights when I wished I wouldn't wake up in the morning, and many days when I planned ways I might die. I sought therapy while I was in college, but by that point, I had gotten good at hiding in plain sight. I finally came out as gay at the age of twenty-three, and while that felt right at the time, I also knew it wasn't the complete picture. I'd had a complicated relationship with gender my entire life, but a lifetime of pain and suppression of my own queerness prevented me from fully mining my gender identity. I am a proud gay, genderqueer person, and this story has been my way of navigating through my complicated relationship with gender; it was through Carey that I realized how deeply my queerness was connected to my own suicidal ideations as a teen. While I'm on the other side of those feelings now, having sought therapy and worked hard to love myself (which is still a work in progress), those memories are phantom pains that sometimes linger in the dark.

Nobody should have to suffer as I did.

While Carey's is just *one* story, their struggles and those of genderqueer, genderfluid, nonbinary, and transgender persons don't exist in a vacuum. According to the Human Rights Campaign's 2018 Youth Report, "73% of LGBTQ youth have experienced verbal threats because of their actual or perceived LGBTQ identity." I wanted desperately to give Carey a drama-free story that had nothing to do with their identity, because as a genderqueer person, I believe with my entire being that all gender nonconforming people deserve to exist in a world free of pain, where our identities are not politicized or reduced to shocking headlines or tweets. But after mining my own experiences and working with many queer students of varying identities in the classroom (and in a volunteer capacity at an LGBTQ center), I knew this had to be an honest, real story that shows how light *can* shine in the dark when young people fight the good fight and push for progress. Carey deserves to live as free as their cisgender counterparts.

There are parts of Carey's story that explore their suicidal ideations as well as a physical assault. If you're experiencing suicidal ideations/thoughts, depression, anxiety, are a young person in crisis, need a safe space to talk with someone, or know someone who is struggling and in need, please do not hesitate to ask for help.

The following services provide free and confidential support (check individual organizations' websites for hours of operations and more information. A comprehensive guide can be found at pflag.org/hotlines):

- The Trevor Project's TrevorLifeline
  866-488-7386
  https://www.thetrevorproject.org

- National Suicide Prevention Lifeline
  800-273-8255
  https://suicidepreventionlifeline.org/help-yourself/lgbtq/

- Crisis Text Line
  Text HOME to 741741 from anywhere in the United States to text with a trained crisis counselor.
  https://www.crisistextline.org

- The LGBT National Youth Talkline
  800-246-7743
  https://www.glbthotline.org/youth-talkline.html

- Trans Lifeline
  877-565-8860
  https://www.translifeline.org

I also highly recommend finding your local LGBTQ center and attending one of the many incredible support groups or events they offer, or volunteering. You can find an LGBTQ center near you by going to www.lgbtcenters.org/LGBTCenters. If you live in Westchester, New York, I can't recommend The LOFT LGBT Center enough! They gave me a sense of purpose when I felt like I didn't have a direction and allowed me the space to feel comfortable in my own skin. You can contact them at www.loftgaycenter.org.

No matter what, you are not alone. Your identity is valid. Your story is worth telling.

You are loved, you are worthy, you are enough.

PHOEBE WRIGHT'S GUIDE TO PROTESTING

Phoebe Wright
Mr. Kelly
Senior English
February 2
Extra Credit

Complacency is not only the enemy of justice, it's the self-made chain that binds people to their beliefs and halts and prevents self-reflection, growth, and progress. Holden Caulfield from J. D. Salinger's *The Catcher in the Rye*, published in 1951, uses his red hunting hat as a way to shield himself from the so-called "phoniness" of the world around him, and many literary critics call it a symbol of his own innocence. However, based on Salinger's own characterization of Caulfield and the level of self-awareness Caulfield possesses, that simply doesn't track. Perhaps Caulfield's reluctance to face the horrible realities around him "works" in a pre-civil rights era context, but that's the privilege afforded to white, (potentially) straight, (presumably) cisgender men, for whom it was easy to overlook, for instance, Jim Crow laws of the time because of the complacency afforded to him by living in New York. In a twenty-first-century context, this is truer than ever before.

A few weeks ago, Mr. Kelly brought up my frustration with his focus on Caulfield's hunting hat and implied that the point of the hat is to represent the moment where Caulfield can no longer use it to shield himself from reality. Mr. Kelly said, "It's those moments when we lose our 'security blankets' and see the world for what it truly is that dictate what we're made of. Do we choose to take the world at face value, accept the phoniness? Or do we push back, try to create a better reality?" To answer that question, I aim to look past Caulfield and his hat because, for me, Caulfield doesn't get brownie points for realizing his hat was a vehicle for complacency (or what many refer to as "innocence"). For me, his hat represents the rose-colored glasses most people wear in order to see the world how they choose to see it, the way that least challenges their privileges and foundational beliefs. I never had a security blanket in terms of how I see the world because I can't afford to see it as anything other than what it is: imperfect, structurally imbalanced for those not in power. I've been attending protests with my mom since I was in diapers, and if I've learned anything over the last few months as a student at Sunnyside High School during the recent protests I helped organize, it's that more people are aware of the harsh realities, the injustices, than we think, and they only need someone to give them permission to remove their "red hunting hats" so that they can jump into the fight and participate. It's okay to take that hat off. This is why I've chosen to write about what I've learned so that maybe it can inspire others to use their voice and power to push back and create a better reality in a step-by-step guide to protesting.

Step One: Pick a cause and focus on that. It's so easy to want to fight everything all at once. The planet is burning from global climate change; racial, LGBTQ+, and gender injustice and inequity run rampant; and gun deaths and mass shootings seem so obviously preventable yet aren't. Channeling your efforts toward one cause at a time will strengthen your purpose. You *can* push back against multiple injustices, but for the sake of a singular demonstration, focusing on one cause can provide more clarity and purpose for all those who attend. It also helps to plan with friends who share in like-minded ideals.

Step Two: Set your goals. What do you want this rally to accomplish? When Carey, Monroe, Joey, Cris, and I sat down to plan our protests, we developed, through planning and strategy sessions, four clear-cut goals:

1. **For Carey to be reinstated as Elphaba in the musical**
2. **For Mr. Kelly to be reinstated as director of the musical**
3. **For Mr. Jackson to be fired due to his obvious bigotry and intolerance making students feel unsafe at school**
4. **For the school board to adopt a no-tolerance policy in the Code of Conduct that mandates all teachers respect the identities of their students. This would apply to both students and teachers, who have to adhere to the Code of Conduct**

Aim high but be realistic. I felt three out of four of our goals were not only possible, but probable. I had my doubts that we could get Mr. Jackson fired, but it was worth the effort. Nothing changes if you don't push back against the systems of injustice that allow for complacency to thrive. Once you have your goal(s), you can begin to strategize and plan *how* to protest.

Step Three: Strategize. Utilize all the tools in your toolbox to organize. Given that we were pushing back against our school, we knew that, in order to get the most impact, we had to think critically about how to achieve our goals. This involved petitioning, walking out, protesting, attending the school board meeting to present our case, and creating a silent picket line. In order for us to get out our message, we knew social media was instrumental in our cause. We created various hashtags to spread news and information and tweeted, snapped, and Instagrammed over and over again until we gained traction. We alerted local news stations, including our own school newspaper. We also got together and made signs to pass out to the crowds.

Once everyone at school knew about it, we also considered ways to keep the crowds involved and motivated once the protest started after the walkout. Carey wanted to sing, and Monroe and Joey made sure to get food donations, and Thom from Exile Records passed out coffee for people who would be standing outside for the bulk of the day. Since it was January, we knew the cold would be working against us. Luckily, the majority of the student body felt as strongly about getting Carey back in the musical as we did, so they fought the cold, but this brings me to my next point . . .

Step Four: Location, location, location! It's crucial to choose a time and place that not only will garner the biggest crowd, but the most impact. Unfortunately, we didn't have the luxury of a warm summer day to protest, but these things can never be timed. We started petitioning at the assembly because we knew there was no better way to get as many signatures as possible than when the entire student body was in the same place at the same time.

We chose to begin our main protest at ten a.m., just after third period, because that time accounted for any late arrivals to school (to maximize attendance) and would disrupt most of the school day. Had we done it later in the day, we would have risked students going home. Had we done it anyplace other than Sunnyside High, we might not have gained the attention we did. Plus, we read bylaws and knew we could peacefully assemble on school grounds, which is crucial. We definitely risked disciplinary action by doing so, but that was the point. Additionally, had we chosen to protest on Main Street or in the park, we would have had to acquire permits.

Step Five: Organize and prepare, mentally and physically. Protests are unpredictable, no matter how much you might prepare. It's easy to get caught up in the excitement of planning a protest and not realize that it's impossible to control who attends and *how* they show up. Emotions run high and people can get physical. While peaceful assembly is effective and may be preferable, it may not always be achievable. Different protests call for different sets of actions, depending on the circumstances and context. I've learned it's necessary to be vigilant, come prepared for anything, and be strong in your resolve. Keep your mind focused on the goal and protect those who need protection.

To this end, self-care is crucial. We experienced an incident where a student made their car backfire to cause panic and disrupt our protest. This is trauma I am still recovering from, and I have sought out therapy to help me work through that. A big part of this process is practicing self-care, whatever that looks like to you: Keep your friends close, laugh, take care of each other.

I've learned so much about myself while planning the #Let-CareySing protests, and while I've never been the type of student who shuts her mouth and goes along with the status quo, I never realized just how many of my peers are just as willing to speak up and push back against that status quo. That's why I push back against Holden Caulfield's hat, because he claims to see the broken world around him, yet he does nothing to challenge that. He embodies the type of passive white supremacy that sees but doesn't act. I may only be a year older than Caulfield in *The Catcher in the Rye*, but I have yet to make up my mind about the world because I believe I can change it in small ways every day.

If I don't, who will?

"CAREY LIKE MARIAH": THE COMPANION PLAYLIST

1. "Close My Eyes" by Mariah Carey
2. "HIM" by Sam Smith
3. "FOOLS" by Troye Sivan
4. "Caution" by Mariah Carey
5. "My All" by Mariah Carey
6. "Always Remember Us This Way" by Lady Gaga
7. "I Want to Break Free" by Queen
8. "Outside" by Mariah Carey
9. "Truth Hurts" by Lizzo
10. "Popular" from *Wicked*
11. "I Have Nothing" by Whitney Houston
12. "Defying Gravity" from *Wicked*
13. "GTFO" by Mariah Carey
14. "How Do You Sleep?" by Sam Smith
15. "Heartbreaker" by Mariah Carey featuring JAY-Z
16. "Rainbow" by Kesha
17. "8th Grade" by Mariah Carey
18. "As Long As You're Mine" from *Wicked*
19. "Looking In" by Mariah Carey
20. "Can't Take That Away (Mariah's Theme)"
    by Mariah Carey

21. "Fantasy" by Mariah Carey
22. "Marry the Night" by Lady Gaga
23. "Everybody Wants to Rule the World" by Tears for Fears
24. "Postcard" by Troye Sivan featuring Gordi
25. "Raising Hell" by Kesha
26. "Wild Hearts Can't Be Broken" by P!nk
27. "Butterfly" by Mariah Carey
28. "We Belong Together" by Mariah Carey
29. "The Wizard and I" from *Wicked*
30. "Always Be My Baby" by Mariah Carey
31. "Runway" by Mariah Carey

ACKNOWLEDGMENTS

For anyone who ever believed in me, an idealistic queer kid with severe self-esteem issues who suffers from anxiety and depression, or offered me a kind word of encouragement: I may not have said it out loud, but you probably saved my life. This book belongs to you.

There's a song on Mariah Carey's 1997 album *Butterfly* called "Outside" that she wrote about being biracial and how she never quite felt as if she belonged anywhere. While I am not biracial, I always felt out of place as a queer person. Listening to Mariah's music, which I discovered at the ripe old age of six when she released "Emotions," has always made me feel like I belonged. Her lyrics spoke to me in ways I'm still processing as an adult. It's because of Mariah's music that I'm alive today. Mariah, if you ever read this, your voice and words saved me, made me feel like I belonged somewhere, and for that, I will always be grateful.

To the incomparable Jess Regel, whose belief in my writing allowed me to breathe. I couldn't possibly ask for a better agent to help guide me through the crazy world of publishing. You're always around to answer questions or soothe anxieties, which is *often*, and none of that goes unnoticed or unappreciated. You pulled me out of a dark place and thrusted me—and Carey—into the spotlight. Thank you from the bottom of my heart.

The GRAMMY for Carey's most vocal champion goes to my brilliant editor, Annette Pollert-Morgan. Getting to work with you was a dream come true, and your fundamental understanding of Carey's story allowed me to fully realize its potential. You gave me all the tools needed to turn the volume all the way up. Major thank-yous to Cindy Loh, whose incredible enthusiasm for this story carried me to the finish line, and to Kate Sederstrom for being equally as wonderful and enthusiastic! I truly am the luckiest author! I am beyond grateful for Bloomsbury, including Phoebe Dyer, Erica Barmash, Erica Loberg, Claire Stetzer, Lex Higbee, Jon Reyes, and the entire team who has made this book a reality. Carey sings because of you all.

If this book could have a second dedication, it would be to Nicolas DiDomizio. You're more than just a great friend/critique partner/beta reader/backboard for ideas; you've kept me going when I wanted to give up, calmed me down when I was convinced I needed to give up, and you've never once allowed me to lose sight of who I am as a writer. We joke that our respective author journeys are somehow synced, but damn if that hasn't been the truth. You were the first person I told when I found out this book was going to auction, so it's only fitting you're the unofficial second dedication. I love you, buddy. It is impossible to look at the last eight (!!!) years and not see how instrumental you were to me writing the book of my heart. There is no way I would be here if it weren't for your friendship, guidance, unmitigated honesty, and the too often mutual spiral. No matter how high the highs or how low the lows, you kept everything in perspective *for* me. You never stopped believing even when I was convinced I wasn't good enough. Guess what? *We're more than good enough.* WE MADE IT!

There aren't enough pages in the world to praise Jess Verdi for being the absolute best person ever. From reading a very early, entirely different version of this book back when it was a "battle of the bands"–type story from Cris' POV before Carey was born (thanks to you and Amy for letting me down gently that it was NOT working at all!) to being there for me whenever I needed to vent about my writing woes (which was probably weekly?). You've been my biggest cheerleader while also keeping it *100* at all times, and that kept me going when I thought about giving up.

Immense gratitude to all my dynamic, beautiful writer friends: A good deal of bravery in this book is inspired by Melissa Tabeek, the Charlie to my Todd: you are the bravest, boldest person I know, and you remind me what's worth fighting for, even when the world seems like a true devastation. I'm consistently inspired by Amy Ewing's magical mind and talent: I don't know how you write the way you do and find the time to be such an amazing friend and resource, but I love you and will forever shower you with all the shirtless Tom Hiddleston GIFs. Jeffrey Guard, you're like a constant ray of sunshine, and your positivity never fails to lift me up. For my sensitivity readers for making certain that my heart and intentions shine most effectively. Morgan Boecher, you inspire me with your incredible stories and gorgeous art, and thank you for reading parts of this book I was uncertain about. Sylvia Zelaya, my first critique partner, I lo' you (you better be writing right now)! And to all my fellow New School alums: Your advice and support has kept me going!

A never-ending well of gratitude goes out to all the incredible mentors and teachers who inspired me the way Mr. Kelly inspires Carey: Beth Holden (I can never thank you enough for growing me from a little seed and allowing me to flower), Nick Smart, David Levithan, Jill Santopolo, Sarah Weeks, Joan Marcus, Diane McPherson, Linda Godfrey, Pat Spencer, Jerry Mirskin, Katharyn Howd Machan, Julie Ippolito, and especially Alicia Adiutori Vonderhorst, who allowed me to eat lunch in her classroom when I had nowhere else to go.

I can't say it loud enough that Hilde Atalanta's artwork on the cover is everything! Carey is truly alive, and not only does your rendition of them sing, it's evocative and gorgeous and dreamy. I'm in awe of your talent, and it was an absolute honor to have your collaboration on the book of my heart!

To Donette Smith, for reminding me week after week that I already had everything I needed.

I wouldn't be half the person I am today if it weren't for my mom and everything she did for me growing up: Mom, you're my Wonder Woman. You believed in me and my talent every step of the way. You encouraged me to draw, paint, sing, write, and be as creative as I could be. Your unconditional love taught me that the world *can* be wonderful, if we choose kindness. For the rest of my big, crazy family, who have always wanted the best for me and were willing to move mountains to help me achieve my goals: Thank you, Giselle, Carole, Dad, Ozzy, Sandy, Missy, Uncle Bobby, Chris, Christopher, Adriana, Mike and Patti,

Queen Maria, Samantha, Jenna and Mama Becky, Carolyn and Joe, Elizabeth (Eddy Lee Ryder), Mama and Papa Alobeid, and everyone else I can't possibly list, but haven't forgotten, I love you all.

Part of Carey's emotional journey begins and ends with their grams, who *is* my grams, and I wish she could see this book. I miss you every single day, Grams. I listen to the recording of you singing "Secret Love" and smile every time you get to the golden daffodils. Don't worry, I haven't forgotten you and never will. You're with me always. #1.

The friendship between Carey, Monroe, and Joey is the backbone of this book, and my sisters by choice, Nikki and Marissa, have forever been *my* backbone. Thank you both for more than I could ever list here. Our stories are the brightest, best parts of me, and your friendship has sustained me in times of incredible darkness. My wish is for everybody to experience the bond we share. *Some things last.* I love you both immensely. Grandma Bev told me this book would sell before it was even written. She knew.

Most of all, this book belongs to my husband, Steve, who is everything to me. You inspire me every single day with your capacity for kindness and love. You've motivated me when I needed a swift kick in the ass, consoled me when I needed a shoulder (or was just being dramatic), and left me alone when you knew I needed to hermit. The universe opened up to me when I met you. This book wouldn't exist if you hadn't been 1,000% behind me, pushing me, cheering me on, and telling people I was "published" even when I didn't have an agent; you spoke it into existence. You see me and make me feel seen. I love you with every fiber of my being, witch. Three squeezes.